GUILT WAS STRONG,
BUT PASSION WAS STRONGER

"Oh, Mr. Tate, I'm such a sorry object for your affection," Emily said.

Her voice was so thick with unhappiness that Will wasn't sure he'd heard her correctly. Then he decided it didn't matter. He tilted her chin so that he could peer into her eyes.

Just before his soft lips captured hers, Emily's aching heart felt an instant of soaring gratitude. He loved her. That knowledge might almost keep her warm as she huddled in a cold-water flat with her impoverished aunt and uncle after they lost everything they owned, as they surely would.

Then her brain shut off, lulled into ecstasy by the wonderful man who held her so tenderly. And Emily, who had never kissed a man before, responded with all the considerable ardor in her being.

By Alice Duncan

One Bright Morning
Texas Lonesome

Published by HarperPaperbacks

Texas Lonesome

ALICE DUNCAN

HarperPaperbacks
A Division of HarperCollins Publishers

HarperPaperbacks   *A Division of* HarperCollins*Publishers*
10 East 53rd Street, New York, N.Y. 10022

Copyright © 1996 by Alice Duncan
All rights reserved. No part of this book may be used or reproduced in any manner whatsoever without written permission of the publisher, except in the case of brief quotations embodied in critical articles and reviews. For information address HarperCollins*Publishers,*
10 East 53rd Street, New York, N.Y. 10022.

Cover illustration by Doreen Minuto

First printing: January 1996

Printed in the United States of America

HarperPaperbacks, HarperMonogram, and colophon are trademarks of HarperCollins*Publishers*

❖ 10 9 8 7 6 5 4 3 2 1

The dogs in this story are modeled down to the last neurosis after two of my own, Eric and Truffles. They have gone on to greater doggy glory now, but I remember them with love.
This story is dedicated to them;
to Thelma Jarvis, who remains my friend
in spite of all the dachshunds she's palmed
off on me over the years;
and to Dr. Daniel Vanderhoof and his wonderful staff
at the Vanderhoof Veterinary Hospital in Altadena, California. If everybody were as kind and caring as they are, the world might just work. (And isn't Vanderhoof a wonderful name for a veterinarian?)

1

San Francisco, California, 1895

Dear Aunt Emily:

I am in deep distress and know not what to do. I have a passionate artistic temperament and am in love with an actor. The object of my love is not just any actor, Aunt Emily, but plays Hamlet on the Stage. My mother says all Theatrical People are trash. She refuses to let me attend the Theatre with my friend Jill and says I must marry a banker. All I can do is weep. Oh, please, please, help me! I am Desperate!

Signed,
In Love with Hamlet

Emily von Plotz glared at the letter clutched in her fingers and muttered, "Affected, sniveling dolt."

Before she could put pencil to paper and answer the correspondent with her own appropriately modified opinions, however, she found herself rudely jerked up from her park bench. Both letter and pencil went flying, and Emily had to grab hard at the leashes straining against her arm. Uncle Ludwig would never forgive her if she lost his dogs.

Will Tate stared at the melee erupting in front of him and squinted to be sure his eyes hadn't deceived him. Shaking his head, he decided they hadn't. Two of the most ridiculous-looking animals he'd ever seen in his entire life were trying to murder his dog.

The ferocious duo were glossy, reddish brown, and about as close to the ground as a mammal could get without slithering on its belly like a snake. They were doing their level best to put an end to poor Fred, who tried without much success to lift all four paws off the ground at the same time in an effort to elude them. The effect was comical, and Will wondered with some amusement if the minute warriors planned to chew their way up to a vital organ from Fred's enormous feet.

The little hellions were being barely kept in check by a slender woman who tugged with all her might at the leashes nominally tethering them. Will figured she must have come to Golden Gate Park on this perfect San Francisco summer morning in order to exercise the dogs. She had obviously been unprepared for their militant streak.

"It's a good thing Fred has a sense of humor," he murmured as he urged Cyclone, his big bay gelding, closer to the action.

He could hear the woman trying to control her wayward pets as he neared.

"Gustav! Helga! Stop it right now. That dog could eat the both of you with one bite!"

That was true, and Will acknowledged the woman's honesty with a smile. Fred was an enormous, though amiable, beast. The latter quality, while generally considered favorable, had apparently gone unappreciated by his present company.

Will reined in Cyclone a few feet from the altercation and whistled for Fred. Then he slipped off the horse's back and waited for his obedient dog to come to him.

Fred took one last peek at the two frenzied hounds and plodded meekly to Will, his tail wagging a happy greeting.

"Good boy, Fred. Sit down now, old fellow." Will gripped him by the collar, then glanced at the woman.

The poor thing was young—Will guessed her age to be somewhere near twenty—and she was a charmer. She had lots of honey-brown hair, a rosebud mouth, and eyes as blue as the sky above them. He almost whistled in appreciation of her perfect Gibson-girl figure. She was something and a half; no mistake. Will grinned in approval and pushed his hat back on his head.

"'Pears to me those two critters lack a certain sense of proportion, ma'am," he said in a friendly drawl owing as much to his understanding of city women as it did to his southwestern roots. That lazy, sun-kissed accent got them every time.

The woman blushed rosily. Will thought she looked pretty as a picture in her blue skirt and short jacket with its puffy sleeves, strapped around by those two crazy animals' leashes, and with her cheeks as pink as a Texas sunset. Her straw hat had been knocked a little cockeyed in her struggle with the dogs, and it now sat at a jaunty angle on her upswept hair. Will's smile broadened, and he doffed his hat politely.

"Oh," she cried in obvious embarrassment. "They're such absurd dogs. My aunt's brother, Ludwig, brought them to her from Germany."

Her voice sounded at once proper and pretty. It caused something in Will to vibrate in appreciation. He plopped his hat back onto his head and gave her a slow nod, as though it all made sense to him now. "German, are they?"

"Yes," the woman said. "But I think these two are actually from Vienna, Austria."

"That explains their dispositions, then, I reckon."

In spite of her embarrassment, the woman allowed a smile to peek out of her flushed face. To Will's further delight, a dimple appeared at the corner of her mouth.

"I suppose it does," she said. "I'm really sorry these idiots attacked your dog, sir."

"That's all right, ma'am," said Will. "Old Fred here's a friendly cuss. And he's got a right lively sense of humor, so I expect he'll just go back home and tell his pals about it and they'll all have a good laugh."

The woman gave him a full-bore smile. Then she stuck out a small hand and said, "Well, I do appreciate your being so understanding, sir. My name is Emily von Plotz."

Her smile was like sunshine on a rainy day. Will doffed his Stetson once more.

"Will Tate, Miss von Plotz. And it's a real pleasure to meet you." After shaking her hand and resettling his hat, Will hooked his thumbs into his back pockets and surveyed Emily von Plotz with a connoisseur's eye. In order to keep her talking for a while, he said,

"These critters always so happy to meet strangers, ma'am?"

Emily smiled at Will's deep drawl, gazed up into his suntanned face, and couldn't suppress a small giggle. It surprised her. She couldn't remember the last time she had uttered a spontaneous giggle. Her life had been rather trying of late.

"They're really awfully sweet dogs once you get to know them," she said. "But Uncle Ludwig says they're bred to be hunters. I guess they take their job in life seriously."

"Well, that's more than a lot of human folks can say, I reckon." Will eyed the two little dogs with a dubious frown. "Hunters, are they?"

Emily watched him, intrigued. Mercy sakes, the man was handsome and so—manly. She felt so warm all of a sudden and she wished she could fan herself.

"Oh, yes," she told him. "They've been bred to hunt small game, like rabbits and such. My uncle says they'll even go after badgers." She gave a firm nod to emphasize her words. "Uncle Ludwig says they've got a lot of heart."

Will seemed impressed. "Badgers are pretty rugged customers. No wonder you two think you're tough." Will squatted and held out a hand to the pair.

The dog Emily had called Gustav immediately rolled himself onto his back. He looked ridiculous with his four tiny legs flapping in the air from both ends of his sausage-shaped body, but Will decided it would be prudent not to point out the fact to Emily.

"Well, now, I guess you're a friendly cuss underneath all that bluster, aren't you, Gustav, ol' boy?" Will scratched Gustav's chest with deft fingers.

The dog named Helga backed up and began to yap

hysterically. She bared her teeth and raised her hackles in a perfect fever of upset.

Will chuckled.

Emily sighed.

"Gustav, you're a complete embarrassment," she told the male severely. "Helga, stop it right now." She looked at Will sheepishly. "At least she tries to earn her keep."

"She's a scrapper, all right," acknowledged Will, peering up into Emily's eyes.

He got lost in her gaze for a moment until Helga intruded again. Edging ever so slowly nearer to Will's lanky thigh, she started to sniff tentatively. Then, after one or two preliminary snuffles, her long snout began a noisy, businesslike inspection of his leg.

Both Will and Emily let sighs of relief escape them.

"Well, now, are you going to try to make up to me after all that hullabaloo?" he asked the dog.

Helga snapped at Will when he ventured to stroke her head with a hand at least as long and almost as brown as her nose. He withdrew his hand to the safety of Gustav's belly in a hurry.

"Helga! Stop that," commanded Emily.

The dog ignored her. Instead, she sniffed Will's hand as it paid attention to an itchy spot on Gustav's deep chest.

"I think she likes you," Emily said. Her voice held little conviction.

Will grinned at her. Emily thought he had a wonderful grin. His lovely hazel eyes crinkled up at the corners, and the creases on his tanned face deepened.

A tingle of excitement surged through her, and she found herself wishing she knew Will Tate. As she was forever telling her correspondents, however, it was not a lady's place to initiate social intimacies with a gentleman. She didn't quite know what to do instead, so she just swallowed hard and smiled back at him.

"What kind of dogs are these, Miss von Plotz? I've never seen their like before. Of course, I'm from Texas. We get mostly working breeds there."

At his mention of Texas, Emily felt a sudden thrill and then tried to tamp it down. *Oh, don't be silly, Emily von Plotz,* she chided herself. *He couldn't be. That would be simply too much luck.*

Then she remembered Will had asked her a question but couldn't recall what it was. She cleared her throat in embarrassment and felt her cheeks get warm.

"I—I'm sorry, Mr. Tate. What did you just ask me?"

Will chuckled. She was absolutely adorable. He wanted to scoop her up and make off with her, but he figured polite society would disapprove. "I asked you what kind of dogs these two are, Miss von Plotz." He also decided Emily deserved a better last name than von Plotz, which sounded kind of ridiculous to him.

"They're dachshunds, Mr. Tate." Then Emily hurried on before Will could speak again. "Did you say you were from Texas?"

Will gave up on Gustav's tummy and stood once more. He realized Emily only came up to his chin, and he liked that a lot. He liked the way she peered up at him with those big blue eyes of hers, too.

"Yep," he said. "Got me a real nice place near San Antone." He didn't usually lay his accent on this thick, as a rule, but he figured that since Emily seemed to like it, he'd oblige her.

Emily did like it, although for a reason completely beyond Will's ken.

She couldn't help but notice what a big man he

was, though. And very appealing. He had just the tall, lanky, lean look about him that Emily so admired. And he had the prettiest, sun-streaked brown hair underneath his big Texas hat.

"Are you—are you here in San Francisco on business, Mr. Tate?" she asked with what she hoped sounded merely like polite interest. What she wanted to do was grab him by the collar and shake him until he told her what she wanted to know.

"Nope. I'm playin'. I'm here on a holiday. And San Francisco sure is different from Texas, Miss von Plotz, I can tell you that."

He seemed like such a sweet man. Emily tried to rein in her excitement. After all, the chances of his being the one she needed were very, very remote. Still, she'd never know for certain unless she asked.

"Mr. Tate," she began, and stopped, unsure exactly how to proceed. Finally she decided just to blurt it out and be done with it. "Mr. Tate, are you Texas Lonesome, by any chance?" Then she flushed a deep, hot crimson.

"Texas lonesome?" Will's brow crinkled. That was a strange way to put it, he thought.

He watched her curiously, taking note of her fervent expression. She sure seemed to want him to be Texas lonesome, whatever that meant. Then he grinned. Will Tate was nothing if not obliging. "Well, Miss von Plotz, I guess you might just say I am."

Emily's heart did a double somersault and began hammering like a woodpecker after a grub. "Oh, Mr. Tate," she cried. She put a small hand on his sleeve and looked up at him earnestly. "I'm Aunt Emily!"

Will's nimble brain assimilated that astonishing

piece of information in only a very few seconds.
When it did, his mouth dropped open.

"You? *You're* Aunt Emily?"

The huge grin following his exclamation nearly
caused Emily's palpitating heart to turn a handspring.
She could only nod. Lord above, the man was handsome. She'd had no idea; would never have suspected, in fact.

Will couldn't believe it for a second. Why, he and
his pal Thomas Crandall had spent this very morning
in stitches over Aunt Emily's advice-to-the-lovelorn-
and-other-fools-who-can't-take-care-of-themselves
column in the *San Francisco Call*. Will found it hard
to believe people actually wrote the hogwash he'd
seen printed in the newspaper. Thomas had almost
spit his coffee all over his breakfast eggs when Will
read some of the letters to him.

"Why, ma'am," he told her honestly, "I just purely
can't believe it. I pictured Aunt Emily as a middle-
aged spinster lady. And hog-fat, to boot."

Emily wasn't entirely sure she appreciated his disclosure. But still, if this man was Texas Lonesome, it
wouldn't do for her to get huffy at him. Too many
intriguing thoughts were beginning to spin about in
her mind for her to risk antagonizing him.

She smiled up at him, sweet as honey on a butter-
milk biscuit. "No, Mr. Tate, I'm sorry to disappoint
you, but she's not. She's me."

Will shook his head slowly. "Don't be sorry, Miss
von Plotz. I'm surely not disappointed."

Emily's smile faded and was replaced by an expression of earnest goodwill. "And, Mr. Tate, if you truly
desire assistance in your endeavor, I can help you. I'm
just certain I can. In truth, nothing would give me

more pleasure than to help Texas Lonesome in this time of need."

By now, Will had come to the conclusion that this Texas Lonesome character must be one of Aunt Emily's lovelorn correspondents. And while it was true Will had adopted a scruple or two since he'd grown up and made his way in the world, it was also true he was quite taken with this little lady. He guessed he wouldn't mind playing fast and loose with honesty for a while. At least for long enough to get to know Miss Emily von Plotz better, especially since she seemed so eager to help him out of whatever fix he was in.

He decided it might behoove him to play the bumpkin better, so he tugged his hat from his head and clutched it in front of him to show off his two big, callused, country hands. "Why, ma'am, I'd just purely appreciate it if you would help me," he said in his best Texas drawl.

Emily's eyes fairly shone. Her expression of relief and happiness almost overwhelmed him. He'd never seen anything quite like little Miss Emily von Plotz in all his born days, in spite of her silly name.

"Oh, Mr. Tate, I'd just love to help you." Emily meant that in all sincerity.

"Well, ma'am, I'd be honored if you would."

He hoped she'd offer a suggestion pretty soon as to how she planned to go about it, since he had no idea what this Texas Lonesome fellow had written to her. It was always possible she might ask a question about his false persona he wouldn't be able to answer, and then where would he be? Alone in Golden Gate Park without her, he reckoned. The thought held little appeal.

Emily thought fast. Will Tate seemed to be an honest and upright fellow. Still, she didn't know him at all, and she certainly didn't want to put herself into any compromising situations—yet. That might come later, after she determined for sure he was truly honorable. All at once, she thought of a brilliant solution to her dilemma.

"Mr. Tate," she said briskly, "I believe we can begin your lessons as soon as tomorrow morning if you'd like to meet me in the park again."

Just in case he might wonder at—or, worse, object to —a young lady's wandering at will and unaccompanied in a public park, she added, "I live nearby, Mr. Tate, and Golden Gate Park is such a well-traveled place. Nobody could possibly object to our meeting here."

It sounded a little weak to her, so she smiled what she hoped was an alluring smile when she added, "I promise to leave Gustav and Helga at home."

Will was lured. In truth, it never entered his head to think it odd that Emily should be out and about all by herself with no chaperone to watch over her. "Why, that sounds just fine to me, ma'am. I'll look forward to it."

"Good. Will nine o'clock be a good time for you?"

Although he had planned to spend a rip-roaring evening in a house of ill repute, gambling and sporting, and not return home until the wee hours of the morning, Will promptly agreed.

"That will be just perfect, ma'am."

Emily was pleased. "Well, then, Mr. Tate, until tomorrow."

"Until tomorrow, Miss von Plotz."

They shook hands on it. Then Emily had to awaken Gustav before she could walk home. Her mind was racing, and she dashed out of Golden Gate Park and practically skipped the few blocks to her aunt's mansion on Hayes Street.

Blodgett, Aunt Gertrude's kind, elderly, deaf, and very dignified butler, greeted her at the door. Emily quickly consigned Helga and Gustav into Blodgett's capable hands, then darted down the threadbare carpet and past the second-best parlor.

The bell-shaped tones of Aunt Gertrude's voice told Emily that Gertrude was in the process of giving an elocution lesson. Emily could picture her standing amid the somewhat shabby furniture in the room, her iron-gray hair wound into a discreet knot at the back of her head, her finger upraised as she imparted the rudiments of proper speech to some bored young lady who didn't care in the least. Emily sighed and wondered if this student was another one of her dear aunt's charity cases, or if Gertrude would manage to get paid for once.

Since her aunt was otherwise occupied and couldn't be disappointed at her improper behavior, Emily took the steps of the wide, curved staircase two at a time. She flung her door open and made a beeline to her desk. Once there, she began rifling through a huge stack of papers. She soon found the one she was looking for, snatched it out of the pile, held it up to the late-morning sunlight streaming through her window, and read it eagerly.

"It does," she breathed with rapture. "It does say what I remember." Then she kissed the piece of paper, hugged it to her bosom, and did a little twirl around her bedroom.

*   *   *

Will watched for a long time, enchanted, as Emily and her two low-slung companions walked away from him. He enjoyed the way Emily's little bottom swished and thought she handled her charges quite well, considering their dispositions. He admired that.

With a pat for Fred and an affectionate stroke of a long, silky ear, Will murmured, "You get an extra bone tonight, Freddy boy. If it weren't for you, I'd never have met Miss Emily von Plotz." He shook his head and chuckled. "Von Plotz. What a name."

When Emily finally ambled out of his sight, he remounted Cyclone, whistled to Fred, and finished his trot around the park.

The place had changed a good deal in the five years since Will had lived in San Francisco. Civic pride had wrought many horticultural changes, in which he took particular pleasure. Will was quite a gardening enthusiast and, therefore, very interested in some of the new gardens planted for the Mid-Winter Exposition the year before. He especially enjoyed roses, and took notes about several new varieties that might grow well in his own elaborate garden back home.

It was around four in the afternoon when he returned to the Nob Hill mansion of Thomas Crandall, his friend and business partner, and made his way into the parlor. There he sat down in an over-stuffed wing chair with his big, booted feet propped on a burgundy velvet ottoman.

When Thomas came home an hour later, Will was shuffling through a huge stack of newspapers piled beside the chair and sipping from a mug of beer. He looked up and smiled. "Home so soon, Thomas?"

Thomas was a few inches shorter than Will, and he

was built along stockier lines, although he was not at all fat. He had thin, curly brown hair and fluffy muttonchop side-whiskers Will accused him of growing to distract the ladies from his receding hairline.

Thomas grinned. "Figured I'd better get back here early to keep you out of trouble."

"Too late for that," Will told him with a grin of his own.

"Oh, great God, what's her name?"

Will laughed and shook his head. "Shoot, Thomas, now what kind of trouble can I get into in one little afternoon?"

Thomas flopped into a chair across from Will. "If I remember right, it took you less than five minutes when we met up with Flaming Polly that time in Virginia City."

There was more than a hint of wistfulness in Will's smile when he admitted, "Yeah. I guess that's true."

"Well, my friend, ladies aside, has the city changed much in five years?"

"It's changed for the better, I'd say," Will told him with a wink. "I found me a fine new polyantha for my rose garden."

Thomas shook his head. "I still can't picture you, of all people, as a damned gardener."

"I like roses. I can't help it. They make me feel refined. Besides, I'm rich. I can do what I want."

"I guess that's so." Thomas shook his head again, this time almost sadly, as though he was ruing their lost youth. "That all you did today? Smell the roses?"

"Well, I had me a right fine time in the gardens. That's true. But I also met up with some of the prettiest scenery I've ever seen in my life."

Thomas sat up straight, all attention. "All right,

Will, I mean it now. What's her name?" Thomas and Will knew each other very well.

Sighing lustily, Will said, "All right. Her name is Miss Emily von Plotz." He eyed his friend over the crinkled newspaper. "Better known to *you* as Aunt Emily."

"Aunt Emily? That old maid who writes the silly advice column for the *Call?* My God, Will, all that digging in the dirt and playing with posies must be making you soft!"

Will peered at Thomas dreamily. "I learned a valuable lesson today, my friend. You should never judge a book by its cover. Or, in this case, you should never judge a columnist by the drivel she writes. Aunt Emily is one prime female. And I saw her first, so don't get any ideas."

Thomas laughed and stretched his legs out to snag the sides of Will's ottoman. It took some clever maneuvering, but he managed to catch it between his feet and jog it toward himself so he could share it. "I assume you're reading old columns so you'll have something to talk about when you meet up with your fair aunt again?"

Will crunched the newspaper up on his lap. "Actually," he admitted, "it's a little more complicated than that."

"Hmmm. Now why am I not surprised to hear you say so?"

"You see, she thinks I'm some lonely cowpoke who calls himself Texas Lonesome. I guess he wrote her a letter saying he needs some kind of help. So I'm trying to figure out just exactly what his problem is so that when Miss Emily tries to help me, I can oblige her by getting better. And I promise to be real grateful, too."

Thomas cocked an eyebrow. "And how, pray tell, did she get the impression you were this correspondent of hers?"

"Why, city feller, I ain't got a clue." Will's drawl was so slow a snail could have beaten it to Thomas's ears.

"Oh, Lordy," sighed Thomas. "Here. Give me a hunk of those papers, and I'll help you look."

So Will divvied up the stack of newspapers, and the two men proceeded to dig through them in search of old Aunt Emily columns. They had been at their task for about ten minutes when Will leapt to his feet.

"I found it!" He stood in front of his wing chair and read the column. Then he read it again. Then he looked over to where Thomas sat expectantly, grinning at him. Will was troubled.

"Uh-oh."

"What do you mean, 'uh-oh'?"

Will didn't respond immediately. He sat down once more and read the column yet a third time to himself. Then he cleared his throat and proceeded to read aloud.

"'Dear Aunt Emily,' it says here. 'I come to San Francisco to get me a wife because this here is where all the real ladies are. I got me a spread in the middle of Texas and a lot of money, but I'm too shy to talk to real ladies. I don't smoke nor chew, nor I don't hardly drink overmuch, but how can I get me a lady for a wife if I can't talk to them? Please help me.'" Will looked at Thomas. "It's signed, 'Texas Lonesome.'"

"Oh, Lord. What does she say back?"

"'Dear Texas Lonesome: You sound like a fine, upright man to Aunt Emily. I believe if you were to study an improving volume on proper deportment, it would help you to feel more at ease with the gentle sex. Ladies always appreciate a gentleman who is polite and kind. Many a young lady would be proud to marry a good man such as the one described in your letter, even if he is deficient in some of the social graces. I must add, however, that a good many proper ladies frown upon the consumption of strong spirits, even if such consumption is not considered by the consumer to be "overmuch." Please accept my best wishes for success in your endeavor. Sincerely, Aunt Emily.'"

Will sat in his chair, the paper spread over his knees, and stared out of Thomas's large parlor window. The window afforded him a splendid view of the city sprawled out at the foot of Nob Hill, but Will wasn't paying any attention to rambunctious San Francisco as it carried on below.

"Maybe this isn't such a good idea after all," he said at last.

Thomas had been trying to stifle his amusement, but he let it go now. He hooted loudly, and then laughed so hard he ended up slapping his knee and clutching his stomach.

Will scowled. "I don't see what's so blamed funny, Thomas."

Thomas leaned back in his chair and wiped his streaming eyes. "Well, I was meaning to talk to you about its being high time you got married and settled down, Will. After all, you don't want to follow in your uncle Mel's footsteps, do you?"

Melchior Tate had reared Will from "infantry to adultery," in his own colorful and not entirely inaccurate words. Mel Tate was a rambling man. He was also a gambling man. And he had a more-than-passing

acquaintance with the bottle. In fact, a good many
shocked schoolmarms who had met Uncle Mel during
Will's several brief attacks at schooling had decried
Mel as a whiskey-soaked reprobate. Uncle Mel had
invariably preened under the flattery.

It wasn't until Will met up with Thomas Crandall
in the gold mines around Virginia City that he learned
not all relationships were based upon what one could
get away with. Still, Will appreciated some of the
lessons Uncle Mel had taught him. He chalked up his
easy way with women to Mel's tutelage.

At his friend's jibe, however, Will shuddered. "I tell
you, Thomas, I didn't know Texas Lonesome wanted
to commit something as foolish as matrimony."

"What did you say she looked like? Maybe I could
take her off your hands."

"The hell you will," Will said gruffly. Then he fell
silent for a few moments, considering.

Thomas lifted the newspaper from Will's lap and
read Texas Lonesome's letter and Aunt Emily's reply
for himself.

"What exactly was it Aunt Emily said to you today
in the park?"

Will lifted his troubled gaze. "She said she'd be
glad to help me."

"Well, that doesn't sound too sinister, does it? It's
not as if she said she wants to marry you herself, is it?
Maybe she's just one of those do-gooders who aren't
happy unless they're rescuing some poor soul from
happiness or feeding him Bible verses."

Will's clouded countenance began to clear a little.
"That may be so."

"So what can it hurt if you pretend to be this lonesome cowboy and learn a few lessons? At least you'd

be in her company. There are worse things to do than keep company with a good woman, you know."

"Think so? I've not had much practice at it."

"Well, it's the truth."

Will offered Thomas a crooked grin. "And how would you know about such a thing, my friend?"

His old pal laughed. "That's what I've heard, at any rate."

By the time the two men sat down to sup upon prime California beefsteak in Thomas Crandall's elegant dining room, Will had decided to keep his appointment with Emily von Plotz at nine o'clock sharp on the morrow.

As for Miss Emily von Plotz herself, Aunt Emily stared at the water-stained ceiling above her bed for hours and hours before she finally managed to fall into a troubled sleep. By the light of the one flickering tallow candle she allowed herself, she considered various ways to entrap a rich, naive Texas rancher into marriage without tipping her hand.

2

Early the next morning, Emily smiled when she read, "Dear Aunt Emily: I took the advice you give me and called a liberry from the telephone in my hotel. I asked about decorum but the lady said they got books on ettyket. What is ettyket? Can I use it instead of decorum? She said so but I don't trust her. I trust you. Thank you for your help, Texas Lonesome."

After thinking for only a moment, Emily wrote, "Dear Texas Lonesome: Your Aunt Emily applauds you for the dedication you display toward the achievement of your goal. Yes, dear sir, etiquette will set you on the proper path toward decorum. The object of your affections will assuredly honor your attempts to better yourself. Aunt Emily knows full well she will."

She stared at her response for a full minute before she heaved a sigh and set the letter aside, her heart strangely stirred.

Moments later, that same heart thumped a frantic tattoo against her ribs as she walked briskly to her editor's office. She had hardly slept the night before, but she was too nervous to be tired.

As usual, Emily was alone on her walk and, as usual, she held her chin high in the air, daring any villain to approach her. She hoped any nonvillainous persons who might spy her would chalk up her solo jaunt to her being a suffragist. She wasn't. But more than anything, she didn't want to advertise the fact that her solitary state was due to her inability to afford a servant to accompany her. If she had nothing else, Emily had her pride.

Mr. Kaplan, her editor, gave Emily a somewhat bloodshot smile when she sailed through his door. "You're here bright and early today, Miss von Plotz."

"Yes, I suppose so. I didn't sleep very well last night, so I got up early and wrote my column." She handed Mr. Kaplan a hefty sheaf of papers.

"Oh, my, you've got a bundle for us today."

"I guess I do at that." Emily had been in such a nervous frenzy that morning, she had read and answered at least five more letters than she usually did. "Can you print them all?"

"Well, if we can't print them today, we'll be able to fit them in eventually. You do good work, Miss von Plotz. Aunt Emily's column is one of our best-read features. The public really loves you."

Emily felt her cheeks get hot. "Thank you, Mr. Kaplan."

"Thank you, Miss von Plotz."

When she left Mr. Kaplan's office and headed toward the park, Emily tugged at the corkscrew sleeves of her half-fitting sailor jacket with nervous fingers. She hoped she cut a fashionably jaunty picture. She also hoped Will Tate would be too innocent to recognize the somewhat faded blue fabric as having once seen service as her aunt's old draperies.

She had sewn the walking outfit from a pattern she copied from a *Ladies' Standard Magazine*, and spiffed it up with striped edging purchased dirt cheap and after much haggling from a grimy shop in Chinatown. She knew she was taking a chance by wearing the same straw hat she had worn the day before, but perhaps Will wouldn't recognize it. She had redecorated it with more of the same striped edging and a big red satin rose.

A huge sigh leaked from between Emily's lips when she thought about the rose. Her dear aunt Gertrude believed she had cut a tremendous bargain when she bought the bushel of satin flowers from a street vendor. Poor Gertrude could never be brought to understand a bargain is only a bargain when one actually needs the goods purchased and has no other use for the funds expended. And, although she resisted the truth at every turn, Gertrude needed many things before she needed satin roses.

Well, if this plan works, Aunt Gertrude can have all the satin flowers she wants, Emily told herself stoutly in order to bolster her resolve.

She still felt more than a little bit guilty about her plot as her footsteps carried her toward Golden Gate Park. She hoped Will wouldn't notice she carried no parasol, or if he did, he would chalk the lack up to personal choice and not penury.

Will was sprawled on a park bench, enjoying the lovely summer weather, when he espied Emily striding toward him purposefully. He decided that foregoing a night of gambling and rutting wasn't really much of a sacrifice when one had such an enchanting companion to look forward to in the morning.

Forgetting his role as crude country lout, he stood up and ripped his wide-brimmed hat from his head. Then he remembered he was supposed to be socially inept and decided Texas Lonesome would probably fidget. So he fingered his hat and shuffled his feet.

Aunt Emily, darlin', you're pretty as a San Antonio summer sky, he thought.

When Emily reached him she held out her hand, trying her best to appear unruffled. "Good morning, Mr. Tate." *My stars, he was a handsome man.*

"Good morning to you, Miss von Plotz," Will said with considerable warmth as his big hand engulfed her much smaller one.

She was nervous, he noticed with some surprise. He was the one who was supposed to be nervous.

Emily cleared her throat. "Well, now, Mr. Tate, shall we have a seat on this bench and begin our lessons?"

"Yes, ma'am," Will agreed, trying his best to sound meek.

Emily gazed at him pensively for a moment or two. She almost wished he weren't such a handsome devil. She was sure she would feel less fluttery about her deception if he were a plain man.

"I believe we should start with manners, Mr. Tate. Or, as some might say, etiquette." She gave him a prim, sideways smile, wondering if she would get a responsive twinkle.

But Will only nodded solemnly. "I reckon, ma'am."

Stifling her sigh, Emily said, "Now, you were perfectly correct when you stood at my approach."

Will tried to make the best of his regrettable lapse into manners.

"Thank you, ma'am," he muttered with as sheepish an expression as he could muster. "My ma taught me that."

"Well, your mother was absolutely correct, Mr. Tate. A gentleman should always rise when a lady enters a room or if he intends to greet her in a forum of public assembly, such as this park."

"Uh-huh."

"And you did very well by removing your hat, too. It was a polite gesture and the very best of manners. Did your mother teach you to do that as well?"

"Uh-huh." Will figured it wasn't too much of a fib. He was sure that if he had ever known his mother, she would have at least tried to teach him that much.

Emily smiled kindly. "One minor point, Mr. Tate. A gentleman usually tries to refrain from grunting in a lady's presence. A lady would generally prefer to hear a gentleman say 'yes' rather than 'uh-huh.'"

Will appeared suitably abashed. "Oh, gol', I guess I never thought of that, ma'am."

"It's quite all right, Mr. Tate. That's what I'm here for." She put a hand on his sleeve. "And please, Mr. Tate, don't take anything I say as an affront. I mean only to help you." As an experiment, she batted her eyelashes, and then felt silly.

Will noticed her fluttering lids and was amused. "You got something in your eye, ma'am?" he asked solicitously. Now why was Aunt Emily trying to flirt with him? he wondered.

Emily dropped her gaze and frowned. "No, Mr. Tate, but thank you for inquiring. It was very polite of you." So much for flirtation, she thought sourly. The man was even more innocent than she had suspected.

"Now, Mr. Tate, I believe it would be a good idea for us to take a small stroll around the park. Then I can point out to you various nuances of polite behavior that are better demonstrated than imparted verbally."

"Thank you kindly, ma'am."

Will stood up. Then he sat down. Then he tried his best to blush, failed, and decided to stutter instead. "D-Do I g-get up first, ma'am?" he asked in what he hoped was a shy, tentative voice.

Emily smiled at him with genuine tenderness, thereby very nearly causing him to forget himself entirely, grab her, and kiss her.

"It is proper for a gentleman to stand first and extend a hand to help the lady rise, Mr. Tate."

Will promptly surged to his feet and stuck out his hand. When Emily held up a limp wrist, he grabbed her by her fingers and hauled her to her feet with such gusto that her made-over hat almost toppled from her head. Emily clamped a quick hand on it to steady it.

"When I said a gentleman helps a lady to rise, Mr. Tate, my words were not to be taken quite so literally," she gasped.

"Oh." Will adopted a crestfallen expression.

"Oh, dear, Mr. Tate, I'm not scolding. You did nothing wrong. You were merely following my instructions. I should have explained to you that your hand is merely for support. Unless the lady in question is very old or infirm, you needn't actually use force to help her to rise."

"Oh." Will still looked rather hangdog. "I'm sorry, Miss von Plotz."

Emily honored him with a smile. "It's quite all right, Mr. Tate. As long as you learn from your mistakes, all will be well."

"Thank you, ma'am."

Emily felt a quick stab of guilt for deceiving this perfect country innocent and then stamped the feeling down with vigor. If she didn't do something soon, she reminded herself, her entire family would be out on the street without a penny to their name. She had to deceive this poor fellow. It was for her family's good. She held the knowledge close to her heart and swallowed the scruples that had suddenly lumped together in her throat.

"Do I hold your hand when we're walkin', ma'am?" Will asked, trying hard to look innocent.

Emily blessed him with an indulgent laugh. "No, Mr. Tate. You would never hold a lady's hand unless the two of you are so well acquainted as to have become engaged. And then you would never do so in public. Such an intimate display of affection is offensive to the public's eye and best kept to the privacy of one's own home. Of course, you must always ask the young lady's parents before you assume such a liberty, as well."

Will nodded, sober as a judge. "Yes, ma'am."

"You may, however, crook your elbow just so." Emily demonstrated by lifting her arm as described. "Then the lady will place her hand on your forearm as you walk."

"Like this, ma'am?" Will crooked his elbow.

Emily placed her hand on his arm and smiled. "Very well done, Mr. Tate."

Will grinned back at her. Saints and angels, this woman was the most adorable little thing he'd ever seen.

His gaze seemed to caress her in the most intimate way, and Emily felt her insides flutter. She had to clear her throat before she could speak again.

"You—you are very quick to learn, Mr. Tate."

"Shucks, ma'am," Will mumbled. "You're awful kind to teach me."

"Well, shall we take our little walk, Mr. Tate?"

"Yes, ma'am."

Will expected to have to slow his long stride a good deal to accommodate his partner. He wasn't prepared for Emily's firm gait.

The park was a delightful place. Emily had liked to go there on fine days to write her column even before she met Will Tate. Today, in his company, the park grounds seemed more beautiful than usual. The summer sky smiled down upon them, and the sun's rays picked out every leaf and petal as though to emphasize each one individually. The paths were raked to perfection, and the shrubbery was pruned into tidy borders.

If she hadn't been so acutely aware of her purpose, Emily might have taken great pleasure in their walk together. She *was* aware of her purpose, however, and didn't dare let down her guard, not for a single instant.

"Now, Mr. Tate, when a gentleman walks out of doors with a lady, he always walks on the outside, if there is an outside. Here in the park, we shall follow the paths, so there is no particular side to consider, but on a street with traffic you would take care to stay on the street side, closer to the traffic. The lady would walk next to the buildings."

"Why is that, ma'am?"

"Well, Mr. Tate, it's an old custom and one relating to matters of chivalry. A gentleman would place himself closer to the source of any danger in order to protect the lady. Also, if the streets are muddy, any mud or water thrown up by a passing carriage would hit the gentleman and not the lady. Ladies, as you know, are more delicate than gentlemen, and more apt to succumb to the ill effects of dampness. And their garments are more easily damaged as well."

A sudden image of Flaming Polly—smoking an enormous black cigar, her ample bosom spilling out over her red harlot's corset, cursing like a sailor and pointing a silver derringer at a drunk—flashed through Will's mind, and he had to stifle a guffaw. He peered down at Emily and discovered her gazing at him with an expression of absolute sincerity. Apparently Miss Emily von Plotz actually believed that folderol about women being more delicate than men.

"Yes, ma'am," he said meekly.

Will and Emily strolled through the park, delighting in the occasional pretty floral displays blossoming in discreet beds here and there. Pansies, even in their ungainly early-summer sprawl, seemed to be particular favorites of Emily's, Will noticed. He tucked the information away, thinking it might prove useful one day.

They meandered through the new Japanese Tea Garden, and Will exclaimed at its exotic beauty. They both enjoyed the majesty of the Huntington Falls as their waters splashed and tumbled down Strawberry Hill. Will itched to take Emily to the new rose garden but held his tongue, since it was she, after all, who was supposed to be showing him around.

They were at surprising ease with each other, and walked along for several minutes without speaking. When Will heard Emily's gusty sigh, he hoped it was one of pleasure.

It was. Emily was very happy with the way things were going. Will Tate was an apt student. Although in his letters he portrayed himself as a shy country lad, he seemed to have a natural gift for the social graces. The unexpected attribute pleased her. Although she would have married him anyway, the thought of spending the rest of her life attached to a rude bumpkin, even for the sake of her beloved family, did not appeal very much.

Also, he seemed to be responding to her even though she had not been flirting—not since the aborted attempt at batting her eyelashes. Emily considered flirting a demeaning, embarrassing activity indulged in only by females of a certain sort. Even so, she was willing to thrust her compunction aside for the sake of winning Texas Lonesome. Now she prayed she would be able to accomplish her goal with at least some of her dignity intact.

Will gazed down at her reworked straw hat and noticed a couple of places where the straw weave had been repaired. It had not escaped his attention, either, that Emily's costume had a look about it with which he was all too familiar: the look of made-over goods. He also acknowledged that whoever had made it over was very skilled at her craft. If he had not been exquisitely aware of all the tricks a person could use to try to disguise poverty, he would never have guessed. However, Uncle Mel, the shrewdest confidence man Will ever met in his life, had taught him well.

Emily's lack of a parasol, that absolutely necessary accoutrement to a lady's toilette, had not gone without his notice, either. And he recalled as well that young ladies of social standing did not traipse around town unaccompanied. He wondered what game Aunt

Emily was up to. His interest, which was already piqued, surged.

"Would you care to look in at the flower gardens, Mr. Tate?" Emily inquired politely. "I believe if you were to escort a young lady on a stroll through the park, it would elevate you in her esteem if you were to exhibit an interest in flowers.

"Not," she added primly, "that I advocate your professing an interest you do not possess, for that would be a falsehood, and a falsehood is never to be tolerated. But, if only for the young lady's sake, I believe it would behoove you to cultivate an interest in—oh, roses, for example."

Since Will Tate was about the only rosarian extant in the state of Texas at the moment, he nearly laughed out loud. He blinked back the sparkle threatening to give him away and nodded as though she had just uttered the One Universal Truth.

"Good idea, Miss von Plotz." He hoped Charley Wong, the gardener with whom he had conferred yesterday, wouldn't be working in the rose garden today.

Emily loved roses. She walked through the rose beds in Golden Gate Park at every opportunity. She thought the blossoms looked particularly beautiful today, for some reason.

"Someday I hope to have a rose garden of my own, Mr. Tate."

The simple confession sounded oddly sad to Will. He subtly steered Emily over to inspect the new polyantha he had taken such a shine to the day before. "What do you think of this one, Miss von Plotz?"

"Oh, Mr. Tate, it's just lovely." She leaned over to sniff the tiny, perfectly shaped soft-pink buds, and their powerfully sweet fragrance surprised her. "And they smell so wonderful. Yet they're so small."

Will had to hold back the information that polyanthas were noted for their heady rose fragrance and clusters of tiny blooms. Instead, he made a show of sniffing at the blossoms, too.

"Well, I'll be hornswoggled," he said in an attempt to sound countrified.

"'Cecile Brunner.' What a lovely name." Emily wished she could have a Cecile Brunner rosebush in her own garden. But, of course, she had no garden now that her uncle Ludwig had turned Aunt Gertrude's backyard into a breeding kennel for dachshunds. Every now and then Emily couldn't help but wish her relatives were just a wee bit less eccentric.

Will noticed her wistful expression and wondered if it would be polite to ask what he wanted to know. He decided Texas Lonesome would probably take the risk. "Can't you have a rosebush at your home, Miss von Plotz?"

Emily gave a little start. She hadn't meant to demonstrate such a transparently hopeful interest in these roses. "Oh, w-well, you see, Mr. Tate," she stammered, "it's—it's that I live with my aunt and uncle, and—and, well, the yard is being used for other purposes."

"Oh." Will thought for a minute. Then he drawled tentatively, "Miss von Plotz, would it be rude for a feller to ask what that purpose is? If a feller wanted to get to know a lady better?" He hoped he sounded sufficiently naive.

But Emily only smiled at him. Her expression was darling, and Will's heart gave an uncharacteristic leap so strong it startled him.

"Of course it wouldn't be rude, Mr. Tate. It is always polite to exhibit concern for a lady's interests and family, as long as you are well enough acquainted to make such an inquiry seem natural."

Merciful heavens. Aunt Emily was certainly a most fetching work of nature. He had to clear his throat before he could speak again.

"Well, then, ma'am, if we're well enough acquainted, maybe you wouldn't mind tellin' me what your yard is being used for, if you don't mind my askin'."

Immediately Emily realized she had talked herself into a tight spot. Then she guessed it didn't matter much. He'd have to find out about her lunatic relatives sooner or later if her plan was to succeed.

"Well, you met Helga and Gustav yesterday, of course."

"Yes, ma'am. Couldn't hardly forget that." Will smiled.

Emily felt mortified all over again about her uncle's dogs' unruly behavior, but she forged ahead. "Yes. Well, you see, Mr. Tate, my uncle, Ludwig von Plotz, believes dachshunds are the coming thing in the dog world."

Will had no trouble at all in looking astonished at her words. "The coming thing, ma'am?"

Abashed, Emily murmured, "I'm afraid so, Mr. Tate. He's certain he will be able to create a market for dachshunds here in America, since they're such wonderfully brave dogs. Even though they're small. In fact, Uncle Ludwig believes their size will be a selling point. People won't expect such a little animal to be so ferocious, and they'll also be cheap to feed. He has the idea that dachshunds will soon be used for all sorts of helpful purposes, from protecting banks to herding sheep. He even envisions them guarding strongboxes transported on railway carriages."

"Oh." Amazed, Will couldn't think of anything else to say.

"You see, Uncle Ludwig has spent most of his life in Europe. He lived in Germany as a young boy, and then Austria until four years ago. The death of the archduke and crown prince, Rudolf, affected him quite deeply, however, and he decided to move to the United States. My aunt Gertrude is his sister. Since she is a widow, she was very pleased that he wanted to join us here."

"I see." Will nodded with what he hoped looked like sympathy, wondering who in hell this Rudolf fellow was. He decided to pose the question at a later date. "Well, I think that's just—just fine, ma'am."

Emily thought it would be a good deal finer if Uncle Ludwig had any concept of the cost of establishing and maintaining a breeding kennel. Or a knack for raising money instead of spending it. Unfortunately, the entire von Plotz family, with the possible exception of Emily herself, seemed to have been born without a single shred of fiscal cunning.

Will noticed her retreat into reticence as they strolled past the rest of the rose beds. He figured she was embarrassed by her uncle's bizarre interests and had a sudden urge to tell her about his own uncle Mel. He had a feeling that he and Emily could spend a year or more swapping tales about their respective eccentric uncles, but he held his tongue. It wasn't time for such disclosures yet.

It was getting on toward midday, and all at once Will's stomach took the opportunity to growl. The fact didn't bother him, but he decided to use it to his advantage. Maybe he could remain in Miss Emily's company a while longer if he played his cards right.

He tried to look ashamed of himself. "I'm sorry, ma'am," he said.

Emily looked up at him, surprised. "You're sorry?"

"Yeah. My belly just grumbled, 'cause I'm hungry. I 'spect a real gentleman's belly don't never do that." Will was proud of that sentence.

Emily laughed. She had a sweet laugh, and Will liked it a lot.

"Oh, my, Mr. Tate, I don't suppose a gentleman has any more control over his stomach than the rest of us do. He would, however," she added in her teacher's voice, "call it his stomach and not his belly—if he referred to it at all, which he probably wouldn't. It is considered indiscreet to refer to one's organs in polite company."

Will gazed at her in honest appreciation. She had a very kind way of imparting these improving lectures of hers.

"Yes, ma'am," he said. "Well, ma'am, since my— my organ is empty and we're here together, would it be proper for me to invite you somewheres to eat? Then you can teach me how to use them forks and knives and such."

Emily was hungry, too. She usually had bread and butter and water at midday because she didn't want to waste her family's rapidly dwindling resources. The thought of eating a real luncheon was quite appealing, especially if she could do it in Will Tate's company and at his expense.

The fact that dining in a restaurant alone, just the two of them, was decidedly improper caused her a

stab or two of unease. She also had to suppress a sub-
stantial twinge of guilt about the cost by reminding
herself that he had described himself as a wealthy
man. She didn't suppose buying her lunch would be
much of a burden for him.

"Why, I think that's a marvelous idea, Mr. Tate.
Thank you very much for the invitation. And you
extended it very prettily." She didn't think she should
quibble about his grammar at the moment. There
were too many other things to teach him first.

Will seemed pleased, and that made her happy.

"Do you know a place close by to eat at, ma'am?"

"I believe there's a small chophouse on Montgomery Street where one can have quite a nice luncheon at a reasonable price, Mr. Tate."

Will felt vaguely troubled. He wanted to take her
someplace nice to eat, not to some dump of a chophouse. "Isn't—" He almost corrected himself and said
"ain't," but decided it would be too obvious. "Isn't
there someplace a little bit finer, Miss von Plotz? I'm
real rich, and I 'spect I'll be takin' my wife to real nice
places, if I ever get me one. A wife. Not an eatin'
place."

Emily looked up at him quickly. The thought of
dining at a fine restaurant was so appealing, she
nearly succumbed to the evil demon tempting her,
but her nobler nature won the day.

"I think perhaps we should start on a small scale,
Mr. Tate. That way, when you do take your lady to a
fine restaurant, you won't have any reason to be
uncomfortable."

Will was a little disgruntled at having his plot
foiled so neatly, but he didn't dare show it. "All right,
Miss von Plotz. That's probably a smart idea. But you

have to promise me you'll let me practice in a fancy place when I get the hang of it."

Emily had seldom met such a nice man. It seemed almost a shame to trick him. Nevertheless, she needed him—her family needed him—too much to allow her conscience to smite her. If she had to harden her heart and play the coy seductress, so be it. Resolute, she trod beside him to Mrs. Flanagan's Kitchen.

During their luncheon, Will discovered he enjoyed Emily's little lessons. He tried very hard to give her plenty of material to work on.

He tucked his napkin into his shirtfront and adopted an expression of chagrin at Emily's kind suggestion that he place it on his lap instead.

He fumbled with the silverware and ate with his knife and was suitably contrite when Emily pointed out to him the reason civilized man had invented forks.

He slurped his soup and dipped his spoon the wrong way, then ducked his head in shame when she taught him the proper way to drink soup.

He reached clear across the table to fetch the salt cellar and recoiled like a scolded puppy when Emily imparted the socially accepted way to ask for salt.

He buttered an entire piece of bread and appeared terribly abashed when Emily told him it was polite to break off little pieces of bread and butter them individually, one at a time, before he popped them into his mouth.

"Why, shucks, ma'am. Ain't that a lot of effort to go to when you can just butter the whole thing once and be done with it?"

Emily's laugh tinkled from her rosy lips. "I suppose it does seem so, Mr. Tate. But you see, polite manners are often holdovers from earlier days, when there were good reasons for them and they really did make sense. The fact that the absolute necessity for such customs may have passed does not absolve one from following the accepted mode."

Will contemplated his companion for a moment. Aunt Emily sure had a way with words, all right.

"I guess that's so, ma'am," he said with what he hoped sounded like uncertainty. When he saw Emily's eyes brighten with pleasure, he knew his answer was appropriate.

Emily couldn't remember ever having had such a wonderful time in a gentleman's company. Of course, the only gentlemen she'd been in company with lately were her uncle and Clarence Pickering, her aunt's financial adviser. And while her uncle was at least a kind man, Pickering was enough to make a saint curse. Suddenly recalling that he was coming to dine at her aunt's home the following evening, Emily made yet another impetuous decision.

"Mr. Tate, how would you like to come to my aunt's house for dinner tomorrow night? You can practice your new table manners there, out of the view of the public. If you make any little mistakes at my aunt's table, it won't matter, and you needn't be embarrassed."

Will stared into Emily's sparkling blue eyes and lost his concentration for a minute. Fortunately he collected himself in time to answer in character. Instead of telling her exactly how charmed he would be to accept such a kind invitation, he made a clumsy show of clearing his throat and then said, "Well, er, gol', ma'am. I ain't never been to no lady's house for dinner before."

Emily put her hand over his as he gripped the edge of the table.

"Please don't be nervous, Mr. Tate. You're a wonderful student. I'm sure you'll do just fine. My aunt and uncle are—are—Well, they're not at all stuffy."

In fact, this was quite an understatement. An image of Uncle Ludwig singing merrily along with "General Knickerbocker" from his seat in the balcony at the opera house nearly made her blush. No. Her relatives were certainly not stuffy.

"You really think I'm a good learner, Miss von Plotz?" Will wished she would leave her little warm hand on his, but she withdrew it and tucked it demurely back into her lap.

"You're an excellent learner, Mr. Tate."

"Well, then, ma'am, if you truly wouldn't mind a big galoot like me invadin' your home, I'd be proud to take supper with you tomorrow."

The smile with which Emily greeted his words almost made him fall off his chair. Lord above, Aunt Emily was some piece of work.

Emily gave him her aunt's address and told him to be at the house at seven the following evening, and they parted company. Both left feeling the day had been well spent.

Later on in the evening, Will had a grand time imparting Emily's lessons in deportment to Thomas Crandall.

"My God, Will, I can't believe you actually made her believe you're a country boy." Thomas laughed so hard and so long, he had to mop tears from his face with his handkerchief.

"If Uncle Mel taught me anything at all, Thomas Crandall, it was how to dissimulate effectively," Will said solemnly. "Besides, Miss Emily is up to something. I'm not quite sure what it is, but I know she's up to something."

"Something devious? You mean she's scheming?"

"Yep."

Thomas frowned. "Well, I guess if anybody could recognize a cheat, it's you, Will. God knows, you cheat better than anybody I've ever met."

Will frowned and thanked Thomas sarcastically for his kind words.

Emily was alternately elated and depressed as she made her way home from the park. On the one hand, her plot seemed to be working even better than she could have hoped. She had noticed the unmistakable signs of interest in Will Tate's eyes during their walk in the park and at luncheon. On the other hand, the better she got to know this big, delightful, lonely Texan, the worse she felt about deceiving him.

"He's such a sweet, simple man," she murmured as she walked along Grant Avenue. The street had been renamed recently in honor of the former President, and Emily sometimes had trouble remembering it was no longer Dupont. She turned up Hayes and frowned when she recognized Clarence Pickering's carriage standing in front of her aunt's house.

Pickering's henchman, Bill Skates, lounged against the carriage and leered at her as she approached. Skates reminded Emily of the villain in a play she had once seen at the California Theater. A tall, reed-thin, almost cadaverous man, he had a long black mustache, which he apparently took great pains to wax and wrap into tight curlicues at the ends. The unpleasant fellow sported a hideous red-and-green plaid cutaway suit. Emily wanted to squeeze her eyes shut against it as she walked past him.

"'Lo, Emily, darlin'," Skates greeted her snidely.

Emily chose to ignore him as she marched up to her aunt's front door. With luck, she wouldn't have to talk to Skates's employer.

She opened the front door slowly and cringed at the loud, grating creak its hinges made. She'd meant to soap those hinges. But it was too late now.

"Emily, my love, come here and say hello to Mr. Pickering," Aunt Gertrude called from the parlor before the door even stopped screeching. At that point, Emily knew luck was visiting elsewhere today.

3

Emily silently uttered as foul a curse as she could think of for failing to take care of the door hinges, braced herself for an unpleasant encounter, and donned a smile before pushing open the parlor door. Without looking to her right or her left, she steered a wide path around Clarence Pickering and tried her best to ignore him. She went over to her aunt and kissed her cheek in greeting.

If Bill Skates was patently evil, Clarence Pickering was even worse. He reeked of sincerity. His handsome face had a sincere smile on it. His dark brown eyes possessed a sincere twinkle. He wore sincere suits of brown gabardine, and his hands were even manicured sincerely.

It was no wonder her aunt had been taken in by him, Emily thought sourly. Aunt Gertrude gloried in good manners and fashionable dress. She was also not one to delve beneath the surface of anything.

But Emily didn't trust Clarence Pickering one bit. He had steered her aunt into one bad investment after another, and Emily was sure he was lining his pockets with pickings from Gertrude's assets.

In the wintertime Pickering invariably wore an elegant black coat with multiple capes. But the weather was fine today, and he was clad in a respectable summer suit. He sported white gaiters and black patent-leather shoes just like those of his henchman, and she wondered if they'd purchased them at a discount, two for the price of one.

But no, she thought with uncharacteristic cynicism. Clarence Pickering had no need to look for bargains, since he had all of her aunt's money.

Aunt Gertrude peered up at her expectantly, and Emily knew she could postpone this unpleasantness no longer. She turned, held out her hand, and said with great formality, "How do you do, Mr. Pickering?"

The man had the effrontery to look her up and down, and Emily longed to smack his handsome face.

"My, my, aren't we formal today, Miss Emily. Call me Clarence, child. You know I'm always telling you to call me Clarence."

Emily tried not to recoil from him because she didn't want to upset her aunt. "Yes, Mr. Pickering, I know you're always telling me that."

He didn't seem inclined to release her hand, so Emily had to tug it from his grip.

"Mr. Pickering has been telling me about a wonderful new investment opportunity, Emily dear. Something about ships. He's sure it will make loads of money for us all. Then you won't have to fuss at me anymore about my finances. Sweet Emily is forever scolding me about money, Mr. Pickering." Aunt Gertrude gifted Emily with a rather vacuous smile and then aimed it at Pickering.

"Well, she's a dutiful niece, Mrs. Schindler. As well as a very pretty one." Pickering waggled his eyebrows at Emily, making sure her aunt couldn't see the gesture, of course.

"Well, you can stop worrying now, Emily darling. Mr. Pickering assures me this new opportunity will turn our luck around."

"I didn't think luck was supposed to have anything to do with it, Aunt. I thought one's financial adviser was supposed to be a font of wisdom." Emily knew the words were catty, but she tried to keep her expression sweet.

She was about half successful. Pickering glared at her, but at least her aunt didn't notice. "Oh, yes!" Gertrude cried. "And Mr. Pickering is *so* wise. Why, these ships sound absolutely marvelous!"

"Oh, really? Your last scheme nearly turned us out of this house, Mr. Pickering. Is this as marvelous an investment opportunity as that one? The Chinese horse herds? The ones that don't exist?"

The target of Emily's acid tongue assumed an air of long-suffering patience, as though he were now going to try to explain a complicated mathematical equation to a four-year-old. "Well, now, Miss von Plotz, I'm sure you know how volatile the financial markets can be. One must sort through all the information one is given and discard the chaff. It was truly unfortunate that communications about those Manchurian herds went awry."

Emily hated this man for weaseling his way into her aunt's confidence. Aunt Gertrude would never allow herself to see through his facade, no matter how thin it was. Emily's aunt invariably accepted everything at its face value, and Pickering's face, unfortunately, looked quite pleasant.

"That's so, Emily dear," Aunt Gertrude said with a sigh. "You know those poor Chinese horses weren't Mr. Pickering's fault. Such an unfortunate thing to have happened. They sounded so pretty, too. I wonder where on earth they went."

Emily could no longer hide her contempt. "Now wherever did I get the impression an investment counselor's purpose in life was to learn about the investments he proposes before he takes your money for them, Aunt? It seems to me that Mr. Pickering needs to research his schemes a little more thoroughly before you give him any more money. After those invisible herds, you know, you don't have much left."

Aunt Gertrude pouted. "That's an unkind thing to say to dear Mr. Pickering. He tries so hard for us. I just hate to hear unkindness spoken in my home." She then addressed Pickering. "My sweet Emily is such a spirited little thing, don't you know."

Pickering ogled Emily. "Isn't she, though?"

Emily sighed. "Well, what is this wonderful investment scheme, then? Did you say ships?"

"Emily, you sound almost snappish. Did you have a bad day, dear? I almost think it would be better for you not to hear about it now, darling, if you can't speak in a more pleasant manner. Poor Mr. Pickering is very upset about those Chinese horse herds. He brought this new idea to me today in an attempt to make up for the lost horses. He's sure investing in these ships built out of that special African wood will recoup all our losses."

Ships made from special African wood? Oh, Lord. Emily gave up. She knew from bitter experience it wouldn't do any good to fight her aunt about Pickering because Aunt Gertrude simply wouldn't listen. Emily knew her family's only hope for financial salvation lay elsewhere.

"You're right, Aunt," she said abruptly. "I don't think I want to hear about any more of Mr. Pickering's plots and schemes right now. I'll just leave you two to discuss them. I have a column to write."

She marched out of the parlor and up to her bedroom fairly quivering with indignation. Once seated at her desk, she was in such a state of frustrated rage that she read and answered another five whole letters.

When she reread the answer she had just penned to yet one more lovelorn adolescent, Emily realized she was taking her anger out on her correspondents. The heartsick girl had sent Aunt Emily a plea for assistance because her mother and father didn't understand the depth of her regard for her young man. The girl came across to Emily as an idiot infatuated with a bounder. In her reply Emily had written:

"Dear Unhappy: You would best recover from your melancholy if you were to turn your energy to some constructive activity rather than whine about lost love at an age when you are too young to know what love means. Mooning helplessly and arguing with your parents about a person who, quite frankly, sounds like a money-grubbing twit will only prolong your misery. Believe me when I tell you a proper gentleman would not press a suit distasteful to his dear heart's parents, nor would he *ever* urge the young lady into deception. Turn your attention outside of yourself, young lady, and you might come to understand that the reason you are unhappy is not your parents but your own present callow, selfish attitude."

Emily actually groaned aloud when she scanned

this particularly vituperative response. She crumpled the piece of paper.

She would have to get a grip on her nerves. It wouldn't do to alienate her readers and lose the only source of income her family had. With a soul-deep sigh, she dipped her pen into the standish and tried again.

She was more pleased when she read her edited reply to the lovelorn miss:

"Dear Unhappy: At age sixteen, I know you believe your heart is broken. Please take advice from your caring Aunt Emily and abide by your parents' wishes with grace. They love you, my dear, and it is their duty as parents to protect you. It is your duty as a good and obedient daughter to trust their judgment. If your young man is a person of character and honor, he will wait for you and not press you into a deceitful alliance. Please accept my best wishes in this time of distress."

"Idiot child," Emily muttered as she completed her reply. "Her parents ought to lock her in a closet until she grows a brain in her head."

Her heart lurched when she picked up the next letter. She read, "Dear Aunt Emily: I think you are a very nice lady to give me such good advice. I wish more ladies was like you. Signed, Texas Lonesome."

Tears stung Emily's eyes, and she swallowed them back. She must not flinch from her purpose. The reason for her resolve was taking tea with her aunt at this very minute. She couldn't fail in her plan. She simply couldn't.

After she had written a gentle reply and finished reading and answering another letter, she gathered her stack of correspondence. She supposed she'd better slow down. Pretty soon she'd have so many columns written, Mr. Kaplan wouldn't need her services anymore.

Feeling very melancholy, she gazed out her bedroom window as the dusky evening settled into dark. The fog curled up from the bay and wound its way around the city, softening its rough edges.

What a fraud she was. Who was she to vilify another's deceit? Here she was, coldly trying to lure poor Will Tate into marriage with her—her!—a woman burdened with debt and two crazy, spendthrift relatives. And he was so kind, so sweet. Emily decided glumly that she was an evil woman. She wiped a tear from her cheek and wished there were another way.

She changed into her evening clothes slowly and wondered what Will Tate was doing for dinner tonight. The uneasy feeling that Clarence Pickering would be joining them at the table gnawed at her, and she wished she'd invited Will to sup with them tonight instead of tomorrow. For some reason, she just knew Pickering wouldn't bother her if Will Tate was around.

Oh, well, she thought. She didn't suppose she could have Will visit every night just to distract her from Pickering.

Emily didn't have a maid to help her dress, so she generally chose gowns that buttoned up the front. She was fastening her basque when she was suddenly struck by the thought that if she married Will, he could button dresses up the back for her. The thought of his long brown fingers brushing against her bare skin brought a flush to her cheeks.

If she did trick him into marrying her, at least she'd be wed to a very handsome man. And he seemed so considerate, too. But it would serve her right if he hauled her off to Texas and she never got to see San Francisco again.

She loved her city by the bay. Every time she thought about Texas, the best her brain could picture was bleak desert dotted with hostile savages, all aiming their bristling arrows straight at her heart. She was nearly in tears by the time she descended the stairs.

But at dinner, as Clarence Pickering tried to play with her feet under the dining room table, Emily's resolve, which had been perilously close to dissolving earlier, began to firm up again. It solidified into a granitelike certainty after the meal when Pickering managed to get her alone in a corner of the parlor.

Uncle Ludwig was, as usual, pontificating about dachshunds. Aunt Gertrude was listening to him with rapt attention.

"I tell you, Gertrude, they're *magnificent* animals. *Marvelous* dogs. They have the spirit of the kaisers in their blood!"

Uncle Ludwig almost always spoke in italics and exclamation points. He had a heavy German accent and a tendency to spit when he was excited. Since he was excited most of the time, chatting with Ludwig could be quite an adventure.

"I'm sure you're right, Ludwig. I'm certain of it." Gertrude gazed adoringly at her beloved brother. He could do no wrong in her eyes.

Gustav and Helga had been allowed into the house after supper and they too were in the parlor. Neither dog cared for Clarence Pickering. While Ludwig spoke to Gertrude, they nipped at Pickering's feet and gradually backed him into a chair by the fire.

"Look at them, Gertrude! Just look at them! They're trying to protect us."

Ludwig's voice was fervent and he gazed at his pets with pride. Pickering managed to raise his feet a bare instant before Helga's sharp teeth could damage his new shoes.

Gertrude's smile wobbled a little. "Perhaps you should call to them, Ludwig dear. They seem to be trying to bite poor Mr. Pickering."

"I think Uncle Ludwig is right, Aunt Gertrude," Emily said. "They certainly do seem to be trying to protect us."

The ferocious hounds ignored Uncle Ludwig's command to leave Pickering alone, but at the offer of a biscuit, Gustav immediately abandoned his quarry. Helga followed him a moment later with a fair show of reluctance.

The dogs' departure gave Pickering an opportunity to rise from his chair and, in one fluid motion, trap Emily by the fireplace.

"Those dogs of your uncle's are a fierce pair, Miss Emily." Pickering's slick voice made Emily shiver.

"They're shrewd judges of character, Mr. Pickering." She stood as rigid as a lance as he approached. She cursed herself for coming over to the fire, because now there was no easy escape.

Pickering gave her a sly smile. "You don't like me much, do you, Miss Emily?"

"You're wrong, Mr. Pickering. I don't like you at all."

Pickering seemed undaunted. In fact, he chuckled when he said, "Aw, now, Miss Emily, I'll bet that if you'd get to know me better, you'd soften your attitude a little bit."

"I seriously doubt it, Mr. Pickering. But we'll never know, because I certainly do not intend to get to know you better."

His smile was sincere and condescending, as though he were a politician speaking to a constituent. If one were observing from afar, Emily was sure, one would think he was only making polite conversation. She knew better, though, especially when he said, "It might be a good idea if you did, Miss Emily. I really do think it would be."

"I'm sure you do, Mr. Pickering," Emily said furiously. "After all, one of these days perhaps my aunt and uncle will listen to me and realize what a villain you are." Actually, she was positive that day would never come, but she didn't want Pickering to know it.

He chuckled. "You're a fine sight when you're riled, Miss Emily."

Her spine stiffened even more. She did not deign to respond to Pickering's offensive comment, but the look on his face began to alarm her.

"You know, sweet Emily, it might really be a good idea if you were to be a little nicer to me." One of Pickering's long, elegant fingers reached out to stroke her cheek, and she turned her face away in disgust.

"Stop it!" she whispered fiercely.

"Oh, my lovely Emily, don't be so rash. I bet you'd like me if you gave me half a chance. And it sure would be good for your aunt and uncle if you sweetened up to me."

"And just what do you mean by that, Mr. Pickering?" Emily tried to move away from him, but he blocked her retreat. She swore to herself that she would never allow this vile creature to back her into a corner again.

"Well, now, Miss Emily, what do you think I mean? If you were to be nice to me, it would be a joy for me to help your family out."

"You're supposed to be helping them now. What does my being nice to you have to do with anything?"

"Aw, Emily, my pet, you know I do right by your aunt and uncle. But if you were to give me some incentive, I'd work even harder. I'll bet you'd like pretty dresses and trinkets. Wouldn't you? All ladies like pretty things. You deserve them, Emily dear. You truly do."

She was flat up against the wall now. She'd slap his face and run out of the room, except she didn't want to upset her aunt and uncle. Frantically she tried to peer over his shoulder, but realized he had chosen his time and place well. They were hidden from Aunt Gertrude and Uncle Ludwig by two enormous wing chairs, and neither her aunt nor her uncle was paying them any mind. Ludwig was too busy glorifying his dogs and Gertrude was too busy agreeing with him to think about Emily.

As usual, Emily thought. She had to swallow a bitter tear or two that surged up behind her guard.

"You're a real, real pretty girl, Miss Emily," Pickering whispered.

His face was getting closer and closer, and Emily finally couldn't stand it a second longer. She gave him a tremendous shove, and he stumbled backward. They were near the fireplace, and Pickering's right ankle banged against the brass firewood basket.

"Oh, dear. How terribly clumsy of me, Mr. Pickering."

Emily watched with pleasure as the basket tipped over and Pickering landed on his elegant rear end among the rolling logs. Using exquisite care, she stepped on his hand with the sharp heel of her evening slipper as she sidled around his sprawled body. Then she ground her heel into his open palm once, just for spite.

"Oh, my goodness, Mr. Pickering, how careless of me," she added sweetly when he let out a bellow of pain. She smiled down at him beatifically and then strolled over to the door.

"My goodness!" Aunt Gertrude cried as Pickering tried to pick himself up. His ascent was seriously impeded by Helga and Gustav, who sniffed a victory and roared over to attack.

As she paused at the doorway and peered at the melee, Emily thought she had seldom enjoyed a scene more. She smiled in satisfaction when she noticed the angry red welt on Pickering's palm as he covered his head to avoid the furious dachshunds' gnashing teeth. Then he staggered up, immediately stepped on a log, and lost his balance once more as it rolled away under his foot.

She nearly giggled when Helga's long canine teeth ripped a big gash in the side of his shiny patent-leather shoe. Gustav tugged at a formerly white gaiter, and two buttons popped off.

Emily was disappointed when Ludwig finally subdued the two small furies, exclaiming, "Now you see what I say is true, Pickering. These dogs are wonderful guardians. Wonderful!"

While he and Aunt Gertrude were occupied in soothing Pickering's ruffled feathers, Emily decided to make her escape.

As she trod up the stairs to her room once more, she realized that she had no choice but to ensnare the

innocent Will Tate. She vowed she would do her best
to be a good wife to him.

The next day was a productive one for Will. He spent
most of it with Charley Wong in the rose garden at
Golden Gate Park, making arrangements to have several roses shipped to his home in San Antonio. Before
he left, he paused before the pink polyantha he'd
shown to Emily the day before.

"Why don't you give me another one of those
Cecile Brunners, too, Charley? Put it in a big pot and
have it delivered to this address." He scribbled
Gertrude Schindler's Hayes Street address on a scrap
of paper and handed it to the gardener.

"Sure thing, Mr. Tate."

"It'll grow all right in a pot, won't it?"

"Oh, it will. Just make sure it gets lots of sunshine
and plenty of water."

Will didn't know it for a fact, but he was fairly certain Emily von Plotz would take good care of anything anybody gave to her.

"Is this a gift, Mr. Tate? Do you want to send a
note with it?"

Will decided then and there that Charley Wong
was a genius. "Good idea, Charley. Yes, I do." He
thought hard for a minute. Then a grin spread across
his face, and he quickly scribbled a note. "Can you
put this on a card for me?"

"Sure thing, Mr. Tate." Charley Wong read the
message, looked up at Will in surprise, and then stuck
the paper into his pocket with a shrug.

*   *   *

Emily felt her cheeks warm with pleasure when she read the note accompanying the lovely potted rose plant that had just been delivered to her aunt's door.

"Dear Miss Aunt Emily," the note ran, "I don't know if it is proper manners, but please accept this here rose and stick it somewheres in the sun. The man says it will grow good in the pot, so's you don't need a yard as long as you pour water on it. Yrs, Will Tate."

"Oh, what a dear, dear man," Emily breathed.

She gave the delivery boy a tip before she directed him to take the big pot out back and deposit it beside the entrance to Gustav and Helga's elaborately constructed living quarters. Emily held the snarling beasts by their collars so they couldn't eat the frightened boy as he did as she bade him.

He eyed the dogs warily. "I ain't never seen no dogs look like that before."

"No, I'm sure you haven't," Emily said with a sigh.

When the boy left and she finally released them, Gustav promptly marked the rose pot as his. Helga sniffed at it with her usual suspicion, then lay down next to it and went to sleep.

"Well, that beautiful rose will look very pretty climbing over your kennel, Gustav and Helga," Emily said.

She stared morosely at the dogs' home, which resembled a miniature Victorian mansion, complete with real glass windows. Uncle Ludwig had certainly spared no expense in building it. Nothing was too good for his dogs, he claimed.

Sometimes she wanted to ask him why his dogs should live better than their owners, but she always restrained herself. She knew better than to expect her relatives to behave sensibly.

Her mood was gloomy when she walked into the house to search for her aunt. She found Gertrude in the best parlor, staring into a globe of clear glass Emily had never seen before.

"What's that, Aunt Gertrude?"

Gertrude peered up at Emily with her usual slightly befuddled smile. "It's a crystal ball, dear. Mrs. Pollifant says you can see the future in it."

Emily held in her groan of exasperation. "And what do you see in your future, Aunt?"

Her aunt stared intently into the ball for a minute or two. "Bubbles," she announced at last.

"Bubbles?"

Gertrude sighed. "The glass has bubbles in it, dear. I can't see a thing. Mrs. Pollifant says it sometimes takes a while for the spirits to warm up to one."

Emily sighed too as she looked down at her aunt's immaculately coiffed gray head, covered this morning with a lacy white cap that must have cost five dollars if it cost a penny.

"Where did you get it, Aunt?"

"Mrs. Pollifant's spiritual advisor sold it to her, and she sold it to me, Emily darling. Mrs. Pollifant never does a thing without consulting Professor Claude, you know. He's a very wise man."

Try as she might, Emily couldn't be cross with Gertrude. She was such a sweet woman, in spite of her often tenuous relationship with reality. Emily could not, however, hide the slightly acid tone to her words when she said, "Well, maybe your crystal ball can tell me if Will Tate will be easy to trick into marrying me, Aunt."

"Will Tate, dear? Are you marrying a gentleman named Will Tate? I don't believe I recall who he is."

Emily sat down. "You haven't met him, Aunt Gertrude. And I was only teasing about marrying him. Sort of. He's coming over to take dinner with us tonight."

Gertrude brightened immediately. "Oh, how lovely, Emily. A gentleman caller. What a treat for you. Is he a *young* man?"

"Yes, Aunt, he's a young man. I expect he's about thirty." Emily had not actually put an age to Will before this. She hadn't much cared how old he was once she found out he was Texas Lonesome.

Gertrude placed a warm, plump hand over Emily's. "I know how difficult it is for you to be confined to this house with us two old people, dear. You have your writing to keep you busy, but I still think it's wonderful that you have a young man to call on you."

Emily's fond smile wavered slightly at the reference to her writing. Aunt Gertrude simply could not be made to understand that the only thing standing between herself and poverty was Emily's newspaper column. And her writing just barely paid for their food, a part-time houseboy, the services of Mr. Blodgett, and those of their cook, Mrs. Blodgett.

The possibility of her aunt's investing in another one of Mr. Pickering's ill-fated schemes and losing everything was a daily worry for Emily. One more disaster like those imaginary Chinese horse herds would find them all out on the street. Her uncle's dachshunds were, literally, eating up the meager interest earned on her aunt's few remaining solid investments. She knew it was useless to talk to her aunt about any of these things, however.

"Well, I'm trying very hard to make a good impression on Mr. Tate, Aunt Gertrude," was all she said.

Gertrude looked puzzled. "Oh. Well, I'm sure you'll do that, Emily. You're perfectly well mannered, dear, and you're quite a lovely girl."

"I only hope Uncle Ludwig will behave himself," Emily said very softly, fussing nervously with the ribbons tied at her waist. She knew she was treading on dangerous ground, but she couldn't help but be concerned.

Gertrude's face crumpled up into a sad little frown. "Oh, Emily, how can you say such a thing? You know your uncle Ludwig is a wonderful man."

Emily felt like a beast, but she still persisted. "Yes, I do know it, Aunt. But you have to admit he can be trying sometimes."

"Now, now, Emily darling. Ludwig is a man with strong interests and opinions. And if you're thinking about that time at the Woodward Gardens, you know that wasn't his fault. Not entirely."

Emily had actually forgotten about Ludwig's run-in with the chief horticulturist at the Woodward Gardens until now. She cringed as the memory flooded back. It had taken all of her charm and an enormous amount of wheedling to prevent the offended horticulturist from having Ludwig arrested for eating the shrubbery.

Ludwig claimed he had been conducting an experiment. The fact that he was telling the absolute truth didn't make the incident any less disconcerting for Emily. Nobody else's relatives ate the plants in public gardens, she thought gloomily.

"Well, I don't suppose there will be anything for him to get into tonight. After all, we'll be here."

Emily wondered suddenly if it was such a good idea for Will to visit. Still, it couldn't be helped. If he was as naive and innocent as he appeared, perhaps he wouldn't notice anything out of the ordinary about her aunt and uncle.

She peered wistfully at her aunt, whose attention had again wandered to her crystal ball. Gertrude now stared into it with rapt concentration.

"I believe I'm beginning to see something, dear," she told her niece in a happy trill as she passed her hand mysteriously over the globe.

Then again, maybe even a shy, innocent Texan would be able to discern a certain off-centeredness about Emily's family. Heaving a deep sigh, Emily rose from the sofa and left the parlor to Gertrude and her spirit friends.

As she climbed the stairs to her room, Emily decided she would use all the feminine wiles at her command on Will Tate tonight, whether such tactics were honorable or not. With any luck at all, he wouldn't even notice Aunt Gertrude and Uncle Ludwig.

4

Dear Aunt Emily:
  *I am going to eat supper with the lady I like
tonight. I hope I know what fork to use when,
and that my decorum is good. Please wish me
luck. I feel like I know you and you are my friend.*
  Signed,
  Texas Lonesome

Emily sighed wistfully and decided this was one
letter she didn't need to answer in her column.

After a busy afternoon spent in the kitchen helping
poor old Mrs. Blodgett prepare a big company dinner,
Emily hurried upstairs to her bedroom.

With trembling fingers, she tugged at her sapphire-
blue satin bodice and surveyed herself in her warped
mirror. She noted with satisfaction the swell of her
firm young bosom.

Both from reading and from gossip, Emily had
gleaned the interesting fact that young gentlemen

enjoyed observing young ladies' bosoms. The information, which might have shocked an innocent maiden in other circumstances, only spurred Emily to action. Desperate times, after all, called for desperate measures. She eased her bodice a tiny bit lower to give herself more cleavage and smiled at the result.

She had made this gown over from one she'd purchased at an estate sale, but she tried not to think about that. The idea of wearing a dead woman's made-over dress was simply too disconcerting.

"There. That should do it. Oh, please, God, forgive me." Her little prayer sneaked out from between her lips unbidden.

She was trying so hard not to feel guilty about this. She almost wished Will Tate weren't such a nice man. She'd feel much less terrible about deceiving a villain. On the other hand, her practical nature reminded her, she was sure to be much happier married to a nice man than to a villain.

The deep, old-fashioned gong of Aunt Gertrude's front doorbell announced somebody's arrival. Emily took as deep a breath as her corset would allow. She hoped it was Will Tate and not Clarence Pickering.

Then she patted her shimmering brown curls once, adjusted the blue satin ribbon holding them in place, and opened the door to her room. She said a little prayer for strength and practiced a charming smile as she gripped the banister and began her descent.

It was Will. She could tell by his deep, beautiful, drawling Texas voice. A little flutter of excitement rippled through her. Then their gazes met as he looked up, and she thought for a terrifying moment that she was going to tumble down the rest of the staircase.

He looked *so* handsome.

Emily remembered herself in time to salvage her seductive smile. Still, she hadn't properly prepared herself for the sight of Will Tate in his sober, elegant black evening clothes. His crisp white shirt with the ruffled front set off his tan face to perfection. His sun-bleached brown hair glimmered in the soft candlelight issuing from the wall sconces in the hall. Clutching a shiny black beaver hat in white-gloved hands, Will Tate looked nothing at all like an illiterate Texas bumpkin.

As for Will, he had never been stricken dumb before. He didn't think he had it in him. But when he glanced up to see Emily von Plotz floating down the stairs toward him in a cloud of blue satin, her eyes reflecting the color of her gown and her cheeks flushed a soft, delicate pink, he felt as though he'd just been punched in the gut. Hard. His mouth dropped open, and for a moment he had no trouble at all feeling like the bashful Texan Emily believed him to be.

Sweet Lord in heaven, she was beautiful.

Emily had recovered nearly all of her composure by the time she got to the bottom of the staircase. There she held out a hand to Will and spoke in a voice that trembled only slightly.

"Good evening, Mr. Tate. It's a pleasure to welcome you to my aunt Gertrude's home." She turned to Blodgett. "Are my aunt and uncle in the parlor, Blodgett?"

"Your uncle is, Miss Emily." The butler's voice was as creaky as those door hinges that Emily still hadn't soaped.

"Well, why don't you take Mr. Tate's hat, Blodgett, and I'll see him into the parlor."

"Very good, miss."

Will shoved his hat into Blodgett's hands and finally found his voice. "You look real fine tonight, Miss von Plotz. Real, real fine." He gazed down at her and realized that, from his height, he had a perfect view of Emily's carefully emphasized cleavage.

"Thank you, Mr. Tate." Emily took his arm and began to guide him toward the parlor. "And thank you so very much for the lovely rose you sent. It was such a sweet, thoughtful thing to do."

She peered up at him and dared to flutter her lashes. The ploy hadn't worked too well in the park, but he seemed a little dazed this evening.

Her flutter broke the spell for Will. He was on the alert in an instant.

Now just what was her game? he wondered. Maybe she really was trying to lure Texas Lonesome into marriage. But why?

His question began to answer itself as soon as Will entered the parlor. He had a quick impression of shabby grandeur before his attention was captured by the two flashes of reddish brown fur running over to greet him.

He smiled at Emily, who dropped her coy demeanor and put her hands to her hot cheeks in embarrassment.

"Oh, Mr. Tate, I'm so sorry. I didn't know these beasts were in here."

Will gave her a wink and knelt to greet the dogs. "It's all right, Miss von Plotz. Gustav and Helga and me are old friends."

Had he just winked at her? Emily stared down at Will in astonishment.

She didn't have time to think any more about it, though, because her uncle interrupted.

"Well, well, well. I see you three have already met." Ludwig von Plotz stepped up to Will and gave him a huge grin. Ludwig approved of people who weren't afraid of his dogs. He thought it indicated not merely good sense but impeccable taste.

Will stood again. "Yes, sir, we met in the park. You have a couple of spirited dogs there, if I do say so."

Ludwig chuckled heartily. "That I do, sir. That I do."

At last Emily collected her wits, which had been seriously scattered by Will's wink. "Uncle Ludwig, this is Mr. Will Tate. Mr. Tate, my uncle, Ludwig von Plotz. Mr. Tate is from Texas, Uncle Ludwig."

Ludwig shook Will's hand with the force a farm wife might use on a butter churn. "Texas, you say? You got any cattle, Mr. Tate?"

Will was amused. So this was the man who wanted to market sausage dogs. He noted, too, that Uncle Ludwig sported a black armband. He decided he'd best not ask about the armband. He didn't want to open any recent wounds.

"I got me a few cows in Texas, I s'pose," he told Ludwig.

Will did not feel it incumbent upon himself to mention he owned the majority interest in three gigantic Texas spreads running thousands of head of cattle. After all, he lived in a mansion outside of San Antonio and didn't have a whole lot to do with bovines himself, except as a meal or an investment. Will preferred his roses and his Thoroughbred horses to cows any day in the week.

"Well, what would you think about trying a new breed of cattle dog, Mr. Tate?"

"Oh, Uncle Ludwig, please don't try to sell your dachshunds to Mr. Tate yet. You only just met him."

Emily's cheeks were flaming red now, Will noticed, and she seemed horribly embarrassed. He decided to rescue her.

"It's perfectly all right, Miss von Plotz. I'm right interested in new innovations."

His smile for Emily was one of such understanding kindness, she almost swooned. She wondered if she should have laced her corset quite so tightly.

Uncle Ludwig looked a bit put out. "Now Emily dear, you know I'm not meaning to shove my dogs onto Mr. Tate. But they're a wonderful breed, Mr. Tate. Wonderful! They can be trained to do anything." Fanatical sincerity throbbed from Ludwig's voice and gleamed in his eyes.

"That's exactly what Miss von Plotz told me, Mr. von Plotz. And I reckon you're both right about that. Although they seem a mite yippy to me. Don't gen'ly want yippy dogs herdin' cows. Cattle, you know. Cattle is pretty brainless critters and startle real easy. Might just start a stampede."

Ludwig's smile suddenly melted into an expression of intense concentration. "Yippy. Yah. They are yippy. Hmmm." He wandered to the sofa, sat down, leaned his elbows on his knees and his chin on his hands, and appeared to be thinking hard.

With concern, Will watched Ludwig walk away. He whispered, "Did I hurt his feelings, Miss von Plotz? I didn't mean to do that."

"No, not at all, Mr. Tate, although it is very polite of you to inquire. You've given him something to think about, though. Don't worry. He'll recover. Not only that, but he'll take your assessment of the dogs and use it to his advantage. Uncle Ludwig is very enterprising."

Will noticed her rueful smile as she gazed at her uncle, and had a sudden yen to tell her about his own uncle Mel's penchant for attaching himself to innovations. Uncle Mel, however, usually went in for snake oil and perpetual-motion machines. He didn't much cotton to animals. You had to feed animals, and that cost money. Since Mel used to use Will as a shill in his confidence routines, he hadn't resented feeding him. Much.

"Do I see you to a chair now, ma'am?" he asked innocently when his companion seemed lost in thought.

Emily gave a little start. "Oh. Oh, yes. I'm sorry, Mr. Tate. I was thinking about—about Uncle Ludwig's dogs."

Will chuckled. "I don't know that I take that as a compliment, ma'am."

"Oh, I'm sorry, Mr. Tate. I didn't mean any comparison."

Emily walked him over to the sofa and sat down at one end with great care. It was touchy work, sitting gracefully while wearing a bustle, but Emily had had lots of practice. She motioned Will to the other end of the sofa and hoped he wouldn't recognize it as a shocking intimacy to be sharing the same piece of furniture after having known each other for only two days.

He did, but her breach of propriety only amused him. *By God, I think she really is trying to snag ol' Texas Lonesome.*

Emily folded her hands in her lap primly and sat up very straight.

Will decided that since he was supposed to be a rustic, it would be all right if he lounged a little. He stretched his long legs out, relaxed against the sofa, and peered at Emily in honest appreciation. She really was something, all right.

"Would it be polite to ask you a question about your uncle, Miss von Plotz?" he asked, keeping his tone as naive as possible.

Emily's heart stopped for an instant and then began thudding with dread. Oh, dear. She'd never in her wildest imaginings believed Will would fail to notice her uncle's eccentricities, although she couldn't help but hope. But she hadn't realized just how worried about them she was until right this second. She cleared her throat almost painfully.

"Why, no, Mr. Tate. I don't believe it would be discourteous to ask a question about Uncle Ludwig." Then she held her breath.

"Well, ma'am, I don't want to bring up any bad memories or nothing, but I couldn't help but notice he's wearing a mourning band."

Emily stifled her groan and smiled at Will. She wondered how she'd explain this one without appearing to belong to a family of certifiable maniacs.

"Er, yes. Well, Mr. Tate, Uncle Ludwig was seriously unsettled by the death of Rudolf, the crown prince and archduke, in 1889. I believe it was the unfortunate circumstances surrounding the tragedy that particularly affected him. He's still in mourning." Emily rendered the information in a confidential whisper and with a sidelong glance at her uncle, as though she didn't want him to overhear her.

"Oh. Er, ma'am?"

"Yes, Mr. Tate?"

"I, er, don't reckon I know what those circumstances were, ma'am."

Emily didn't mean to sigh. It just leaked out by itself before she realized it. She knew her cheeks were growing pink and wished she'd thought not to mention there was anything unusual about the archduke's death.

Then she took a deep breath and plunged in. "The crown prince died a suicide, Mr. Tate. He shot his youthful mistress and then took his own life in Mayerling. It was a terrible tragedy for the Austrians. And for Uncle Ludwig. They had all looked to Rudolf, you see, as a leader to march them into the new century and the new age."

By the time she was through with her little speech, her cheeks burned. Talking about mistresses! The poor man must think her a total wanton.

It took every ounce of strength Will possessed not to snatch Emily up, plop her on his lap, and hug her in delight. She was absolutely adorable, blushing like that over the defunct crown prince's mistress. He opted for a brief "Oh" and said no more.

"Would you like to go over your company manners for a minute or two, Mr. Tate, before dinner is served?" Emily's cheeks still felt hot. She spoke with a brightness she did not feel in order to cover her discomposure.

"Why, I'd take that as a real kindness, Miss Emily. Kin I call you Miss Emily now, ma'am?"

After recovering from his heart-stopping smile, which took a second or two, Emily replied in a shaky voice, "I believe we are well enough acquainted to make the familiarity not improper, Mr. Tate."

"Kin you call me Will, ma'am?"

Emily was spared an answer by the abrupt entry of her aunt Gertrude, who burst into the room in a dither and with her crystal ball clutched tightly in her hands.

"Oh, Ludwig! Emily! I've just established successful communication with a spirit! I'm so thrilled!"

If there were a merciful God in heaven, Emily thought, He would strike her dead right now. Her heart sank, her gaze made a brief visit to the ceiling, and she uttered a silent prayer for fortitude before she said to Will, "Let me introduce you to my aunt Gertrude, Mr. Tate."

Will had stood up at Gertrude's precipitate entrance. He took a look at the fluttery woman clutching the glass globe, blinking in a somewhat dazed fashion around the room, and decided that Emily had her hands full with these two daffy relatives of hers.

Gertrude was the picture of plump elegance. Her black taffeta dress was studded with shining ebony beads, and she wore ostrich feathers in her softly piled silver-gray hair. She was a tall, somewhat fluffy woman, making Emily look particularly tiny and delicate in contrast.

"Aunt Gertrude," Emily said, thereby riveting her aunt's wobbly attention upon herself.

"Oh, Emily," Gertrude cried. "I've just received a spirit message!"

Emily prayed once more for guidance and decided nonchalance was her best defense. "That's very nice, Aunt. But please let me introduce you to Mr. Will Tate. Mr. Tate has come to dine with us this evening. Mr. Tate, this is my aunt, Gertrude Schindler."

Gertrude stared in blank astonishment at Will for

a second or two, then gave him a glorious smile. She thrust her crystal ball into Emily's arms before holding out an elegantly gloved hand for Will to shake.

"Of course. I had forgotten. It's so nice to meet you, Mr. Blake. Emily spoke of you to me just today."

"My pleasure, ma'am," Will drawled. He found it difficult to contain his laughter. "It's real nice of you to have me over."

"Oh, Mr. Blake, we just love to have visitors. Don't we, Emily dear?"

"Yes, Aunt. We do. But our visitor's name is Tate, Aunt Gertrude, not Blake." Emily had no idea what to do with the stupid crystal ball, which had been consigned to her. She decided to try to ignore it.

"Tate Blake," murmured Gertrude. "What an unusual name."

Deciding to give up on Will's name for the moment, Emily said, "Mr. Tate is visiting San Francisco from Texas, Aunt."

"Texas!" Gertrude breathed the word with reverence, as though Texas were the most exotic place on earth. "How exciting."

Will did chuckle at that. He couldn't help it. "Well, ma'am, I don't know as to how exciting it is, but I like it."

"I'm sure you do, Mr. Blake. Texas? My, it sounds so—so rugged."

"Mr. Tate says my dogs won't do to herd cattle, Gertrude. They're too yippy," Uncle Ludwig said, sounding genuinely disappointed.

Aunt Gertrude's face fell. "Oh, dear. Well, Ludwig, I'm sure he must be wrong. Not that I doubt your trustworthiness, Mr. Blake. But you must know that Ludwig sets a great deal of store by his dogs, and he's certain the possibilities for their usefulness are limitless."

"I'm sure they're very useful dogs, Mrs. Schindler, Mr. von Plotz." Will decided he'd never met such a charming pair of lunatics in his life.

Emily finally set her aunt's crystal ball down on a chair cushion. "Mr. Tate is the one who sent us the beautiful rosebush today, Aunt Gertrude. Wasn't that a sweet thing to do?"

"Rose? Oh, of course. Of course! The rose!" Gertrude seemed very pleased with herself for remembering. "It was a perfectly lovely thing to do, Mr. Blake. Our Emily loves flowers. We used to have a very pretty garden in our backyard." She glanced nervously at her brother and added, "Not that we at all begrudge Ludwig the use of the yard for his kennel. After all, his enterprise is terribly important."

Will nodded. Right then he decided Emily deserved all the flowers she could get.

Gertrude returned to her original subject. "Have you ever used a crystal ball, Mr. Blake? I just received a spirit message on mine."

Will noticed Emily shut her eyes tightly for a second and appeared to be praying. He wanted to hug her and tell her it was all right, that if anybody in the world understood crazy relatives, he did.

He didn't do it, but he did try to alleviate Emily's anxieties by answering Gertrude as if she were a normal human being who had just asked about the weather. "No, ma'am, but I'm right interested in hearing about your message. Do you commune with the spirits often?"

Emily's eyes popped open, and she looked at Will with such relief that he winked once more.

He did it again! He winked at me! For a startled second, Emily wondered just exactly who and what Will Tate was. It seemed inconceivable to her that the Texas Lonesome who had written those forlorn, illiterate letters to Aunt Emily would have the social grace to accept her aunt's spirit friends. Emily suddenly had the unwelcome thought that perhaps Texas Lonesome was more complicated than he had made himself out to be.

Well, she simply couldn't afford to worry about it. He was her last hope, and that was that.

She didn't have time to fret, anyway, because Blodgett appeared at the parlor door to announce Mr. Clarence Pickering's arrival.

Will noticed Emily stiffen perceptibly as Pickering's name was intoned by the butler. He wanted to assure her that he wouldn't let Pickering— whoever he was—hurt her, but he didn't. He did, however, pay very close attention to the man who entered the room, and he didn't like what he saw.

Clarence Pickering was clad in a maroon velvet dinner jacket, black evening trousers with maroon velvet stripes up the sides, a white shirt with about a thousand starched ruffles, and a maroon silk tie. His costume might have been considered elegant by some, but to Will he looked like nothing so much as a pimp.

Gertrude rushed over to him. "Oh, Mr. Pickering, we have a guest this evening. Let me introduce you to Emily's new gentleman caller."

Will decided that was an interesting way of putting it and turned to see Emily's reaction. He noticed the utter horror with which she greeted her aunt's words.

"Aunt! Mr. Tate is just visiting us this evening.

He's not my gentleman caller," she said. Then she felt stupid, and wished she'd kept her mouth shut.

"Oh, but Emily, I'm sure you said you were the one who knew Mr. Blake. I'm sure I don't. At least, I don't think I do. Or I didn't until right now. Ludwig, are you the one who knows Mr. Blake?"

Gertrude seemed very puzzled as she executed a slow circle in the room, speaking to everyone in it one by one. Then she apparently decided she was being rude to Will, because she dashed over and grabbed him by the arm. "Not that you aren't very welcome here, Mr. Blake. Especially since you must have many wonderful tales to tell us about Arizona, but I'm just certain *somebody* must know you. I thought it was Emily."

Emily wanted to die.

Before she could find her uncle Ludwig's silver letter-opener and slit an artery, however, Will came to her rescue yet again.

"It's all right, ma'am. Miss Emily and I met in the park. She invited me here, and I suppose that makes me her gentleman caller, all right."

His smile for Emily was very warm, and she didn't burst into tears. Instead, she returned it with a rather uncertain one of her own, and wished she could just sink through the floor and hide for a couple of centuries.

Clarence Pickering was used to Aunt Gertrude and apparently didn't find her introduction at all odd. It was obvious, however, that he considered Will Tate an unwelcome interloper into his territory. He held out his hand and said with a somewhat grim attempt at one of his sincere smiles, "Pleased to meet you, Mr. Blake. You're from Arizona?"

"I'm visiting, all right, but from Texas, Mr. Pickering, not Arizona. And the name's actually Tate. Will Tate."

Very early in life Will had learned to read people quickly. Having assessed Pickering as an enemy, he decided to play Texas Lonesome to the hilt. He certainly didn't like the way the man seemed to leer at Emily.

"A friend of our little Emily's, are you?"

Pickering's tone sounded possessive and patronizing, and Will noticed Emily's lips pinch together. It looked to him as though she was trying not to scream. He judged this evening to have been rather hard on her so far.

"Well, now, I didn't rightly know she was your little Emily, Mr. Pickering," he said in a sweet voice.

Emily wondered if he knew how challenging his words really were. She decided to use whatever advantage Will had just given her, however. "I'm not, Mr. Tate. Mr. Pickering is my aunt's financial adviser. He recently advised her to invest in a bunch of nonexistent horse herds in China."

Pickering's eyes narrowed. "That was indeed rather unfortunate. But, you know, sometimes things of such a nature do happen."

Emily responded with a humph.

Will decided not to press that issue right away. He did resolve to ask Thomas Crandall what he knew about Clarence Pickering, though, at his first opportunity.

Gertrude favored her guests with a vacuous smile and sat down on the chair where Emily had dumped her glass globe.

"Oh! Oh, my goodness, what on earth is this?" She

stood up again in a rush and peered down at the ball. "Oh, dear, now how did that get there?"

With a gallant sweep of his arm, Will rescued the ball from the chair. "Is this yours, ma'am?" he asked politely.

Gertrude beamed at him. "Yes, Mr. Blake. This is my crystal ball. And although at first all I could see was bubbles, I just received a spirit message through its medium. I'm terribly thrilled about it."

Suddenly Emily felt as though all the fates in the universe were conspiring against her. She had just begun to pray for a quick bolt of lightning to rescue her from this awful evening when Blodgett appeared at the parlor door to announce that dinner was served.

"May I escort you to dinner, Miss Emily?" Will asked courteously.

Emily smiled at him, and was alarmed as a sudden electric tingle shot through her body when his gaze collided with hers. She had to clear her throat before she could speak.

"That would be very kind of you, Mr. Tate," she murmured.

Will noticed Clarence Pickering scowl when he crooked his elbow, as Emily had earlier instructed him to do, and Emily placed her small hand on his forearm. He also noticed Emily shoot Pickering a cold frown in return.

Dinner at Gertrude Schindler's house was an enlightening experience for Will. Uncle Ludwig spoke of nothing but dachshunds. Aunt Gertrude chattered about her spirit friends and the slipshod enunciation she so deplored in modern young ladies. Clarence Pickering made snide remarks about Texas and cowboys during the entire meal. Emily tried her very best to shield Will from Pickering's nasty barbs and, at the same time, distract him from her two bizarre relatives' disordered conversation.

He admired her grit. He was sure he wouldn't have had the skill and fortitude required to juggle this many loose ends so effectively.

It also became very plain to him that the family's fortunes, while once obviously grand, had declined a great deal. Gertrude Schindler's elegant French china was chipped in places, and although someone—probably Emily, Will guessed—had done a very good job of matching colors, two cheap serving dishes had been substituted for the ones that came with the set. He suspected the originals had been broken and the family did not possess the resources to purchase replacements in the same pattern. The silver was polished to a fare-thee-well, and was an exquisite, old-fashioned pattern. Will had selected a much more modern design for the silver in his new home.

Emily was absolutely exhausted by the time the meal finally dragged to a close. Then she felt spasms of worry while she and her aunt retired to the parlor and Will remained in the dining room to take brandy and cigars with her uncle and Clarence Pickering. When the gentlemen at long last emerged, she scanned Will's face for any indication that he was about to turn tail and run.

But he seemed perfectly serene as he followed Uncle Ludwig and Pickering into the parlor, where Emily was by now in a hand-wringing state of anxiety. She sighed with relief when he gave her a smile as sweet as honey.

Thank God! she thought. *He must be too innocent to realize what crazy people these are.*

Will almost laughed at his first sight of Emily's earnest, worried expression. But he wasn't at all surprised. He had learned a lot this evening, and none of it had done a thing to lower Emily in his esteem. Far from it. How she had survived in this nest of loonies—and criminals, too, as Will believed Pickering to be—was an amazing puzzle to him. He silently honored her for it.

"Did—did you have a pleasant chat, Mr. Tate?" Emily asked breathlessly when she dashed over to his side.

"Yes, ma'am," he replied. "Your uncle is a mighty entertaining man."

Entertaining? Emily's nerves were now strung so taut, she wanted to scream at Will and demand to know what he meant.

She didn't. Instead she took a deep breath, gave him what she hoped was an enchanting smile, and said, "Yes, he certainly is, isn't he?"

"Yes'm. But that Mr. Pickering feller don't seem to cotton much to Texans."

Emily's face paled. She would not invite this man to her home again until she was safely married to him, she decided. Then she almost burst into tears when she realized she'd probably be in Texas by that time and couldn't invite him anywhere, anyway.

Will followed her to the sofa at a lazy amble. He was very curious to see what the rest of the evening held in store for him, although he was a little worried about Emily. She looked almost sick with apprehension.

In fact, she was. Her hands even shook when she gently placed one of them on Will's arm and asked in a tiny voice, "Would you care to take the air with me, Mr. Tate?"

Her suggestion was terribly improper, but all at once it had become imperative to Emily that she get Will away from her bizarre family and the leering Clarence Pickering. She was so nervous, she felt like a fiddle string about to snap. She trusted Will's innocence would keep him from realizing how brazen she was being.

He tried to hide his twinkle when he said, "I'd be purely honored to take the air with you, Miss Emily." He stood and crooked his elbow politely once more, just to prove what a fine student he was.

Emily felt an almost overwhelming sense of relief when it looked as though they were going to escape the room without being detected.

"Emily darling? Mr. Blake? Wherever are you going? I'm just about to summon Raja Kinjiput. Don't you want to ask him a question?"

Will felt Emily stiffen. When he glanced over his shoulder, he saw Gertrude perched in sparkling taffeta elegance on the edge of her chair, her beringed hands passing over her crystal ball in grand circles and her somewhat myopic blue eyes peering at them eagerly.

"Well, ma'am, that sounds right nice, but Miss Emily here is feeling a mite peaked. I thought she might need some fresh air."

Emily stared up at him in astonishment when her aunt answered, "Oh, of course, Mr. Blake. What a kind man you are." Gertrude dismissed them with an airy wave of her hand. "I'll just talk to the raja myself, then."

"Thank you, ma'am," Will said. He guided Emily through the side parlor door and onto the little terrace overlooking Hayes Street.

The night was clear for once; no gray fog misted the city. They had a perfect view of the rather seedy neighborhood surrounding Gertrude Schindler's formerly elegant address. The full moon hung above them like a shiny silver dollar, and softened the sometimes crude outlines of the city.

Emily felt her cheeks burn as the cool night air washed over her. She looked at the peeling paint on the railing and hoped Will wouldn't notice.

"Thank you, Mr. Tate. That was very diplomatic of you."

"Diplomatic, ma'am?" Will asked innocently.

Emily took a deep, steadying breath, bracing herself to wrap Will more tightly around her finger. She didn't much like herself for it.

"Yes, Mr. Tate. Diplomatic. I know my aunt and uncle are—are unusual people." She stopped all at once, uncertain how to explain Gertrude and Ludwig in a manner that might mitigate their eccentricities.

"That they are, ma'am."

He looked down at her, and his breath caught somewhere between his heart and his throat. The moon had bathed Emily's flushed cheeks in its silvery light, and she looked utterly enchanting, a fairy princess out of a storybook. The deep sapphire satin of her gown set off her smooth, pale skin to perfection. He found himself having to forcibly restrain his arms, which felt compelled to reach out and draw her to him. He ached to caress the bosom she had so artfully plumped up for his benefit.

Emily couldn't meet his gaze. She felt completely humiliated—both embarrassed about her aunt and uncle, and ashamed of herself for her embarrassment. And she was utterly aghast at herself for her own duplicity. But she had no choice. The image of Clarence Pickering flashed through her mind. She couldn't quit now, no matter how villainous her plot. She simply couldn't.

She opened her mouth to speak, but her words died unspoken as she found herself trapped by Will's gaze. Her lips parted slightly, and she could only stare at him, stunned. All at once, Will Tate looked like the very picture of the man of her dreams. The planes of his face were picked out by the moonlight, and the shadows etched his strength to granitelike perfection. In the books she'd read, in the fantasies she'd spun, the hero always looked exactly as Will Tate looked now.

The invitation she offered was too much for Will to resist. "You're just the prettiest thing, Miss Emily."

Emily felt gooseflesh in the most embarrassing places when Will's finger nudged her chin up even further.

"Mr. Tate, I—" She couldn't go on.

"Just the prettiest thing."

His whisper sent ripples coursing through Emily's body from her ears to her toes, which were tucked away in their dainty, though well-worn, evening slippers, and which suddenly curled in reaction.

She couldn't breathe as she saw Will's face slowly draw nearer and nearer to hers. Her gaze fastened on his full mouth, and she was sure she would faint when he kissed her. And although she knew she must be beyond redemption by this time, she wanted him to. More than anything else on earth, she wanted to feel those wonderful lips on hers. Her eyes fluttered shut, and she felt his warm, sweet breath on her cheek.

Then she almost fainted dead away when the parlor door suddenly swung open and Clarence Pickering's mocking voice flayed her senses like the lash of a whip.

"Well, well, well. Now I just wonder what's going on out here."

Will dropped his hands and straightened up fast.

Emily's eyes popped open, and she whirled around to find Pickering leering at the two of them, a thin cigar clamped in his sincere white teeth.

5

"*Tell me, Thomas,* do you know a Clarence Pickering, by any chance?"

Will had shed his black silk tie and dinner jacket. He now tossed his elegant beaver onto the undignified heap they made on the seat of Thomas Crandall's sofa. Then he stood before his friend's fire, warming his hands.

He had walked home from Emily's house. He needed a good dose of night air to cool his ardor, which had not been altogether dampened by Pickering's untimely interruption. In fact, his unruly sex still had an unfortunate tendency to thicken up on him whenever he remembered how Emily had looked as they stood on that rickety porch, bathed in soft moonlight. Lord above, she was beautiful.

Although it had annoyed him awfully at the time, he was now grateful for Clarence Pickering's jealousy. That's what it had been, Will was sure. Just as he was sure Pickering was up to no good with Emily's aunt Gertrude's financial affairs.

Still, Will was glad he hadn't kissed Emily. A kiss, to a proper young lady like Miss Emily von Plotz, was akin to a proposal. And Will was not at all sure he wanted to make a proposal.

Thomas Crandall, wearing a brocaded blue dressing gown, stroked his fluffy muttonchop side-whiskers as he stared hard at his friend. Then he frowned with distaste. "Clarence Pickering? How the devil do you know that vulture?"

"A vulture, is he?" Will had already pegged Pickering for a bad one, but his innards clutched at the expression on his friend's face.

"The worst. He sniffs around until he finds people who're about to go belly up. Then he helps them do it and feeds on the remains. Why? Don't tell me Pickering has something to do with our Aunt Emily."

Will sighed. This was trouble, all right. "He's her aunt's financial adviser. Apparently he recently advised her to invest in some horse herds that don't exist. Now he wants her to invest in ships made of some special African wood."

Thomas eyed Will quizzically. "Do you suppose Aunt Emily really *is* trying to snag you into marrying her? If Pickering's nosing around, you can be sure the family's in deep waters. Maybe her motives aren't purely noble after all."

"Maybe not."

Will wasn't sure exactly how he felt about that. He could have sworn Emily von Plotz was an upright, honest young woman. He also figured her for being none too wealthy. If anybody in the world could detect twice-turned clothes, it was Will Tate; and Miss Emily had definitely worn at least two reworked gowns in the two days since he'd met her. Still, he couldn't quite believe she was an out-and-out fortune hunter.

On the other hand, he could, better than most, appreciate a well-laid confidence scheme. If it was Miss Emily's goal to seduce him into marriage, she was doing a good job of it. But he couldn't quite help feeling a bit—just a little bit, mind you—hurt, if she was indeed pretending an interest in him she didn't really feel. She certainly didn't seem to be pretending.

Will knew it was ironic. Who was he to belittle a cheat? He'd grown up with a man who truly believed cheating was the only way to get along in the world, and who had imparted the belief to Will. And Will had been an apt student, too. Not for the first time he wondered if his family had a streak of Romany blood in their veins.

Besides, he himself was posing as Texas Lonesome, whoever that was. So he was just as guilty of dissimulation as Emily. If she was scheming.

Lord, all this thinking was making his head ache.

Then Thomas laughed and snapped Will's attention away from his unsettled thoughts.

"Well, Will. You figured her for a gold digger as soon as you saw that letter from the Lonely Texan, or whatever he called himself." Thomas's laugh died when he encountered Will's sharp frown.

"Texas Lonesome," Will muttered. He glared into the toasty fire, which was flickering and crackling, making the cozy room seem even more snug and inviting. "And she's not a gold digger, either."

"Well, whatever she is, if her aunt is being advised by Clarence Pickering, the family's done for. That's one thing I *am* sure of. Pickering," he said once more, "is a vulture."

Neither man spoke again for several minutes. Will continued to ponder the dying fire, and Thomas studied him closely.

Finally he ventured, "Don't bite me, Will, but I can't recall your ever paying particular mind to anything a female did or said before, or to care about anything that befell one of them. But you sure seem to be spending a lot of time and thought on our fair Aunt Emily. Don't tell me she's managed to pierce that steel armor of yours."

Will, lost in thought, gave a little start at Thomas's words. Then he broke into a reluctant grin and flopped himself into the chair opposite Thomas.

"Hell, Thomas, even *I* don't know that. I never met anybody like Miss Emily von Plotz before. It's not my fault. I'm sure I'll get over it. I just don't like the thought of a vulture hurting her or her family." He shook his head as he recalled the events of the evening.

"Lord, what a family. And the funny thing is, she really cares about them." Since Will had never experienced much in the way of family feelings himself, he didn't quite understand them, but they touched a raw place in him. It was a place he'd packed away so securely, he'd even forgotten it was there. Until now.

He sounded more chipper when he said, "Did you know her uncle Ludwig thinks dachshunds are the next big craze in the dog world? That they can be trained to herd cattle? He's turned their backyard into a breeding kennel." He chuckled at the memory.

"What the hell's a dock-soont?"

Will's grin widened. "It's a dog, Thomas. It's about as tall as a weasel, it's shaped like a sausage, it yaps constantly, and it has one hell of a mean disposition."

It was obvious Thomas didn't know if Will was teasing him or not. "That doesn't sound like much of a herd dog to me, Will."

An honest-to-goodness belly laugh was all the response Thomas got for his astute observation. In fact, Will was so tickled, he actually had to wipe a tear away when he finally managed to choke out, "Do you know the man is wearing a black armband? He's been wearing it for six years now. Still in mourning for the Crown Prince and Archduke Rudolf." Will doubled over in laughter again. Thomas only stared at him.

When he could catch his breath, Will went on. "And her aunt got a spiritual message from some raja named Kinjiput on her crystal ball right before I arrived there this evening, too."

Thomas was dumbfounded for a minute before he, too, began to smile. "Who in God's name are the Crown Prince and Archduke Rudolf and Raja Kinji—whatever you said?"

Will could barely talk through his strangling laughter. "The—the Austrian crown prince who shot himself and his mistress, and I don't know who the raja was."

"Are you trying to tell me Aunt Emily's relatives are not playing with a full deck?"

"A full deck?" Will whooped. "They're each short an ace, king, queen, and jack—at least—if what I saw tonight is any indication."

Thomas stopped laughing before Will did. "You know, Will, maybe we shouldn't be too hard on Aunt Emily if that's what she's up against every day. Especially if Pickering is lurking in the background waiting to snap up the leavings."

Thomas's words sobered Will up right quick. He remembered Pickering's unsavory leer every time he looked at Emily, and the recollection turned his good humor sour.

"Yes," he said. "And he wants to snap her up, too."

"You think so?" Thomas closed the Sherlock Holmes book he'd been reading, apparently finding real life more intriguing at the moment than the realm of detective fiction. "Well, and just what do you aim to do about that, my friend?"

Will stretched his long legs out in front of him and folded his hands behind his head. "I don't know yet, Thomas. But I aim to do something."

"You don't like the idea of Pickering's swindling the fair Emily's relatives?"

"I don't like the idea of Pickering's coming within fifty miles of Emily."

Thomas didn't say anything but opened his book to the page he had kept marked with his index finger. Before he sank back in his chair and hied himself once again to the misty English countryside, he remarked mildly, "I think you've been smitten, Will Tate."

Will glanced up to find Thomas's nose buried behind his book. He didn't respond but wondered if his friend was right. Texas Lonesome aside, he didn't aim to let Emily be hurt by Clarence Pickering or anybody else on this earth if he could help it.

Before he left the Schindler home that night, Will had had the presence of mind to make Emily promise to meet him in the park the next day for more lessons in good manners. Now, as he pondered little Miss Emily and life in general while he stared at Thomas Crandall's cozy fireplace, he looked forward to their meeting in the park with interest liberally laced with confusion.

With a defeated sigh, he gave up trying to reason with himself and decided to pay a call on Ludwig von Plotz before he kept his appointment with Emily in the park.

Emily stared at her reflection in her scratched vanity mirror for a long time before she crawled between the old patched quilts covering her bed. The warped mirror showed many gray splotches, which clearly indicated it needed to be resilvered. It was probably a hundred years old, Emily thought, a relic from her aunt Gertrude's days as a wealthy young bride in Germany. It had belonged to Gertrude's husband's family.

"I don't know what to do," Emily whispered to her wavery reflection.

She was surprised that the overwhelming confusion of the evening did not show in her face. She had expected herself to look ravaged, but she didn't. Instead, as she peered pensively at her reflection, she beheld an Emily whose cheeks were flushed a delicate pink, whose clear blue eyes were bright, whose full lips appeared rosy, and who was prettier than she ever remembered being. She beheld, in short, a stranger.

And he'd almost kissed her.

A tentative finger reached up to press her lips, and her eyes slid shut when she considered it might have been Will Tate's lips resting there. She felt at once more wonderful than she had any right to be and more wicked than she perhaps was.

She wished he had kissed her.

Emily was at this moment so confused she

wouldn't have been surprised if a streak of lightning burst through her bedroom window to cleave her in half. She already felt torn in two.

When she set out to deceive Will Tate, she'd hoped he'd fall in love with her. But she hadn't even considered the possibility that she might begin to care for him. She did, though. Somehow it felt even worse to deceive a man she cared about than it did to trick the bumpkinish Texas Lonesome she had once known only through the newspaper.

Not only that, but he must have seen through her ruse tonight. There was no way to disguise the shabbiness of the furnishings in the Schindler home. And there was no way to disguise the patent craziness of her family—or the villainy of Clarence Pickering. She knew she was being uncharitable when she suddenly wished Gertrude and Ludwig could just disappear until Will Tate's ring was firmly on her finger. They were so—so—*eccentric* was the kindest word Emily could think of.

That was the crux of the matter. Right there, in plain, unvarnished words, Emily had hit the nail solidly on its head. Oh, Lord. What if he didn't care to associate with her after this evening? What on earth would she do then?

Emily was so overwrought, she would have thrown herself onto her bed to sob if her corset had not been laced so tightly. She heaved a deep, morose sigh as she unbuttoned the dozens of tiny buttons holding her satin bodice together. Then she unsnapped her corset and, in spite of her roiling emotions, breathed in and released a deep, refreshing gust of contentment.

"I wonder who invented corsets," she muttered.

She loosened the lacings in the back, and a tear slid down her cheek when she considered what she should wear to the park the following day.

She was no better than a trollop, she decided with exaggerated melancholy as she stared into the dim atmosphere of her bedroom. She'd deliberately laced her corset too tightly in order to swell her bosom and make her waist smaller in an attempt to ensnare Will Tate. She wondered what he would think of her feminine endowments.

A doleful sniff escaped her. It didn't much matter, for once he discovered her unscrupulous plan after they were married, he'd surely hate her forever.

On that dismal note, Emily succumbed to her desire and flung herself on her bed to sob. The old springs creaked ominously, and for a heart-stopping second she was afraid the whole bed would collapse. It wouldn't have surprised her much. This whole evening, simply because it had been so marvelous in spots, was a disaster.

But the bed frame held, and Emily indulged herself. Finally her flood of hot tears subsided into unhappy hiccups, and she drifted off to sleep without having decided on her next day's costume.

Her oversight created an hour's worth of real panic the following morning. She ultimately donned an old cherry-red Spencer waist and a walking skirt of cream-and-red stripes, then ripped the blue ribbon off her straw hat and attached a matching red one. Finally she pinned the universal bonnet to her glossy locks.

She angled the hat so that it looked jaunty, and her heart clutched at the sporty vision she had created of herself. No one, she decided, would be able to tell that underneath this facade of healthy, modern young womanhood beat the broken heart of a miserable seductress.

Then she heard Clarence Pickering's voice waft up the stairs and felt her insides tighten. What on earth was he doing here at this hour of the morning?

Deceiver or not, she had no choice. She braced herself for the sight of Clarence Pickering before she traipsed down the stairs and into the breakfast room. Sure enough, there he was, munching on a muffin and chatting with her aunt.

"Good morning, Emily darling!" cried Gertrude. "Look who's taking breakfast with us today." Gertrude smiled at her financial adviser as though she hadn't seen him for a year or more.

"So I see." Emily raked Pickering with an icy glare. "Are you paying my aunt for board, Mr. Pickering? You seem to be taking all your meals with us lately."

She saw a flicker of anger pass over his face and smiled inside. She just loved it when her barbs found their target.

Pickering apparently decided to ignore her rude jibe. "You look pretty as a picture this morning, Miss Emily."

His voice was smug, and it made Emily's insides shudder.

"Why, what an original observation, Mr. Pickering." She tried her best to ignore him after that.

As she eyed the ham on the sideboard she wanted to ask her aunt why she was wasting expensive ham on a weekday, but she held her tongue and took a small piece. She hesitated over the toast a moment too long and stiffened when she realized Pickering was standing at her side.

"You should try being nicer to me, Miss Emily," he

murmured into her ear. "I could make your life very, very easy, if you'd let me."

"I would kill myself and you too before I would allow you to do anything at all to me, Mr. Pickering." Emily's furious whisper was a little bit too loud.

"What did you say, dear?" Gertrude looked up from her ham and eggs.

"Nothing, Aunt. I just stepped on Mr. Pickering's toe and was apologizing."

So saying, Emily executed a sharp turn and ground her heel into Pickering's instep. He grunted in pain, and Emily smiled as she made her way to the breakfast table.

"What are you going to do with yourself today, dear?"

"Just what I usually do, Aunt. First I'm going to take my latest column to Mr. Kaplan. Then I'm going to visit the park." She decided not to mention Will Tate.

It didn't make any difference, for Gertrude said, "That Mr. Blake was a terribly nice man, Emily dear. He seemed quite taken with you, too. Did you say he was from Texas?"

"His last name is Tate, Aunt Gertrude, and yes, he is from Texas."

"The fellow seemed rather dumb to me," muttered Pickering as he limped back to the table.

The fury that arose in Emily at Pickering's words surprised her. After all, what did she care what the swindling viper thought of Will Tate? Still, she found herself snapping, "I'm astonished at your assessment, Mr. Pickering. On the other hand, I suppose you, of all people, could recognize dumbness." Emily herself deplored the use of the word to signify stupidity, but she used it now out of spite.

Pickering shot her an ironic smile. "Why, Miss Emily, you sound rather snippy this morning."

Emily chose not to answer. She didn't want to upset her aunt. Instead, she stared at her plate while she finished her breakfast in as little time as possible. Then she excused herself, kissed her aunt's soft cheek, went back upstairs, gathered her column together, and set out for Mr. Kaplan's office.

She had no idea Will Tate was walking up Hayes Street at the same time, saw her leave the house, ducked into a nearby alleyway, and waited until she was out of sight before he continued on his way to Mrs. Schindler's front door. Once there, he tugged the bellpull and asked Blodgett if he could be taken to Mr. von Plotz.

He found Uncle Ludwig in the backyard on his hands and knees, his shirtsleeves rolled up to his black mourning band. Ludwig was tidying Helga and Gustav's elaborate home. The two little hounds tried to help by nibbling on his nose and ears while he chuckled in appreciation.

Ludwig was delighted to see Will. The two men spent a fruitful morning together, and Will left an hour or so later very pleased with himself. That hour or so had also served to further Will's enormous respect for Emily.

"I'll be damned," he murmured as he strode to Golden Gate Park. He couldn't imagine how she'd managed to do it so far.

The sudden burst of pleasure Emily felt when she spied Will Tate sitting on the park bench startled her.

It didn't surprise Will one little bit when he saw Emily walking toward him and felt his insides stir. He had come to expect this reaction to her. He rose, whipped his hat off, and stood, smiling broadly at her approach and thinking that little Miss Emily von Plotz would make a monk want to sin.

His smile was warm enough to bake bread. It burned through Emily in no time at all, and she was blushing by the time she reached him.

"Good morning, Mr. Tate."

She felt shy and fluttery today and was sure her jitters were in direct reaction to the promise of last night's unfulfilled kiss. She wondered how she'd feel if Will really had managed to kiss her, and wished she knew. Then she felt her cheeks burn even hotter.

"Miss Emily, I swear, you get prettier every time I see you." The heat Emily was experiencing was nothing compared to that threatening to incinerate Will. He felt himself get hard and held his hat in front of him in an "aw, shucks" pose, grateful for once for his false persona.

"Thank you, Mr. Tate. That was very prettily said."

"I think I'm getting better at this manners stuff, ma'am." He grinned and gestured her onto the park bench.

Emily smiled at him. "I believe you are indeed, Mr. Tate."

Will had considered long and hard how he was going to maneuver Emily into spending most of the day with him. At last he had come up with what he believed to be a brilliant idea, and he used it on her now.

"M-Miss Emily, ma'am?" His stutter had been

practiced until it was absolute perfection. He was proud of himself.

"Yes, Mr. Tate?" With a demure look—which she had rehearsed for hours for just such an occasion—Emily peered into his face. Then she nearly lost control of her studied pose when she encountered his glorious hazel eyes. Good heavens, the man was more than handsome. He was beautiful.

"Well, ma'am, I'd consider it a real kindness on your part if you was to accompany me to Nathan-Dohrmann's Crockery Emporium in Union Square, so's you can teach me the right way to go on in a big-city place like that."

The truth was, Will needed to restock his dinner-ware and linens back home. The selection of such goods to be found in San Francisco was ever so much more elegant than that to be had in San Antonio. He was also curious about Emily von Plotz's taste. Not, he admitted to himself in a fit of honesty, that it much mattered anymore. If she wanted purple sheets, orange pillow slips, and green curtains, he most likely wouldn't object. The realization hit him square between the eyes and almost made him laugh.

"Why, Mr. Tate, I'd be delighted." Emily tamped down her wry smile with difficulty. But while it was true she had spent a good deal of time in Nathan-Dohrmann's, her hours there were much akin to those spent poring over fashion periodicals in the public library.

The library, as well as Nathan-Dohrmann's, Gump's, Magnin's, and other stores like them, was where Emily did her research. After she had deter-mined everything she needed to know about the very latest fashion trends in apparel and home decor through her studies, she would hie herself off to Chinatown and buy everything she needed to create facsimiles at a fraction of the price Nathan-Dohrmann's or an expensive modiste would charge.

She elected to spare Texas Lonesome that information. There was a vast difference between genteel poverty and desperation, she told herself. She didn't want him even to guess at how straitened her circumstances really were, or else he would certainly cotton on to her devious scheme.

They took a cab to Nathan-Dohrmann's, chatting as companionably as lifelong friends. When they alit, Will very properly took her arm in his and kept to the outside of the sidewalk in order to protect her from mud flung up by passing carriages or random violence that might erupt on the street.

Nathan-Dohrmann's bustled with activity. Emily, who had no idea Will knew his way around the store, led him to the linens.

"What is it you need, Mr. Tate?"

"Well, ma'am, I got me a new table in my dining room back home, and I wanted to find a nice cloth for it. For big dinners and such. You know?"

In truth, he had built his home outside San Antonio on a massive scale, and his new dining room could seat a horde of hungry diners with ease. He had just received a wire from the manager of his estate that the mahogany table he'd ordered from New York had arrived. He wanted to purchase not merely linens, but everyday crockery and a formal china service as well. But as much as he delighted in Emily's company, he figured he'd better try her out on the linens before he trusted her to spend perhaps thousands of his dollars on porcelain dinnerware and fine china.

He was not disappointed.

"Are you sure, Mr. Tate?" Emily asked uncertainly when he told her he had no budget limits.

"Yes, ma'am," he said, trying his best to look innocent.

"Well . . ." Emily peered around at the wares displayed before them. "And how many people does your new table seat, Mr. Tate?"

"Fifty."

Emily gasped. *"Fifty?"*

"Yes, ma'am." Will was surprised at his sudden urge to scoop her up and whirl her around, and then kiss her astonished little mouth. It was puckered up in surprise, just perfect for a kiss.

"I got me a lot of friendly neighbors," he added with what he hoped was appropriate sheepishness.

Emily swallowed and tried to recapture her air of nonchalant authority. She couldn't even imagine the fortune it must take to build a home equipped with a dining room suitable for entertaining fifty people at a sit-down dinner. But, she told herself with a firmness she intended to hold on to, she aimed to find out firsthand.

"Well," she said when she could speak, "I don't suppose you'll need any everyday linens for such a grand room. You must have a breakfast room for your daily meals."

"Yes, ma'am, I got me a breakfast room. At least the architect called it a breakfast room," he added confidentially, not caring to pass up an opportunity to appear unsophisticated. "Actually, I eat there all the time, 'cause I didn't have a table for the other room until now. My house is new, you know."

"Oh. No, Mr. Tate, I didn't know." Until this minute, Emily hadn't actually considered where Will might have made his fortune or how long he'd had it.

"Yep. I had it built special."

It didn't seem the right time to let Emily know about his roses. Judging from Thomas's reaction when Will began studying rose culture, people didn't consider gardening a manly pastime. Will figured he'd rather demonstrate to Emily exactly how manly he was before he sprang the roses on her.

"You—you didn't inherit—I mean—Oh, I'm sorry, Mr. Tate. Here I am, supposed to be teaching you proper manners, and I very nearly asked you a terribly impolite, personal question."

She felt her cheeks get hot and could have kicked herself for her slip. All at once, though, she found herself monumentally curious about Will's money. She had just sort of assumed he'd grown up in Texas and carried on with the family ranching business, although she wasn't altogether sure how she'd come to the conclusion. Now, however, it seemed her assumptions were completely wrong.

"Miss Emily, ma'am, you couldn't ask me a question I'd think was impolite." That was the truth. "And no, I didn't inherit anything, 'cept the urge to wander a bit. No. I made my own money, fair and square, and I built me my house in San Antone just last year. Not all of the furniture's even been delivered yet. My house agent wired me about the table. That's why I figgered to buy me some linens."

Emily wished she could make up for her lapse into curiosity. It was, of course, certainly understandable that a young lady might express an interest in the financial circumstances of the young man she intended to marry. Generally, however, the young man in question was aware of his status as potential bridegroom before the probing began. Emily was annoyed at herself for her slip.

Her tone was businesslike when she spoke again. "Well, Mr. Tate, with such a grand new home, I'm sure you will want to furnish it tastefully."

The awful thought that he was one of those newly rich cowboys who gloried in garish displays of wealth crossed her mind, only to be discarded almost immediately. Even though Will Tate seemed on occasion to be shy and unlettered, he certainly didn't appear to flash his wealth around. What's more, he dressed with impeccable taste. Emily was very grateful for that. She would have married him in any case, but the thought of being wed to a loud, boorish, rambunctious man did not appeal to her. In fact, it went flat up against her highly polished sense of propriety, gleaned from her tastefully impoverished aunt and everything she read in the high-toned fashion journals she lapped up as a kitten laps cream.

"Oh, yes, Miss Emily. I want it to be tasteful, all right." Will nodded solemnly. What he actually wanted to do was laugh. She'd looked truly scared there for a minute, as though she expected him to select crimson velvet and gold for his dining room table. The very thought made him shudder.

"Well, Mr. Tate, here is a lovely display of Irish linen. Irish and Belgian linens are supposed to be the best kinds," she told him in a confidential aside.

After a good deal of discussion, they decided Will's new table would look splendid under a covering of embroidered white linen. And, just in case he held two elaborate dinner parties in a row—a scenario Will proposed with an innocent, wide-eyed stare his uncle Mel would have applauded—he asked Emily to choose a second cloth. He was pleased as punch when she selected a beautiful creamy French lace, tatted by nuns in some nameless convent in Rouen, to go over a plain linen cloth.

Her wistful expression did not escape his notice. Nor did her shock when the haughty salesman told them the total cost of the items they had selected. He feared for a dreadful moment she might faint, but she just clutched spasmodically at her tiny handbag and tried to stifle her outrage. He could almost see her protest forming, and it both amused and pleased him.

So his little Emily, even if she was trying to snag a rich husband, was not a spendthrift. The knowledge nestled in his heart and made him happy.

She still looked a trifle peaked when they left the linen department, and her little fingers dug into his arm like claws.

"Thank you very much, Miss Emily. I'm right pleased with those tablecloths. I can't wait to hold a real big shindig when I get home."

Since she was still reeling from the knowledge that she had just caused this dear man to spend almost a hundred and fifty of his hard-earned dollars, Emily found it difficult to speak at first. When she could at last form coherent words, they came out in sort of a croak.

"I had no idea they would be so expensive, Mr. Tate."

Will smiled down at her with genuine pleasure and did risk a small pat on her tiny hand.

"It don't matter none, ma'am. I got lots of money."

How nice, Emily thought. How nice it would be to be able to spend a hundred and fifty dollars on table linens and not even blink.

She didn't dare answer him for fear she would croak again.

"Now I need to get me some chinaware, ma'am. Do you know whereabouts in this store I could do that?"

Emily took a deep breath. That was one thing she could do, she thought. She could at least save him money on china.

"Yes, Mr. Tate. I believe I do know where you can get china for your new home."

"The price don't matter, ma'am. I got lots of money."

Emily gave him a very small smile. "That's wonderful, Mr. Tate. You're truly a fortunate man. But I don't think you really need to spend all of your money on china, now do you?"

Will wanted to hug her. "No, ma'am, I don't guess I got to do that."

"Then perhaps you would like to come with me to Chinatown. I know of a few places there where one can purchase wonderful crockery at a bargain."

"I'd like that just fine, ma'am."

And he did. They spent a delightful couple of hours in Chinatown. Will was impressed not only with Emily's taste but also with her ability to dicker. He'd never known a woman with a better eye for quality or a better sense of when and how much to haggle.

Emily herself was a little worried lest her shrewd tongue give Will too sharp a picture of her nature. But she couldn't bear the thought that he might be taken advantage of by anyone besides herself. So she talked Mr. Woo down from his first outrageous suggestion to a mere fraction thereof. Then she made the merchant throw in a serving platter and a teapot for good measure. When she was through, she looked up at Will rather bashfully.

"You probably think I'm an awful shrew, Mr. Tate," came her mournful little whisper as Mr. Woo shuffled to the back of his shop, still grumbling, to pack up Will's purchases.

"No, ma'am. Not at all."

The truth of the matter was that Will had seldom been so impressed. Emily had just made as careful a bargain as any he had seen, and he had seen the best. He honestly doubted if even his uncle Mel could have done better. Of course, Mel didn't do too many things honestly.

Yet Emily had never once shed her dignity, raised her voice, or been anything less than ladylike. She hadn't gone all prim and prissy, either, a feat Will appreciated almost more than her skill at haggling. It was a fine line Miss Emily had walked, and she had done it with skill and consummate grace. Will was, in fact, more than impressed. He was very nearly in awe.

"It's just," Emily hastened to explain, "that I can't bear to see you spend more of your hard-earned money than you need to. And the sad truth is that many San Francisco merchants will take advantage of a visitor to our city."

It sounded to Will as though she was ashamed to admit to the flaw in her city's merchant population. He stifled his grin.

"I suspect it's like that all over the world, Miss Emily. You have to watch out for yourself no matter where you are, or people will try to cheat you."

Will's uncle Mel had taught him that, although in Mel's case he was working from the opposite direction.

Mel had at the time been teaching Will the best ways to take advantage of his fellow man, not ways in which to protect himself. Will had known how to protect himself by the time he was four or five.

"I guess that's so." Emily's sigh was from the heart. "I wish it weren't, though."

A phenomenal rush of tenderness nearly overwhelmed Will at her wistful words. The image of Clarence Pickering hit his mind's eye like a fist, and he had a sudden urge to slay the man who was causing his little Emily such distress.

After their business with Mr. Woo had been accomplished, Will took Emily back to her aunt's house in a cab. He didn't want to let her leave his company yet, but Emily said she needed to write her column.

"Well, ma'am, I surely do appreciate your help today."

As they stood on the walkway outside the Schindler residence, Emily discovered an amazing disinclination to leave Will's side to go indoors. She had no idea how very plainly her vivid features captured her emotions.

Will read her reluctance with a soaring heart. Damn, she cared about *him*. It wasn't just because she thought he was Texas Lonesome. The knowledge fostered within him a conflagration of emotions so strong, it made breathing difficult.

"Will you meet me again tomorrow, Miss Emily?" he managed to ask at last in a voice he barely recognized as his own.

"Why, certainly, Mr. Tate. I'd be delighted. We can review your lessons. And I'd be very happy to help you shop for anything else you might need. I—I enjoyed your shopping spree today." She wasn't sure, but she didn't think her small confession would give her away.

"So did I, ma'am. So did I."

Then he kissed her hand before they parted. Emily was utterly charmed. She pressed her hand to her heart as she climbed the staircase to her room.

Will fairly skipped back to Nob Hill on a cloud of happiness. He realized with a start that he'd never had such a good time with a woman in his life—and they hadn't even gotten near a bed.

Astonishing. It was absolutely astonishing.

6

Dear Miss Aunt Emily:

You was right. I think I found the female I aim to marry. She is perfect and I love her. Thank you for all your help. Thank you also for not making fun when I spelled etiquette *wrong. You are a kind lady.*

Signed,
Texas Lonesome

My dear Texas Lonesome:

Your letter made my heart sing. I dearly hope you are right and that this lady is the bride for you. I am certain she returns your regard.

Affectionately,
Aunt Emily

P.S. Please know that I will never, ever disparage a gentleman who is earnest in his efforts to better himself.

The following morning Will spotted Emily walking toward him between the herbaceous borders lining the raked paths of Golden Gate Park, as beautiful as an angel in soft green.

Emily decided the special care she had taken with her toilette this morning had been worthwhile when she saw the expression of adoration in her quarry's eyes. She did not begrudge him the few hours of lost sleep required to retrim her old green calico with new ribbons, or to reset the sleeves with an added length of cream-colored cotton to achieve a modern, sporty look.

"Good morning, Mr. Tate. I trust you had a pleasant evening." She found it telling that he kept her hand in his for several moments longer than was absolutely necessary. It was working. Her sinful scheme was working. Even his letter said so.

"Very pleasant, ma'am," Will managed to say. "And how about you? Was your evening pleasant?"

He didn't fail to notice her expression sour for a second before it resumed its studied cheerfulness.

Emily's recollection of her evening was not at all pleasant, although she didn't intend to tell Will so. Clarence Pickering had once again paid a call, and the man was becoming more obnoxious by the hour. He had apparently decided she would soon realize she had no other choice than to succumb to his scandalous advances, and his insinuations became more pointed as each day passed.

She recovered her composure in a hurry, however, and did not realize Will had caught her eloquent expression. "My evening was quite pleasant, Mr. Tate. Thank you."

Will didn't believe it for a second, and he wanted

to get to the root of her distress. And once he discovered what or who it was, he wanted to kill it. With his bare hands.

"Did that Mr. Pickering feller visit you again, Miss Emily?"

"Why, yes, he did, Mr. Tate. As my aunt's financial adviser, I'm afraid—or rather, I mean—Oh, dear. I didn't mean 'I'm afraid'—I mean that Mr. Pickering visits us often." There. That was noncommittal enough.

It was also too late. The sudden, overpowering urge Will had to strangle Clarence Pickering made his fingers curl in anticipation. He was obliged to wage a mighty struggle with his emotions before he could form his next question without bellowing.

"Well, ma'am, I reckon it's not polite of me to say so, but I didn't cotton much to that Pickering feller." Of all the falsehoods Will had uttered in his colorful life, that one was the falsest. In reality, he hated Pickering's black soul with a loathing greater than any he had ever experienced.

When he caught Emily's startled but grateful smile, though, he supposed his prevarication didn't matter.

"Oh, no, Mr. Tate. You're not being impolite. You are merely demonstrating good sense. I think Mr. Pickering is—is simply awful."

Her flush of embarrassment was just exactly what Will needed. All at once he decided he wasn't going to be denied a second time.

"Miss Emily, I'd take it as a pure insult if you said you wouldn't go to a fancy restaurant with me if I asked you now, after all the manners you taught me at your place the night before last. And I know you don't mean to insult me. So I'm askin' you again, ma'am. Will you allow me to escort you to the Palace for dinner tonight?"

Emily hesitated for only a second before a wild, reckless feeling with which she was completely unfamiliar nearly swamped her. She threw caution to the four winds. So what if she was a single lady and he was a single gentleman? So what if his accompanying her to the Palace would be considered scandalous by San Francisco's stuffy upper crust? What did she have to do with those crusty, boring people anyway?

With a radiant smile, she said, "I think dining with you at the Palace would be simply delightful."

She did, too. In fact, Emily realized all of a sudden, her time spent in company with Will Tate had become the most precious hours of her day. She wondered how on earth it had happened so quickly. Was this love? Emily quickly set the question aside to be pondered alone and in private. Then she cleared her throat and began the day's lessons.

Since they were going to visit the Palace for dinner, those lessons centered around table manners. It occurred to Emily that Will Tate was a particularly apt student. More than once he drifted out of his rustic Texas accent, too. He also seemed genuinely interested in many different subjects, a circumstance Emily appreciated, since if her devious plan worked, she would be spending a good deal more time with him. It was pleasant to know they would have more to talk about than cows when she was ensconced in the wilds of Texas as his bride.

Then it occurred to her that so far he hadn't once mentioned cows. She wondered what exactly Will Tate did in Texas. All he had told her was that he had a "spread," whatever that was.

When Will suggested a walk around the park, Emily accepted readily. They strolled along in amicable companionship for several minutes, enjoying the fine weather and each other, neither one speaking and neither one bothered by the quiet that settled like a fine, delectable radiance upon them.

Finally Emily asked, "Can you tell me a little bit about Texas, Mr. Tate? It sounds so—so wild and rugged to me. I've always lived here in the city, except for every now and again when we go to the woods for a small holiday. We haven't done that for a long time, I'm afraid." There was no more money in the till for holiday trips, but she didn't tell Will that. She missed those rural trips.

Although she hadn't intended to, she sounded wistful, and Will found himself wishing he could take her to the woods right now to make up for her family's oversight. His wish brought, hard on its heels, the pleasant notion that if he did carry her off to the woods, he could teach her a couple lessons of his own. He decided he'd better not pursue that line of thought if he expected to walk much farther.

He cleared his throat. "Well, ma'am, Texas is a big place. Some parts of it is pretty much desert. Up where I live, near San Antone, it's greener than some of the other parts. My place is outside the city, by a river, and it's pretty as anything."

This was encouraging news indeed, she thought. If she had to leave San Francisco, Emily was glad to know she'd be living in a pretty place.

"Is it—is it wild there, Mr. Tate?"

Emily wasn't at all sure how she felt about wildness. On the one hand, she deplored violence. On the other hand, she'd led a subdued existence, living as she did with her elderly aunt and uncle. She wouldn't mind a little excitement; indeed, sometimes she almost craved it. She most particularly didn't think she'd mind excitement if Will Tate would be there to protect her.

Will smiled down at her. She had put her hand on his arm, and now he covered her hand with his. He tried to look innocent when Emily's startled gaze met his. He didn't press his luck, but dropped his hand at once and with regret.

"It ain't what I'd call wild, ma'am. San Antonio's no more wild than San Francisco, I suppose. There's rough elements there, just like there's rough elements here. It's just that here, most of the rough customers spend their time around the wharf. In Texas, we get rough cowboys and bandits and such.

"Why, Miss Emily, we're downright almost civilized in Texas these days. There ain't too many desperadoes in those parts any longer. Leastways not in Texas, so long as you stay away from the borderlands. Most of the desperate characters have run to the Territories—New Mexico and Arizona. I expect them places is still pretty rugged."

"I see." Emily felt vaguely disappointed and wasn't sure why. "I've always sort of wanted to see a real desperado," she admitted at last. Then she blushed at her shocking disclosure.

Will only laughed. He considered telling her that if she wanted to see a real desperate character, she had to look no further than her aunt's financial adviser, but decided he'd better not.

"I 'spect a desperado or two might still call Texas home, but I don't suppose you'd really like to meet up with one of 'em, right up close and all."

"I suppose not. Have you always lived there, Mr. Tate?"

Her polite question brought Will face to face with a quandary. He didn't particularly want to confess he had spent a good many years in San Francisco. On the other hand, he didn't want to lie to her, either. He opted for a partial truth.

"I've lived quite a few places in my life, ma'am. I was raised from a tadpole by my uncle Mel, you see, and he was—he was— Well, Miss Emily, Uncle Mel didn't like to sit too long in one place." It would have been more honest to say that Mel didn't dare sit too long in one place, but Will thought better of telling her so right now.

"Really?"

"Yes, ma'am."

Emily frowned. "Did you and your mother live with your uncle, Mr. Tate?"

"My mother, ma'am? I never knew my mother."

Now Emily was more than a little puzzled. "But Mr. Tate, I'm sure you told me your mother had taught you to stand in a lady's presence."

The lilt in her voice and the question in her eyes slapped Will right on his conscience. *Criminy!* He'd gotten his fibs mixed up. He'd never done that before in his life. Uncle Mel would have been appalled.

Well, there was no hope for it. He'd just have to 'fess up. As if in shame, he hung his head.

"Ma'am," he said as though admitting to a mortal sin, "I'm afeared that was a stretcher."

Emily's eyes opened wide. "A stretcher, Mr. Tate?"

He hung his head a little lower. "It was a lie, ma'am."

"Oh!"

Lordy, if he wasn't careful, he'd be a fallen man in no time at all. Swallowing hard, he nodded somberly, slowly.

"Yes, ma'am. I was afeared you wouldn't cotton to a feller who's got no folks."

Emily's tender heart gave a painful squeeze. "Oh, Mr. Tate!" she exclaimed softly. "Having no parents is not your fault. And it's certainly nothing to be ashamed of." She pressed his arm gently in a comforting gesture.

Nothing to be ashamed of, she'd said. Well, that was a novel idea, coming from the lips of a proper young lady like Miss Emily von Plotz. As he gazed into her sweet, smiling face, Will realized she meant it, too. All at once he found himself thanking the fates, or whoever was responsible, for having sent Aunt Emily his way.

He was still trying his best to sound abashed when he said, "I'm right sorry I fibbed to you, ma'am. I don't reckon it was something a gentleman would do."

Emily, who had a shrewd notion most gentlemen fibbed whenever it jolly well suited them, shook her head. "It's all right, Mr. Tate. While it's understandable that you might like to impress the lady of your choice, she is almost certain to find out sooner or later that you perpetrated a prevarication. It is my belief that one is almost always best advised to tell the truth at the outset. If one is honest from the beginning, the object of one's admiration is less apt to feel—well, exploited."

And who was *she*, she wondered, to be giving such advice to Will Tate, the object of her devious scheme to spare her family the vicissitudes of poverty? Emily tried not to think about it. She cleared her throat with some difficulty.

"So, Mr. Tate, you lived with your uncle. And you say you and he moved around quite a bit during your youth?"

"Yes, ma'am. My uncle Mel liked to keep on the move, all right."

A memory so strong Will could almost taste it barreled into his mind—of his uncle and him hightailing it out of a little Missouri hill town, hotly pursued by a mob of angry townsfolk carrying pitch torches and buckets of tar. Will, just a little boy then, thought he'd caught a whiff of hell that night. It was a long time before the nightmare resulting from the escapade left him alone to sleep a full night through.

"I can't say I always liked being on the move," he said in a mild voice at tremendous odds with the turmoil the recollection had stirred up in him. "I 'spect that's why I finally got me a piece of land in Texas, built me a house on it, and aim to squat there until I either blow away or die."

Emily noticed he had a faraway, and not particularly happy, expression on his face. Her heart was tugged yet again.

"It must be hard on a little boy to be always moving. I—I think children need the security of a settled home, surrounded by people who love them. And friends. It's hard to have friends if you're always picking up stakes and traveling around." Emily's voice was gentle; her hand stirred on his arm and gave it another small squeeze.

Will was more than a little surprised at her response. Most of the "ladies" he'd met in his life, far from being touched, were faintly disgusted when they learned his early years had been spent on the run in the company of a wily vagabond. Of course, he reminded himself, Emily hadn't been given any particulars yet.

"Well, ma'am, my uncle was an unusual person."

"Even compared to *my* uncle?" she asked with a little smile. Her heart began to palpitate in a crazy manner, and she realized that what she really wanted was for Will's uncle to be as eccentric as her own. Then maybe he'd understand her dilemma and feel more sympathetic toward her when he discovered her perfidy. If it was perfidy.

Emily wasn't sure of anything anymore. What had at first appeared to be a wicked plan to entrap an innocent cowboy, who needed a bride with whom to share his wealth, seemed to have undergone a transformation. Now Emily found herself actually looking forward to being with Will Tate, not because he was Texas Lonesome, but because he was Will Tate.

A deep chuckle rumbled out of Will's throat. "Compared to my uncle, Miss Emily, your uncle Ludwig is just an amiable, kind of odd old feller."

"Really?" It was difficult to imagine. "What about Aunt Gertrude? Was your uncle any worse—I mean, not worse, but, well—you know, um—odder than she is?"

She felt herself blush. What kind of a cold, hard-hearted, ungrateful niece did she think she was, to be talking about her dear aunt and uncle this way? Emily was ashamed of herself.

But Will only laughed. "Miss Emily, I think your aunt and uncle are very nice people. They're surely not dull and ordinary."

A hint of amusement began to override Emily's shame. "No, I guess they're not that."

"I think you're lucky to have relatives who love you, ma'am," Will continued, correctly assessing the state of Emily's nerves and trying to set her at ease.

Those nerves were still jangling a good deal, although his words soothed her. But it was his choice of words that caught Emily's attention. She looked up at his strong profile and wondered what he must have been like as a little boy. It was difficult to remember, she thought, that adults had been children once and had suffered all the trials and tribulations of growing up.

"Do you mind my asking you another personal question, Mr. Tate?" she asked timidly.

When he smiled at her, Emily just about melted on the spot. *Oh, my,* she thought. He had such an alarming effect on her nerves.

"I don't reckon you could ask me any question I'd mind." He hesitated for a couple of seconds. "Of course, I guess I also reckon some of the answers might not be purely to your liking."

He wondered if Aunt Emily would drop his acquaintance like a slimy worm if she knew he had spent his youth selling snake oil and trying his damnedest to cheat honest folks out of their hard-earned money. He wasn't sure, but he suspected more than one family had suffered dire consequences as a result of his youthful employment. Before he'd learned better.

"Well, I just wondered if you ever knew your parents, Mr. Tate. I only ask," she hurried to explain, "because I—I remember my mother and father, and sometimes I still miss them. It's certainly not that I don't love my aunt and uncle. It's just—" All at once Emily felt tears sting her eyes, and she looked away, embarrassed.

Will saw her tuck her little chin in close to her collar, and he felt a tremendous urge to hug her tight and tell her everything was going to be all right. Instead, he covered her hand with his once more.

"No, ma'am, I don't reckon I recall my ma and pa at all. My uncle Mel—his name is Melchior—told me they both died when I was just a babe in arms. I never knew them."

"How sad." Emily's voice was a tiny whisper. Then she blinked back her tears, donned her brightest smile, and said, striving for a light note, "Melchior? What an unusual name, Mr. Tate. Like the Wise Man?" She was acutely conscious of Will's hand covering hers; it felt so good. Protective. Comforting.

Her words produced another chuckle, somewhat tainted this time by recollections too painful to mention. "Wise Man? I reckon. Don't know as how I'd call Uncle Mel awful wise, though." Of course, if Will took Mel at his own assessment, he would have called him not merely wise, but sharp, shrewd, and cunning as well. But Will no longer considered the ability to swindle one's fellow man a virtue.

He could tell Emily was still in some kind of distress. And while he didn't understand it, he sure wished he could help her.

"Well, anyway, I don't guess I have to worry none about Uncle Mel haulin' me all over the country anymore. And I'm right glad about that. It's much nicer to be a man grown and to be able to take a pretty lady like you to the Palace of an evening, Miss Emily."

The grateful smile with which she greeted his words was all the thanks Will figured he'd ever need for steering the conversation out of the maudlin depths of painful memory.

"Do you suppose we could go over my manners one more time, ma'am?"

A sigh of pure happiness escaped Emily's lips before she could stop it. "I think that's a perfectly delightful idea, Mr. Tate. Would you care to walk me home while we have our review? I need to let my aunt know I won't be at home this evening and then prepare tomorrow's column before we dine."

She also had to scurry about and fix herself a costume suitable for a visit to the Palace, too, but she didn't expect Will needed to know it. Fortunately Emily, having had years of practice, was ready for almost any clothing contingency life had to offer, and she had a fair notion of what she was going to wear.

"That sounds like a fine idea to me, Miss Emily."

So the two of them strolled toward Hayes Street slowly, arm in arm, soaking up the day and each other's company. They paid no mind to the happy nods of people they passed along the way, who saw the couple, recognized a splendid match, and smiled in approval.

Emily's sunny mood lasted until after Will left her and she had almost reached the foot of the stairs in her aunt's house. When she passed the second-best parlor, her smile of amusement and love was genuine when she heard a muffled thump, as of a thick book hitting the carpeted floor. She recognized that thump and knew her aunt was assisting yet another young lady to attain the pinnacle of perfect posture.

Emily's own favorite volumes had been rescued long ago and were now safely tucked away in her room. Although she admired her aunt's industry, however ill rewarded, she didn't particularly care to have Mr. Shakespeare or Mr. Wordsworth fall from an unsteady head and land, pages crimped, upside down on the parlor floor.

It was her uncle Ludwig who inadvertently caused her mood to blacken. He didn't mean to do it, either. His only purpose in stopping Emily before she skipped up the stairs to her room was to share some wonderful news with her.

"Emily!" he cried. "That wonderful young man of yours visited me this *Morgen* and told me he's interested in investing in my dogs!" Ludwig was so excited his feet scarcely touched the shabby carpet as he rushed toward her.

"*What?*" The word burst out of Emily's mouth in a gust of incredulity.

Ludwig didn't notice. Anything that did not directly affect his dogs had little ability to puncture his enthusiasm. "Yah, yah! It's true. That nice Will Tate wants to invest in my dogs!"

Ludwig grabbed Emily and did a little dance while she stared at him, dumbfounded, and turned in a circle as he led. He didn't notice he was the only one dancing.

"Oh, my God," Emily whispered.

She watched Ludwig waltz himself off down the hallway and felt her heart, which had been soaring, suddenly wheel like an arrow-pierced dove and spiral to a slow, miserable plop on the tattered hall carpet.

"Oh, my God," she repeated as she trudged up the stairs. Tears burned her eyes when she pushed her door open and stepped into her room.

She allowed herself only five minutes or so of unrelieved unhappiness, though, as she sat at her desk and stared out onto the crowded street below. A brief thought that she could solve all of her problems by flinging herself out the window crossed her mind, only to be immediately rejected with no little disgust.

"What are you thinking of, Emily von Plotz, you selfish, ungrateful girl? If you were gone, there would be nothing at all standing between your aunt and uncle and miserable want. No. You must be strong. You must set scruples aside and work with firm diligence toward your goal. You can't allow honor to stand in your way. If Will Tate wants to invest in Uncle Ludwig's dachshunds, he's a grown man with a grown man's will, and he's made the decision of his own accord. It's not your responsibility."

Her stern self-lecture got her off her desk chair and over to her wardrobe, even if it didn't do a thing to mitigate her overwhelming feeling of guilt.

If only she hadn't allowed herself to care. She'd been willing—no, *happy*—to deceive him when she thought he was nothing but a crude country bumpkin. Now that she knew what a kind, wonderful man he was, she felt guilty. Hah!

What an unscrupulous fraud she was. It didn't matter what kind of man he was. She was a miserable, wretched, deceiving cheat.

On that cheerful note, Emily began to haul gowns out of her closet and fling them onto her bed. Ruthlessly she sought to create the one perfect costume that would leave Will Tate—country boy or hero, it mattered not—helpless at her feet.

She had three evening ensembles from which to choose, and a whole paperboard carton full of laces, trims, frills, and embellishments she had rescued from a variety of sources. Ultimately she decided upon her most daring, revealing gown. Over it she would wear a burgundy evening basque trimmed with ivory lace.

She had a feeling the lace had, in its youth, been white. But it was cream-colored now, and it would do very well. Emily was nothing if not practical.

After an hour or so she was happy enough, if such bitter satisfaction could be termed happiness, with her ensemble so as to feel ready to tackle her column. It took no time at all to get the morrow's words ready for Mr. Kaplan, although she did find herself having to curb her unsteady temper once again.

"Dear Aunt Emily," one heartsick correspondent wrote. "My husband is a wealthy businessman in the city. I'm sure he loves me, but he pays me no mind. He gives me money as though to make up for his lack of attention. I sit all day long, wishing for him to be with me. When I cry, he gets upset. Whatever shall I do to win his eye again? I am so unhappy. Signed, Lonely."

Gritting her teeth, Emily did not allow herself the pleasure of telling the writer exactly what she thought of a rich woman who had nothing better to do with her time and money than pine away for a husband who was, no doubt, spending all his energy earning her more money. Instead, she was rather pleased with her tepid response.

"Dear Lonely: Whenever Aunt Emily finds herself lonely, despondent, and in need of attention, she takes comfort from helping her fellow creatures in distress. She also takes long walks in the park, where she gathers ideas for her garden. I believe if you will look about you, you will discover any number of benevolent causes, from abandoned dogs and cats to orphaned children, all of which will benefit from your attention. Your husband is doing his duty by providing well for you. I believe you might do yours somewhat better by not trying to make him feel guilty about it."

The last sentence bothered her after she read it aloud, and she decided, although she meant every word, to scratch it out. "Well, at least Mr. Kaplan will be pleased," she sighed.

The next letter she picked up was from Texas Lonesome. She recognized the writing on the envelope immediately and ripped it open.

"Dear Aunt Emily: I think you are the nicest lady in the world. I think I am in love and hope to know for sure soon. It is you who helped me, and I thank you."

She didn't know what on earth to write back. At last she decided not even to try.

7

Will Tate was a happy man. He had left Emily at her aunt's front door with a promise to pick her up, in a carriage, at seven-thirty.

Then he'd whistled his way over to the Palace, where he spent a fruitful half hour or so arranging for the evening's entertainment. Those arrangements required a good deal of diplomacy and the liberal greasing of several palms, but Will didn't begrudge a single gold coin. He wanted tonight to be special.

After his dealings with the folks at the Palace, he strolled back to Thomas Crandall's mansion on Nob Hill. There he was greeted by his faithful canine companion, Fred.

"Freddy, old boy, you're about the best friend a man could ever have. If it hadn't been for you, I'd never have met my little Emily."

It didn't occur to Will to examine exactly when he had decided she was his little Emily. He only knew she was.

Fred seemed pleased.

*   *   *

"Do I *what?*" Thomas Crandall's mouth dropped open and stayed open after the three words tumbled out.

"Do you want to invest in dachshunds? They're the coming thing in the dog world, you know."

Will gave his black silk evening cravat a little twitch and positioned his diamond-and-pearl stickpin among its elegant folds with great care. The pin was expensive but tasteful, and Will thought it gave his appearance just the right touch to impress Miss Emily von Plotz, if she needed further impressing. He suspected she didn't.

"Have you completely lost your mind, Will Tate?"

Will chuckled. "Well, now, I'm not sure. I don't think so. Not completely, anyway; maybe only a little."

"I'd really like to meet the woman who's got you investing in mean-tempered weasel-hounds and dressing like an East Coast dandy." Thomas's voice held genuine awe.

"We're dining at the Palace tonight, if you want to drop by. As long as you don't stay too long."

"You're taking her to dinner at the Palace? I don't remember your ever taking a lady out to dinner before."

"I've taken lots of women to dinner, Thomas, and you know it." Will was just the tiniest bit embarrassed as he dusted off his tall beaver hat.

"I said a *lady*, Will, not a *woman*. There's a difference, my friend."

Will gave Thomas a lopsided smile. "You told me yourself there were worse things in life than spending time with a lady, Thomas. I remember your saying it."

"So do I, Will, but I didn't know you were going to

make a career of it. I've hardly seen you since you met Aunt Emily."

"Miss Emily is different," Will said on a sigh.

"She must be."

Will turned with a flourish of black cape and cane. "How do I look, Thomas?"

"And I've never known you to care how you looked, either. But if you must know, you look like a courting lover."

Will laughed in real amusement. "Maybe I am at that, Thomas. Maybe I am."

After Will's arrival at the Schindler residence was announced that evening, he and Emily assessed each other with candid pleasure, she from the upper landing and he from the somewhat musty elegance of her aunt's foyer.

The only adornment to her person, save the lace on her basque, was the two carved ivory combs holding her hair in place. The fact that the combs looked as though they might be old, expensive family heirlooms appealed to Emily. In reality, she had bought them, after much strenuous bargaining, from yet another estate sale. This evening she had piled her hair into an upswept do copied directly from one of Mr. Gibson's ubiquitous drawings, and she was very pleased with the result.

So was Will.

In a determined effort to seduce Will Tate—for such was her admitted intention at this point—Emily had once again plumped her bosom and laced her corset tight. Although she felt anything but confident, she gave the appearance of a sophisticated, self-assured young lady as she descended the stairs to greet him.

Will had no idea what her intentions were, but he heartily approved of the result of her efforts. He had ever admired the soft curves of the womanly form; seldom had he seen them displayed to better advantage. What's more, he had an almost overwhelming desire to explore these particular ones by hand.

"My saints and stars, Miss Emily, you are the prettiest thing I've ever seen." He peered down into her brilliant blue eyes and decided he wanted to sweep her up into his arms and carry her away with him forever.

As for Emily, she forgot for a moment that she had set herself on a course of deception and deceit. Her first impulse upon seeing Will in his dashing evening finery was to fling herself into his arms and beg him to have his way with her—with or without marriage vows and financial rescue attached. She could hardly believe it of herself.

"Thank you, Mr. Tate." Her tongue felt dry, as though she had left it outside in the sun while she'd been about her business indoors. "You look—you look truly elegant this evening."

"Thank you, ma'am." Will gaped at her in perfect imitation of a tongue-tied country lad; only he wasn't pretending. She had just about deprived him of speech.

Thomas Crandall's town carriage was a splendid vehicle, and his coachman was a master. He opened the door and flipped down the stairs for Emily in one smooth movement. Emily was terribly impressed. She placed a hand on Will's arm and stepped daintily into the carriage.

Thanks to Will's clever planning, liberal tips, and prior patronage, the Palace was expecting them and was prepared with its best. The maître d' welcomed them with a low bow and then preceded them to a candlelit table tucked away in a romantic corner.

Emily scarcely had time to appreciate the setting before a white-gloved waiter arrived with an ice bucket and a bottle of the restaurant's best champagne.

"Oh, Mr. Tate," she whispered, "this is so elegant." She felt a little silly, since it was she who was supposed to be teaching him things about fine living. But she couldn't help it.

"Well, ma'am, I came over here this afternoon after I saw you home and fixed it up with the staff. They got right nice, obliging folks workin' here."

Emily, who had long been under the impression that the Palace was the most snobbish establishment in San Francisco, was pleased to hear him say so.

"I'm so glad, Mr. Tate. I think it's very important for people to be courteous and easy to work with when one has to do business with them." Emily's soft voice held absolute sincerity.

It took a good deal of effort to suppress his laughter, but Will managed. He had a vivid recollection of the Palace's haughty chef staring down his nose as Mr. Potter, the manager, handed him Will's request for this evening's dinner. Will didn't mind. The expression on Emily's face was worth having to deal with a stuffy French chef any day of the week.

"To you, Miss Emily."

He held up his champagne glass and tilted it ever so slightly toward her. The look in his eyes was one Emily wished she could store in a locket and keep with her forever.

"Thank you, Mr. Tate," she whispered.

Their glasses clinked, and Emily took a tiny sip of her champagne. It tickled her throat wonderfully.

The Palace was meant for evenings like this. The carpeting was thick and elegant, muffling the sound of the waiters' shoes as they toted viands back and forth. Although gas lighting was in common use in the metropolis, the table at which Will and Emily sat was lit by the soft, flickering glimmer of candle lamps.

The gentle light from the lamp at their table cast a delicate, warm glow over Emily. Will liked the way she looked at him across the table, as though she was not quite sure of herself.

He found himself oddly glad to discover that Aunt Emily, the capable, efficient newspaper columnist, could be so easily transformed, by his own meager efforts, into this creature of delightful fragility. Although, he acknowledged, she was assuredly *not* fragile. Anybody who had managed to keep her crazy relatives solvent and Clarence Pickering at bay for so long was definitely a person of infinite strength. But she was a fetching, feminine little thing in spite of that.

A waiter brought them their first course, a wonderful concoction of crab in a puff of delicate pastry, and then silently departed. Will took another appreciative eyeful of Miss Emily von Plotz and dipped his fork.

"I hope you like this, Miss Emily. It's one of my favorites."

"I'm sure I shall, Mr. Tate."

They spoke then of things of little consequence. Will told her a few of his more repeatable, amusing adventures in growing up, and Emily spurred him to more than one out-and-out belly laugh as she related tales of her family's doings. Will's genuine appreciation, the restaurant's pleasant ambiance, and, perhaps, the champagne seemed to lull her into revealing more than she had intended to.

"You mean he was actually eating the plants?" Will had to wipe his eyes, he was laughing so hard.

"Oh, my, yes, Mr. Tate. Uncle Ludwig is often given to spur-of-the-moment scientific experimentation. I'm afraid the chief horticulturist was not sympathetic. I had to beg him not to press charges. It was very embarrassing at the time."

A giggle rendered Emily's last words somewhat wobbly, and she watched Will with a warm welling up of emotion in her breast. Nobody had ever made her feel like this before, as though there was nothing inherently wrong with her because her relatives were batty.

"That, of course, was before he took up dachshunds," she added.

The words were spoken with such delicate inflection that at first Will didn't know whether she understood how ironic they sounded. One peek at her twinkling eyes told him she did, though, and his mind almost boggled at a sudden realization: He wasn't bored. Will Tate, who found the empty, endless chatter of the more refined members of the female sex almost brain-numbing, was not bored. He was listening to Miss Emily von Plotz tell him stories about her crazy aunt and uncle, and he was hanging on every word that tripped from her perfect rosebud mouth. He, who had to suppress yawns every time he was in polite female company, was laughing now as much as he had ever laughed with Flaming Polly, and with infinitely more genuine pleasure.

Will had to admit that Flaming Polly, while amusing, was rather crude and a little weak of intellect. But Emily did not suffer from either of those two shortcomings. Far from it. There was nothing the slightest bit crude about Emily, yet she wasn't prudish. And she was smart as the proverbial whip, but she was not at all starchy.

And pretty? *Lord have mercy.* Will looked at her creamy shoulders and collarbone and peered with real longing at the very discreet swell that foretold the delights of her satiny bosom, and his throat tightened. He could have feasted his eyes on her all night long and for the rest of his life.

The realization almost made him laugh out loud in irony. He, who had been reared to look upon his fellow human beings with a predator's eye; who had been taught that women served only one useful purpose; who had been brought up from his earliest days on this earth to be a freewheeling bachelor; whose every childhood lesson, in short, had taught him to take what he wanted and to need nobody, suddenly found himself being sucked under by a quicksand of need. And, more amazing than anything else, he realized that if he had known this feeling Emily evoked within him existed before now, he would have sought her out, dived in headfirst, and not waited to stumble into the quicksand by accident.

He absolutely adored her.

Emily had been regaling Will with tales of her aunt's ill-fated attempts to teach young ladies proper elocution. She stopped all at once, alarmed by the expression on his face.

"Oh, I'm sorry, Mr. Tate. I didn't mean to rattle on and on so."

Will blinked, astonished by her interpretation of his worshipful gaze. "Ma'am—Miss Emily, ma'am, you can go ahead and talk to me forever. I didn't think you were rattling on. I'm not bored. I've never been less bored in my life."

He was absolutely certain now, after meeting her relatives and Clarence Pickering, that little Miss Emily had set out to entrap him, as Texas Lonesome, into marriage. As little as a week ago such an idea would have made him guffaw at its very absurdity. Now he couldn't repress the images flickering through his brain of himself and Emily nestling together as sweetly as a couple of doves and sharing moments like this for the rest of their lives.

Will Tate, a domesticated animal. Good grief, maybe he *was* losing his mind.

That possibility had just entered his head when both he and Emily were ripped out of their cozy intimacy by the booming and entirely too amused voice of Thomas Crandall.

"Why, Will Tate, you old son of a buck! Now what on earth are you doing here?" The appreciative gleam in Thomas's eyes as he looked at Emily irritated Will.

Will made an effort to suppress his annoyance. "I was trying to eat dinner, Thomas, which should be obvious even to you. Not that you didn't know I'd be here, since I told you this afternoon."

Then he added with somewhat grumpy civility, "Miss Emily von Plotz, this is Thomas Crandall. Thomas and I have known each other for several years, and I'm staying with him in San Francisco."

The hand Emily extended to Thomas was very dainty indeed. "I'm so pleased to make your acquaintance, Mr. Crandall."

Thomas had to clear his throat before he could answer Emily with the appropriate degree of politeness. Somehow or other, she seemed to have deprived him of his usual suave urbanity.

"M-Miss von Plotz," he finally stammered, "this is truly a pleasure."

Emily smiled at Thomas, who stared at her in open admiration. Will's initial amusement quickly soured the longer Thomas gawked, and he soon began to glare. Thus they remained for a full minute or more, until Emily, becoming uncomfortable in the lingering silence, finally spoke.

"And how did the two of you become acquainted, Mr. Crandall?"

After a gulp and a blink or two, Thomas managed to croak, "I—we—we met in the mines, Miss von Plotz. In Virginia City. We've known each other for years."

"How nice it must be to have friends of such long standing. Good friendship is rare in today's hectic environment." Emily smiled sweetly at Thomas, then glanced at Will. She hoped somebody would take up the conversational gauntlet soon, because she didn't know what to say now.

The poisonous viper of jealousy slithering through Will both startled and infuriated him. *Damn Thomas Crandall to blazes.*

Completely forgetting he had as much as dared Thomas to come see for himself the manifold charms of his little Emily, Will's inventive mind immediately indicted his best friend.

Then, in his irrational fit, he misunderstood the expression on Emily's face. Instead of a clear wish to be rescued from an uncomfortable social situation,

Will read into her gaze a harpy's shrewd appraisal of yet another wealthy victim.

Hah! Did the sharp-as-a-tack Aunt Emily find rich-as-Croesus Thomas Crandall more to her liking than she did Will himself? Was her nimble brain assessing Thomas's fine clothing and urbane manner and deciding marriage to him would be more to her advantage than marriage to the country-bred Texas Lonesome? If so, that was just too damned bad. She was his, and that was that.

"Well, Thomas, I guess you have things to attend to this evening, don't you?"

Emily looked at Will in undisguised astonishment.

As for Thomas, he finally realized he had been staring with fixed intensity at Emily for some time. When his gaze lit once again on Will, he recognized his best friend's undisguised jealousy. He laughed, thereby startling Emily into further confusion.

"Well, I can tell I'm not wanted here," Thomas said with a grin. "Miss von Plotz, I can't tell you how happy I am to have met you at last. Will has spoken of you often, and I didn't believe him. But I can see now that he was right and I was wrong. You're every bit as charming and lovely as he told me you were."

"Why, Mr. Crandall, what a kind thing to say."

Emily's cheeks went pink under the praise. Will glowered at Thomas.

"Go away now, Thomas," he hissed.

"All right, Will. Guess I can't ignore that blunt request. Good evening, Miss von Plotz."

"Good evening, Mr. Crandall."

Thomas tipped his hat and sauntered off.

Will eyed Emily, who was watching Thomas stroll away. He didn't care for the look on her face, which he assumed to be one of cunning.

Emily, however, although she was consciously doing her very best to ensnare Will Tate, was not vain. She never suspected she could inspire awe in more than one man.

At last she gave up trying to figure out why Will's friend had behaved in such an odd manner and returned her attention to Will. Her smile died a quick death.

Oh, dear. What had seemed an almost magical atmosphere before Thomas Crandall's interruption now crackled with something unspoken and ugly. She didn't understand it, but she wanted to do away with it at once. She wanted the magic back, and she wanted her pleasant companion, Will Tate, back with it.

In an attempt to restore their former blissful harmony, Emily said, "My, it must be nice to have such a good friend as Mr. Crandall, Mr. Tate."

Will was still stewing in the bitter juices of jealousy. "He's a lot richer than I am, Miss von Plotz. And he's not married, either. He'd be a great catch." There. Let the miserable vixen choose between them, then, if that was the way she wanted it.

"Oh!" Emily blinked and wondered why on earth Will had said such an odd thing. An incredible possibility hit her like a bolt of lightning. Good heavens, could Will Tate be jealous? Of his best friend? Because of her? She would have to reassure him that he had no cause to be.

Those same unerring instincts that had guided Aunt Emily into becoming the best-read columnist in San Francisco now led her to say in a confidential tone, "Mr. Crandall is a good-looking man, Mr. Tate, but if he is truly seeking a wife, perhaps you should give him a little hint. I believe it would behoove him to trim his side-whiskers just a tiny bit. I'm sure he grows them to distract ladies from his bald spot, but honestly, I believe most ladies find thinning hair less objectionable than bushy side-whiskers."

She smiled guilelessly and added, "I hope you don't think me bold, Mr. Tate. It's just that although Mr. Crandall doesn't possess your charm, he does seem to be a rather nice, solid sort of man." Then she paused, as if chagrined, and went on. "Oh, I'm sorry, Mr. Tate. I certainly don't wish to criticize your friend. How terribly rude of me!"

All at once the bubbling cauldron of Will's jealousy evaporated as if it had never existed. The magical aura of the evening settled about them once more. Will felt his sudden flame of anger smother and die as though it had never flared up.

The smile he gave Emily was so warm, she was reduced to quivering aspic. Lord, the man had a smile that could melt ice. And Emily was definitely not ice.

"I keep telling him that myself, Miss Emily. He thinks the ladies won't notice his hair if they're occupied with his muttonchops."

Breathless as she now was, it was difficult for Emily to speak. "Well, Mr. Tate, I—I think Mr. Crandall could learn a thing or two from you. You've never pretended to be anything other than what you are, yet you are a perfectly charming companion. Any young lady would find delight in your company. I certainly do."

Emily felt herself flush from her toes to her ears as soon as the words tripped from her tongue. They were the truth, though, and her heart clenched with anguish. This dear, dear man was so honest and sincere and open, and she was such a deceitful, fraudulent wretch. Her behavior didn't bear thinking of.

Will's warm smile did not waver. Just as the waiter arrived with the roasted ducklings nestled upon a bed of French truffles, asparagus spears Polonaise, potato croquettes, and tiny green peas in butter, however, a thought smote him. Actually, there were two thoughts, but the second arrived with such blinding speed and so hard on the other's heels that Will could not have said which came first.

Both were delectable in their irony and completely unnerving. All at once, he realized he was every bit as much a cheat as little Emily von Plotz, and with much less noble motives.

The other realization, which settled like a golden aura upon his senses, was that even though he had been wise to her game almost from the very beginning, she had succeeded. Little Miss Emily von Plotz had snared him with as much ease and finesse as if he had been any green boy of sixteen. He, Will Tate, his uncle's nephew, one of the world's most accomplished confidence men, now fluttered in her beguiling feminine net as helpless as a butterfly. What's more, he liked it there. A lot. And he didn't want out.

Will had been smiling at her and saying nothing for so long, Emily was becoming nervous. She was afraid of that smile. It was so deliciously inviting, she wanted to curl up in it and snuggle like a kitten in its warmth. It was too late to tell herself not to care about Will Tate; she knew that with dismal certainty. But if she planned to succeed in her plot to rescue her aunt and uncle from ruin, she had to keep her wits about her.

Those wits told her to be very careful; they told her Will Tate was on the brink now, that he was just about to tumble. She took a larger gulp of champagne than she had intended, and it startled her. Fortunately the waiters were settling delicacies before them, so she could speak of food instead of the disturbing emotions churning within her.

"Oh, my, Mr. Tate, this looks absolutely delicious."

Emily's prosaic words snapped Will out of his reverie. It had been such a pleasant one, too, with his vision filled with Emily in her evening finery, the soft expanse of flesh from her delicate shoulders to the delicious hint of bosom swelling provocatively above her burgundy-and-cream costume.

It suddenly mattered not at all to Will that Emily had deceived him. Hell, he had deceived her, too.

"I'm glad you think so, Miss Emily," he said when he could speak. "I chose everything just for you."

"What a sweet thing to say, Mr. Tate," Emily breathed. "How terribly kind of you."

Will gave his head a little shake. "It wasn't kind, Emily. I wanted this evening to be special for you. For both of us."

The briefest thought that Will Tate's country accent had suddenly gone visiting elsewhere flickered through Emily's mind and was instantly extinguished. She didn't want to wonder about anything tonight. She just wanted to enjoy the magic Will had created for them.

"It is special, Mr. Tate. Thank you." The words were a mere whisper.

"Thank *you*, ma'am."

They stared into each other's eyes as if the waiters didn't exist, as if they were not seated in a public restaurant in the bustling metropolis of San Francisco . . . as if they were lovers. For a moment neither of them considered their false personas; they were Will and Emily, Emily and Will, and they were in love.

The truth rose like the sun above them, and they both recognized it at the same instant. Emily's eyes got big, and she blinked hard. Will gave a visible start and sat up straight in his chair.

Oh, my Lord in heaven, Emily thought.

Son of a gun, thought Will.

Then he grinned. Will Tate wasn't one to waste time in idle regrets, and even if he were, it was too late. He was already in love with her. It felt good, too. It felt *damned* good.

Will hadn't anticipated this reaction and considered it odd. His uncle Mel had warned him from infancy to beware the fair sex. Uncle Mel had even told him that love was the absolute worst thing that could befall a man.

Uncle Mel, it was now obvious, had been wrong, wrong, wrong.

Well, it shouldn't surprise him any, Will thought as the very last one of Uncle Mel's teachings withered up and blew away like so many autumn leaves in a strong breeze. He refilled Emily's glass and lifted his own.

Emily saw the warm light in his lovely hazel eyes, and her own eyes filled with tears when he said, "To you, Miss Emily. To us."

It was all she could do to keep from bursting into sobs.

8

Emily had regained control of her emotions by the time Will guided her into their waiting carriage. Pangs of conscience still plagued her, though. How on earth could she continue her evil deception of this wonderful man? She loved him. God help her, she loved him.

Emily couldn't recall ever being so unhappy in her entire life.

"A penny for your thoughts, Miss Emily."

Will's soft voice caressed her ears like a kiss, and Emily had the sudden awful fear that she would cry. With a monumental effort, she smiled at him.

The light filtering from the gas lamps on the street through the windows of the carriage was dim. Will had not drawn the curtains, though, and he could see Emily's wistful expression.

He really did wonder what she was thinking. She looked almost sad; he would have expected her to appear triumphant. After all, he was making no secret of his adoration. She had won. He was hers. He'd gladly marry her and take her off to Texas—and her aunt and uncle and all those stupid little dogs of his, too, if that's what she wanted. He'd do anything for his darling Emily. Anything.

"Oh, I'm sorry, Mr. Tate. I—I was just thinking what a perfectly lovely evening this has been." Her voice cracked a little bit.

Suddenly throwing restraint out the window, Will crossed the carriage in one graceful movement and sat beside her. He swept her hands up in his and held them in his secure grip.

"What is it, Emily? What's wrong? Have I done something to distress you?"

Emily looked up into his face, which was solemn now with concern for her, and her control snapped.

"Oh, Mr. Tate, you haven't done a thing wrong. You've done everything exactly right."

The words poured out of Emily's heart along with a flood of guilty tears. She was frantically trying to find her lacy handkerchief—purchased at a tremendous bargain from a charity shop run by nuns in Chinatown—when she felt Will's long, strong arms surround her. She surrendered herself to his care in a wash of misery.

"Oh, Mr. Tate," she mumbled into his broad chest.

"Don't cry, Emily. Don't cry." It broke Will's heart to see her so unhappy. He hugged her close, feeling as though she had been created for his embrace, she fit so perfectly. Her warmth mingled with his heat to send his senses soaring.

"Please don't cry, love. Oh, Emily, I love you so much."

If he had been listening to himself, Will would

have been astounded to hear those words issue from his lips. But he was too busy comforting his Emily to pay attention. God almighty, she felt good.

The admission of his love for her was Emily's complete undoing. She sobbed with unrestrained misery into his shirt, her tears making his starched ruffles wilt.

"Oh, Mr. Tate, I'm such a sorry object for your affection."

Her voice was so thick with unhappiness, Will wasn't sure he'd heard her correctly. Then he decided it didn't matter. Very carefully he tilted her chin so he could peer into her glistening eyes.

"Miss Emily, you're the most wonderful woman I've ever met in my whole life."

Just before his soft lips captured hers, Emily's aching heart registered an instant of soaring gratitude. He loved her. That knowledge might almost keep her warm as she huddled in a cold-water flat with her impoverished aunt and uncle after they lost everything they owned.

Then her brain shut off, lulled into ecstasy by the wonderful man who held her so tenderly. Emily, who had never kissed a man before, responded with all the considerable ardor in her being.

She loved him passionately, completely, permanently. She loved him so much she could never carry out her deceitful plan. Her arms, which had been folded up against his chest, sneaked out of their bondage to wrap themselves around his strong, broad shoulders. She pressed herself shamelessly against him and sighed as the most complete bliss she had ever felt swallowed her whole.

Her candid surrender shook Will Tate to the soles

of his expensive patent-leather evening shoes. Although he had suspected a passionate nature lay beneath Emily's proper, ladylike demeanor, he had not dared hope it would be so *very* passionate. He was thrilled.

Pausing only briefly for breath, he renewed his kiss with gusto. The heat of their embrace caused every nerve ending in his body to vibrate in ecstasy. What this woman did to him!

As for Emily, she was lost. Not all the lessons her aunt had carefully imparted about the merits of Virtue and the importance of Propriety could stop the feelings Will stirred within her. Her body sang. Without her being aware of it, she tightened her arms around him and snuggled closer, feeling an unfamiliar and almost irresistible urge to become one with him. For a moment Emily felt as though her troubles had never existed, that nothing could ever hurt her now that she had found sanctuary in Will's arms.

Will had never felt more of a man. As much experience as he'd had with the gentle sex, and it was considerable, he had never experienced the overpowering need to possess and protect that he felt at this moment. The incredible urge to make Emily *his*, body and soul, caused his entire large frame to shake.

It was with a good deal of difficulty that he finally broke the kiss. He knew he had to do it, though, or end up taking her right here, right now, in Thomas Crandall's carriage as it rumbled along a busy San Francisco thoroughfare. He squeezed Emily's small body tightly to his, enfolding her in an embrace he wished would never end, and just held her while he tried to calm down. He could feel her soft sigh of surrender. She was no longer crying.

When he could speak, his voice was no more than a ragged whisper. "Great God, Emily, I've never felt anything as good as you feel right now. God, I love you."

Emily was shaken to the depths of her being, both by his declaration and by the blissful kiss they had just shared. Too stricken to respond, she pressed closer to him and wished they could stay locked in each other's arms forever.

It was Thomas Crandall's very proper coachman, discreetly clearing his throat outside the carriage doors, who finally caused Will to release Emily. Noticing her eyes looked dazed by the feelings that had just attacked her, he gave her a crooked smile.

"I guess we're back at your house, Miss Emily," he said, once again Texas Lonesome, although his eyes twinkled.

Emily couldn't speak yet. Her breath came in panting gasps. She wanted to cling to Will's shoulders for the rest of her life. The impossibility of that pleasant scenario began once more to register in her brain. Reluctantly she edged away from him, although it tormented her to do so.

"Oh," she managed to squeak. "Are we?"

"I'm afraid so, ma'am."

Will eyed her with concern. He didn't want her weeping spell to show and cause her discomfort in front of her aunt and uncle. He realized he still hadn't gotten to the bottom of the puzzle of those tears, either. One look at the coachman, though, decided him against pursuing it at the moment.

Emily patted her hair back into shape. She gratefully accepted the handkerchief Will dangled in front of her, wiped her eyes and cheeks, and blew her nose. Then she noticed that his shirt ruffles were drooping from her teary onslaught, and she tried to fluff them up again.

"Oh, Mr. Tate, I'm so sorry. Look at your poor ruffles. Goodness. I'm so embarrassed." Her voice was a little whisper and it almost died before it reached his ears.

He smiled at her forlorn gesture. "It's all right, ma'am. I don't reckon my shirt will suffer any permanent damage. And I guess I should apologize for kissin' you, although I do know what came over me, and I'm not sorry. You're just about the sweetest thing I've ever come across in all my days, Miss Emily."

He saw her swallow hard, and her eyes looked a little misty when her gaze met his. It was all he could do to suppress the base urge to haul her into his arms and kiss her again—and again and again and again, until the sorrowful expression left her face.

"Are you all right, ma'am? I'm sorry if I frightened you."

"You didn't frighten me, Mr. Tate."

He reached out and caressed her soft cheek with the backs of his knuckles. "Then can you give me a smile, ma'am? I'd feel less like a brute if you'd give me a smile."

Emily reacted to his stroking fingers like a cat. She might even have purred; she didn't know. She did know that her sigh was deep and heartfelt. How she would miss Will Tate. The thought almost made her weep again. Instead, she slowly straightened her shoulders and forced a smile.

"I'm so sorry for my indelicate fit, Mr. Tate. I declare, I don't know what came over me."

Will didn't particularly want to be Texas

Lonesome just then, but until he figured out how to tell Emily he wasn't, he guessed he was stuck with the role. "I—I reckon it was wrong of me to kiss you, Miss Emily, but I couldn't help it." That, at least, was the truth.

Emily's sad smile tugged at his heartstrings. "No, Mr. Tate, it was I who was wrong. I should not have responded so—so—so enthusiastically. I—I don't generally behave in this scandalous manner. You must think me no better than a hussy."

The thought of Miss Emily von Plotz being anything even close to resembling a hussy was so comical, Will couldn't repress a chuckle. "Why, no, ma'am, I don't think anything of the sort."

"Well, then, good. Thank you, Mr. Tate. It is very gentlemanly of you to say so."

Will's thoughts were far from gentlemanly when he helped Emily descend from the coach. In spite of her recent bout with whatever sadness had possessed her, she looked ethereally lovely under the soft, foggy glow of the streetlamps.

Will told the coachman to go on along home; he'd walk back to Nob Hill. He figured he'd need the walk to cool him down. Then he took Emily by the arm and led her up the walkway toward her aunt's home. They heard Gustav and Helga vigorously hailing their return to the Schindler house before they reached the door.

"Are those two critters always so, ah, alert, Miss Emily?" Will asked.

"I'm afraid so, Mr. Tate. They're very good watchdogs. Except, of course, that they don't quiet down very quickly after they've ascertained there is no danger."

Will shook his head in wonder as he escorted

Emily onto her aunt's porch. Blodgett opened the door just as they reached the top step. The two glossy animals hurtled out of the door and leapt upon them, yapping a gleeful welcome.

He let go of Emily's arm and knelt down to the hounds. He didn't want them to jump up on Emily and muss her gown.

"Oh, dear, I do apologize for the dogs, Mr. Tate." Emily's hands pressed her burning cheeks as she watched her uncle's undisciplined charges climb all over Will. The smile he gave her from his knees almost sent her heart flip-flopping out of her breast.

"Emily! Emily! Oh, Emily, something terrible has happened!"

Ludwig von Plotz's heavy, booming German accent startled them both.

Emily whirled at Uncle Ludwig's dramatic declaration and was horrified to find him running toward them, truly upset. His long side-whiskers bristled, his smoking jacket was askew, and his appearance was atypically ruffled.

"What's the matter, Mr. von Plotz?" Will asked, forgetting all about Texas Lonesome for the moment.

"Somebody tried to burn down Gustav and Helga's kennel!"

Emily could manage only a stricken gasp.

"When did this happen, Mr. von Plotz?"

"Right after the two of you left. It had just gone dark, and Gertrude and I were sitting down to supper. I heard noises, and these two wonderful watchdogs started barking, and I rushed outside to see what was what."

The pallor of Emily's cheeks worried Will. He put a comforting arm around her waist, in spite of

Ludwig's presence. "So you put the fire out before any damage could be done?"

Ludwig had no thought to spare for whether or not it was proper for Will to be hugging his niece. "Yah, yah. In fact, Helga took a piece out of the man's trousers before anything could be burned. It's what I tell you, Mr. Tate. *Nobody* creeps up on these wonderful dogs. The fellow must have been kneeling to light the fire when Helga attacked him."

"Mr. von Plotz, I think I know who's behind this. If you'll let me intrude on your business, I'd like to talk to you about it later."

"Oh, no, Mr. Tate. This isn't your concern," Emily replied immediately. Oh, Lord, what had she done? To involve this dear, dear man in her family's maniacal schemes seemed the ultimate in perfidy right now.

But Will's words brightened Ludwig up at least a hundred percent. "Oh, yah, Mr. Tate. You take care of it. I know you can take care of it." Ludwig's head nodded up and down as if he were bobbing for apples. Then he rubbed his hands together briskly, thrust all unpleasant thoughts from his head, and smiled at the perfect couple.

"Well, well, well. Now that that's settled, let's see what we have here. Back from the Palace, are you?"

"But—" Emily felt as though everything in her life was slipping out of her control.

"Yes, we are indeed, Mr. von Plotz."

Will gave Emily a gentle nudge to let her know it was wiser to drop the subject of the kennel attack.

Still unhappy, Emily glanced up at him. When she read the request in his eyes, she gave up. She said, "Yes, Uncle Ludwig, we're back." Then she sighed, "It was just wonderful."

Her honest, breathless confession made Will smile with pure male satisfaction. That was the sign he'd been waiting for: the unmistakable note proclaiming she was his. He had never heard it before from a woman—had never wanted to hear it—but he recognized it with an innate, animal instinct for possession. She was *his,* and he was going to keep her, come hell, high water, crazy relatives, Clarence Pickering, Gustav, Helga, or kennel arsonists.

"Well, well, well," said Ludwig once more. "Come into the parlor and visit with your old uncle, Emily darling. Your auntie is there with her spirit friends. We can have a nice chat."

Ludwig smiled broadly at the both of them. Emily felt like a miserable coward for cringing from his voluble good humor after having almost died from heart failure at his report of arson. She knew she had no just cause to feel such embarrassment. All at once, though, the thought of sitting in the parlor with Will while her uncle lectured them about dachshunds and her aunt conversed with the Raja Kinjiput was too much to bear.

"Oh, no!" she cried. "Oh, no, I can't, Uncle Ludwig."

Her cheeks burned with shame when she saw her uncle's crestfallen expression.

"Oh, Uncle Ludwig, Mr. Tate, I'm so sorry. I didn't mean to sound like that. It's just—it's just— I'm so tired all of a sudden. Why, I simply can't seem to keep my eyes open a second longer." She gave a ridiculous titter and knew they knew she was lying.

Will understood. He'd felt the same way a time or two around boyhood chums when in his own uncle's presence, especially when Mel had been tippling. He smiled to let her know he wasn't offended, neither by her retreat nor by her falsehood.

"It's all right, Miss Emily. You go on up to bed. I know it's late." Will didn't figure a little fib to help her out would earn him any more years in purgatory than he was already facing. Her grateful smile was all the thanks he figured he'd ever need.

She murmured, "Thank you, Mr. Tate," so sweetly that he wanted to follow her right on up the stairs.

"It's all right, ma'am." He also wanted to kiss her good night. He didn't, of course.

Emily turned toward the staircase, then suddenly whirled around and grabbed Will's hand. She pressed it fervently as she said, "Mr. Tate, I can't thank you enough for the wonderful evening you've given me. I can't remember ever having such a delightful time. Thank you."

She wanted to kiss him, to snatch one last, blissful buss before leaving him for what would be, if not the last time, at least close to it. But she didn't dare. All of her proper upbringing rose as would a steel barricade to stop her.

When Will lifted her hand to his lips and kissed it, she thought for a moment she might faint.

"Miss Emily, the pleasure was entirely my own. Believe me."

The speaking look in his eyes convinced Emily he was telling her the truth. She supposed her blush must be as deep as the pickled beets her uncle loved so much. "Thank you, Mr. Tate."

"Thank *you*, ma'am." He didn't release her hand. Instead, he squeezed it more tightly and said, "Please let me call on you tomorrow, Miss Emily. I'd like to see you again."

This was the end of the road for Will, and he knew it. He figured he might as well get it over with. He was going to propose to her, damn it, and that was that.

Emily hesitated for a second. The idea of seeing him the next day was as tempting as the promise of candy to a child, even if it meant saying good-bye forever. She knew beyond the shadow of a doubt she could not marry him. She couldn't do such a patently evil thing to such a perfect, wonderful man. But the thought of never seeing him again almost made her heart snap right in two.

One last time, she told herself. Just one last little time. Then she would leave him alone and not darken his life anymore with her vile, deceitful schemes.

"All right, Mr. Tate. I'd love to see you tomorrow."

She shook his hand with the utmost propriety and hurried up the stairs. To Will, who had no idea her heart was breaking, it looked as though she were skipping upstairs on a cloud of happiness. He knew she loved him. He had read it in her eyes.

He had also completely forgotten Uncle Ludwig was anywhere in his vicinity until he heard the man's discreet cough.

"Come into the parlor and have a glass of brandy with me, Mr. Tate. I've got some excellent cherry brandy. Brought it with me from Austria. It's the best."

"I'd like that fine, Mr. von Plotz."

This would be his opportunity, Will realized, to kill two birds with one stone. He could finalize plans for his investment in Ludwig's dachshund scheme and, at the same time, be a proper gentleman and ask Emily's aunt and uncle if he could call upon her on the morrow to ask for her hand in marriage. He knew Emily would appreciate that gesture.

He wanted nothing but the best for his Emily, and would cut his own throat before he did anything even remotely smacking of disrespect. He supposed the kiss they'd shared in the carriage might be considered disrespectful by some stuffy moralists. But Will himself remembered it with too much awe to believe it had been anything but wonderful, even worshipful.

His first glance at Aunt Gertrude once he crossed the threshold into the parlor made him stare in amusement. She was gazing with shortsighted intensity into her crystal ball, and her hands were passing in mystical-looking circles through the air above it, as though she were attempting to polish the globe without touching it.

"Gertrude, look who's come to take brandy with us." Ludwig interrupted Gertrude's spiritual communication without so much as a by-your-leave, Will noticed. It seemed to him these two relatives of Emily's were so wrapped up in their own little foibles that neither had a thought to spare for anyone else, least of all their niece, who was struggling so valiantly on their behalf.

He bit back the unkind thought. They were Emily's family and precious to her. As such, they were also precious to him. He would be happy to take them under his wealthy wing and thereby spare his Emily the trials they must cause her. Poor Emily. His admiration for her grew every day as the knowledge of her many struggles became evident to him.

Speaking of struggles, Gustav had managed to locate a shoe buckle from somewhere. Will saw him gnawing it under one of the sofa's end tables. Ludwig noticed it at the same time, uttered a loud cluck, and stooped to retrieve it.

Both Ludwig and Gustav held on tight to either end of the buckle, Gustav growling ferociously, Ludwig pleading. Ludwig finally won after a brief but intense struggle. Gustav stared after him with what Will could have sworn was resentment in his beady brown eyes when Ludwig stood and carted off the now-ruined buckle.

Good God almighty, Will thought. *Who in his right mind would ever want a dog like that?*

He did not give voice to his doubts. Instead, he accepted Ludwig's proffered brandy and sipped politely.

"This is very good, Mr. von Plotz."

"Yah. It's the best."

Gertrude had by this time put her crystal ball aside and joined the gentlemen. Sipping with appropriate delicacy, she said, "It was so kind of you to take our Emily to the Palace this evening, Mr. Blake. I know she thinks a lot of you. I think it's simply marvelous that you have managed to find your way so easily around our huge city, being from Arizona and all. It must be so different here for you."

Will discovered with surprise that he was honestly beginning to like these people, even if they did cause Emily a lot of worry. "Well, ma'am, my name is Tate, and I'm from Texas. And as for San Francisco, I actually lived here before I moved to Texas."

"Really?" Gertrude seemed to find the information fascinating. Or maybe she was just trying to focus her nearsighted eyes. Whatever the cause, her gaze was now fixed as firmly on Will as it had been on the crystal ball a few moments before. Some people might have found her stare disconcerting, but Will, who had grown up with much worse than Gertrude, didn't mind at all.

"Yes, ma'am. I like it here just fine. Always have. As a matter of fact, I'm partnered in a business here."

"Ach, a businessman! Didn't I tell you, Gertrude? Mr. Tate is a man of parts. I said so, Mr. Tate. I told my sister that." Ludwig's head bobbed up and down like an India-rubber ball.

"Why, yes, Ludwig dear. I believe you did say something of the sort." Gertrude smiled vaguely.

"Yes, ma'am. My partner's name is Thomas Crandall, and the business is Crandall and Tate. Maybe you've heard of it."

"Crandall and Tate?" Ludwig's mouth dropped open.

"Crandall and Tate?" Gertrude's eyes blinked so fast, Will nearly got dizzy.

"Yes, ma'am."

"Why, my goodness, Mr. Blake, you must be positively wealthy. Crandall and Tate is the biggest import house in the United States."

"Well, maybe not the entire United States, ma'am, but it's pretty big, all right."

Will wondered why he was trying to make his business enterprise sound like a trifling matter. What he really wanted was to show these people he had so much money, he could support Emily, Gertrude, Ludwig, and a hundred dachshunds. He didn't want there to exist the slightest possibility that either one of them might object to his suit. He was positive Emily loved him, but he also knew her sense of duty would prevent her from going against her aunt and uncle's wishes. Or, at least, any objections on their part would make her sad, and he didn't want his Emily to be sad again. Ever.

"Wonderful! That's wonderful, Mr. Tate. No wonder you want to invest in my dogs. You're a shrewd man. You know the coming thing when you see it."

"Yes, sir," he answered.

Ludwig nodded with vigor. "I told you, Gertrude. I told you Mr. Tate was a man of parts."

"Well, Mr. von Plotz, Mrs. Schindler, I don't like to boast, but I did want you to know I'm no mere Texas vagabond. I've got plenty of money to support a wife."

Gertrude's sweet smile faded somewhat. "Oh, Mr. Blake, I didn't know you had a wife. Is she in Arizona? I'm not sure it's quite the thing for you to be escorting our Emily to dinner all alone if you have a wife, sir. I'm quite certain it is not, in fact." A small frown was the most Gertrude, who deplored unpleasantness, could manage.

Will felt himself losing his audience and wondered how on earth it had happened. He hurried to explain.

"No, no, ma'am, I don't have a wife. That's what I want to talk to you about tonight."

"About not having a wife?" Gertrude looked suitably puzzled.

"Wait, Gertrude. I understand. Mr. Tate wants to call on our Emily!"

"Exactly!" Will exclaimed in relief.

"Well, of course he wants to call on her. He's *been* calling on her, Ludwig dear. What I'm saying is that it's not proper for him to call on her if he has a wife in Arizona already."

"I don't have a wife, ma'am, in Arizona or anywhere else," Will said, deciding bluntness in this circumstance was more appropriate than *politesse*. "I want to marry Emily, and I've come to ask if you will allow me to court her properly."

"Oh!" Gertrude's face lit up with comprehension. "Oh, how sweet." Then she asked, obviously touched, "Did your other wife die, Mr. Blake? How terribly sad for you."

If Will hadn't seen tears of genuine sympathy in her eyes, he would have cursed in frustration. "I've never been married, ma'am. If Emily agrees to be my wife, she'll be my first. My first and only."

Gertrude looked dreadfully confused.

Not so Ludwig. "That's wonderful, Mr. Tate! I'm happy for both of you. You couldn't find a more darling girl than our Emily. And I'm sure you'll be a fine husband for her. Anybody with your good sense about my magnificent dogs has got to be a brilliant provider."

Ludwig's happiness was apparently contagious, because Gertrude smiled, too. "How lovely," she sighed. "Our Emily to be married. Oh, what a beautiful bride she will make."

"Well, Mrs. Schindler and Mr. von Plotz, she hasn't accepted me yet," Will reminded them.

"She will," Ludwig said with certainty.

Privately Will thought so, too, but he didn't say so aloud. Instead, he decided the time was ripe to finalize plans for his investment in Ludwig's dogs, so he steered the conversation in that direction. Ludwig was, as ever, eager to oblige.

About an hour later Will walked home feeling quite chipper. After dinner with Emily and brandy with her relatives, there was no doubt in his mind that Emily was the woman for him. He shook his head in awe.

"God almighty," he whispered to the foggy night sky.

Family feeling was not an emotion his uncle Mel had fostered in Will's breast. The fact that Emily harbored such devout feelings for her own family, even in the face of their lunatic propensities, both puzzled and touched him. In fact, if he hadn't already loved her to distraction, those feelings of hers would have pushed him over the edge.

"She's amazing," he told himself. Then he told the same thing to Thomas Crandall when he got home, completely forgetting that Thomas had annoyed him almost to the point of homicide not four hours earlier.

Thomas had been reading peacefully in his upstairs sitting room, once again engrossed in the seamier streets of London, when Will intruded on him.

"You're a fallen man, Will Tate. I recognize the symptoms."

Will didn't even bother to deny it. "Damned right I am. I'm going to propose to her tomorrow."

Thomas stood up and stuck out his hand. "Congratulations, Will. I didn't think I'd ever see the day."

"I didn't think so, either, Thomas. I surely didn't."

Will decided the only thing that could possibly make him happier that night would be to have Emily next to him in bed.

Soon, he promised himself. Very, very soon.

Emily felt as though her body were cast of lead when at last she reached her bedroom. She went mechanically through the motions of disrobing, sighing wretchedly as she hung up her gown. The dress had done its duty well, she guessed, for all the good it was going to do her.

The night should be clear, she thought as she gazed out her bedroom window at the sky. She wanted to see stars, not this hideous fog that hid the heavens from her. She was depressed enough without this wretched fog clouding her vision.

Oh, how she would love to marry Will Tate. She sighed again into the mist. How she would love to go to Texas with him and be his wife and help him herd his cows—or whatever it was a ranch wife did. "I could learn," she declared soulfully to the cold, uncaring night. "I know I could learn."

But it was not to be. She positively could not deceive Will Tate another minute longer. She would confess her sin tomorrow, in fact, when he came to call.

Well, maybe she would wait until after his visit ended and he was leaving. It was cowardly of her, she knew, but she couldn't bear to lose him without one last, happy hour in his presence.

When she finally dragged her soul-weary self to bed, she stared at the ceiling for a long time before sleep claimed her.

9

Dear Aunt Emily:

I am in love with a sailor whose ship departs for Singapore on the morrow. He says he loves me, although I would not give him his heart's desire even when he begged. I shall wait for him until the end of time, but waiting is so hard. My mother does not understand. She believes, as I am only fifteen, I am being silly. How can I convince her I am not silly?

Signed,
Mermaid

Dear Mermaid:

While your caring Aunt Emily is pleased you think you have found your one true love, she is concerned about your planned course of action. She believes you would be better advised to participate in the activities common to other fifteen-year-old young ladies rather than wait and

*pine for your sailor. Perhaps if you prove to
your mother you are not merely a silly girl, but
an obedient, thoughtful one, she will begin to
treat you differently.*

    Love,
    Aunt Emily

    *P.S. Please, darling Mermaid, never grant a
gentleman his heart's desire unless and until his
ring is firmly affixed upon your finger and the
minister has pronounced the holy words.*

Emily reread her latest letter and sighed. "Why is
life so hard?"

The window, to which she had addressed the question, did not answer.

When she tired of working on her column, she
gave herself a firm lecture before she stepped out of
her room. Marriage to Texas Lonesome was no longer
an option now that she had come to care so deeply for
Will Tate. She absolutely *had* to determine the exact
state of her aunt and uncle's financial affairs if she
ever hoped to set them straight. The thought held no
appeal. In fact, it was downright depressing.

Nevertheless, directly after luncheon, she padded
to her aunt's office and sat herself down at Gertrude's
big desk. The clutter was appalling, Emily realized
with drooping spirits as she scanned the mess.

But she told herself it had to be done.

Sorting through the heap of papers took over an
hour. Modistes' statements and butchers' bills were
piled together with the intimacy of long acquaintance,
along with Gertrude's *Daily Star Guide for Aquarius,
Year of Our Lord 1893* and a Sterling Safety Bicycle

manual. Emily racked her brain to think of where on earth a bicycle could be hiding itself, but she couldn't come up with a location or a single other thing to account for the presence of the manual.

A carpenter's statement for the building of Gustav and Helga's fancy quarters nearly made Emily burst into tears. She wanted to scream in frustration when she discovered a bill from Clarence Pickering for financial services rendered, lying underneath a notice dunning Gertrude for unpaid grocers' charges.

Then there were the overdue taxes on Gertrude's property. Emily's hand trembled as she scanned the document.

"Oh, my Lord," she whispered when the full extent of her aunt's financial ruin lay in front of her in neat little piles of stark black and white. "What on earth can I do now?"

She wanted to cry, but knew tears would be a useless waste of energy. She couldn't afford to fall apart now. She had to think of something.

The house would have to be sacrificed. Of course, that meant Uncle Ludwig's dogs would have to go. Emily shook her head in despair as she contemplated how on earth she could accomplish that maneuver short of waiting until the courts did it for her. It would be best if she could convince them to sell the place before it was taken over for taxes, but she knew that her aunt and uncle could not be made to listen to reason.

"At least I have my column."

Even as she said the words, Emily knew them to be empty. The money she earned from her column wouldn't make the tiniest dent in the stacks and stacks of debt staring back at her.

Emily tried to tamp down her despair as she left the room in search of her aunt. She mustn't allow herself to abandon hope, or else all would be lost. She simply had to talk to Aunt Gertrude again.

Her resolve nearly died when she stepped into the best parlor only to be brought up short by the appalling specter of Clarence Pickering.

He was leaning against the fireplace as though he already owned the place, stroking his upper lip and looking very relaxed. His handsome face creased into a sincere-looking smile at Emily's entrance, and she couldn't repress her distaste.

"Where's my aunt?" she asked without preamble.

"Why, good morning, Miss Emily, my sweet." The look Pickering gave her was so near an ogle, it made her want to vomit.

"Where's my aunt?" she asked again. Her repugnance seemed only to amuse Pickering.

"Why, Emily, you sweet child, don't you even have a 'good day' for me?

"No, Mr. Pickering, I do not."

"I declare, I don't think you like me at all, do you?"

"No, I most certainly don't."

She turned to leave the room, but he was too quick for her. His hand closed around her arm in such a tight grip that she winced.

"I think it would behoove you to be a little nicer to me, my darling," Pickering crooned into her ear, "if you know what's good for you and your family. I don't believe you can count on your aunt and uncle to help themselves, do you? Of course you don't. You're too clever for that. You know they're crazy, don't you?" His whispered words were murmured with the smoothness of a caressing endearment. He tried to turn her around and pull her closer to his chest, but Emily resisted.

"I'm sure they'll be happy to learn your assessment of their character, Mr. Pickering." Emily's voice was tight with barely controlled fury.

He chuckled. "Now, Miss Emily, you know your aunt isn't going to believe anything bad about me, don't you?"

Unfortunately, Emily did know it. She wanted to make a scathing reply, but her innate honesty—the same honesty that now thwarted her scheme to marry Will Tate—made her bite it back.

Instead of lying to him, she wrenched her arm from his grip and said, "Don't you ever touch me again, Mr. Pickering, or you'll be very sorry."

The threat was an idle one, and even Emily knew it. Before Pickering could laugh at her, however, he found himself suddenly hurtling across the room. His back slammed against the wall next to the fireplace, and he slid down to land on the same pile of logs that had caused him to go sprawling several nights before.

"If you ever so much as lay a finger on her again, I'll kill you, Pickering. Don't doubt it for a second."

Emily's startled gaze went from Pickering's undignified sprawl to Will Tate, who stood at the door, fists clenched at his sides. He seemed to be struggling with the urge to do further harm to Clarence Pickering.

"Mr. Tate," breathed Emily. "Oh, Mr. Tate." Then, before she was aware of what she was doing, she found herself throwing herself into his welcoming arms.

Will forgot all about slaughtering Pickering as he hugged Emily close to his chest.

"Are you all right, sweetheart?"

"I—I think so."

They were so wrapped up in each other that they didn't notice Pickering shake his immaculately pomaded head as if to clear it of cobwebs, stand up, test his bones for breaks, and finally march out of the room. On his way out he glared at the two lovers, but his efforts were wasted since neither Emily nor Will was watching.

"What did he do to you, Emily?"

"N-nothing. He just grabbed me, and I think he was going to kiss me, and—and—oh, Mr. Tate, he's such an awful man!"

That was it, as far as Will was concerned. He'd just have to follow Pickering and kill him right now. He told Emily as much as he peeled her arms from around his waist and turned to storm out of the room in pursuit of his quarry.

"Oh, no, Mr. Tate. Please don't. You'll just get yourself in trouble. That awful man isn't worth it." Emily once more threw her arms around his waist.

Since Emily had asked him not to, Will guessed he'd forgo the pleasure of strangling Pickering, but it went against his better judgment. Then, when his angry gaze again met Emily's, it softened in a hurry.

Since her arms were already wrapped around him, it was an easy matter for Will to pick her up and carry her to the sofa. He sat down with a whump, Emily firmly ensconced on his lap, and their lips met in a kiss they would both remember for the rest of their lives.

As Will's mouth scorched across hers, his possession was so fierce she gasped. Emily had never even suspected that she, a mere woman, could feel this much heat. Will's touch ignited a desire that curled through her body, causing her to ache to be even closer to him. She snuggled restlessly on his lap, thereby creating for Will no end of delicious torment.

The prevailing fashion in this enlightened age had done away with the bustle except for formal evening occasions, so Emily was not wearing the beastly annoyance today. She had donned a practical cotton skirt and shirtwaist, and her soft bottom pressing against his arousal was nearly Will's undoing. Of course, no proper lady would face the day without her corset, so he did encounter that impediment to his exploring hands. But her sweet breasts tumbled over the top of her corset and camisole so provocatively, Will thought he might just die on the spot.

"My God, Emily. Oh, my God, you feel good."

"So do you, Will." Emily couldn't believe her own proper lips had formed those words no matter how true they were. She didn't give herself time to think about them, though.

When Will's mouth left hers to go exploring, Emily was sure she would swoon. His searing touch traced a path over her chin and down the sensitive column of her throat.

Somehow Will had managed to unbutton the first few buttons of Emily's shirtwaist, so when his hand brushed aside her high collar and rested on her tender flesh, Emily nearly shrieked with pleasure. When his tongue sought out the pulse beating in her neck, she groaned. Her head fell back and she lay in his arms, exposed to his touch and eager to experience whatever he wanted to do to her next. She had never felt anything so wonderful in her entire life, and she was terribly disappointed when Will drew away.

He didn't want to. Nevertheless, he decided he'd have to stop what he was doing or disgrace them both beyond redemption. He withdrew his mouth from her sweet neck and tightened his arms around her while he rested his chin on her head, trying to regain his breath and his composure.

It was the yapping of Gustav and Helga that ultimately forced Will to gather his wits and quickly button up Emily's collar. This surprised her, for she had been so involved in their activity, she hadn't realized he had unbuttoned it in the first place.

When the door to the parlor opened, the two dachshunds raced in and jumped up on Will and Emily in an enthusiastic doggy greeting.

"Well, hello, you two." Will couldn't help but laugh at their exuberant display. These dogs might not be good for very much, but at least they made one feel welcome.

Emily was still too shaken to say a word.

"Oh, here you are, Emily dear. I just saw Mr. Pickering leave. He looked as though he was in a hurry. I hope you didn't upset him."

The expression on Gertrude's face spoke so eloquently of worry that Emily felt guilty.

Will, who had stood politely at Gertrude's entrance into the parlor, forestalled any apology on Emily's part, however. He said with great force, "You've got it exactly backward, Mrs. Schindler. Pickering was trying to take advantage of Miss von Plotz when I happened to come into the room. I sent him flying." Will chose not to explain that his use of the word was literal.

"My goodness, Mr. Blake! I had no idea. How terrible!"

Emily, who hated to see her aunt upset, intervened in haste. "It's all right, Aunt. Mr. Tate was very kind and took care of everything. I must tell you, though, that Mr. Pickering was most unpleasant to me."

"I shall speak to him severely about this, Emily dear. Yes, I certainly shall."

Gertrude squared her shoulders and marched out of the parlor, full of purpose. Where she was going, neither Emily nor Will knew, since Pickering was long gone by this time. The two dachshunds followed at her heels, no doubt hoping for a treat when they got to wherever she was going.

"She'll probably forget all about it by the time he comes over again," Emily said forlornly.

"Well, I won't."

When Emily gazed up at him, Will looked ready for battle again. It gave her a fluttery feeling to know he was willing to fight evil men on her behalf. She'd never had anyone offer to help her before. It felt good, even though she knew it could not continue.

"Will you walk out to the backyard with me, Mr. Tate? There's something I must tell you." Her voice almost broke on the words.

"I need to tell you something, too, Miss Emily." Now that he'd decided Emily was the one for him, Will couldn't wait to propose.

They walked outside, arm in arm. The Cecile Brunner rose Will had sent Emily was doing very well in its special spot next to Gustav and Helga's elaborate kennel. Will was impressed.

"Why, that rosebush looks just perfect there, Miss Emily."

Emily, who watered her rose every day and tended it like a mother hen, sighed. "Yes. Sending that rose

was so kind of you, Mr. Tate." Her voice did crack a
little bit when she recalled all the wonderful ways
Will had about him.

Helga and Gustav were outside already, having
preceded Emily and Will. They dashed up to say hello
once more, as if they hadn't seen these two humans in
a month of Sundays instead of barely five minutes
before.

Will couldn't help but laugh at them. "You know,
Miss Emily, these critters are really kind of nice once
you get to know them."

Emily's heart gave a painful tug. "Yes, they are
endearing dogs. Uncle Ludwig certainly loves them."

"He tells me he's trying to breed them. I'll bet a
bucketful of dachshund puppies would be about the
cutest thing on the face of the earth. Do you think
he'll be able to make dachshunds the next craze in the
dog world with just the two of them?"

Such a feat didn't sound feasible to Will, although
he didn't know much about dogs. So far, however, he
had been unable to wheedle any details out of
Ludwig. Ludwig's only interest seemed to lie in reciting the hounds' many virtues and accepting money
for his grand idea. He was, Will had discovered, perilously short on details.

"Well, he hopes to start with Gustav and Helga,
and then send for more animals from Germany when
he sells the pups. So far, though, nothing much has
happened."

Will had been kneeling beside the hounds in order
to deflect some of their affection from Emily's skirts.
Now he looked up at her and wondered if she knew
how puppies were made. The thought that she very
well might not amused him. He knew many proper

young ladies had scant knowledge of how the breeding process was accomplished in animals. He'd sure be happy when he could teach Emily how humans mated. Soon, he promised himself as he stood again. Very, very soon.

"You know, Miss Emily, dogs aren't like people. They can't make babies just any old time." He paused then, wondering how Emily would react to his shocking statement.

She blushed, then looked at her shoes, which peeked out from underneath her skirt. "I know, Mr. Tate. I read a book about it."

"Really? You had to read a book? Your uncle didn't tell you?" Will forced himself not to smile.

"Of course not," Emily declared. Her cheeks were as hot as two live coals. "Uncle Ludwig is a gentleman. Gentlemen can't—can't speak to ladies about such things. It isn't proper. He gave me a book."

Will nodded. "Well, do you know if Helga has gone into heat yet?"

He wasn't sure if it was a proper thing to ask a lady like Emily, but he was curious. Besides, he was going to be spending a lot of money on these creatures, and it was mighty difficult getting information out of Ludwig.

"Yes, I do. She has."

"Ah." Emily looked so adorably embarrassed, it took all the control at Will's command not to reach out, grab her, and squeeze her tight. "So she's had her first heat. But she didn't have any puppies?"

"No."

"Did Gustav seem, ah, interested in her at the time?"

Emily wished she would stop blushing. She took a deep breath. "Yes. He was—quite interested."

In fact, the interest Gustav displayed in Helga at the time had shocked Emily.

Will didn't say anything for a second or two; he just watched Emily and enjoyed the pretty picture she made as she changed color. Then he began to feel a little guilty about causing her such anxiety.

"Hmmm. That doesn't sound too good to me. Maybe poor old Helga can't have puppies. Or maybe it's Gustav. Maybe it's just the combination. I'm sure they'll try again when the time is ripe."

"Yes."

"I guess ol' Gustav knows how to do the thing right."

"I'm sure he does. At least, I hope so. At least, he seemed to. At least—well, I mean, they *do* sleep together every night, after all." Emily hoped Will would drop the subject now, before she became the first documented case of spontaneous combustion in San Francisco's colorful history.

Emily's ingenuous comment was enough for Will, who decided this was it. He didn't figure there would ever come a better time than right this minute. And he was going to do it the proper way, too. Nothing was too good for his Emily. He dropped to one knee in front of her and took her hand in his.

Emily froze in shock when she realized Will Tate had just adopted the classic, time-honored pose a respectable gentleman assumed in circumstances of a certain nature.

My heavens, he's going to propose! The knowledge ricocheted through Emily's brain, setting off alarm bells. She longed to stop him, to confess her many sins before he could do the rash deed. She couldn't bear to deceive him one more instant, yet she knew he'd hate her once he learned of her foul behavior.

She opened her mouth to protest, only to discover her words had all clumped together like soggy bread in her throat. Nothing escaped her lips but a sigh.

Will took that as a good sign.

"Miss Emily, I'm here today to ask you the most important question a man can ask a lady. I'm in love with you, Emily, and I want to spend the rest of my days with you."

Emily squeaked.

"Say you'll marry me, Emily. Please say you will. I'll take care of you and your aunt and uncle, and even your uncle's dogs. You'll never have to worry about anything again as long as you live, if you'll only be mine."

She gasped.

"Marry me, Emily. Please. I'm asking you to be my wife."

"Oh!"

For the life of her, the one inadequate syllable was all Emily could shove past the lump in her throat. She swallowed hard and stared at Will, aghast.

Will couldn't figure out what the problem was. He knew she loved him. She knew he loved her. They both knew she needed him. Why didn't she just say yes, throw her arms around him, and be done with it?

For a moment time seemed to stop for them. Then, when it started again, it did so as though it were slogging through a streamlet of cold molasses. Emily's mouth opened and shut uselessly several times. Will stared up at her. Gustav decided to chew on Will's boot. Helga flopped down to take a nap.

"I can't!" The words finally pushed themselves

past the clot of misery in Emily's throat and popped out of her mouth.

Will was astonished. He stood up in haste, flinging Gustav's long body away from him to land in a heap upon Helga, who took immediate exception. As the two dogs growled and snapped at each other, Will demanded, "What the hell do you mean, you can't?"

"I—I can't, Mr. Tate."

Emily grabbed Will's hand. She wanted to tell him about her wicked deceit. She knew she should tell him how she had tricked him. But when she looked up into his face and read the hurt, bewilderment, and anger in it, words failed her. She was already reviling herself as a craven wretch, but it was no use. She couldn't make herself confess.

"Oh, Mr. Tate," she cried, "I'm so sorry!"

Then she burst into tears, flung herself away from him, and dashed into the house, up the stairs, and into her room, where she threw herself onto her bed and sobbed as though her heart was broken. Which it was.

Will could only stare after her, mystified.

"Well, I'll be goddamned," he muttered. He stood in the backyard with his hands on his hips, not believing what he'd just heard.

"Now what in the Sam Hill got into her?"

Helga and Gustav were in the midst of a bloodthirsty battle at his feet. "Shut up!" he hollered at them. They subsided at once.

"I don't understand it," he mumbled. "She loves me. She needs me. I love her. I need her."

The admission cost him a good deal of pride, although he knew it was merely the truth.

Not only that, but he admired the hell out of her. She'd set out to get him and, by God, she'd gotten him. Him! Will Tate, nephew to Melchior Tate, smoothest confidence man this side of the Hudson River and sometimes on the other side of it, too. She'd won, for God's sake! Just what in hell was going on, anyway?

It was too much for him to figure out right now. He picked up his Stetson, which he had cast aside long before, and crammed it on his head. Stalking into the house, he hoped to escape without meeting up with either of Emily's lunatic relatives, but luck was not on his side.

"Well, well, Mr. Tate. And did you and our little Emily set a date for the happy event?" Ludwig asked when he spotted him.

The man's smile was sincere. Will knew it, but the knowledge didn't help. He was so frustrated and angry, he didn't want to talk to anybody.

"No! She won't have me." Will felt guilty over his outburst as soon as he saw Ludwig's face crumple up. Then he sighed and said, "I'm sorry, Mr. von Plotz. I'm a little shaken right now. I thought for sure she would agree to marry me."

"I thought so, too, Mr. Tate. I don't understand it." Ludwig scratched his head. "I could have sworn she was head over heels in love with you. I *saw* it, Mr. Tate. I swear to you, I *saw* it!"

A rueful chuckle leaked out of Will's throat. Good old Ludwig was earnest about everything, he supposed. "I thought I saw it, too, Mr. von Plotz."

The pitiful expression on Ludwig's face brought something else to Will's mind, and he reached into his breast pocket to withdraw the draft he'd had the bank prepare earlier in the day.

"Here, Mr. von Plotz. I think it would behoove you to get yourself some more dogs if you really want to breed them. You can use this."

Ludwig's eyes widened when he took the draft from Will and saw the amount written on the paper.

"Mr. Tate, I swear to you in the name of our beloved, departed Rudolf, I will use this money to create the best damned string of dachshunds in the world. No. In the universe!" Tears stood in Ludwig's eyes when he uttered his impassioned phrases, and Will was touched in spite of himself.

"I'd like to help you do just that, Mr. von Plotz. Would you care to talk about it now?"

Ludwig had to dab at his eyes with a handkerchief quickly yanked from a pocket before he could answer. "Anything, Mr. Tate. For you, anything." He blew his nose with a huge honk and ushered Will into the parlor.

Since it was very nearly impossible to get Ludwig to concentrate on business long enough to accomplish anything worthwhile, it was up to Will to compose the letter to Ludwig's breeder in Germany. Ludwig happily translated the missive into German once it had been written.

Then the two men collaborated on an advertisement Will proposed they publish in both San Francisco daily newspapers. He also suggested having promotional posters printed, an idea Ludwig endorsed with glee.

Will was fascinated to discover that although Emily's uncle was a complete flop when it came to practicalities such as bill-paying and letter-writing, his obsession could be used to create very effective publicity for his dogs. Will stored the useful piece of information away for the future, glad to know Ludwig might prove to be good for something after all.

"I'll call again tomorrow, Mr. von Plotz, and tell you how things are going," Will promised as he prepared to leave the Schindler home. "With any luck, I can visit the papers this afternoon, and your ad will appear in the morning."

Ludwig shook Will's hand fervently. "I don't know how to thank you, Mr. Tate. Your support for my wonderful dogs will make all the difference. You'll see. They'll take off like skyrockets once people learn about them."

Although Will harbored many doubts on the issue, he would not for the world let Ludwig know it. He wasn't about to do anything that might lessen his chances of turning Emily's no into a yes. He figured the sooner her relatives were out of financial hot water, the sooner he could make her listen to reason. Once she saw how valiantly he was working to rescue her batty aunt and uncle, she was sure to marry him—out of gratitude, if nothing deeper.

But she loved him. He knew she loved him.

With that thought at the forefront of his mind, he left her home to go place the ad at the newspaper offices. That didn't take any time at all, but he had slightly more trouble with the artist he sought out to prepare the artwork for their poster. After Will drew a rough sketch and then convinced the man he hadn't made a mistake—the dogs really *did* look like that—things went more smoothly. By the time he left, Will was sure the artist thought he was out of his mind. He was satisfied the man would carry out the assignment to his specifications, however, and that was all that mattered.

From the artist's studio, Will walked to Thomas Crandall's house on Nob Hill. Only today he was not walking on air. Instead, he slouched along the San Francisco streets, staring at the road in front of him, pondering the perversity of women, and feeling like a very dejected young man.

10

Dear Aunt Emily:
I know I have found the girl. She is perfect and I love her. Thank you for your help. I think it was etiquette that done it.
Signed,
Texas Lonesome

For the life of her, Emily couldn't formulate a response. Tears kept blinding her.

"I'll never understand it as long as I live, Thomas. I swear to God, she loves me. I can see it in her eyes every damned time she looks at me."

Will shook his head as he paced back and forth in front of Thomas Crandall's elaborate fireplace in the upstairs sitting room. Thomas hadn't even had a chance to delve into his Sherlock Holmes mystery today before Will cornered him.

He had never seen his friend so upset; indeed, he hadn't even known Will could become this over-wrought, over a mere woman. Thomas held in his laughter out of respect for Will's broken heart.

"I mean, look at the whole situation, Thomas. Just take a good look at it," Will said. "She met me in the park. She found out I was from Texas. She asked me if I was Texas Lonesome. I swear, Thomas, she nearly fainted on the spot when I said I was. I know she planned right then to snag me. *You* even said that was probably her game."

Thomas felt obliged to agree. "That's so, Will. I believe I did."

Will nodded miserably. "That's what I mean. I remember, because I thought you were wrong. Then, when I knew you were right, I could only be amazed at how damned smart she was. So why in God's name did she refuse to marry me? I mean, Thomas, she won! I swear to God, I'm hers, body and soul. I can't even imagine being with another woman now that I've fallen in love with Emily."

"I don't blame you, Will. She's really something, all right."

"And she loves me. I know she loves me. You may think I'm being foolish, but I can tell. For God's sake, I spent my entire childhood reading people's expressions and gestures. I was taught by an expert in the field! I can tell the real thing from a good act-ing job any day of the week. Emily doesn't have it in her to dissimulate. She loves me, goddamn it!" Will was yelling now, even though Thomas had not con-tradicted him.

"I believe you, Will. You don't have to holler. I believe you. Although," he couldn't help adding, since he found the whole situation so funny, "I guess she did dissimulate a little bit when she tried to trap you."

Will frowned. "Well, I guess she did. A little, tiny bit. But she wasn't very good at it."

"No?"

"No." When Will recalled the first time Emily had tried batting her eyelashes at him, he almost cried. The thought of losing her now was so horrible, he wouldn't allow himself to think about it. He had to concentrate on winning her.

"But how can I win her if I've already won her, and she still won't marry me?"

Will was hollering again, and Fred, who had been snoring blissfully in front of the fireplace, looked at his master in concern. Will absently bent to pat his dog's head.

"Sorry, old friend."

"Will," Thomas said at last, "has it ever occurred to you that she refused to marry you precisely because she *is* honorable?"

Will straightened. "That's crazy, Thomas."

"No, it isn't." Thomas sounded very sure of himself.

"Yes, it is." So did Will.

"Will Tate, you've come a long way since you broke your connection with your uncle Mel, but you still have a habit of thinking like him. Did you know that?"

"The hell I do!" Will's disclaimer bounced from wall to wall in Thomas's sitting room like a ricocheting bullet. "I rejected every damned thing my uncle ever taught me, and you know it, Thomas. And then I rejected him! You just insulted me worse than I've ever been insulted in my life."

"I didn't mean it the way you're taking it, Will. What I mean is that even though your better nature tells you different, you can't, deep down in your soul, really believe people aren't out for what they can get."

Will glared at Thomas and didn't answer.

Thomas went on. "Now we both know Aunt Emily started out by trying to get Texas Lonesome to marry her. When you think about it, it was a reasoned, sensible action on her part. The man wrote to her saying he was rich and wanted a wife. It's not her fault you're not Texas Lonesome."

"Of course it isn't." Will had no idea what Thomas's ultimate point might turn out to be.

"The problem, my friend, is that she's started to care about *you*."

"Well, of course she has. That's what I just told you."

"There. You see? My point exactly." Thomas settled back in his wing chair, a smug smile on his handsome face.

"What point?" Will's bellow made Thomas flinch. "Just what the hell kind of point are you trying to make? She loves me? That's why she won't marry me? That doesn't make a lick of sense, Thomas, and you know it!"

Thomas sighed. "Of course it does."

It took all the patience Will could draw upon not to grab Thomas by his pleated shirtfront and shake a proper explanation out of him. "Tell me," he demanded through gritted teeth. "Why does it make sense?"

"Don't you see it yet, Will? It's so simple. In spite of what your uncle Mel taught you, not everybody in the world is comfortable fooling people. In fact, most of us try our very best to be honest with others. Emily is obviously a woman of high moral principle."

"Yes."

Thomas smiled. "All right. So you see, once she realized she'd begun to care for you, she began to feel guilty about tricking you. She probably refused you because she's afraid you'll hate her forever when you find out her family is in financial trouble. She knows you'll find out, since there's no avoiding it, and I bet she can't stand the thought of facing your contempt once her true scheme is revealed.

"After all," Thomas went on wryly, "she had no way in the world of knowing you only love her all the more for having succeeded in her confidence game. Most people would actually frown on such a scheme, you know. I don't mean to disparage you or your family, Will, but your uncle's standards are not necessarily those the rest of the world runs by. Barring politicians and lawyers, of course."

Comprehension burst across Will's face. "Of course!" Then he grabbed Thomas's hand and nearly shook it off his arm. "I don't know how to thank you, Thomas. Of course that's it. God almighty, I don't know why I didn't realize it sooner."

"It probably never even entered your brain."

"No. It didn't." The admission caused a clutching sensation in Will's chest, and he shook his head. "I wonder if I'll ever completely recover from Uncle Mel."

"Probably not, but that's not all bad, you know. After all, he taught you some things that have helped you in business much more than what most of us were taught in childhood. Hell, we're both rich now, thanks in large part to your devious brain."

"I suppose so," Will agreed glumly. "But how am I

going to get Emily to stop feeling guilty and marry me?"

"Well, what about those stupid dogs of her uncle's? What if you made his business so successful he begins to get rich on his own?"

"I'm already helping hom, Thomas."

"You've just given him a little money, Will. What I mean is that you need to make the man *really, really* rich. If anybody in the world can make people want something completely useless, it's you, Will. If you do a little more work, I'll bet you can even make weasel dogs attractive."

Will began to perk up a little. "I've already designed a poster."

"Perfect! The business is already on its way then. We can think of more sales opportunities, too, if we put our minds to it. If her uncle's business becomes fabulously successful and it looks as though it's all his doing, then she can settle her own debts and won't need your money. That way she won't feel she's deceived you. I bet she'll agree to marry you then." Thomas sat back and smiled.

"Just think of it, Will. Leland Stanford walking his sausage hounds on the grounds of that college he built. Mrs. Crocker taking her dachshunds for a ride in her new horseless carriage. Collis Huntington using a weasel dog as the mascot for one of his midnight specials." His grin broadened. "Why, the possibilities are endless."

Will's smile was so full of affection, Thomas looked away, feeling self-conscious.

"You're the best friend I've ever had in my life, Thomas. You know that, don't you?"

"Actually, Will, I think I'm the only friend you've ever had in your life."

"Well, I guess that's true, too. But still, I don't know what I'd do without you. I really don't."

"Ah, hell, Will. Just cut me in on the sausage-dog profits, is all I ask." Thomas reached into his breast pocket and plucked out a banknote. "After I met your little Emily, I decided to invest in those silly critters after all. Shoot, we've always done things together. I didn't want only one of us to be a fool."

Will took the banknote and had to blink quickly. He'd never cried in his adult life and didn't intend to start now.

"Thanks, Thomas." His voice was thick.

"It's all right, Will. But now let's start thinking about how to market those stupid dogs. I don't want to lose my investment."

So the two men spent several hours in Thomas's sitting room plotting marketing techniques for a breed of small, mean-tempered, low-slung dogs, for which neither one of them could think of a legitimate use. When their brainstorming session concluded, Will was whistling and Thomas was grinning from ear to ear. Both men went to bed that night feeling very pleased with themselves.

"'Sleep no more. Von Plotz does murder sleep,'" Emily muttered mournfully, fracturing Mr. Shakespeare's famous words. She stood in front of her blotchy mirror and stared with melancholy at the huge purple rings under her eyes.

Her night had been spent tossing, turning, wishing, despairing, and constantly thinking about Will Tate. She felt as though she had been flung headfirst into a bubbling vat of emotion. One moment she told herself she might just as well go ahead and marry him, only to revile herself the next moment as a vicious harpy without a shred of honor in her soul. Such inconsistencies had not made for a restful night.

"At least I have my column."

Those words, which only yesterday she had uttered in an attempt to make herself believe she had some control over the morass of her aunt and uncle's failing fortunes, were now being used for another purpose entirely. Faced with a bleak lifetime alone, unloved, and with no Will Tate, Emily's column was the one solid thing to which she could still cling. She could write, if nothing else, and pass away a listless lifetime giving advice to the lovelorn.

The irony did not escape her. "I? Who am I to give advice to anybody?" Two enormous tears rolled down her cheeks, and she chastised herself for being a miserable fraud.

It was her own fault. She was a fool and a cheat, and she had nobody but herself to blame for her unhappiness. "So, Miss Emily von Plotz, what are you going to do now? Stand here and whine? Or face the day with fortitude?"

Her pep talk didn't have much of an effect on her sick heart, but she forced herself to lift her stubborn little chin, don a defiant expression, and nod firmly into her mirror.

As a precaution against nosy relatives who might ask overly personal questions about her ragged appearance, she rubbed face powder over the shadows under her eyes in an attempt to hide them. Then she pinched her cheeks with unnecessary viciousness to give them some color, picked up the pages of her column, and headed out of her bedroom. She stopped off in the kitchen to grab some bread and cheese, and then left the house.

Her spirits did not improve as Emily walked toward her editor's office, but she did manage to contain her agony until it was a more manageable, steady ache. From some previously untapped inner resource, she was able to force a smile as she knocked on Mr. Kaplan's door.

"Why, Miss Emily, my star columnist. It's so good to see you, dear. You're always so prompt. Always so conscientious."

Mr. Kaplan rose and gestured Emily into the chair in front of his desk. Then he sat back and smiled at her.

Her editor's honest appreciation usually made Emily feel good about herself. Today, however, his praise pierced her throbbing heart like a poisoned dart. *If he only knew,* she thought with terrible bitterness. *Oh, if he only knew.*

She did, however, manage to keep her smile in place when she handed him her work. "Thank you, Mr. Kaplan. Here are six letters. I'm not sure whether you can use all of them, but I seem to be getting more mail than usual lately."

"That's because people love you, my dear. Aunt Emily is becoming quite famous in San Francisco. As a matter of fact," he added with a twinkle, "what would you think if we were to expand your column space?"

A mere day before, such news would have sent Emily's heart soaring. But now that same heart felt cold and untouched by her editor's words. "How wonderful," she said listlessly.

Even those two words sounded forced to her, but Mr. Kaplan drew his own conclusions. "Are you feeling well, Emily? You look a little pale."

Wonderful. Just wonderful. She'd even donned makeup, a practice she, as a respectable, moral young lady, deplored, and people still thought she was sick. Well, by grace, if she looked sick, then she'd play sick. Nobody needed to know her sickness was of the heart and not of the body.

"I believe I've come down with a small malady, Mr. Kaplan. I'm sure it will soon pass." Her sweet smile belied her inner turmoil. Only she knew that her little malady probably would indeed soon pass— into a deep, lifelong melancholy.

"Well, you take care of yourself, Emily. We can't have our favorite aunt laid up."

Mr. Kaplan's small show of levity was accompanied by such an expression of genuine concern that Emily was touched. He was a truly nice man.

"Thank you, Mr. Kaplan. I certainly shall." The fact that he cared about her almost made her burst into tears, and that aggravated Emily a good deal. "How many lines do you think you'll need for my column, Mr. Kaplan?"

"We'll be giving you another twenty, my dear."

Surprised, Emily cried, "My goodness, Mr. Kaplan, are you expanding the paper?"

Mr. Kaplan's sigh sounded as though it had been torn from his scuffed shoes. "I'm afraid Mrs. Puddingstone will be leaving us, Emily. You'll take over her space, since your column is so popular."

"Oh!"

Emily was distressed to hear Mr. Kaplan's news. She enjoyed reading Mrs. Puddingstone's recipes. In fact, she used to clip them and save them in a little booklet in the hope that one day, when she married, she could use them in her own household. Since the possibility of her ever marrying was now a thing of the past, she didn't suppose it mattered.

"Why is Mrs. Puddingstone leaving?"

Mr. Kaplan looked at his closed office door as if to assess the possibility they might be overheard. His surreptitious gesture made Emily's eyes open wide, and she leaned forward, her own unhappiness momentarily forgotten.

"Mrs. Puddingstone," Mr. Kaplan whispered confidentially, "is, I'm afraid, much given to the consumption of strong spirits."

"Oh!"

The editor nodded somberly. "Aye, it's too bad. But she's simply become too undependable, and unless she decides to take a cure, she can't stay on. We can't run a newspaper if our columnists are unreliable, now, can we? Mrs. Puddingstone, I regret to tell you, is a dipsomaniac."

For a bare moment Emily's worries seemed to pale beside those of the unfortunate Mrs. Puddingstone. "How sad."

Rising from his chair, Mr. Kaplan smiled once more. "Yes, it is sad, my dear, but one must try to master one's baser impulses, you know, or all is lost."

Emily rose, too. "Yes. All is lost," she whispered.

After she left Mr. Kaplan's office, Emily wandered to the park and sat on a bench. As she sadly munched her bread and cheese, she reviewed every second she had spent in Will Tate's company. A morose smile played on her lips when she recalled Gustav and Helga's initial attack on his big dog. When she remembered the two glorious kisses they had shared, a tear slid down her cheek, and she wiped it away angrily.

Stop it, Emily von Plotz, you unnatural girl. Just stop it. It's your own fault. Mr. Kaplan was right when he said we must all master our baser impulses. You gave in to yours, and just look at where that course of action has gotten you now. Foolish, foolish Emily.

She paid a short visit to the rose garden before she left the park, remembering every single second of her time spent there with Will. Then she slowly walked home, grateful for her additional column space, even if it was due to poor Mrs. Puddingstone's affliction. At least, she thought, there was a Mr. Puddingstone to help her through this time of trial. Emily hoped he would be kind to his errant spouse.

She was astonished to see a wagon from the San Francisco Municipal Telephone Company parked in front of her aunt's door when she got back home. Inside her aunt's office she found a harried telephone installation man being instructed by her uncle Ludwig. Ludwig, of course, had no idea on earth how to install telephones, but little things like that never stopped him.

"Emily," he cried when he spotted her in the doorway. "Come see! Your Mr. Tate is having them install a telephone in the house. For our dogs."

"For the dogs?"

Emily knew her uncle was fond of his pets, but she didn't think even *he* would expect them to be able to use a telephone. And what on earth did Will have to do with it? She steered Ludwig out of the office and into the hall so the poor telephone man could finish his job in peace.

"Yah, yah. For the dogs. Mr. Tate has put advertisements in all the newspapers, and he says people will begin to call soon, wanting our wonderful dogs."

"But Uncle, you don't have any dogs except Gustav and Helga." She didn't want to burst his happy bubble; still, she felt certain facts must be faced.

"Oh, yah, I know that. But Mr. Tate has already written a letter to Germany. Within six months we'll have more dogs, Emily. More wonderful dachshunds. I tell you, they're the coming thing. Everybody will want our dogs. Everybody!"

"What will you do in the meantime?"

"Ach, Mr. Tate has explained it all to me. What I do now is, I take orders!"

"Take orders?"

"Yah, take orders. I take orders and tell people their dogs are coming to them direct from Germany. He says that will make them even more coveted. That Mr. Tate of yours is wonderful! A genius!"

Ludwig skipped off back to the office to confuse the telephone installation man further, leaving Emily to stare after him.

"'My Mr. Tate,'" she whispered. "That sounds so nice."

But she knew it wasn't to be.

When Will called at the Schindler home later in the day, he did not ask to see Emily. He ached to hold her again, but thanks to Thomas Crandall's insightful instruction, he understood her now.

It had never before occurred to him somebody might feel guilty about winning just because he or she had played dirty. Will had always just assumed a person who played dirty was happy to win, period. His personal opinion was that Emily had played her game brilliantly, had won it, and should be proud of herself. The good Lord knew he was proud of her. He'd never seen anything to rival the art she'd used in snaring him.

He himself possessed no such scruples. By fair means or foul, he planned to win Emily von Plotz. If it meant playing Texas Lonesome until the day he died, he would do it. If it meant a crazy project such as the marketing and sale of a useless breed of nervous, foul-tempered, noisy hounds, he would do it.

"Here's the artwork for the poster, Mr. von Plotz. I think it looks pretty good." Will handed Ludwig a poster and watched Ludwig's reaction with genuine pleasure.

"Oh, my, Mr. Tate. It's wonderful. Just wonderful."

Will saw tears glittering in Ludwig's eyes and had to choke back a laugh. He'd never seen anybody quite as fanatical about anything as Ludwig von Plotz was about his beloved dogs.

"I've brought copies of both newspapers, too. The ad is there, bold as brass."

"Mr. Tate, you're a genius. You're a real genius." Ludwig took the papers and wandered into the parlor to gaze at them further.

Will followed him and sat on the sofa. "I see they're installing the telephone. You should be getting calls pretty soon. The posters will start going up this afternoon, and the ads are already out in today's papers. Do you remember what to do?"

"Yah, I remember, Mr. Tate." Ludwig nodded energetically. "I take the name and address and send the flyer and order form as soon as I get them from the printer."

"And?" Will prompted.

"And when I'm not here to answer the telephone, I

instruct our sweet Emily or Mr. Blodgett what to say and what to do. I don't let Gertrude talk to the clients."

Between them, they had decided Gertrude's association with the everyday world was too slippery for them to trust her with the important business of dachshund marketing. She didn't mind, for she much preferred communing with her spirit friends through her crystal ball now that she had gotten past the bubbles.

While Ludwig and Will were discussing business in the parlor, Clarence Pickering came to call once again. Blodgett showed him in.

Pickering stiffened perceptibly when he saw Will Tate and then stepped pointedly toward Ludwig, giving Will a wide berth.

The glare Will shot him could have withered spring leaves, but Pickering was made of impenetrable stuff and he ignored it.

"Good afternoon, Mr. Pickering," Ludwig said with a smile. "Look what we're doing here. You should advise Gertrude to invest in my dogs now. They're going to be famous."

"Indeed?" Pickering's sneer might have been intended to be polite.

"Yah, yah. Mr. Tate here is running the business now. He's a genius, Mr. Pickering. Our dogs are going to be selling like hotcakes pretty darned soon."

"Is that so?"

"That's so, Pickering." Will shot him a challenging scowl, and Pickering seemed to draw even farther away from him.

"Well, isn't that grand? I think that's just fine."

How Pickering managed to make his voice sound

so damned sincere, Will didn't know. The financial adviser even manufactured a sincere smile for Ludwig. "I can tell you're very happy about this, Mr. von Plotz."

"He will be," Will told him, usurping Ludwig's answer. His voice was full of meaning. "This will spell an end to any debts in the Schindler home, that's for sure."

With any luck, the blasted vulture would go away if he thought his pickings were going to dry up. Especially if he knew Will Tate would be watching him like a buzzard hawk.

"Yah, yah. Mr. Tate's got posters and ads and fly-ers and letters and everything," Ludwig put in, seem-ingly oblivious to the tension between the other two men in the room.

"Well, isn't that just fine," Pickering repeated. Although he sounded sincere, he apparently pos-sessed no turn for a creative phrase.

"Yah, it's real fine."

Will only glowered stonily at his adversary, daring Pickering to try any further tricks such as disappear-ing horse herds, ships built from African wood, or, worse, kennel-burning.

It looked to him as though Pickering got the mes-sage. He stood up after a second or two of uncomfort-able silence, and said, "Well, I'll just go on along and visit Mrs. Schindler. She asked me to call this after-noon."

Will stood up, towering over Pickering. He knew his height was intimidating. His uncle Mel had taught him to use every advantage he possessed. Pickering seemed to shrink into himself when he looked up at Will.

"Just be careful with your advice, Pickering. And be careful where you put your hands."

Will's message was unmistakable. Pickering scowled at him and then made an exit that strove for dignity but didn't quite make it.

A good half hour later, Will and Ludwig were still discussing the dachshund business when Gertrude Schindler floated into the room, waving a telegram in her hand.

"Ludwig dear, look what we just got. Oh, Mr. Blake!" she cried when she noticed Will. "What a pleasant surprise."

Will had, of course, stood at Gertrude's entrance. He wondered wryly if she would ever get his name right. When—not if, since he refused to think about that possibility—he had his way and married Emily, he supposed Gertrude would be introducing her as "Mrs. Blake" for the rest of her days.

"Howdy, ma'am. How are you today?"

"Oh, I'm fine, I think, Mr. Blake. Or, rather, not fine, but all right, I suppose. Oh, perhaps not even that. It's just that we got this—Oh, Mr. Blake, weren't you going to marry our Emily?"

Will felt an uncharacteristic twinge of sorrow. He stamped it down vigorously, refusing to admit to anything but a slight setback in his plans. She *would* be his, one day. He produced a smile for Gertrude.

"Well, ma'am, she hasn't said yes yet, I'm afraid."

Gertrude frowned. "Do you suppose she found out about your other wife, Mr. Blake?"

"I don't have any other wife, Mrs. Schindler."

Will repressed a sigh and wondered how on earth Emily had managed to survive so beautifully with these two people for so long. His admiration for her grew ever greater with each fresh encounter with Ludwig and Gertrude.

"Oh." Gertrude looked very confused. "I thought you had a wife in Arizona, Mr. Blake. Perhaps I'm confusing her with somebody else."

The paper in her hand recaptured Gertrude's wandering attention before she could become any more addled, and she held it up for Ludwig to see. "Oh, Ludwig dear, we just got a wire from Gretchen."

Ludwig raised his eyebrows. "Gretchen? What's to do with Gretchen?"

"I'm afraid her poor Wilhelm is very ill, dear, and she has asked us to come and visit her for a short stay."

"Ach. But I can't leave now, Gertrude. I have my business to run. My wonderful dogs need me now more than ever."

"But Ludwig, she *is* our sister. I do believe we should honor this little request. After all, we haven't visited her for the longest time, and if Wilhelm should happen to pass on to another dimension, I would feel terribly guilty if we weren't there to comfort her."

Ludwig's attention was caught by Will's discreetly cleared throat. "Gretchen is our sister, Mr. Tate. She lives in Redwood City. Not far away, but it would be a shame to leave San Francisco now, when we're on the edge of success."

"I don't think you need to worry about the business too much right now, Mr. von Plotz. I can make sure Blodgett knows how to take messages properly. And I'll stop by every day to make sure everything is going smoothly and take care of answering any requests Blodgett writes down. If things get really busy, I can send over a clerk to handle the telephone."

Besides, although Will didn't want to say so, if he could maneuver a little time alone with Emily, he might just get her to listen to reason.

"That's a very sensible plan, Mr. Blake," Gertrude said with a smile. "What sort of request do you expect to be receiving, Ludwig darling? I'm sure that snappish man at the Woodward Gardens has already requested at least a thousand times that you not visit there again."

"Ach, Gertrude, not that kind of request. Requests for my dogs! Mr. Tate is helping me with my business, and we should be getting requests to buy dogs starting any day now!"

"Oh." Gertrude's vague, myopic gaze slid from Ludwig to Will and back again. "But you have only the two dogs. If somebody buys them, then you won't have any more left."

"Not to worry, Gertrude. Mr. Tate is taking care of everything. Soon we will have a kennel full of dogs. A glorious, glorious kennel full of the most wonderful dogs in the world. Mr. Tate knows just what to do."

Will was moved by Ludwig's obvious faith in his business acumen. Not that it was misplaced, for Will was well aware of both his strengths and his weaknesses, and business acumen was at the top of his list of strengths. He planned to have San Francisco, and then the rest of the country, groveling at Ludwig von Plotz's large feet for dachshunds.

"You two just go on along to your sister's place. I'll take care of everything here. We shouldn't be getting much of a response to the ads for a few days, anyway. I expect the posters to have more of an impact."

The posters, which illustrated the glossiest, most noble-looking dachshund ever born, would have appealed to his uncle. The print below the image extolled the virtues of dachshunds in terms that had made Ludwig weep in ecstasy and would have had Uncle Mel roaring with cynical amusement.

Will knew those posters would do the trick. As Thomas had said, if there was one thing Will understood to perfection, it was how to create a throbbing need for a useless object in the breast of his fellow man. Once the need was established, he and Ludwig would fill it and rake in the profits.

"Well," said Ludwig, still obviously unsettled, "if you really think so, Mr. Tate . . . "

"I know so, Mr. von Plotz."

It was thus decided that Gertrude and Ludwig would depart the next evening for Redwood City on a trip to visit their sister, Gretchen, and her ailing husband, Wilhelm. They told Emily about their trip over supper. The meal was taken, for once, unmarred by the presence of Clarence Pickering.

Emily felt guilty for not being more worried about her uncle Wilhelm, but she couldn't help it. Her poor heart had become an aching, wrinkled shadow of its formerly full self, and there wasn't any more room in it for concern about relatives. It was already stuffed to the brim with grief over Will Tate.

11

The following afternoon a subdued, unhappy Emily helped Gertrude pack for her trip.

"Are you sure you won't need me to go with you?" she asked as she watched her aunt.

"No, Emily dear. I'm sure it will be more pleasant for you if you remain here. Ill health can be so depressing. A young lady shouldn't be unnecessarily exposed to it."

Gertrude gave Emily's cheek a distracted pat, then returned her attention to searching for her gloves. Eventually she found them under a shoe that had somehow or other found its way to the top shelf of her closet. She stared blankly at the gloves and the shoe, then pulled on the gloves and put the shoe back on the closet shelf.

Emily retrieved the shoe and placed in its proper rack on the floor of the closet. "All right, Aunt Gertrude, if you really think so."

In truth, Emily was glad. She needed solitude right

now. She could write her column and think over her many transgressions in peace, and nobody would be around to watch her cry. Blodgett and Mrs. Blodgett would be in the house, but if she stayed away from the kitchen, neither of the kind old retainers need know of her distress.

And as for Will Tate's trips to gather messages from Blodgett, well, she'd just be sure to be away when he visited.

Of course, Clarence Pickering might be a nuisance, but Emily could deal with him, too. If she could be out to Will Tate, she most assuredly could be out to the awful Mr. Pickering. The mere thought of him made her shudder.

The phone began to ring in the afternoon, just after her aunt and uncle left for Redwood City. The unfamiliar noise made Emily, in the parlor trying without much success to read, jump.

"Good grief, what a terrible racket." The commotion only increased when Blodgett answered the telephone and proceeded to take a message, making up for his bad hearing by yelling into the receiver.

And it didn't stop with the one call. Blodgett finally gave up trying to attend to his regular household duties and assumed residence in Gertrude's office. He soon had a stack of messages piled up, and Emily had a headache.

"Mr. Blodgett, you have too many other things to do to be in here monitoring this ridiculous contraption all day long. Let me help."

"Well, Miss Emily, Mr. Tate has given me particular instructions as to how to go on with this telephone machine. I daren't shirk my duty to him and your uncle, you know. They're depending on me."

The old man looked very serious, and Emily's heart stirred. She gave him her sweetest smile and said, "I'm sure that's so, Mr. Blodgett. But you can teach me what to do, and then I can stay here and take messages. I can write my column from here, and read, and mend—why, I can carry out my entire life from this office. You, on the other hand, cannot get anything done if you're trapped in here answering the telephone."

Eventually she convinced Blodgett to relinquish the telephone duties to her, but only after he grilled her long and hard on proper telephone etiquette and the approved method of taking notes.

Emily was amazed at the growing number of requests for dachshund information spread out before her. Maybe her uncle Ludwig had been right all along, and people really would want his silly dogs.

It did not take her long, however, to realize that were it not for Will Tate's timely interference, her uncle's dogs would have remained undiscovered. Every single caller referred to Will's newspaper ads or to the colorful posters he'd had printed. To his other manifold virtues, Emily unhappily had to add a true genius for marketing.

The man was simply perfect, and she had been a fool to believe she could have lived with herself if she'd tricked him into marrying her. He was too good for her. The admission cost Emily a watery sniffle and a teary blot on the letter she was trying to answer in the moments when she was not on the phone.

Fortunately, the busy telephone did not allow her to slip further into melancholy. In between calls, she continued to answer letters to Aunt Emily. One of those letters startled her into a gasp.

"Dear Aunt Emily," she read. "The advice you give me was good, but it didn't work. My girl says she won't marry me. I guess she don't like me after all and my heart is broke. What do I do now?" It was signed, "Texas Lonesome."

Oh, Lord. Emily supposed he felt he had to speak to her through her column since she had as much as run away from him yesterday.

It then occurred to her that this letter seemed to have arrived at the newspaper very quickly. She scanned it for a date and found none. Frowning, she considered the puzzling circumstance and decided he must have delivered the missive by hand to the newspaper office. Such things happened often.

Still, it was odd he hadn't just brought the letter to her home. But no. Emily sighed. He seemed to delight in these sweet little letters. Another tear dripped down her cheek.

She penned her response from the depths of her soul. "Dear Texas Lonesome: I am so sorry you feel hurt by your lady's rejection. Perhaps, dear friend, the lady feels she does not deserve such a very, very wonderful man. Please accept my deepest affection and all best wishes for your future. Perhaps one day you will find another lady to love."

When she was through answering the letter, it was drenched with her tears, and she had to rewrite it on a clean piece of paper. Then she picked up his letter and peered at it for a long time. After a while, she grew even more puzzled.

Why, she wondered, did Will Tate's letters seem so much less literate than he was in person? Thinking over her dealings with him, she acknowledged that he lapsed into bad grammar occasionally. But more often than not, he was a perfect gentleman, marvelously self-assured and grammatically correct. She wondered why such a discrepancy existed.

But as her concentration was constantly being shattered by the jarring ring of the telephone, Emily decided she'd just have to contemplate the enigma of Will Tate's literacy another day. Besides, thinking about him only made her sad.

Her sadness took an abrupt tumble into anger when Clarence Pickering came into the office a few minutes later. His smile looked as though it had been painted onto his face, and it made Emily's teeth clench.

"My aunt and uncle are gone to the country, Mr. Pickering, and I do not care to speak to you. Please go away."

"Now, Miss Emily, you know I didn't mean to upset you yesterday." His smile was so sincere, Emily almost gagged. "I just want to help you, my dear. I could be of great service to you and your family, you know. If you would just give me a small chance, I'm sure I could make you happy."

His smile disgusted her. Before today, it would have made her insides ball up into a tight knot of despair. But now, she realized, there was a faint glimmering of hope on the horizon for her family. Thanks to Will Tate's brilliant business mind, Emily almost dared hope her aunt and uncle might have a sound financial future after all.

"I'm sure you're absolutely wrong, Mr. Pickering. Besides, your threats mean nothing to me any longer."

"Threats? I can't imagine why you should even use the word, my dear. Threats, indeed."

"Oh, you villain!" she cried. "I know your game, and it won't work! You'll never get me, and you'll never get my aunt and uncle's resources, either! My uncle's dog business is—is flourishing. It's positively booming. Why, just look at all these orders!"

Her hand swept over the desk, indicating the pile of messages she and Blodgett had taken. It was true most of the messages were merely requests for information, but Emily wasn't about to let Pickering know that. Let him think they were actual orders. Then maybe he'd realize that his suit—if it was a suit and not a prelude to a less savory proposition—was hopeless and leave her alone.

She was gratified when his sincere smile changed into a disgruntled frown. In fact, Pickering was so miffed he forgot to be suave for a moment. He snarled, "Oh, yeah?"

"Yeah!" Emily hated the way Pickering made her forget propriety and use disgusting street cant.

"Well, I'd suggest you not place all your hopes on those dogs of your uncle's, Emily dear, because you never know what might happen to them."

With those ominous words, Pickering turned and exited the office, leaving Emily to fume at his impudence and finger her uncle's heavy glass paperweight. The idea of flinging it at his back entered her mind only to be rejected as too violent and unladylike. Still, the thought held great appeal. Another glance at the satisfying stack of messages, however, soothed her.

"You odious man," she whispered to the empty space where Picking had just stood. "You just watch. I may never have Will Tate, but you'll never get me. Never!"

*   *   *

Only later that night did it occur to Emily that Clarence Pickering might be evil enough to sabotage her uncle's dogs.

She had lived with Gustav and Helga for quite long enough to be able to distinguish differences among their various, nearly incessant barks. The dogs loved to bark. But at about one-thirty in the morning, the piercing, high-pitched, keening yaps of a dachshund sounding an alarm penetrated Emily's sleep-fogged brain. She sat up in her bed and rubbed her eyes.

Oh, dear Lord, what now? she wondered. As she tucked her feet into her slippers and donned her well-worn robe, shreds of Clarence Pickering's parting words began to slink into her brain, very much as Clarence Pickering himself slunk. Emily frowned, suspicious.

"Now, I just wonder if that awful man is trying to hurt Gustav and Helga."

The very idea infuriated her. Realizing that neither one of the Blodgetts, who were both hard of hearing, would be of any help to her, Emily quickly tied the belt of her robe, flung her tousled hair out of her face, and ran out of her room and down the big staircase. Pausing only to grab one of Uncle Ludwig's stout German walking sticks, she dashed out to the back-yard.

"Aha!" she cried when she spotted a shadowy figure. It seemed to be trying to dodge the vicious fangs of the two frenzied hounds attempting to murder him from the feet up.

"Get them off me!"

It wasn't Pickering, Emily realized, disgruntled, when she heard the man's terrified wail. She'd hoped it would be, so that she could hit him with her uncle's heavy stick. Oh, well. She would just have to hit this person instead.

She advanced upon the intruder with a firm tread. He cowered in a corner, trying in vain to ward off the furious dachshunds.

"You'd better get out of here right now, mister, or you'll be sorry."

"Get them off me!" the man cried again.

Emily could tell the plea was torn from his gut, but she harbored no mercy in her heart for him. "I don't know what you think you're doing in our backyard, mister, but I do know you're up to no good. Now get out!"

She swung Ludwig's walking stick hard, catching the man's ear with a vicious blow. He screamed.

"I don't care if it hurts, you horrid saboteur! You just get out of here. And after you get out, you go tell Clarence Pickering he can't win by theft or violence, either. What did you think you were going to do here, anyway? Kidnap the dogs? Kill them?"

The possibility that Pickering had sent someone to do away with her uncle's beloved pets fueled Emily's fury. Again and again she swung the stick, connecting with various parts of the man's anatomy.

The interloper, attacked on all fronts, finally lurched away from the corner. He shoved Emily hard, causing her to lose her balance and back up. With Gustav firmly attached to his ankle and Helga in hot pursuit, the man made a mad scramble for the back wall.

"Emily!"

A shot rang out. Emily heard the interloper's bellow of pain right before he disappeared over the wall, leaving Gustav behind bearing a shredded red-and-green plaid trouser cuff in his teeth as a proud trophy. She whirled around to find Will Tate charging toward her, his pistol smoking.

"Damn! Must have only winged him."

The agitation thrumming through Emily's body made it difficult for her to sort out the images and emotions hurtling around inside her. She dimly perceived that Will Tate must have come to aid her in thwarting the trespasser, but she didn't understand how he had gotten there.

"Mr. Tate?" Her breath came in ragged gasps, and her bosom heaved under the hand she pressed to it.

"Are you all right, Emily?" Will grabbed her by her arms and squeezed her.

He peered down at her with loving concern, and Emily could only stare up at him for a moment, baffled. Uncle Ludwig's walking stick dropped from her numb fingers onto Gustav's head, making him yelp.

"I'm all right." Emily's voice was no more than a feathery whisper.

"Oh, God, Emily darling, I was so afraid when I saw you out here, fighting that man off."

The fact that the poor man had been cowering from the dachshunds' attack and Emily's deftly wielded weapon had apparently slipped Will's mind. He threw propriety to the winds and clasped his beloved to his chest.

Emily didn't mind. Her thoughts whirled in mad confusion. Who was the intruder? What was Will doing there? How could anything feel more wonderful than his arms felt around her at that moment? She felt his heart thunder in his breast like stampeding cattle, and knew fear for her safety had caused the tumult. The knowledge created a surge of triumph within her. She flung her arms around his waist and squeezed him tight.

"Oh, Will," she whispered. "Oh, Will, my darling."

"Come inside, Emily, sweetheart. It's cold out here."

Will scooped her up and carried her toward the back door. Neither one of them thought about Ludwig's walking stick. It had been discovered by Gustav and Helga, each of whom grabbed an end and began to gnaw with delight.

"Oh, Will," Emily sighed once more.

She nestled her head on his shoulder, feeling overwhelmed by the absolute bliss of being cared for. Emily had not been cared for in a long, long time, if ever; she had been doing all the caring for others. It felt like heaven to relinquish her heavy load of responsibility for a moment or two and give herself up to this strong, brave man who loved her.

Will carried Emily into the parlor and sat down with her on his lap. He didn't give two hoots about whether or not his conduct might be considered improper.

Emily sighed rapturously. Her arms slid to Will's shoulders, and she melted against his strength with a surrender so sweet, she could almost taste it.

So could Will.

"Lord, Emily, when I heard that racket, I thought for sure Pickering had sneaked in here and was trying to kill the dogs."

"So did I, Will. But it wasn't Pickering." Emily sounded almost grumpy about it.

"Well, I'll bet you anything he was behind it."

"Oh, I know it, Will. I'm sure of it. I think it might have been that creature who works for him."

Neither of them spoke for another minute or two. Their hearts had calmed down some and soon seemed to beat in a harmonious duet as timeless as life itself. Emily tucked her head under Will's chin, and he rested his chin on her soft, tumbling curls. They were as comfortable as if they'd been created for each other at the beginning of time.

When Emily spoke, the peace was not disturbed. Her voice fit into the companionable silence perfectly, as though flowing into a space designed just for it.

"I was so surprised to see you, Will. How on earth did you come to be here?"

Will's gentle chuckle settled over them like an eiderdown quilt.

"Pickering came over today when your uncle and I were making plans. I think he's worried our business is going to be a success and spoil his rotten scheme to profit by your aunt and uncle's financial ruin. I decided it might be worthwhile to keep an eye on things."

"I can't stand that awful man. He's so evil."

"I'm afraid you're right, my love. Your aunt has taken up with a real villain in Pickering. He's known as a veritable vulture in some circles here in San Francisco. I suppose you can guess the reason."

"Yes." The word was a little sigh.

"I won't let it happen, Emily. I swear to you I won't. That's why I was here tonight."

"So you—you were actually guarding our house?" The idea brought tears to Emily's eyes, and she had to sniff them back.

"Yes. I didn't want anything to happen to the dogs, Emily. Or to you."

"Oh, Will."

It was a few moments before Emily could speak again. She dabbed her moist eyes with Will's tie.

"Pickering came by again this afternoon, Will, when I was taking telephone messages. I bragged about the business, and I guess it worried him."

Will pulled back slightly and peered at Emily in surprise. "You mean people are calling already?"

"Oh, my, yes. There must be a hundred messages, all from people who either read your ads or saw your posters. They all want information about Uncle Ludwig's dogs. Uncle Ludwig says your posters are going to do for dachshunds what Mr. Gibson's drawings have done for the New American Woman."

As he tucked Emily's head under his chin once more, Will's heart soared in triumph. "I knew we could do it, Emily, but I had no idea it would happen so fast. I hope the new dogs arrive from Germany soon."

"Oh, Will, it's not 'we,' and you know it. It's you. You're the one. If Uncle Ludwig's dogs are a success, it will be because of you and you alone."

"Aw, Emily . . . "

"It's true. Uncle Ludwig is a dear, dear man, but you must admit he's a—well, a little eccentric. And you, of all people, must know he has no business sense. It's you, Will. You're the one."

Silence fell once more between them, a silence as sweet and warm as hot cocoa on a snowy winter's evening.

"And I think it may be time to start thinking about puppies from Helga and Gustav again, too, Will."

Emily's head was still tucked demurely under his chin, so Will didn't see her blush, but he felt it. For some reason he had become exquisitely sensitive to every single flutter of emotion emanating from his Emily. He squeezed her tight.

"She's gone into heat again?"

"I think so. At least Gustav was—was very attentive to her this afternoon."

Will squeezed her again, loving the way she got embarrassed about these things. Thinking about Gustav's interest in Helga caused his mind to veer in a direction he recognized as being treacherous. But it was too late. Already, now that the danger posed by the intruder was past and their initial reactions had settled, he was becoming uncomfortably aware of the delightful bundle of femininity he cradled on his lap.

In an effort to get his mind away from baser matters, he said, "You were very brave, Emily, to tackle that man alone."

"Well, I wanted to protect Gustav and Helga. Uncle Ludwig would be heartbroken if anything happened to them, you know. He worships those dogs."

"Yes."

"I didn't know what was going on at first. Their barking woke me up, and I just had time to slip into my robe and slippers and grab Uncle Ludwig's walking stick."

"The man might have been armed, Emily. You took an awful chance."

The mere thought of what might have happened to her if the trespasser had carried a gun made Will wrap her up more snugly. The effort brought her soft bottom into even closer contact with his already turgid maleness. It was only with great effort that he suppressed his groan.

When Emily's arms tightened around his neck, Will did groan. He could feel her breasts, ill disguised

under her well-worn robe and nightie, pressing
against him, her nipples puckered tight under the layers of fabric like two pebbles.

Emily knew she should leave Will's lap at once,
but she couldn't have moved if she wanted to—which
she didn't.

Her soft sigh pierced Will's senses like a knife.
"You're—you're wearing your nightgown, Emily."
Will didn't know why he said that.

"Yes." Emily sighed again and cuddled even closer
against his strength and warmth.

"Oh, Lord." It was a little prayer for guidance.

"You're so strong, Will."

Emily's words were a caress, stroking every nerve
ending in Will's body. "And you're so soft," he
moaned.

Knowing he was taking a monumental step in the
wrong direction but unable to stop himself, Will
tucked a finger under Emily's chin and lifted her face.
Her succulent mouth and half-closed eyes were all the
invitation he needed. His lips descended upon hers,
soft as a feather and hot as molten metal.

Emily sighed into his kiss, surrendering any lingering thoughts of restraint to the bliss of the moment.
In the very, very back of her mind was the understanding of where this kiss would lead, and she gloried in it. She loved Will Tate with her whole heart
and mind and body. Even though her honorable
nature would never allow her to marry him, she knew
that if they could share this one night together, her
entire life would have been worth it. Perhaps she
could savor its delectable memory in the long, cold,
lonely years to come.

"God, Emily, you taste so good. You feel so good."

"So do you, Will. Oh, so do you."

Emily had only been kissed twice before in her entire life, both times by Will Tate, but she was an excellent student. Taking hints from Will and guided by her own needs and desires, she met the thrust of his tongue with an ardor that made Will growl with delight.

When his lips left hers to mosey their way to her soft throat, Emily nibbled his earlobes and used her tongue in so many delightful ways that Will was sure he was going to die from pleasure before the night was over. One of his hands stroked a hot path from her shoulders to the small of her back while his other one explored beneath her robe.

Emily's sensitive breasts ached for his touch. When a large hand covered one of them, she cried out in pleasure.

"Great God in heaven, Emily, you're perfect."

The reverent words were wrenched from Will's soul. He'd never before felt the aching need to make a woman his that he felt at this moment. With exquisite care, he lowered Emily to the sofa.

Somehow or other, probably because Emily grabbed the ribbons and tugged, her robe became untied. It fell off her shoulders as Will laid her down, and she shrugged it off as an annoying impediment to their mutual desire.

"Oh, Will." The tiny gasp escaped Emily's throat at the first touch of his tongue to her sensitive nipple.

She arched toward him in wanton innocence. Will wasn't sure he could maintain his control long enough even to get his trousers unbuttoned. "Emily, I love you so much. I want you so much."

Suddenly the enormity of what he was doing hit

him full between the eyes. Will sat up, bringing Emily with him, hanging on to his shoulders.

A tremendous fear that Will's scruples were going to interfere assailed Emily, and she almost wept. She clutched him convulsively and tried very hard to form coherent words. Such an effort was difficult under the circumstances, when all she wanted to do was mew like a kitten.

"Don't stop now, Will. Please don't stop."

"But Emily, you're a—you're a virgin. We're not married. It's not proper. I can't do it."

"Yes, you can!" Emily could hear the barely suppressed panic in her voice. "You can too, Will. Oh, I know you can! You must!"

Emily was a complete innocent in the ways of men and women, but she had watched Gustav and Helga with fascination on more than one occasion. She had also once caught a very fleeting glimpse of a shocking book hidden on a bookshelf in her aunt Gretchen's adolescent son's room. She knew at least something about the equipment a man used to accomplish what she wanted Will to accomplish this heavenly night.

When he felt Emily's hot little hand stroke the rigid proof of his desire through the coarse twill of his trousers, Will uttered a startled, "Damn!"

Afraid she'd done something wrong, Emily drew back. Her hand flew away from Will's crotch to press her cheek. "Oh, Will, did I hurt you?"

Will's eyes closed in an agony of thwarted desire. He tried valiantly to convince himself that he could stop now, before he accomplished the deflowering of the woman he loved. With a tremendous effort, he managed to say, "No, Emily, you didn't hurt me. It felt so good, I thought I was going to die there for a minute, though."

Emily smiled in triumph. "Oh, good," she said. And her hand left her cheek to assume its former occupation of driving Will Tate crazy.

Will groaned. "Emily, do you know what you're asking for? Do you really, really know? Because if I don't quit now, I'm not going to be able to. I want you so much, it hurts."

"I want you, too, Will," she whispered. Just to make sure he heard her properly, she pushed her words into his ear with a delicate poke from the tip of her tongue.

The very last of Will's honorable resolve deserted him in an overpowering surge of desire. "Oh, God, Emily." Those were the last words he uttered for a long time.

Emily was on her back on the sofa before she knew what she was about. Her nightgown vanished as if by magic. If she had not been so busy feeling new and exquisite sensations, she might have been shocked.

Will's shirt followed Emily's nightgown on the floor. Her fingers found blissful delight in burrowing through the soft, springy light brown fur on his chest. When she discovered his nipple and nipped at it, Will groaned his approval and pleasure.

As Will suckled one of her tender breasts, his hands were not idle. They stroked the sensitive skin on Emily's silky thighs until his fingers delved between the petals of her secret treasure and found her damp, hot, and ready for him.

It was Emily who unbuttoned Will's trousers at last. The proof of his passion leapt out into her hands. She was amazed at the satiny smoothness of it, but any verbal reaction was smothered by Will's fervent kiss as he positioned himself over her.

With a sigh of pleasure as old as time itself, Will eased himself into Emily's tight sheath. When he came to her maiden's barrier, he hesitated a moment too long for the impatient Emily, who couldn't wait to be completely filled by him. She pressed her hips up and, with one strong thrust, became his. They both groaned in satisfaction.

The pain of his invasion did not pass unnoticed, but Emily was too involved with the incredible fire of pleasure and need Will had stoked within her to bother about pain. An ache of longing overwhelmed the sting of her lost maidenhood.

Will had been with any number of women in his colorful life, beginning at age thirteen when a lady friend of his uncle Mel's decided he was too pretty and ripe to go untasted. In the twenty years since his delightful introduction into the mysteries of carnal love, Will had never felt the pleasure he felt now. He had become, over the years, a skillful and thoughtful lover. Yet all his lessons nearly failed him tonight in the arms of the woman he loved.

Emily's unstudied, candid response to his touch ignited him utterly. He had always held a little bit of himself back from his partners before, always kept a smidgen of himself locked away, safe from harm.

Not tonight. Tonight, everything he was and everything he ever would be was laid bare before his Emily. He gave her his all, and his all was almost more than he could handle. He rode her like a stallion, thrusting deeply, unable to be gentle, passion driving him.

In her wildest erotic dreams—and she'd had many—Emily never guessed the act of love could be so all-consuming and wonderful. She adored Will's almost brutal, piercing plunges into her, and strove to meet them, thrust for thrust. And she loved the sharp, musky scent of their passion. Her nails raked his back, and she didn't realize she was biting his shoulder as she reached for her final, shattering climax.

It came to her in a wild starburst of clenching pleasure, and took her completely by surprise. She cried his name, startled, and then her body convulsed under his.

"Oh, God, Emily." When Will felt her contractions suck the very life force out of him, he finally found his own release.

Afterwards Emily subsided into a sated heap in Will's arms. It was a full five minutes before she could speak, and even then her voice was breathless. "Did I hurt you, Will?"

It cost Will a good deal of effort to lift his head and look into Emily's worried blue eyes. As crazy as it seemed, he wondered if she was laughing at him. Had *she* hurt *him?* When he read only honest concern in her expression, he knew she had really meant to ask the incredible question.

"No, Emily, you didn't hurt me. I'm the one who's supposed to ask you that."

He smiled so tenderly, Emily was hard pressed to keep from crying. She loved him so much.

"I—I bit you, Will," she confessed in a tiny, guilty voice. Again she brought a hand up to stroke the marks of her passion.

"You did?" Will craned his neck to look at his shoulder. He smiled when he realized she had indeed. "By damn, you did at that," he breathed.

"Does it hurt?" Emily was afraid she had done

something awful. She hadn't realized how carried away one could become while in the throes of passion. She was very embarrassed.

But the expression on Will's face wiped away her every fear. "No, Emily, it doesn't hurt. It feels just wonderful."

When Will again lowered himself onto her body, Emily sighed with pleasure. Her arms circled his back once more, and she stroked him from his bitten shoulder to his sweat-drenched buttocks, trying her best to memorize every rugged, muscular inch of his hard flesh. She didn't expect she would ever get the opportunity again. She wanted—needed—to remember everything about this night.

"Aw, Emily, I love you so much. I don't want to leave you tonight."

"Please don't, Will. I don't want you to go."

She didn't, either. The thought of his leaving her now almost broke her heart. It was bad enough to know they could never share this glory again. But at least they could savor it and make the night last as long as possible. Emily didn't want to sleep again tonight. She wanted to stay awake in the circle of Will's embrace until the cruel morning parted them.

"I can't stay, Emily. It wouldn't be proper."

"Oh, rot propriety!" The words popped out of Emily's very proper mouth in a burst of honesty, causing Will to chuckle in delight. Emily felt her cheeks get hot, but she didn't regret her outburst.

"My aunt and uncle are away, Will. What will one night matter?"

He knew it was a mistake, but Will couldn't resist the longing he heard in Emily's voice. So he made a circuit of the parlor, picking up all of their clothing, while Emily lay back on the sofa, looking for all the world like Mr. Goya's famous painting, and not giving a hang about it, either.

As he stood before her, clothing draped over his arms, Will drank in the sight of her and knew he would be a happy man when he married his little Emily. The idea of being able to wake up beside this womanly treasure every day for the rest of his life made his heart sing.

Emily giggled when he transferred their clothing to her stomach and scooped her and it into his arms. She wriggled in his embrace, trying to feel as much of him as she could against her naked flesh.

By the time he had carried her to the top of the staircase, Emily probably could have balanced herself on a certain part of Will's anatomy, it had grown to such stiff, impressive proportions.

"Which is your room?" he asked huskily.

"This one."

He barely got her to the rumpled bed before his flesh was buried in hers again, and she was once more digging her nails into his back and whimpering in ecstasy beneath him. This time Will was able to exercise somewhat greater control over his rampaging desire, but not much. When he felt Emily's teeth nip his shoulder, he growled like a lion.

His fingers rubbing the nub of her pleasure very nearly caused Emily to buck them both off her bed. Her orgasm was so quick and so powerful, she screamed.

It wasn't until after his body stopped shuddering from his heavenly release that Will began to worry about her scream. "Hush, love," he managed to gasp. "We don't want to wake the Blodgetts."

"Nothing wakes the Blodgetts, Will darling. They're both deaf as posts."

"Oh, good." It was all he could manage to say before collapsing on Emily and hugging her until he could bear to release her. Then he flopped to her side, pulled her tight against him, and sighed into slumber.

Emily yawned in contentment and allowed herself to relish, one more time, the hard length of Will's huge, hairy body cradling her soft, smooth one. Before she joined him in the arms of Morpheus, she decided this one night might just keep her from despair in the long, lonely years to come.

When Emily stretched herself awake in the morning, her feeling of well-being lasted until she realized she was alone in her bed. Then her eyes flew open, and she frantically scanned the room for Will. She longed to see him one last time. But he was gone.

Her heart fell, but then she found the note he had left her. With trembling fingers, she opened it.

"My love," the letter began, "I didn't want to cause you any embarrassment in front of the servants, so I left before you awoke. (I kissed you soundly first, you may believe it.) I will be back later today. I know you will marry me now, Emily, and when you do, you will make me the happiest man on earth. I love you with all my heart. Will."

"Oh, my," Emily breathed. Tears that might have been from happiness or might have been from unhappiness filled her eyes. The emotions warring in her breast were so contradictory, even Emily didn't know what lay behind her tears.

Had she confessed her feelings for him? Had she

told him how very much she loved him? How much she would always love him, even though they were destined to part?

Emily couldn't remember. She slowly made her way out of bed, wincing slightly at the tug of pain between her thighs and feeling a distinct twinge of embarrassment at her nakedness. She couldn't remember ever being naked before, except in her bath. How odd, she thought, that she hadn't been the least bit embarrassed to be naked in front of Will Tate.

Her practical nature asserted itself with the thought that the only thing she had ever been told before regarding the act of love was about the pain. Nobody had ever mentioned the phenomenal pleasure a man and a woman could share with each other.

It was to keep people pure, she decided almost at once. If people knew how good it felt, nobody would wait until they got married, and then where would the world be?

Lazily she donned her robe and went over to the window to stare out onto Hayes Street below.

She should be in the country, she thought as she gazed at the morning fog. Such a perfect night should be followed by birdsong, sunlight, and green trees, not gray mist, ugly city walls, and grimy pavement.

She clutched Will's note to her breast, then lifted it and read it again. Her eyes filled with tears of love and loss.

Maybe she could marry him after all. Maybe it wouldn't be evil of her to marry him. Not now.

Even as she thought the words, she knew they were a lie. She had tricked him. She hated herself for it, too; and she couldn't imagine that he wouldn't hate her when he found out about her perfidy.

TEXAS LONESOME   217 ☙

She couldn't bear to see the love in his eyes turn to hate. She simply couldn't bear it.

Emily succumbed to a mournful sniffle and swallowed her tears. At least they had had one night.

She made quick work of her morning ablutions, and as hot water spurted from the tap she was grateful that her aunt had indulged in this extravagance. It wasn't everybody who had hot and cold running water, but Aunt Gertrude did. Emily hoped that with Will's timely intervention into their affairs, she and her relatives would at least be spared a move into a shabby cold-water flat.

It was amazing how quickly luxuries could become necessities, Emily realized as she brushed her long hair into a soft knot, à la Mr. Gibson, and pinned it up on the top of her head.

When she got to the backyard, Gustav greeted her with a furor of happy barking. Then she discovered her uncle Ludwig's walking stick, which she'd forgotten about in the commotion of the previous night. It was now a gnawed stump of its former solid, Germanic self. If she hadn't known it in its prior incarnation, Emily would not have recognized it at all. Helga was still blissfully chewing on it, and Emily had a battle on her hands to get it away from her.

"I might just as well let you finish it off now, I suppose," she muttered as she tugged on one end of the stick. "Although I guess that would only be teaching you it's all right to chew walking sticks."

She eyed the two canines at her feet and decided that the assumption one could teach them anything at all was perhaps absurd. Still, they were adorable, if one could get past their dispositions. She knelt in the yard and petted the two animals.

"I do love the two of you, really. And you were very brave last night to attack that awful man. I guess you deserve to chew on Uncle Ludwig's walking stick. I'm sure he won't mind, anyway."

The loud ringing of the telephone startled Emily out of her reverie. She dashed into the house and into her aunt's office only to lift the receiver a second too late. The line was dead.

She just wasn't used to telephones, she guessed. But she planned to do everything in her power to make sure Uncle Ludwig's business became successful.

With that firm resolve, Emily made a quick trip to her room. There she fetched materials for another column, a book to read when her column was finished, and some mending she had been putting off.

Then she took a deep breath, seated herself at her aunt's desk, and, with a heart aching with grief, penned the most difficult letter she had ever composed in her life. She reminded herself it was the only honorable thing to do. It took her a long time to dry her eyes, and even longer before she dared face her aunt's part-time houseboy, Chung Li, with instructions to carry the missive to Thomas Crandall's Nob Hill mansion. The letter was addressed to Will Tate.

She watched Chung Li until he was swallowed up by the milling throngs on Hayes Street. It was the jangling of the telephone that finally drew her back inside the house. Emily resumed her seat at her aunt's desk knowing she would never be happy again.

12

Dear Aunt Emily:

My beloved Henry and I will be married in the spring. Neither of us has much money, but Henry works very hard and will surely be a success. My mother and father do not approve of him because he is not wealthy. But he is everything I've ever wanted, Aunt Emily. He is so kind, and he attends church with me every Sunday. How can I make my parents realize Henry is the man of my dreams, even if he isn't rich?

Love,
An Unhappy Maiden

Dear Maiden:

God bless the both of you, my dear. Aunt Emily believes the best way to educate is by example. I am certain that, in time, you and your young man will teach your parents you have made the right decision. Please accept

*your loving Aunt Emily's best wishes for a
happy lifetime with your Henry.*

Emily's throat ached when she put down her pen
to answer the telephone.

Will sat in Thomas Crandall's breakfast room and
tried to concentrate on eating.

It had taken all the control at his command to
force himself to leave Emily's bed that morning. He'd
wanted to make love to her again and again and
again, until neither one of them could stand. But he
would kill himself before he caused her a second's
embarrassment, and he knew that having him discovered in her bed would be embarrassing to her.

"You mean he hired somebody to kidnap the
dogs?" Thomas Crandall asked, intruding on Will's
thoughts.

"Kidnap or kill. Emily thwarted him, though."

The real pride in Will's voice made Thomas smile
as he stuck a forkful of eggs in his mouth and
chewed. "And how did your enterprising Aunt Emily
do such a thing?"

"She nearly battered him to death with a big stick.
She had a little help from the dogs."

Thomas swallowed quickly so he wouldn't choke
on his breakfast. "I'd like to have seen it. A little girl
like her and a couple of dogs that look like ferrets . . .
It must have been something to behold."

For some reason, the thought of his friend viewing
Emily in her nightie and robe did not sit well with Will.

His sudden scowl made Thomas stop laughing.
"What's the matter, Will?"

"Nothing."

Thomas noticed it was a harsh, grumpy reply. "So what time did you get to bed, anyway? I didn't hear you come in."

Since Will had never blushed before in his life, he didn't recognize the sudden surge of heat flushing his cheeks and dampening his collar. He wondered if he had suddenly been taken ill.

But Thomas recognized a blush when he saw one. "Good grief! You spent the night with her!"

"That's enough, Thomas. We're going to be married. She asked me to stay because she's alone in the house and there had just been a break-in, for God's sake."

"Of course."

Will eyed his friend uncertainly for a moment or two. But he felt too wonderful this morning to hold a grudge. He was also too full of energy to sit still, so he jumped up and helped himself to some more bacon and toast from the sideboard.

"I know Pickering was behind that break-in, Thomas. Emily thinks so, too. He's afraid because now that you and I are involved, those dogs are becoming popular. They're already getting telephone calls about them." He spoke with pride.

"I knew we could do it, Will. Did you doubt it?"

"Not really, I guess."

"Well, I should hope not. We're great at making money together. I guess it's a gift."

"I guess." Will quirked a brow. "You know, it wasn't until I met Emily that I really understood honor and decency. She's just so—so real, so pure."

"Pure?" Thomas raised his eyebrows, and Will blushed for the second time in his life.

"You know what I mean. She tried her damnedest to trick me into marrying her, but she couldn't make herself do it in the end. And I don't think it's just because she loves me, either, even though I know she does. It's because she's too decent to dupe a man into matrimony, no matter how desperate she is. And I know damned good and well she was desperate."

"I knew it, too, the minute you told me Clarence Pickering was on the scene."

"Yes. And that's another thing. I'm going to put an end to that man's career. I'm not sure how, but I'm going to."

"Well, let me know if you need help. He's a certified evil man and deserves to be put away," Thomas said with a snap of his napkin as he stood up. "I don't suppose your little Emily has any friends, do you? I can't stand the thought of your being married and my being single, Will. It just doesn't seem right."

"I think she's been too busy keeping her aunt and uncle out of trouble to make many friends."

"That sounds like a pretty lonely path for a young woman to have traveled during her youth, Will."

"It was, Thomas. I don't know all the details, but I'm going to do my best to make up for it, believe me."

Thomas had never seen such a look on his friend's face before in all the time the two of them had played together and worked together and even mourned together. Will Tate was genuinely, honestly in love. It was amazing.

"I believe you, Will," Thomas said with a lopsided grin.

Just then his butler entered the breakfast room to

deliver Emily's letter into Will's hands. Will had to read the epistle twice before he could believe his eyes hadn't deceived him the first time.

"Well, hell!"

The expletive shot out of his mouth in a burst of fury that made Thomas jump. "What is it?"

Will glared at the letter and then at Thomas, and then back at the letter. "Decency," he snarled.

Since Thomas didn't know how he was supposed to respond to that, he said nothing.

Will's furious gaze scorched the paper in his hand for another minute before he began to read it aloud to his friend. "'Dear Mr. Tate.' Goddamn it, Thomas, she was calling me Will last night." He took a deep breath and went on.

"'Dear Mr. Tate: Please accept my deepest apologies for not telling you this in person, but I don't believe my slight courage would bear up under the weight of my words, and I don't dare take the chance. I cannot marry you, Mr. Tate, as much as it would give me the greatest pleasure to do so. I'm afraid I am not what you believe me to be. It is beyond my feeble strength to confess *all* to you, but please believe me when I tell you I love you with all my heart. It is that love which prevents me from allowing you to make the biggest mistake of your life. Please believe me also when I tell you that when you return to Texas, you will be taking my heart with you. Farewell. Emily von Plotz.'

"Well, shit." Will crumpled the letter up in his fist, then uncrumpled it again and smoothed it flat. It made his heart hurt to wrinkle anything sent him by his Emily.

Thomas shook his head. "Told you so. Told you she was honorable."

"If she's so blasted honorable, why doesn't she just tell me she's been trying to trick me and let me choose for myself?"

"She's probably ashamed of herself and afraid you'll hate her."

Will snorted. "I never did understand shame."

"Of course not."

The men looked at each other for a second and then uttered two words together: "Uncle Mel."

Emily's gloom did not abate when Clarence Pickering came to call in the afternoon. She knew Will had received her letter by this time and must hate her. It was difficult to keep her voice bright when she answered the telephone because she kept wanting to cry. When Pickering opened the door to her aunt's office and stepped inside without so much as a by-your-leave, however, her unhappiness immediately transformed itself into fury.

"How dare you show your face in this house after your villainy of last night?" she cried in indignation. It was all she could do to keep from picking up the heavy telephone and flinging it at Pickering's head.

"Why, Emily, my dear, what on earth do you mean by that?"

Pickering's smile was one of absolute sincerity, and his words were disgustingly sweet, as usual. He even had the temerity to look surprised at her outburst.

"Get out of this house, Mr. Pickering, and don't ever show your face here again. After trying to kidnap Uncle Ludwig's beloved dogs last night, how dare you even enter these portals?"

"Me?" Pickering placed a manicured hand on the

expensive summer suit that lay over what passed for his heart. "Emily, my dear, you know I'd never do anything to hurt your uncle's dogs. I wasn't within a mile of this house last night. What on earth are you talking about?"

"Of course you weren't here. You hired somebody to do your evil work for you."

"I don't know what you're talking about, my dear. Did something happen to your uncle's darling doggies?"

Emily stood up and pressed her hands down on her aunt's desk. Her breasts heaved with wrath, which doubled when she saw Pickering's gaze slide to her chest. When the telephone rang, she lifted the receiver from its cradle with a grip that would have crushed a less well constructed object.

"Hello!" she bellowed into the instrument. Then she realized what she had done, and her face flamed.

Pickering fell silent, apparently deciding he didn't dare rile her further. Emily glared at him as she spoke to the caller.

"Oh, hello, Aunt Gertrude. . . . No, I'm fine, Aunt, really. I didn't know Aunt Gretchen had a telephone in her house. . . . Oh, how nice. I'm glad. This evening? . . . Yes, everything is fine here, Aunt, except for a little disturbance overnight." She cast Pickering a scalding glance. "Everything is all right now. . . . Yes, Aunt. Good. I'll see you then. Please give my love to Aunt Gretchen and Uncle Wilhelm. . . . All right. . . . Yes. Good-bye."

Emily replaced the receiver with great delicacy.

"My aunt and uncle are coming home this evening, Mr. Pickering, and you may be sure they will hear about your perfidy. And don't you even *dare* to think

I don't know you were the one behind that man's attempt to hurt Gustav and Helga."

"My darling Miss Emily, I can't conceive of why you hold me in such slight regard. Nor can I imagine why you think I should have anything at all to do with hurting your uncle's precious dogs. Why, my dear, I'd never do such a vile thing."

Pickering's attempt to look crushed made Emily want to scream. Instead, she said, "Get out of here, Mr. Pickering. My aunt will soon learn what an evil man you are. If she didn't believe me before, she certainly will now."

"I have no idea what you're talking about, Emily dear, but I shall take my leave now, as you seem too perturbed to listen to reason. Your aunt," he said with a smile that tried to be sincere but looked merely sly to Emily, "will believe *me.*" That was Pickering's parting shot.

Emily glared at the door as it shut behind him, and had the morose thought he was probably right. The knowledge settled in her belly like curdled cream.

Well, like it or not, her aunt Gertrude would finally be made to sit down and listen to her. Emily still had not had the chance to confront Gertrude with the reality of her disastrous financial situation. At least, she thought with some relief, now that Will was helping Uncle Ludwig, their financial problem might be on the way to being solved.

When she thought about Will, Emily's heart felt as though it were being squeezed by a giant fist. She forced herself to think calmly.

She was going to make Gertrude understand about money, and about Clarence Pickering. She simply had to listen to her this time.

With that firm resolve, Emily left her aunt's office. She needed to find Blodgett and recruit him to tend to the telephone while she delivered today's column to Mr. Kaplan.

When she entered her aunt's kitchen, Emily had a brief, dazzling image of what her life with Will Tate might have been like had she not set herself upon a course of deceit and untruth. The two Blodgetts were cozily chatting with the comfort that comes of having spent a lifetime together. Mr. Blodgett was polishing the silver while Mrs. Blodgett cooked.

The Blodgetts had been married for at least forty years. They'd had children together, and now they had grandchildren. They had grown old as a couple and fit together as comfortably as a pair of old shoes. Emily nearly burst into tears as the reality of what she had thrown away washed over her.

It took a moment before she could make herself respond to Mrs. Blodgett's happy "Good morning, Miss Emily."

"Good morning, Mrs. Blodgett, Mr. Blodgett."

"You didn't ask for breakfast this morning, dear. Do you want something now?"

The very thought of food made Emily feel peckish. Her misery filled her much more effectively than food ever could.

"No, thank you. I'm not very hungry. But I do need to walk my column to Mr. Kaplan's office, if you wouldn't mind taking over the telephone for a couple of hours, Mr. Blodgett."

"Certainly, Miss Emily. Just let me finish up the silver here, and I'll be right along."

"Thank you." Emily eyed the old couple with love and longing. They had been employed by her aunt

when she was a young bride just come from
Germany. They must have worked for Gertrude
Schindler for thirty-five years or more. She didn't
realize she had sighed aloud.

"Is there anything else you need, dear?"

Mrs. Blodgett looked at her with a question in her
old, tired eyes, and Emily realized she had been staring into space.

"Oh, no. No, nothing." Before she shut the kitchen
door, though, Emily did think of something. She
turned in the doorway and asked, "Did either one of
you hear anything last night?"

The Blodgetts exchanged puzzled glances. "Hear
anything, dear? Hear what? I guess our old ears
aren't as good as they once were." Mrs. Blodgett
chuckled.

"Well, somebody sneaked into the backyard and
into the kennel. I think they were trying to either
hurt or kidnap Gustav and Helga. I chased whoever
it was away." If neither Blodgett had heard Will's
gunshot, Emily didn't see any reason to bring him
into the picture.

"Good gracious, Emily, why didn't you wake us?
Now that we have a telephone, we could have called
the police."

"Oh, my goodness. I didn't even think of that." It
was a foolish oversight, all right. And by now, she
supposed, all evidence of the intruder had been long
since rubbed out by the incessant pattering of little
dachshund feet.

"If you really think somebody is after those dogs,
I'd better make sure Chung Li watches them until
your uncle gets back."

Blodgett gave a final swipe to the silver teapot he

had been polishing and then rose slowly to his feet. Emily could hear the various cricks and pops as his joints straightened out, and wondered who would be at Will Tate's side to listen to his joints creak when he got old. Or hers, for that matter. It didn't bear thinking of, so she stuffed the thought away.

By the time she got back from her editor's office, her aunt and uncle had returned from their visit to Aunt Gretchen's. Emily found Gertrude fluttering over baggage in the hallway. Uncle Ludwig was, of course, out back being greeted by his canine friends.

"Oh, Emily darling, I'm so glad you're here. I seem to have misplaced something."

A quick glance at the jumble of suitcases and boxes littering the hallway was enough to make Emily shudder. As usual, though, she braced herself and tackled the challenge with a calm demeanor. At least dealing with her aunt's luggage would keep her mind off Will Tate. And after this problem was solved, she would *force* Gertrude to sit down and talk to her about her monetary situation. It simply had to be done.

"What is it you've misplaced, Aunt Gertrude?"

"I'm not sure, dear, but I'll know what it is when we find it."

Watching her aunt kneel beside a huge trunk, dip her arms inside, and begin to fling clothes hither and yon, Emily discovered her patience was running perilously thin today.

"Aunt," she said in a sharper voice than usual, "why don't we get the bags up to your room? Then you can look through them. You're tossing your things all over the front hallway."

Gertrude's faded blue eyes looked startled. "Oh! Oh, yes. I hadn't thought of that. Perhaps it would be a good idea."

With a huge sigh, Emily began picking up the strewn items and returning them to her aunt's trunk.

"Why on earth did you have to take this much luggage to Aunt Gretchen's? You were there for only a day." Emily could have bitten her tongue when she heard how snippy she sounded.

"Why, Emily darling, you sound positively peeved. Are you feeling unwell?" Aunt Gertrude pressed her hand against Emily's forehead. "You don't feel hot."

"I'm not sick, Aunt." Not unless heartsickness counted, she supposed. "I'm just upset. We had an intruder last night, and I need to speak to you about it."

"An intruder? How appalling. Oh, Emily, are you all right? Did he harm you?"

Gertrude's concern for her welfare was almost Emily's undoing. She felt a sob well up in her throat, and she slammed it back down with the greatest of difficulty. What a miserable, ungrateful, unkind, unfeeling girl she was. First she had tried to deceive the only man in the world she would ever love, and now she was being mean to her beloved, if slightly crazy, aunt Gertrude.

"I'm sorry, Aunt Gertrude. I didn't mean to be short with you. I'm just upset about the dogs."

"The dogs?" Gertrude stared at Emily blankly. "What do the dogs have to do with anything, dear? I thought the intruder was a person."

"He was, Aunt. He tried to hurt the dogs."

"Oh, dear, dear, dear. Your uncle won't be happy to hear this."

"No. But Gustav and Helga weren't harmed, thank God."

"Thank God." Gertrude continued to eye Emily closely, though. "Are you certain you're all right, dear. You don't look well at all."

Wonderful, thought Emily. Her wretchedness was probably written all over her face.

"Well, I am a little bit worried, Aunt. I do need to talk to you as soon as you have a minute."

"Of course, dear. Just help me find whatever it is I've misplaced, and then we can chat for as long as you like."

Apparently forgetting her resolve to take her bags to her room before she went through them, Gertrude began to fling their contents on the hall carpet once more. "I wish I could remember what it is I'm missing. It would be so much easier to find it if I could remember."

Heaving a gusty sigh, Emily gave up and began carrying her aunt's luggage upstairs while Gertrude disemboweled the contents of the largest trunk. The bags weighed a ton, and Emily just knew that if Will had been there, he would have relieved her of the heavy work. Another gigantic sigh and a tear followed her unhappy thought.

By the time she finally managed to settle her aunt in a comfortable chair in the parlor, Emily had determined upon a course that, with any luck and a lot of patience, would not be too difficult for her aunt to follow.

She decided to tackle the bills first and postpone explaining about the intruder and her suspicion he had been hired by Clarence Pickering until later. She didn't want her aunt upset before they discussed money, and at the moment money was even more important than Clarence Pickering.

"We must discuss the state of your financial affairs, Aunt Gertrude. I know this will be difficult for you, but it must be done," Emily began, seating herself opposite Gertrude with a large pile of bills on the table between them.

Gertrude's face fell. "Oh, Emily dear, I know how distressing all of this must be to you. But you know, darling, your uncle Ludwig said your nice Mr. Blake told him he was going to try to help us out of our woes." A tear zigzagged its way along the wrinkles lining Gertrude's sweet face, and Emily felt a tremendous tug of guilt. "I'm so sorry to be such trouble to you, Emily."

"You're not any trouble, Aunt Gertrude," Emily said, lying fervently. "It's just that we must try to work our way through this—this mess, or you're going to lose your home. You don't want that to happen, do you?"

"Oh, dear, no. That would be dreadful." Brightening perceptibly, Gertrude added, "But Ludwig said your dear Mr. Blake told him he would take care of our money troubles, Emily, after the two of you are married."

The painful gripping in her breast did not allow Emily to respond to her aunt's cheerful comment at first. She had to swallow hard once or twice and blink her tears back.

"Mr. Tate and I will not be marrying, Aunt," she whispered at last.

Gertrude's eyes widened in astonishment. "But Emily dear, surely you must be wrong. Mr. Blake said he doesn't have a wife in Arizona, so there's abso-

lutely no reason for you not to marry him. He seems
to be a very nice young man. And even if he did have
a wife once, apparently he doesn't have one any
longer. I can't imagine he would have fibbed about
such a thing. And he seemed so sincere when he
asked our permission to call on you."

"He asked to call on me?"

Emily knew better than to try to make sense of the
first part of her aunt's ramble, but she did seize upon
Gertrude's last sentence. So Will had actually gone to
the trouble of asking her aunt and uncle, properly, if he
could woo her. The very thought made her throat catch.

"Oh, yes, dear. He certainly did. He loves you,
Emily. He told us so."

Emily had to look down in a hurry. She didn't want
her aunt to know how close to a fit of tears she was.

"I don't understand why you say you won't be married, dear. I'm sure you care for him. At least, you
certainly seem to, and I don't believe you would tease
a gentleman about something of such importance. I'm
sure we've reared you to behave better than that."

With a doleful sniff, Emily said, "Oh, yes, Aunt.
You have. But unfortunately I have committed a
dreadful deceit. I can't allow Mr. Tate to marry me. It
wouldn't be fair to him."

Silence reigned for several seconds as Gertrude
digested Emily's confession. At last Gertrude said,
"I'm very sorry to hear it, dear. I don't recall your
ever being deceitful before."

Emily could only shake her head. She was too miserable to speak.

"Don't you think you could simply apologize to
Mr. Blake? He seems like such a fine young man. I'm
sure he would understand and forgive you."

"I can't tell him, Aunt. I can't. And if I can't even forgive myself, how on earth can I expect him to forgive me?"

Although Emily didn't expect an answer to her question, Gertrude seemed to be trying to think of one. Emily forestalled her by leaning over the table laden with bills and putting a hand on her arm.

"There is no way I can ever tell him of my awful duplicity, Aunt. And the subject is too painful for me to discuss right now. Let's just understand that Mr. Tate will not be taking direct care of your debts, and continue our discussion. Now, it is true," she added, "that his help with Uncle Ludwig's dachshund business will undoubtedly assist us a lot, but I'm afraid there is much remaining to be done in the meantime."

Gertrude still looked troubled. "Well, all right, dear. But you may rest assured, I shall communicate with Raja Kinjiput about the matter between you and dear Mr. Blake. I'm sure the raja will give you guidance."

Emily smiled indulgently at Gertrude. "Thank you, Aunt. I do appreciate your help."

So Emily and Gertrude spent an hour or more muddling over debts in the parlor. At the end of their time together, Emily was even more depressed, and her aunt Gertrude was in tears.

And after Emily had wrestled her aunt's debts to a standstill, Gertrude would hear nothing against Clarence Pickering.

The only thing that could drive Emily even closer to the brink of despair was the note from Will Tate that Blodgett brought her that evening.

"My dearest Emily," the note read, "I received your

letter today, my love, and I want you to know it doesn't matter to me what you've done. I love you. I want to marry you. Please say you will be mine. After last night, how can you doubt we belong together? Please tell me you have changed your mind. We can be married immediately, if it is to your liking, or we can wait. For you, Emily, I will do anything. If you want us to live in San Francisco, even, we can do that. I love you. Will."

It was all Emily could do to compose her answer to Will's letter. She gave it to Thomas Crandall's house-boy, who was waiting patiently and didn't seem at all disconcerted by Emily's tears.

"I'll be a toad-eyed son of a bitch!" Will bellowed when he read Emily's response, which arrived an hour or so after he'd sent his message to her.

Emily had written: "My dearest Will: I love you with all my heart. Please try to understand it is my love for you that prevents me from accepting your proposal of marriage. I have done something unforgivable and used you terribly. I don't deserve you. Please, please forgive me and know I will always love you. Emily." The missive was liberally speckled with poorly blotted teardrops.

"Bad news, Will?" Thomas Crandall asked.

Will hurtled his large frame out of his chair and flung himself around the room, snatching up his vest, coat, and hat, confusing poor Fred. The dog woofed once and then settled back to watch his master in concern.

As Will stomped out of the house Thomas thought he heard him say, "Goddamn it, I'm going to make her listen to reason if I have to shake her."

Thomas shrugged at Fred. Fred just closed his eyes and went back to sleep.

13

When Will stormed up to the Schindler residence, it was almost eleven o'clock. He was glad to find the house dark and everyone gone to bed.

The only qualm he experienced as he struggled up the tree outside Emily's bedroom window was that a member of the crack San Francisco police force might notice his ascent and arrest him as a housebreaker. Other than that, Will didn't much care how shocking his conduct appeared. He was going to talk to Emily, by himself, just the two of them, and make her listen to reason. And he was going to do it tonight, hang the consequences.

He had intended to stomp over to her bed and demand she tell him the truth about how she, as Aunt Emily, had tried to snare him, as Texas Lonesome, into marriage. Then he was going to tell her he already knew everything there was to know about her deception. He was going to let her know it was all right with him; he loved her madly and still wanted to marry her. In fact, he was going to demand she marry him.

But when he finally managed to pull himself over the windowsill and into her room, he was so out of breath he couldn't manage to stomp. Instead, he tiptoed, panting, to her bedside, and peered down at her. The pitiful sight of her damp cheeks was more than he could bear.

The moon had waned from its former fullness, but it was bright still and shone through Emily's window to bathe her pale face with its silvery blessing. Will's breath caught in the back of his throat as he gazed at his heart's desire. For the life of him he couldn't imagine allowing her to get away from him. He could scarcely remember what his life had been like before he met her, and they had known each other for only a week or so.

Suddenly his resolve to tell her he already knew about her plot began to waver. Even if she could be made to understand the truth, she would still feel herself to be at fault. Perhaps if he were to confess his own ruse, that he was not Texas Lonesome, she would forgive herself, and him, and agree to be his.

Just then Emily stirred softly in her sleep. She had been lying on her side with her cheek nestled in a hand. Now she cast her arm across her eyes and turned over to lie on her back. Will heard her give a miserable sniffle in her sleep, and he realized the hand that had cushioned her head was clutching the note he had sent her earlier in the evening. He also noticed with an aching heart that her tears had wet it until it was quite soggy and its inky message was smeared.

"Ah, hell, Emily. I can't shake you. I just can't."

Very carefully, so as not to awaken her, he knelt beside her bed. His thumb reached out to gently smooth away the tears still dampening her soft cheeks.

Emily thought she was in the throes of a heavenly dream when she felt Will's lips brush her forehead. An enormous sigh escaped her, and even though she realized it was a dream, she reached for the broad shoulders she knew couldn't be there. When her arms encountered the very solid, very manly form of Will Tate, her eyelids fluttered open to find her only love right there, in her room, beside her bed. She thought she had lost her mind for a moment, until Will spoke.

"Oh, God, Emily, I can't let you go. You've just got to change your mind. You've got to."

One look at her eyes, swollen from weeping, was enough to make Will long to slay those responsible for plunging his own sweet darling into such agony. If only the people who were supposed to have taken care of her had done their jobs, she never would have been tempted to lower her standards and try to deceive him into marriage. No girl Emily's age should be asked to shoulder such heavy burdens. He had never felt such empathy for a fellow human being before in his life.

He would have loved to tell her the truth: that the success of her magnificent plan only made him love her all the more. But if Thomas Crandall had taught him nothing else, he had finally convinced him most people did not consider the ability to swindle a virtue. Will figured he'd better not let her in on his little secret.

"Will?" Emily's whisper caressed his senses and made every single one of his body cells quiver.

"I'm here, my love. I'm here. Nobody can hurt you. I'm here."

"Oh, Will!" Emily cried, and flung herself into his arms.

"It's all right, Emily. It's all right. Everything will be all right."

"Oh, Will, I'm so sorry. I love you so much."

Her blurted confession was enough to send any remaining thought of reasoning with her flying out of Will's head. As he felt her soft body melt against his, the only thing he wanted to do was give her comfort. Well, perhaps not the only thing, he realized as his own body came to attention.

"I'm so sorry, Will. I've treated you horribly. How can you even bear to speak to me?"

Since she had not as yet found the courage to tell him why she believed she had treated him horribly— and Will did not think it was his place to tell her he had found her out anyway—he wasn't exactly sure what to say. He solved the problem by stroking her tenderly from her neck to her soft bottom and whispering over and over again how much he loved her.

He wondered if she would ever stop crying onto his leather vest and began to consider the advisability of moving her sweet face an inch or two over to rest against his cotton shirt. He was sure cotton wouldn't mind tears as much as leather. But at long last Emily hiccuped into silence. He tightened his hug and let her rest, sure that she needed it after her energetic outburst.

It had been at least fifteen years since Emily had felt protected and loved—not since before her parents died in a terrible accident when she was five. From the very beginnings of her life with her aunt after that, even at her tender age, Emily had taken charge. She'd had to. The blissful protection of Will's strong arms was a comfort she hadn't even realized she'd missed until now. She gave a giant sigh of contentment.

"Better now?" Will's soft question was accompanied by a kiss.

"I—I think so." Emily's throat felt as though it had been scraped with sandpaper. "I'm so glad you're here. Even though I know you must hate me now."

"Hate you? How could I possibly hate you?"

Emily bowed her head in shame. "I'm a fraud, Will."

"Aw, Emily." Will wrapped her up again. Since it seemed expedient and she was tugging on his arms, he lay down beside her. "You're not a fraud, love."

"Yes, I am."

"Oh, Emily. Please, tell me what I can do to make you feel better. I can't bear to see you this unhappy."

Emily peeked up at him as a wonderful idea suddenly struck her. She might not have Will Tate forever, but he was here now. Perhaps she could snatch one more heavenly night of bliss to remember in her dotage.

"Do you mean it, Will?"

"Anything, Emily darling. Anything I can do to make you stop being miserable. Please tell me."

He saw a tiny smile play upon her formerly unhappy lips, and his spirits lifted. Then she began to unbutton his shirt. When she kissed his chest, Will groaned.

He hadn't intended to allow himself to get this carried away. After all, they weren't married yet. This was infamous conduct on his part, making beautiful love to the woman of his dreams before the ceremony had even been performed. Oh, he knew he would wear her defenses down sooner or later and make her agree to marry him, but this still seemed wrong somehow.

Then Emily kissed him again, on the mouth this time, teasing his tongue with hers. She pressed her perfect breasts into his chest until he was sure his shirt was going to catch fire. Suddenly what they were doing didn't seem quite so wrong after all.

"Emily, love." His voice was ragged. "You'd better not do that anymore."

Emily drew back and asked, bewildered, "Why not, Will?"

"Because when you do that, I can barely control myself. I want to make love to you, Emily, but it's not proper. You've been trying to teach me propriety, and I'm just as sure as anything this isn't proper."

But Emily would have none of it. "There's a time for propriety, Will Tate, and a time to let propriety go hang. This is one of the times when it's suitable to let propriety go hang." She used her prim teacher's voice and emphasized her instructions with a gentle stroke along his arousal.

"Oh, Lord," he groaned.

"Let me, Will," Emily said softly, continuing to unbutton his shirt. She had no trouble at all with his cuff links, and in a jiffy his shirt and vest were off. She had a little more trouble with his belt buckle.

"Stand up, Will," she commanded.

With another anguished groan, Will did as he was told.

The heavenly agony of having Emily undress him was taking its toll. A fine sheen of sweat erupted on Will's brow. His hands clenched into tight fists at his sides. He was almost afraid to move for fear he would explode before he'd done his manly duty. But Emily managed to remove first his pants, then his drawers. When she began to press tiny, rapturous kisses along his shaft, he uttered such a growl of desperate longing as he had never heard from his throat. His hands buried themselves in her shining tresses, and he knew he couldn't stand it any longer.

With one fluid motion, he picked Emily up, flopped himself flat on her bed, and pulled her over his hard body. She smiled down at him, and he felt like weeping for joy.

"Oh, God, Emily, I love you so much."

Emily had to kiss him for those sweet words, so she did. When she opened her eyes again, she discovered their positions had somehow become reversed. She now lay on her back with Will sprawled over her. She arched like a cat when he kissed a throbbing path to the curls hiding her secrets. When she felt his tongue stroke her there, she had to cram her hand into her mouth to keep from screaming.

The sweet torment was incredible. When Will finally drove his flesh into hers, they groaned a passionate duet of pleasure. Deeper and faster, with Emily matching each thrust with a fervent arch of her hips, they drove each other higher and higher until, as one, they burst into a sparkling cascade of fulfillment.

It was a long time before they cooled down sufficiently to continue the conversation Will had come to her room to initiate. When at last he rolled to Emily's side and drew her close to him, his senses rioted in the pleasure of her softness pressed against him.

Lord above, he loved her. More than he'd ever thought it was possible for one human being to love another human being. His uncle Mel had prepared him for lots of painful eventualities in life, but he sure hadn't prepared him for the magnificence of love. It briefly occurred to Will to wonder about the gap in his education, and to feel a little bit sorry for his wily uncle.

Emily's small hand stroked his chest. She buried her fingers in his curly hair and teased his hard, flat nipples.

"Keep that up, love, and you'll be on your back again in a minute."

Emily sighed with pleasure. "Would that be so awful, Will?"

Will's hard kiss let her know exactly how awful he thought it would be.

"But we still have to talk, darling," he said when he finally managed to pry his lips from hers.

He felt her take a deep breath, as though bracing herself for something unpleasant, and he tried to preclude any further objections on her part.

"Emily, my love, I'm a very rich man. I made my money honestly, by my own enterprise."

"Well, of course you did, Will. I never doubted it for a moment."

Emily sounded surprised he would even have to say such a thing, and Will chuckled. "When you learn more about me, love, you might not wonder why I need you to know that."

"All right, Will." Somehow it didn't seem like the right moment for her to question him. A big yawn escaped her lips along with her assent.

"Of course, like most lucky fellows, I had help. I made my fortune by honest means and with the help of my best friend, Thomas Crandall."

"That nice man we met in the restaurant?"

"The same. Thomas and I started a business—here in San Francisco, as a matter of fact—about ten years ago. It's been more successful than either one of us ever imagined it would be."

"You and Mr. Crandall . . . "

Emily's words trickled to a stop, and Will felt her stiffen at his side.

"Mr. Crandall," Emily whispered. "Mr. Crandall and Will Tate. Crandall and Tate."

Suddenly she sat up straight as a plumb line and pinned Will with a stare of absolute awe. "*Crandall and Tate?*"

She was so damned lovely, looking at him like that. Will could only grin with appreciation for several seconds.

"Yes," he managed to say at last. He couldn't stop his hand from lifting to cup one of her perfect breasts. "God, Emily, you're so beautiful."

But Emily no longer heeded Will's words of love. She was too busy being flabbergasted by his revelation. She did not, however, remove his hand.

"Will Tate. You're *that* Tate?"

"Yes," he said again. His voice was getting a little thick as Emily continued to present him with the luxurious display of her womanly charms. The red haze of his passion cleared slightly when she frowned.

"But you said you have a spread in Texas."

Will was just honest enough to look guilty. "Well, I do," he said. "But it's not a ranch or anything, although I do have a majority share of three large ranches in the area. Basically it's a big estate I built for myself 'cause I never had a real home when I was a kid, and I always wanted one. It can be our children's inheritance, Emily. One that will mean even more because I built it up myself by the sweat of honest work."

It didn't seem as though Emily had heard him after the "not a ranch" part.

"My God," she whispered. "Crandall and Tate is the biggest importer in the West. One of the largest in the nation. Oh, Will." Her expression held dazed incredulity.

He wasn't entirely sure whether being dazed was good or not under the circumstances, but he said, "Yes. So you see, helping your aunt and uncle isn't a problem for me. I've got so much money, I'll never be able to spend it all, even with their help. And it just keeps multiplying. That's the funny thing about money."

There was a lull in the conversation. Eventually Emily said, "I've never been able to find anything at all funny about money, Will."

He couldn't stand it anymore. He grabbed her by her supple waist and pulled her down so that she lay on him, breast to chest.

"I can't marry you, Will," Emily told him sadly. "I can't possibly allow you to waste your money on my family. It wouldn't be fair."

But he was prepared for her this time. By now he had been able to think up a perfect answer, fit to stifle any further protest on her part.

"It's too late, Emily."

"*What?*"

Emily struggled to sit up again, but he wouldn't let her. He held her captive in his arms, his warm hands stroking her back. His undisciplined male parts both appreciated and reacted strongly to the feel of her body wriggling against his.

His soothing massage had its effect. Emily stopped struggling after only a very few of his long, gentle strokes. "I don't understand, Will," she whispered against his neck.

"I've already got your uncle's business on its way toward profitability. There's no way to avoid its becoming a success now. I have a golden touch. Don't know why. It's a gift, I guess. I'm sorry. I didn't realize you wanted your family to founder in poverty and lose everything. If I'd known, I wouldn't have meddled."

His ridiculous statement brought on a fit of soft giggles, a result very much to Will's liking. "Oh, Will, I do love you so awfully much."

"Good. Then if you can't come up with any further objections to it, will you marry me, Emily darling?"

She didn't answer him. She couldn't. Oh, she knew he was right: His interference for the good would save her uncle's business. She was almost positive of it now.

But that didn't negate her own villainy. As she stared into his beautiful hazel eyes, Emily knew she could not refuse him again tonight, even though they would have to part at dawn. Instead, she kissed him. She kissed him soundly, and continued to kiss him until he was at her mercy. Then she kissed him some more, until she was at his mercy.

By the time Will lifted her and pulled her down upon his aching body, they were so besotted with each other that it took only a very few glorious minutes before they hurtled once again into the shattering ecstasy of completion.

"I love you, Will," Emily murmured after they both came back down to earth. She snuggled into the cra-

dle of his arm to go to sleep. She had never even considered what sleeping in the arms of a man must be
like before she met Will, but she liked it. A lot. Fancy
enjoying falling asleep in a man's armpit, she mused.

His strong arms encircled her, and his heart
swelled with adoration. "And I love you, love," he
whispered.

Then he guessed that was redundant. He chuckled
with pleasure. Great God almighty, he was a happy man.

Thus they drifted off to sleep.

It was very late the next morning when Emily was
awakened by the sound of a gentle tapping at her door.

When her eyes fluttered open, she was delighted to
find herself still encircled by Will's strong arms. Her
delight tumbled downhill into panic when she noticed
the sunlight streaming through her window, illumi-
nating the tiny dust motes in the air. It was late; much
later than she usually awoke. Not only that, but somebody was knocking on her door.

She sat up, startled, and stared down at Will, who
stirred sleepily as she jostled him.

"Somebody's at the door, Will," she hissed.

"Uh-oh." With the quick reflexes born of a youth
spent on the lam, Will scrambled out from under the
covers, grabbed his clothes, and dove under the bed.

Emily snatched up her robe in a hurry, looked at
herself in the mirror, and decided her hair and face
were both hopeless. After checking to make sure no
sign of Will Tate still remained discernible, she went
to the door.

"Who is it?"

"It's me, darling." It was Gertrude. "Are you all

right, Emily? I know you were upset yesterday. And it's so late, and you weren't up yet, and I just wanted to know if you're all right."

Emily cracked the door open and peeked out. "Oh, Aunt Gertrude, thank you. I guess I overslept."

"Emily, you look terrible!"

Although she wasn't sure she appreciated her aunt's candor, especially with her beloved Will hiding under the bed, Emily was actually sort of glad she didn't look well. Besides, she was sure she would soon look worse. As soon as Will left her for the last time.

"N-no, I'm not feeling too well, Aunt. I think I'll sleep a while longer." Emily yawned and rubbed her eyes for effect.

"I should go fetch you a tonic. You know, my darling, I really think you should reconsider your decision about not marrying that nice Mr. Blake if refusing him is going to make you this sick and unhappy."

Without waiting to hear her answer—which was just as well, since Emily's eyes suddenly filled with tears—Gertrude left. Presumably she went to fetch Emily's tonic, although Emily suspected Gertrude would forget her errand before she got to the kitchen.

Although she didn't expect further interruptions, Emily took the precaution of locking her door before she tiptoed over to the bed and lifted the counterpane.

"Will . . ."

"Is it safe?"

In spite of her underlying misery, Emily was startled into a ripple of laughter when Will poked his head, a little fluffy from the dust it had picked up, out from under the bed.

"It's safe."

"Are you laughing at me, Emily von Plotz? Soon to be Emily Tate?"

His show of mock grumpiness made her heart squeeze, and she sighed.

Will didn't like the sound of that. "What is it, Emily?"

She gazed at his face for a moment or two. Then she turned away resolutely. Clasping her hands to her breast, she said stolidly, "Please leave now, Will. I—I don't want to keep you from your business."

"What?" Will stopped in the process of cramming a long leg into his trousers. "What did you say?"

She whirled around and cried, "Oh, Will, please! Just go! Go away! Never come back! I can't bear to love you so and to know you can never be mine!"

Flinging herself on her bed, which squeaked a loud protest, Emily succumbed to a violent fit of tears.

Will stared at her, dumbfounded. "What the hell . . . ?" Then he frowned. "Goddamn." His violent curse got lost in the frenzy of Emily's sobs. "Do you mean to say," he said in a very controlled voice, "that you *still* refuse to marry me?"

Emily could not speak. She only nodded, driving her nose into her pillow and nearly smothering herself.

Will continued to stare at her miserable form for several more seconds. Then he muttered, "Well, hell and damnation. I can't even believe this." He threw on his shirt and vest.

"I love you, damn it all to blazes!" Will hollered. Then he jammed his hat on his head, scanned the street below for policemen, and hastily climbed out the window and down the tree, taking most of its leaves and a good many small branches with him.

14

Dear Aunt Emily:

My girl still says she won't marry me. I even told her I don't care that she don't think she deserves me. It is making me mad and sad, and I don't know what to do. I think I need a drink.
   Signed,
   Texas Lonesome

Dear Texas Lonesome:

I am more certain of this than I am of anything else in the world: Your young lady is too honorable to marry a man whom she feels she has deceived. Please forgive her. I know she is miserable.
   All my love,
   Aunt Emily

P.S. And please, dear Texas Lonesome, do not take refuge in the bottle. Your loving Aunt

Emily will never forgive herself if such a dire consequence should occur.

Once Emily finally stopped crying and came to grips with her appearance, she trudged wearily down the stairs. She had scrubbed her face until it glowed, and pressed a cold washcloth over her swollen eyelids to try to soothe them. Her lids were still puffy, though, and she decided she probably should ask Mrs. Blodgett if she had any cucumbers.

She had read in a fashion magazine that both cucumber slices and mashed strawberries could be used to soothe swollen eyelids. The thought of wasting expensive strawberries on her eyes made her squirm. Cucumbers, on the other hand, grew by the million on the vines in Mrs. Blodgett's tiny kitchen garden.

Then she washed her hair, since there was no doing anything else with it, and had to wait until it dried before she managed to wrangle it into her favorite upswept do.

She was more pleased than she expected to be with the result of her efforts. Unless one looked closely, the ravages of the terrible past couple of days—before Will climbed through her window and after he climbed back out again—were almost invisible.

She donned her prettiest day dress, a two-piece creation she had crafted herself from a pattern copied from *McCall's*. The fabric was a calico print, blue as bachelor's buttons, purchased at her favorite cheap shop in Chinatown. On any normal day, she would have been pleased to have the blue of her eyes emphasized. Today, she didn't even care.

Although her emotional crisis had not allowed her to eat a single thing the day before, the thought of food still made her feel ill. Nevertheless, she knew she must keep up her strength. She might yet be the only hope her family had. It was her duty to stay alive, however bleak the prospect of another forty or so years without Will Tate seemed.

"Oh, Lord, help me," she whispered as she paused at the kitchen door. Then she drew a deep breath and pushed the door open.

"Why, good day, Emily darling," Mrs. Blodgett said. "Your aunt said you weren't feeling well this morning, but you certainly look fit to me."

Emily kissed the kind old woman's cheek. "I feel a little better now. Thank you, Mrs. Blodgett. I guess there's a lot to be said for getting plenty of rest."

Mrs. Blodgett eyed her keenly. "Well, you just sit right down and I'll fix you a big breakfast, Miss Emily. How about ham and potatoes and eggs?"

Though the very mention of the succulent meal made Emily feel sick, she said, "Oh, that sounds wonderful, Mrs. Blodgett," and felt like a fool when she heard herself.

Mrs. Blodgett gave her another curious look, but kept up a cheerful stream of chatter while she cooked. Emily wondered if she would have cooked for Will if they had married. She was a good cook, thanks to having to help Mrs. Blodgett. But Will would never know of her skill in the kitchen now. Emily wanted to rest her head in her arms and cry.

Soon Mrs. Blodgett plopped a steaming plate before her and said, "It looks to me as though you're lost in a fog this morning, my dear. Is everything all right?"

Emily jerked to attention. "Oh, I'm sorry, Mrs. Blodgett." She tried for a smile. "I guess I'm not quite feeling tip-top yet."

"Well, I'm sure you'll be feeling more the thing after you eat, dear. I don't think you ate a bite yesterday."

"No," Emily sighed. "I don't believe I did."

Mrs. Blodgett rattled a pan and frowned. "Now, Miss Emily, I don't suppose it's my place to say so, but I don't know why you won't have that Mr. Tate. Mr. Blodgett says he's the nicest man. And he wants to marry you, dear. I wouldn't be at all surprised if that's the reason you feel so poorly."

Emily had to dash a tear away. "Oh, I *wish* everybody would stop plaguing me about Will Tate!"

"It's only because we care about you, Miss Emily," Mrs. Blodgett said, looking hurt.

When Emily saw Mrs. Blodgett's pinched face, she repented. "I'm sorry. I—I'm not happy about it. You're right." She took another nibble of her potatoes Lyonnaise. "But there are reasons I am unable to marry Mr. Tate, Mrs. Blodgett."

The housekeeper's eyes widened. She pressed a wrinkled hand to her bosom. "Oh, dear, Emily. You don't mean to tell me he's a bounder?"

"Good heavens, no!" Taking note of the other woman's horrified expression, Emily added, "Mr. Tate is a perfect gentleman. He's—he's—well—" She had to pause and blow her nose on her napkin. "He's a wonderful man." She tucked her hands in her lap and stared mournfully at the half-eaten breakfast in front of her. "It is I who am to blame," she whispered miserably.

The housekeeper stared at Emily as if she'd lost her mind. "Miss Emily, I can't believe that for a minute. Not for a single minute."

"Nonetheless . . ." She couldn't finish: neither her sentence nor her meal. She pushed her plate away with another sad sigh.

"Well, there's something fishy going on here, if you ask me. Mr. Blodgett says Mr. Tate is a true gentleman, and I've never known Mr. Blodgett to be wrong in the forty-five years we've been married. And he thinks *you*"—she tapped Emily's shoulder with her spatula—"are a fine young lady."

Emily couldn't find the heart to answer. The Blodgetts just didn't know, that was all. She picked up one last potato with her fingers and realized she must really be in a state. She hadn't eaten with her fingers since she was two years old. Sighing, she put it back on the plate, then snatched it back and flung it into her mouth.

There. Sustenance. She felt as if she wanted to die.

"Well, I wish you'd make up with Mr. Tate, Miss Emily. With him coming to call, I'll wager your aunt wouldn't be plagued by that awful Mr. Pickering so much. She's in the parlor with him right now." Mrs. Blodgett's voice held a distinctly sour note.

"He's here now?" Suddenly alarmed, Emily forgot her miseries. A bitter misgiving began to gnaw at her almost-empty innards.

"Oh, my, yes, miss. Mr. Blodgett told me he's been with your aunt for a good hour or more."

"Oh, Lord." Emily pushed her chair back from the table. "I'd better go in there and investigate. I don't trust that man."

"Well, be careful, Miss Emily. Mr. Blodgett says the man is a scoundrel."

"Mr. Blodgett," said Emily with conviction, "is absolutely correct."

Emily forgot all about asking the cook for a cucumber. Giving up heartbreak for anger, she strode firmly away from the kitchen, headed down the ragged carpet to the parlor, and opened the door. The startled—and slightly guilty—expression on her aunt's face when she entered the room did not escape Emily's attention. Rather than launching a bitter attack on Pickering or, better still, stabbing him with her uncle's letter opener, however, she forced a complacent look.

Pickering had the effrontery to wink at her. Emily's insides recoiled in disgust. Since she didn't want to upset her aunt, who already looked pale and drawn, Emily didn't slap Pickering's sincere face, as she wanted to do. Instead, she gave Gertrude a smile and ignored Pickering altogether. Until this minute, Emily hadn't known she possessed such theatrical talent.

"Good day, Aunt Gertrude. Thank you for asking about my health this morning. I'm feeling ever so much better now."

Gertrude looked puzzled for a second or two. Then she brightened, apparently recalling that Emily had earlier been unwell.

"I'm so glad, dear. Er, won't you say hello to Mr. Pickering?"

Emily turned toward him, held out a stiff hand, and said, "How do you do, Mr. Pickering?" With an effort, she repressed her shudder as he took her hand.

"I'm just fine, Miss Emily," he crooned. "Just swell, in fact."

Snatching her hand back, Emily said primly, "I do not believe it appropriate to use street jargon in the presence of my aunt, Mr. Pickering."

As soon as the words left her lips, she wished she could call them back. Aunt Gertrude got so upset whenever Emily demonstrated her obvious dislike for Pickering.

But this morning Aunt Gertrude didn't even appear to be listening. Her vague gaze skittered around the room, and it seemed she was trying to avoid looking at Emily. She appeared nervous, as though she were expecting news about the outbreak of a war.

"Is anything the matter, Aunt?"

"N-No, Emily darling. Everything is just grand."

Emily directed a scowl at Pickering, which, if he'd had a heart, would have caused it to frizzle up into a crisp, smoking lump. He smiled and shrugged at her. Emily wished the law took a more tolerant view of manslaughter.

It didn't, however, so she left off glaring at Pickering and put a comforting hand on Gertrude's arm. "Has Mr. Pickering done something to upset you, Aunt?"

"Why, Miss Emily, my sweet, how you do take on. I haven't done a thing to your beloved auntie."

"Oh, that's not true, Mr. Pickering," Gertrude interjected hastily. "You've probably saved my very life." With those dramatic words, Gertrude gave him a glorious smile.

Gertrude's words, however, did nothing to comfort Emily. A feeling of unease began to nibble at the back of her neck. The only thing on earth she could imagine provoking a comment of such a nature from her aunt would have been some sort of financial rescue. *Oh, Lord,* Emily thought, and began to wonder what it was. She knew Gertrude felt guilty about her spendthrift ways.

Pickering, however, did not seem inclined to stick around long enough for Emily to discover what he'd done to create this frightening gratitude in her aunt.

With another slick smile, he said, "Well, now, I guess I'd better trot along. I'm a busy man, you know."

"Yes," Emily said with barely suppressed violence, "it must take a good deal of time to think up the various outrageous schemes you propound, Mr. Pickering."

He leaned close and pinched Emily's cheek. The uncharacteristically bold gesture shocked her, and she felt her face burn with indignation.

"How dare you—" she began, but nipped her words off before she said more. She refused to allow herself to upset her aunt, no matter what this man did. Come hell or high water, Pickering would not defeat her. If she had to beg in the streets, she wouldn't lower herself to his level. At least she'd be an honest beggar!

"I'll just mosey on along now," Pickering repeated with an endearing smile for Gertrude and a sly wink for Emily.

She couldn't believe his audacity. Pickering had ever been a thorn in her side, and she'd always done her best to avoid him and his disgusting advances. But he had never, until this very day, flaunted his interest in her before her aunt. Her uneasiness suddenly erupted into sickening suspicion.

"Good day, Mr. Pickering. I just don't know how to thank you." Gertrude's myopic eyes filled with tears. She squeezed Pickering's hand between both of hers.

Pickering gave Gertrude one of his most sincere smiles and pecked her cheek. "Take care, Mrs. Schindler."

If Emily had closed her eyes and only listened to him, he would have sounded like a kindhearted, well-intentioned gentleman. But she knew better.

Once he was gone she addressed her aunt. "Aunt Gertrude, why was Mr. Pickering here?"

Her voice was sharp, and Emily at once regretted not taking more care with her tone. One had to ease information out of Gertrude gently, as one might milk a cow with a tender udder.

When Gertrude did not reply, Emily tried again. "Did Mr. Pickering come here for anything in particular this morning, Aunt?"

"Why, no, dear. He just dropped in." Gertrude stood up from the sofa. "I think I'll just go to the other parlor now. I—I think one of my students is here."

Gertrude fluttered and twittered like a frightened sparrow. Emily's emotions began a perilous slide toward dread. She watched her aunt trip out the parlor door and knew she had to get to the bottom of the lady's strange behavior.

"Aunt Gertrude!" Emily dashed out of the parlor after her aunt. "Wait! We need to talk."

"No, we don't, dear," Gertrude shot back too quickly. "We don't need to talk at all. Not about a thing. Nothing to talk about. Ha ha ha. We talked yesterday, remember? And I thought I was the one with the bad memory. Now I have a student, dear."

But Emily, pursuing her down the hall, would have none of it. "You don't have a student, Aunt Gertrude, and something *is* wrong. You must tell me. Have you let that terrible Mr. Pickering lend you more money?"

Although she knew her aunt shied away from brutal honesty, Emily's uneasy prickles had by now turned into a veritable hailstorm of dread. She slammed her hand flat against the door Gertrude tried to shut in her face, pushing it open.

"Emily, how could you even ask me such a thing, after the terrible scolding you gave me yesterday?"

Her aunt's anguish stabbed at Emily. She took a deep breath, striving for a calm she did not feel. "All right, Aunt Gertrude. I'm sorry for suggesting you might have asked Mr. Pickering for more money. But something is troubling you. Please tell me what it is. I want to help you. To help us all. We really shouldn't look to other people—Mr. Pickering or Mr. Tate or anybody else—to solve our problems for us, you know."

When her aunt's plump, wrinkled face crumpled up like a discarded picnic-sandwich paper, Emily felt like the biggest brute in nature. "Oh, Aunt Gertrude, please don't cry! I didn't mean to make you cry when I tried to talk to you about money. Truly I didn't. I was just trying to help us out of our troubles."

But it was too late. Gertrude collapsed onto a frayed wing chair, clutching her lacy handkerchief, and wept. "Oh, Emily, I'm such a burden to you. Such a trial. I'm so very sorry."

Stricken to the core, Emily knelt on the floor in front of her aunt and took Gertrude's hands in hers. "Aunt Gertrude, you're not. You're not a burden. You just aren't—aren't very good with money, is all." Emily taxed her rattled brain to think of something else nice to say. She finally came up with, "You're a wonderful, wonderful aunt, Aunt Gertrude. And you have the most beautiful speaking voice and the best posture in San Francisco. I love you so very much." That last part, at least, was the absolute truth.

A wobbly smile made its way to Gertrude's face. She patted Emily's hand. "Thank you, dear," she sniffed. "But I have too been a burden to you. You're a beautiful young girl. You should have beaux and pretty things. You should attend fancy balls, dine in the finest restaurants, go to dances and to the theater. But you have to work hard and make your clothes over from dead people's leavings and haggle with those awful merchants in Chinatown."

At Emily's horrified, wordless exclamation, Gertrude pressed a finger against her lips before her niece could utter a protest.

"It's the truth, dear, and I know it. Mrs. Blodgett told me how you help her with the marketing and the cooking and how you're always having to make do. Oh, Emily, I'm so sorry. I've been such a sore trial to you. I, who was supposed to be your guide and support."

Finally Gertrude's sobs got the better of her, and she couldn't continue.

If Emily had ever felt worse in her life, it could only have been earlier that morning when she watched Will Tate climb out her bedroom window, knowing he was lost to her forever. To see her aunt weeping her poor heart out on her behalf cut her to the quick. Only a mean, ungrateful child would create this much distress in such a softhearted creature as her aunt Gertrude. Tears of shame prickled Emily's eyes.

"Oh, Aunt, please don't cry. I'm so sorry I hurt your feelings. It was wrong of me. It was because I was so unhappy about not marrying Mr. Tate and so worried about you and Uncle Ludwig losing everything you love so much."

A wail of grief greeted her words. "What a terrible aunt I have been to you!"

"No, no, Aunt Gertrude. You're a wonderful aunt.

I know you love me. That's the most important thing. I know you find money matters"—Emily groped furiously for a word that wouldn't seem to accuse her aunt of carelessness—"troublesome. Many people do." She supposed that might be true. "But you don't have to feel guilty anymore. Now that Mr. Tate has taken over running Uncle Ludwig's dachshund business, I'm sure everything will be all right again soon. You'll see. He is gifted in business matters." As he was gifted in making her heart sing and her body tremble with joy. Emily tried not to think about that.

"Oh, but Emily," Gertrude sobbed, "you said you won't marry him. And he loves you. And you love him. And it's all because of me!"

Emily's heart gave an enormous spasm of agony, cutting off speech for a minute. When she spoke, her words sounded pinched. "It's all my fault. If I hadn't set out to deceive Mr. Tate . . . well, it's my fault. Not yours."

Gertrude's hankie dropped from her eyes to her nose, and she peered at Emily over the damp lace. "Really?"

With a heartbroken nod, Emily whispered, "Yes."

Since her knees were getting sore, Emily edged herself onto the chair next to her aunt. With a cry that must have meant something, although Emily didn't know what, Gertrude threw her arms around her and wept onto Emily's freshly pressed dress.

After a good cry Gertrude began to babble. "Our financial situation will be just fine, dear, I know it. Perhaps you will change your mind about that dear Mr. Tate once our finances are straightened out. I believe it is the worry about money that has overset

you. So, you see, even though he will own my share of
the business—"

"What?"

Emily hadn't meant to shout. Her aunt's sniffling
confession had taken her by surprise, though, and
although she wasn't sure she had heard it correctly,
she had a sinking feeling it boded ill.

With a small, disapproving frown, Gertrude
dabbed at her red nose before she responded. "You
needn't raise your voice, Emily. I'm not hard of hearing, no matter what my other faults may be."

"I'm sorry, Aunt. Would you please repeat what
you just said? I promise my attention will not wander
this time."

Gertrude patted Emily's hand. "You're such a
good girl, Emily, such a comfort to me. I said I'm sure
you'll come to your senses about Mr. Tate once our
money problems are over."

"Yes, yes. Maybe I will," Emily said mechanically.
"But what did you say about somebody owning your
share of the business. What business? Who?" Then it
hit her. Her aunt owned seventy-five percent of the
dachshunds—Helga and half of Gustav.

*Oh, please, God, don't let it be Pickering and the
dogs.*

Emily's brief, fervent prayer was for naught. She
felt her insides begin to shrivel when Gertrude started
to fiddle with her hankie and look guilty.

"Now, Emily, I don't want you to start fussing at
me again. I was terribly upset yesterday after your
tremendous scolding, you know."

"I know, Aunt Gertrude," Emily replied through
gritted teeth.

"And you *did* tell me you weren't going to marry

that nice Mr. Blake, you know. You know you did, dear. I didn't imagine that, Emily."

"Of course not, Aunt."

"And I just couldn't stand seeing you so upset over something like—like money, darling." Gertrude spoke the word *money* as though it signified something vile, dirty, and completely beneath her.

"Yes, Aunt. I know. I apologize for upsetting you yesterday."

Gertrude continued to fidget. "I just hate to see you so upset, dear."

Emily, whose nerves now crackled like Mrs. Blodgett's potato slices being dropped into hot oil, made a stalwart effort not to scream. "Aunt Gertrude," she said gently but firmly, "what was it you just said?"

"About what, darling?"

The sweet, vague smile accompanying Gertrude's question made Emily press her hands together in frustration. She loved her aunt, she reminded herself. It would be a sin to grip her by her starched collar and shake an answer out of her. With the fortitude borne of exhaustive practice, Emily suppressed her shriek and forged onward.

"Who exactly owns your part of what, Aunt Gertrude? You said you sold somebody your part of the interest in something."

But Gertrude shook her fluffy head vigorously at Emily's words. "No, no, no. No, I'm sure I didn't say any such thing, dear. I'm sure I merely said he *owned* my part of the business, dear. I couldn't have said I sold it to him, because I didn't. And you know, Emily, that no matter what my other faults may be, I never prevaricate. I *gave* him my share of the business in return for forgiving some of what I owe him."

"Who?"

Even as the word left her lips, Emily knew who. And she knew what. Her aunt Gertrude had just handed over her share of Ludwig's breeding kennel to Clarence Pickering. Emily was as certain of that as she was she would die one day—and hopefully soon.

Apparently her conviction, as well as the anger and frustration that accompanied it, leaked out in her expression. Gertrude began to look frightened again.

"Please don't take on, Emily. I know you don't care for Mr. Pickering, but he's really a very nice man."

"Clarence Pickering is not a nice man, Aunt. He's a sneaky, hateful scoundrel." Emily's teeth had set so rigidly, it was an effort for her to shove the words through them. Her assurance that, even though she could never be his bride, Will Tate's interference in her family's affairs would set them to rights had just been blown to smithereens in her face. And it was her own beloved aunt, of all people, who had set the bomb and lit the fuse.

Emily kept her fists pressed firmly into her lap to keep them from getting away from her and pummeling Gertrude. She had never felt like this before—as though she just couldn't take one more little, tiny thing. And this wasn't just a little, tiny thing, either. This was a huge, colossal disaster.

"Oh, Aunt Gertrude, how could you?" Emily made no attempt to hide her choler and disappointment. Even when Gertrude's lips quivered and her cheeks wrinkled up, Emily felt only icy rage.

"But I thought you would be pleased."

"*Pleased?*" Emily leapt out of the chair and began

to pace the room, kneading her hands together. *"Pleased!"*

Her shriek, which defied every elocution technique she'd ever learned, made Gertrude wince. Emily didn't care. Pleased? She couldn't stand it.

Gertrude tugged her handkerchief unmercifully between her fingers. The lacy creation was not designed for such strenuous treatment. "I thought I was doing something good for us."

Her aunt's disconsolate statement brought Emily's violent pacing to a dead standstill. She stared at Gertrude hard. "No, you didn't, Aunt Gertrude. Otherwise you wouldn't look so guilty. You did not think you were doing something good." Emily pointed a trembling finger at Gertrude's heart. "You're fibbing to me." Never in her life had Emily uttered such a shocking accusation.

"Oh, Emily." Gertrude's voice was a mere whisper of its former full, rounded, bell-shaped self.

"Don't 'oh, Emily' me, Aunt Gertrude. If you don't feel guilty, why do you *look* guilty?" Emily strode up to her aunt and stood before her, fists held rigid at her sides. Although she was only five feet two inches tall, she loomed over Gertrude like a giant. "Why were you afraid to tell me what you'd done? Why did you try to run out of the other parlor? You *knew* you'd done wrong! You *knew* it! *Why didn't you talk to me before you did something so incredibly stupid?"*

"Oh, Em—" Gertrude didn't dare continue. Stunned to her very core, she could only stare at her niece. From a sweet, loving child, Emily had suddenly transformed into a blazing inferno of indignation.

"I'm sorry, Emily. I thought you'd be pleased that

I'd gotten rid of some of those horrid bills," she whispered miserably.

"*At the cost of your own brother's business? At the cost of your family's well-being?*"

Emily knew she should stop shouting at her aunt. She knew poor Gertrude couldn't help herself. But at that moment Emily couldn't help herself, either. To think that the business Will Tate had barely begun to make profitable was now in the hands of Clarence Pickering was more than she could contemplate with equanimity.

"*Clarence Pickering wanted to make me his mistress, Aunt Gertrude!*"

Gertrude's mouth dropped open. "No," she whispered. Her lips quivered pathetically.

"*Yes!* Yes, Aunt Gertrude. Yes, yes, yes! He's trying to *ruin* us, for heaven's sake! And you just handed him Uncle Ludwig's business! Your own brother's dream!"

Gertrude gasped. "Surely not that, Emily. Surely the business is safe."

Exasperated beyond endurance, Emily flung herself away from her aunt and resumed pacing. "Oh, Aunt Gertrude, wake up! Please wake up! Clarence Pickering is a vicious, evil fraud! Of course, *now* he wants Uncle Ludwig's business to succeed. Now that he knows he can't ruin it. He tried to burn it down once. When that didn't work, he tried to kidnap poor Gustav and Helga. Since neither of those vile plans worked, I guess he just figured he'd latch on to it for himself."

"Emily, no!" Gertrude's tiny protest might not have been uttered, for all the attention Emily paid to it.

"I can't believe you did it, Aunt. I simply can't believe it."

And without sparing a thought for her aunt's shattered nerves, Emily spun around and stomped out of the room.

This was the worst thing that could possibly have happened. Emily could imagine many things, but she couldn't imagine summoning the nerve to explain to Will Tate that his new business partner was Clarence Pickering, a man they both hated. Will knew Pickering was behind the foiled attempts to burn the business to the ground and then kidnap or kill the business's principal assets.

Her beloved Will. Emily wondered how she could tell him about this. There was no way. Even Will, who was as honorable and perfect as a man could be, must have his limits. He'd never agree to work with Clarence Pickering. Then where would Uncle Ludwig and his stupid dogs be? On the street is where.

Emily ran up the stairs. Then she ran down the stairs. Then she stood still and kneaded her hands together again. There had to be a way of solving this terrible dilemma without having Will find out about it. She'd already committed the dreadful sin of trying to deceive him. She wouldn't allow Gertrude to ruin his business plans.

"Uncle Ludwig," she whispered. "I must find Uncle Ludwig."

15

Uncle Ludwig was, as usual, out back with Gustav and Helga, "putting the darlings through their paces," as he liked to call it. To Emily, it looked more as if Gustav and Helga were training Uncle Ludwig—an easier task, she was sure, than training them.

"Yah, yah, you darlings, you stay there where I put you. No, you don't get a cookie until you stay put. Oh, well, maybe just one. Just one, and then you stay."

Although she had stormed out of the house in a rage, Emily's mouth tugged up at the corners when she saw the ridiculous lesson taking place in the kennel yard.

"Uncle Ludwig, you'll never teach them anything that way," she chided.

"Ach, Emily, good day to you." Ludwig honored her with his twinkling smile. "Sure, I am training them, Emily. I am training them to cheat me out of my cookies."

Emily's brief smile was followed immediately by a distracted frown. This part was risky. Ludwig wasn't much more grounded in reality than Gertrude; perhaps not as much. But it was his business that was in jeopardy. If there was one thing Ludwig cared about passionately, it was his dogs.

"Uncle Ludwig, I need to speak with you."

Emily hoped the urgency she felt would transmit itself through her tone of voice into Ludwig's consciousness. Of course, she was wrong. Ludwig didn't even hear her.

"Good boy, Gustav. Good girl, Helga. What wonderful puppies you are."

Ludwig knelt down in front of the dogs and patted his thighs. They promptly leapt onto his lap and began to bathe him with doggy kisses.

Emily's patience had been strained beyond endurance today. "*Uncle Ludwig!*"

Her bellow startled the dogs. Gustav rolled onto his back in submission, while Helga bared her teeth and snarled viciously at Emily from the safety of Ludwig's arms. Ludwig finally looked up at her.

"Whatever is the matter?"

"We need to talk, Uncle Ludwig."

Gently disengaging the animals, Ludwig stood and dusted off the seat of his trousers. "Certainly we can talk, Emily. We can talk now. Yah?"

He looked at her as though she were a lunatic who needed to be humored. Emily didn't care. She grabbed him by a lapel so he wouldn't wander off.

"Something terrible has happened, Uncle Ludwig, and it concerns your dogs."

For once Ludwig was alert. "The dogs?"

Emily knew she would have to be dramatic to keep

his attention. "You're in danger of losing Gustav and Helga and your entire business, Uncle Ludwig."

"No!"

"Yes. And we need to plot a strategy to avert such a calamity."

Emily was afraid she'd gone too far when her uncle's face turned as white as Aunt Gretchen's French poodle and he clamped a hand over his heart. Quickly she steadied him.

"What are you saying, Emily?"

The absolute terror vibrating in Ludwig's voice smote Emily's conscience severely, but she didn't dare offer him any comfort until they had talked. She helped him up and steered him into the house, where she led him to the best parlor and made him sit down. Then she rang for tea.

"Uncle Ludwig, we have to talk. And as we talk, you must pay very close attention to me." Emily felt as though she were dealing with a tiny child.

His eyes wide with horror, Ludwig whispered, "Of course. Of course. Oh, *mein Gott,* Emily. What can you mean, lose my beloved dogs? Such a thing cannot be."

"Oh, yes, it can." With a soul-deep sigh, Emily sat on the chair opposite Uncle Ludwig. When old Mr. Blodgett tottered in with tea, she thanked him and waited until he left the room before she started speaking.

"Uncle Ludwig, Aunt Gertrude has given her part of your business to Clarence Pickering."

"Yah?"

When he stared at her blankly, Emily wanted to scream. How, oh how, could she make him understand? "The fact that Aunt Gertrude gave Mr. Pickering her share of your business is a catastrophe, Uncle Ludwig,

and I'll tell you why." Without waiting for him to protest
or ask a question, she hurried on. "Mr. Pickering is the
person behind the attempt to burn the kennel. When
that didn't work, he tried to kidnap the dogs."

"But—"

"I know it's true, Uncle Ludwig. No matter what
you and Aunt Gertrude want to believe about
Clarence Pickering, the man is a villain. A criminal
and a villain!"

There was a long period of silence. Finally it was
Ludwig who spoke.

"Do you really think so, Emily?"

"Yes, Uncle Ludwig. I *know* so. And so does
Mr. Tate."

Ludwig's eyes got a faraway look with which Emily
was quite familiar, although she didn't know yet
whether to applaud or to groan. At least he was
thinking. When he spoke again, he sounded troubled.

"And what did you say Gertrude did with
Mr. Pickering, Emily?"

"She gave him her share of your breeding kennel in
exchange for some of the money she owed him. Oh,
Uncle Ludwig, we have to do something! Aunt
Gertrude owned seventy-five percent of the business!
And Mr. Tate was trying so hard to help you. Why,
with his help, your dogs were sure to succeed. But
now that Gertrude gave Pickering most of the business, he'll ruin it!"

Ludwig had been staring at the floor, but when
Emily finished her impassioned speech, he lifted his
gaze and eyed her glumly.

"But what can we do, Emily? Maybe we should ask
Mr. Tate?"

"*No!*"

The explosive syllable made Ludwig wince.

More softly, Emily went on, "No, Uncle Ludwig, we can't tell Mr. Tate. Poor Mr. Tate has already done enough for us. I—I'd just feel terrible if I had to confess to him that my aunt gave away a part of his business to a person who has already tried to ruin it twice. I just can't do it."

When tears began to leak from her eyes, Ludwig sat up straight and looked scared.

"Don't cry, Emily. Please don't cry. We won't tell Mr. Tate. Just don't cry." He patted her knee once or twice, then withdrew his hand and stared at her in trepidation.

Emily dabbed at her eyes with a crocheted antimacassar. "I'm sorry, Uncle Ludwig. It's just that I'm so worried. Mr. Tate simply must not find out about this. We have to think of some way to get Mr. Pickering to relinquish his share of the kennel."

"But how do we do that, Emily? Maybe we could ask him? If we give back the bills, he will give us back the business?"

Emily uttered a most unladylike snort. "Well, I can try it, Uncle, but I doubt if I'll have any success."

"No? You don't think if we just go to Pickering and explain it was a mistake, he'll do the honorable thing?"

"Honorable? Clarence Pickering? I think not."

Recollections of the many unsavory suggestions Pickering had offered her roiled in Emily's brain. The thought of going to his house and begging made her flesh crawl. Still, she thought gloomily, that was probably the first thing they should try.

"I suppose we should at least make the attempt," Emily said with a sigh.

"I shall come with you, Emily."

He sounded noble, and Emily was touched. Then she recalled the disastrous other times when Ludwig had tried to be helpful.

Quickly she said, "Oh, no. It's all right, Uncle Ludwig. I think it would be better if I went by myself." The thought of meeting with Pickering alone made her insides knot up, but it would be better than trying to deal with him and her uncle at the same time.

"Yah. Well, while you do that, I will think, Emily. I don't know what to think about, but I will think."

Ludwig nodded vigorously. He was, Emily knew, trying to look thoughtful—but he succeeded only in looking as though he had a tic.

"Thank you, Uncle Ludwig."

"Yah." Ludwig appeared distracted. "Think. I don't know what about."

"I don't know either, Uncle Ludwig, but we must. Think. Please think. And I'll think, too, and between us I'm sure we'll come up with something."

It suddenly occurred to Emily that the telephone was not being tended by either herself or her uncle.

"What about the telephone?"

With great care, Uncle Ludwig scrunched himself back in his chair, trying to get as far away from her as possible. "The telephone, Emily?"

"Yes. Who's tending to the telephone—taking messages—if you and I are in here, and Blodgett just brought us tea?"

"Tea?" Ludwig's glance shot from Emily to the teapot and back again. "Mr. Tate sent a young man this morning to take care of the telephone, Emily.

He's setting up an office for me in Gertrude's old office. Gertrude said it's fine with her."

Mr. Tate. To the rescue yet again. Oh, how she loved him. She would die before she told him her aunt had just jeopardized everything he was trying to do for them. For her. Emily knew good and well Will was helping them because of her. Because he cared about her, and because he was such a wonderful man.

Disconsolately she shook her head. She would love to marry him, but she could never do such a despicable thing. Why, just look at this latest catastrophe. How could she subject him to such a nest of lunatics and wretches? Well, one wretch, Emily thought miserably. Her relatives might be crazy, but she was the only dishonorable one. She swallowed the lump in her throat.

"Oh, Uncle Ludwig," she cried, "we must think of something!"

"Yah, Emily. I will think."

When Emily stood and began pacing, wringing her antimacassar for all it was worth, Ludwig got up and sidled toward the door.

"I shall go now and check on the telephone messages, Emily. But I will be thinking. You know I will be thinking."

With those words, he left. And Emily knew beyond a doubt she was alone with this problem. Poor Ludwig was no more capable of helping her wrest those papers from Clarence Pickering than her aunt Gertrude was.

"Oh, Lord," she whispered to the musty atmosphere of the parlor. "Oh, Lord."

But she wouldn't allow herself to sink into

despair. No. She needed to pay a call on Clarence
Pickering. And when she failed to obtain the papers
from him by that means—she knew better than to
think it would succeed—she would just have to think
of another way.

With a heavy tread she marched once more up the
wide staircase to her room. She sat down at her desk
and stared out onto Hayes Street, wishing traitorously
that she could somehow start over again, this time
belonging to a different family.

"Enough, Emily von Plotz," she scolded after
she had moped for only a few seconds. "You must
not even think of despairing. If you despair, all will
be lost."

As soon as Will got home from Emily's house, he sent
Thomas Crandall's junior secretary over to the
Schindler residence to tend to the telephone and start
organizing an office. Money was no object. By God,
he was going to win Emily by fair means or foul—
and, as fair means seemed the most expedient at the
moment, he planned to use them.

He was going to make that damned dog business
so successful, Emily wouldn't have an argument left
in her repertoire. Damn it, she *would* marry him!

"Will, I heard something today I think you'll be
interested in," Thomas began as he pushed the door
of his upstairs parlor open. When he found Will
scowling malevolently at two pieces of jewelry, he
stared at him in surprise.

"What on earth are you doing, Will?"

Will turned around and transferred his glare to
Thomas. "I'm trying to decide whether Emily would

rather have a diamond bracelet or a pearl-and-sapphire brooch," he growled.

Thomas was taken aback. Carefully he hung up his hat and coat, watching Will the entire time. At last he ventured, "Er, and have you formed a preference yet?"

"No. I'm going to give her both of them." He slammed the two jewelry boxes down on Thomas's sitting room table. "Shreve brought 'em over," he added angrily. "I called him on the telephone."

Thomas cleared his throat. "Shreve came himself?"

"Yeah." Will glowered at Thomas again. "It's 'cause I'm rich, Thomas. If I'd been nobody, he'd have sent someone else."

"Well, you don't seem very happy about it."

In the space of a heartbeat Will's expression changed from fury to despondency. "She won't marry me. I couldn't persuade her."

Will flopped down on the easy chair and dropped his chin into his hands. He looked more melancholy than Thomas had ever seen him.

"I don't know what to do," he said miserably. "But I'm going to make the damned business successful. I figure once she's out of debt, she won't feel so guilty about tricking me." Will looked up at Thomas for approval.

"Oh, dear," was all Thomas said.

Will frowned again, wavering between broken-heartedness and fury. "What the hell does that mean, Thomas? What the hell does 'oh, dear' mean? You sound like a damned pantywaist parson or something. Do you think it will work? If I make her uncle's stupid dogs a success, she'll marry me, won't she? And don't give me any more damned 'oh, dears,' blast it!"

In all the years they'd known each other, Thomas had never seen Will Tate in such a state. He sat on the footstool in front of his friend and said, "Will, listen to me."

"I'm listening," Will growled.

"She loves you. I saw it in her eyes that night at the Palace."

Will still looked grumpy, but his left eyebrow lifted. "You could see it? Really?"

"Yes."

"Well, so what? She even admits she loves me. But she still won't marry me."

"I'm sure you'll bring her around, Will." Thomas actually patted Will's knee and then wondered what on earth had possessed him to do such a sissy thing.

Will didn't seem to mind. "Thanks, Thomas. I hope you're right. Your trust means a lot to me."

"Thanks. But Will, you have to listen to me. Something's come up that might make it harder."

"Criminy! What on earth could possibly be harder than this?"

"Abe Warner told me he saw Clarence Pickering and Bill Skates in the Cobweb Palace this afternoon. Skates's arm was in a sling."

Abe Warner had owned the Cobweb Palace for as long as Will could remember. The place got its name because of old Abe's fervent belief that all God's creatures deserved respect. He demonstrated his personal respect for spiders by not allowing anybody to disturb their webs. Abe didn't like Clarence Pickering any more than Thomas or Will did; he claimed Pickering ruined the ambiance in his drinking establishment.

"I knew I'd shot the guy," Will said with a hint of satisfaction in his voice.

"Abe said he was bruised all to hell, too."

A grim smile quirked the corners of Will's mouth. "Emily beat him with a stick." He sounded very proud of her.

Thomas allowed himself a moment of surprise. "Really? My goodness. But that's not the bad part, Will. Abe said Pickering was flashing an official paper around the saloon and telling everybody he's got control of the dogs at last. Now, I can't imagine what dogs he was talking about, except Emily's uncle's. I figured you should know about it."

Will shot out of his chair. "*What?*"

"That's what Abe told me." Thomas trusted that friendship would prevent Will from killing the bearer of the bad tidings.

"How the hell can that be?" Will hollered. He stormed to the fireplace and kicked the stone hearth. "I swear, I just got von Plotz's dog business squared away. Pickering didn't have anything to do with it as late as the day before yesterday. It took forever to figure everything out, too. God, what a mess." Will ran his fingers through his hair and then shook his head. "The mere thought of dealing with that god-awful mess gives me a stomachache, Thomas. I'm *sure* I didn't overlook anything. I made sure of it because I didn't want to have to do it again!"

"I'm sure you didn't, Will. You're too smart to overlook anything. But Abe says that Pickering claims he's got a crazy old lady's signature on a paper confirming that her share of the dogs has been turned over to him. It must be Gertrude Schindler, because he's been bragging about how he's going to own everything that belongs to them, including your Emily, pretty soon."

"Damn."

Will took another agitated turn around the sitting room. Thomas eyed him with concern.

"Will, don't kill me, but . . . well, are you absolutely certain you want to marry into that family? I mean, those two relatives of Emily's don't seem too, uh, right in their heads to me."

As far as Will knew, nobody had ever uttered such an understatement before. "They're both crazy as loons, Thomas," he growled.

"Ah." Thomas paused, uncertain how to phrase the next part of his concern. He finally just blurted it out. "Will, do you have any worries that it might be an inherited condition?"

Will's jaw dropped. Then, for the first time since Thomas had entered the room, he smiled.

"Lord above, Thomas, you don't know my Emily yet. She's the most levelheaded woman I've ever met in my life. I know her relatives are crazy, but honest to God, she's all that's saved them from ruin these many years. They're crazy as loons, Thomas, but Emily loves them."

As soon as he spoke the words, Will experienced a moment of swift, unexpected, almost earthshaking comprehension. He stopped pacing.

"Yeah," he murmured, more to himself than to Thomas. "She loves them. She loves them because they're her family."

"Right," Thomas said uncertainly.

"Don't you see, Thomas? She loves them because they're her *family*." Will turned away, shaken to the core by his new understanding. He walked to the window and stared outside, unseeing. "I never had any family, Thomas. Not family to love, come hell or high water, feast or famine, sanity or lunacy. Until right this second, it never even struck me such feelings could exist in this world. But they do. In good people, with good hearts, they do."

Will turned around and eyed Thomas intensely. "Emily and I are going to be a family like that. Somehow, some way, we will be. We're going to *make* a family like that. Emily knows how to do it, too, because she's already done it. And I'm not going to let Clarence Pickering play fast and loose with Emily's family. I'll be damned if I will."

"Right," Thomas said again.

Will straightened up. No lingering worries about Emily's unwillingness to marry him marred his determination. He knew what he had to do. Nothing else mattered.

"Somehow or other, Pickering has tricked Emily's aunt into giving him those papers, Thomas," he said briskly. "I'm going to get them back."

Happy to have the old, trusty, businesslike Will back again, Thomas asked, "How? Are you going to try to buy them from him?"

"*Buy* them? I'll eat hog swill before I'll give that bastard a single red cent of my money."

"Then what do you plan to do? Steal them? I've known you for years, Will, and I've known you to do some of the damnedest things, but I've never known you to thieve before."

"Steal? Hell, Thomas, I haven't had to outright steal anything from a person since I was knee-high to a toadstool and had to borrow a blanket in order not to freeze to death."

Thomas would have laughed, but Will's words pierced more deeply than his usual jolly bantering did.

"You had a pretty hard time of it, didn't you, Will, with your uncle Mel?" There was an edge to his voice.

Will looked uncomfortable. "Hell, Thomas, all I know is, Emily's not going to suffer for her family, that's all."

A memory struck Thomas of all those times in gold-mining camps when the two of them had sat by the fire surrounded by strangers, all of them roaring with laughter at Will Tate's stories about growing up with Uncle Mel. Will had padded and protected himself with such a thick layer of humor over the years that even Thomas had never thought about how deep his hurt must go.

He thought about it now, though. Thomas knew he was the only friend Will had ever allowed himself. He'd never thought about that before, either. Suddenly Thomas felt greatly honored.

"Well, Will, whatever you do, I'm going with you."

"What for, Thomas? I know what I'm doing."

"Maybe. But you've got to deal with Pickering. While you're doing that, I'm going to be watching your back."

For a split second, Will had it in his mind to protest. Then he noted the look of determination on Thomas's face. *For Emily,* he thought, and decided that for once in his life he'd let another human being help him.

"Thanks, Thomas," he said.

"Hell, Will, what are friends for?"

"Don't reckon I ever thought about it until right this minute, Thomas."

"Well, you don't have to think about it now, either, Will, because I'm coming whether you want me or not."

Will had to talk around the lump in his throat. "I want you to come with me, Thomas. Thank you."

They grinned at each other for several ₋econds before shaking hands and getting down to business. They spent the next three hours hatching a brilliant plot.

"Ready, Thomas?" Will asked, cocking his Texas hat at an appropriate angle.

"Ready, Will." Thomas tweaked his cravat and stood back to survey his elegant form in the mirror.

"Well, then, let's go."

As night fell and the fog rolled in, Will Tate and Thomas Crandall, partners in business and in life, left the Nob Hill mansion arm in arm. They were ready.

Innocent of the plans being spun on her behalf, Emily von Plotz marched up to Clarence Pickering's rented lodgings on Powell Street, determination fueling her every step. She considered the dirty surroundings with distaste. Not that Emily was a snob; far from it. But her aunt's home, situated as it was in an area characterized by a somewhat fallen grandeur, was a far cry from the run-down buildings in Pickering's squalid neighborhood.

Taking great care, she picked her way over the bottles and trash littering the sidewalk. Then she had to lift her skirts to step over a drunk sleeping it off on the stairs. Her heart palpitated wildly. She was glad she had thought to arm herself with a stout walking stick.

With a brisk yank, she tugged the bellpull next to the tacked-up card designating one suite of rooms as that of Clarence Pickering. Since the moment she had formed the resolve to do this until right this minute, she had not considered what on earth she would do if Pickering was not at home. She did so now and frowned.

Fortunately or unfortunately, she did not have to think of an alternative plan. She had just begun to consider her oversight when Bill Skates, complete with one black eye and one arm in a sling, opened the door.

Although Emily recognized Bill Skates as the brash, uncouth employee of her nemesis, she could not identify him as the person who had tried to kidnap her uncle's dogs. She noticed his bruised face but didn't associate it with the assault the other night. She figured he'd been in a barroom brawl.

"Is Mr. Pickering at home, please, Mr. Skates?" she asked primly.

Once Skates realized Emily didn't mark him as the perpetrator of the kennel break-in, he relaxed. "Yeah, he's here," he said insolently. "What do you want?"

It was not for nothing Emily von Plotz had been drilled mercilessly by her aunt in the proper way for a lady to behave. There were rules for everything, Aunt Gertrude had taught her. Included among them were rules intended to suppress the pretensions of sullen household servants.

At Skates's surly question, Emily drew herself up to her full height, all five feet two inches of it. She said in a cold voice, "Please take me to him. I wish to speak to him. At once."

Skates had never encountered a bearing like Emily's before, having only ogled her from a distance until this minute. Her presence actually cowed him.

"Yes'm," he muttered, and turned to lead Emily into Pickering's rooms.

They were a mess, Emily saw immediately. Newspapers were scattered everywhere, interspersed with old woolen socks, dirty shirts, bread crumbs, and empty bottles.

As soon as Pickering realized who had come to call on him, he made an attempt to sweep the filth behind his tatty sofa. Emily caught him in the act and was not surprised. Her insides recognized this as just the sort of thing one might expect from Clarence Pickering. *This* was the man behind the sincere, polished facade. She felt a quick surge of triumph at having discovered herself to be right as to his true colors. She wished Aunt Gertrude could see him now.

Before he turned to greet her, he tugged his coat-tails straight. "Well, well, well, if it isn't Miss Emily," he murmured. "And what brings you here, my dear? Have you reconsidered my offer?"

"I will drink poison before I reconsider your disgusting offer, Mr. Pickering," Emily announced, not mincing her words.

Pickering's smile tilted slightly askew, and he looked a little less sincere. "Now, Miss Emily, you shouldn't talk to your old friend Clarence that way. I can help you, you know."

"You are *not* my friend, old or otherwise, and the only way in which you can help me, Mr. Pickering, is by returning my aunt's share of my uncle's business in exchange for these notes. It's the same deal you gave Aunt Gertrude; obviously you consider it a fair one, or you would never have offered it to her."

Emily held up the envelope containing her aunt's notes. She'd just managed to rescue them before Gertrude could burn them. She clutched the envelope tightly now, not about to wave it in front of Pickering for fear he'd snatch it from her. Nothing of an under-handed nature was beyond him, Emily knew. She'd never before encountered anybody with such a well-honed sense of dishonor.

Opening his eyes wide, Pickering said innocently, "Why would I do a thing like that?"

"Why wouldn't you, Mr. Pickering? You'll not be losing a thing. It's a square deal, the same one you offered my aunt. We'll just reverse it now."

Pickering put an elegant finger to his cheek and tapped, as though he were actually considering her offer.

"Well, now, Miss Emily, what if I've suddenly developed a yen to invest in those dogs of your uncle's? Have you considered that possibility, my dear?"

His smile was slick enough to grease an axle, and it made Emily's stomach knot up. "Not for a minute, Mr. Pickering," she declared. "You have no interest at all in my uncle's dogs, and you know it as well as I do. They hate you and you hate them; it's a known fact."

Emily noticed he was wearing the same patent-leather shoes he had worn to her aunt's home for dinner the night Helga bit him. She stared pointedly at the jagged tooth mark on the leather.

Pickering stopped even pretending to smile. He frowned at her. "Is that so? Well, then, maybe you're right, Miss holier-than-thou von Plotz. Maybe you're just right at that. Maybe I do hate those dogs. And maybe I hate the way you sneer at me all the time, too. But you won't be sneering very much longer, my sweet, because I've got your idiot aunt right where I want her. Your precious Texas country boy won't be able to help you now, Emily, my darling girl, because it's too damned late. He's going to have to deal with *me* now. I own three quarters of his damned business, and I'm no damned pussyfooter like your crazy uncle Ludwig."

He looked quite petulant when he added, "And I hate Texans."

Emily was profoundly shocked. Never in her entire life had a gentleman actually used profanity at her in this way. Then she scolded herself for her reaction. Clarence Pickering, she reminded herself, was *not* a gentleman.

"How dare you speak to me that way?" she demanded. "Why, you're nothing but a miserable blackguard, Mr. Pickering. If you won't trade back those papers for my aunt's debts to you, I'll—I'll—"

She had no idea what she'd do, in fact; a circumstance Clarence Pickering realized in an instant. At once he found his lost smile, which slithered back onto his face.

"You'll what, my darling little Emily? You'll offer me something else for the papers? Perhaps the possibilities for a trade are improving, my dear." His leer was almost grotesque.

Until this moment, Emily had not been truly frightened. But now, as Pickering began to inch across the room toward her, her steady nerves began to quiver. She stepped back a pace.

"Keep away from me, Mr. Pickering," she said. "You just keep away from me, or you'll be sorry."

"I don't think so. Just think of your loving aunt and uncle, Emily. Just think of them, and I'm sure you'll find my offer appealing. I find *you* appealing, my darling. And, my sweet, I have a feeling you'd like it quite well if you tried it."

Pickering's words snaked their way through the air

to settle like slime in Emily's ears. She shuddered, appalled. In the next instant, though, she dragged her courage up and stood her ground.

"Stay where you are, Mr. Pickering, or you'll be sorry," she declared once more in a resolute voice.

But Pickering only chuckled. His chuckle was as sincere and disgusting as the rest of him. "Now, now, now, you darling little thing. Why don't you just give me one little peck on the cheek now? We can call it a promise. Just to see what you're going to be getting lots more of if you want to keep your auntie and uncle from losing everything they own to me. Because if you're not nice to me, Emily, it's going to happen. You can bet your pretty little bottom on that."

Emily gasped in outrage. She had taken quite enough of this horrible man's disgusting advances. She followed her gasp with a vicious swipe of her uncle's walking stick, the twin to the one she had wielded with such stunning effect against Bill Skates. As Pickering reached out to grab her, she caught him with a bruising blow to the arm.

At his roar of pain, Emily decided her visit was at an end. She fled from his lodgings at a dead run, using her walking stick as knights of old used their lances. Bill Skates just missed being skewered by executing a deft leap aside, thereby bumping his wounded arm against a wall. His bellow blended with that of Clarence Pickering to create a regular cacophony of pain. The noise accompanied Emily down the stairs and outside to Powell Street.

"Hell!" The imprecation was the worst Emily had ever uttered in her entire life.

Her irate exclamation seemed to amuse a sailor walking along Powell. He snickered and winked at her.

His mistake earned him an outraged "How *dare* you?" and a sharp poke from Emily's stick. As she made her way down Powell and turned up Geary, everyone else she encountered very intelligently avoided her.

"Well, it's as I suspected, at any rate," Emily muttered as she stormed along. "And at least I found out what I needed to know."

She stopped at a secondhand shop operated by the Sisters of Benevolence in Chinatown. There she spent forty-five minutes choosing a rather startling costume. The outfit consisted of a pair of boy's knickerbockers, a large plaid flannel shirt, a pair of sturdy brown boy's shoes, and a floppy cloth cap.

Thus armed, she made her determined way back home.

16

When Will and Thomas arrived at Abe Warner's Cobweb Palace around ten o'clock that evening, Clarence Pickering and his crony Bill Skates were already there.

Pickering had dropped his sincere demeanor for the evening. He looked sulky as a poked bear as he smoked a knobby cigar. He was also sucking up whiskey and playing cards, two circumstances that made Will smile. He winked at Thomas, who winked back.

The two newcomers moseyed over to the bar, where Abe acknowledged them with a knowing nod as he poured them a couple of beers. Then Will made his way through the crowded room while Thomas leaned against the bar and watched.

Acting as though he were merely interested in observing the game, Will stopped beside Pickering's table. Pickering had his sleeves rolled up, thereby giving Will a perfect view of the livid bruise Emily had inflicted on his forearm earlier in the day.

Pickering glowered at the cards in front of him. It was some time before he realized who was standing beside him, sipping beer and peering with all apparent innocence at the card game.

"Well, if it isn't the Texas cowboy," he said sourly, blowing a huge puff of acrid cigar smoke in the general direction of Will's face. He didn't bother to smile.

Will, who was used to much worse than cigar smoke from his adversaries, gave Pickering a guileless grin. "Howdy, Mr. Pickering. Playin' cards tonight, I see."

"Clever devil, aren't you?"

Will chuckled. "How're ya doin', Mr. Pickering? Winnin'?"

"I always win at cards, Tex," Pickering said with a sneer.

"That so?" Will tried his best to sound impressed.

Pickering's words were music to Will's ears. One of his uncle Mel's guiding principles was that a man in the throes of a vanity attack was easy pickings. Especially one who was drinking. And Pickering was in the midst of just such an attack right now, and drinking like a fish.

He scratched his chin in an attempt to look both bashful and eager at the same time. "Can I join you gents? I ain't a big-city feller like you, but I like to play me a game of cards every now and agin."

Pickering eyed him. "I don't know that I care to play cards with a Texan," he said.

"It'd give you a chance to get back at me for throwin' you acrost that room, Mr. Pickering." He watched contentedly as Pickering stiffened up like setting cement.

"Damn you," Pickering muttered.

"I ain't the best, but I'd like to try."

Will could tell Pickering was furious. "Well, now, I guess we could find room for a country boy at this table. How about it, gents?"

The other men nodded, obviously uninterested in Pickering's private animosities, and Will pulled out a chair and sat down.

As was his wont, Will started out slowly, assessing the skill of his fellow players carefully. He lost the first two hands, although it took a good deal of effort to do so. His respect for Clarence Pickering, already dim, flickered and died out entirely when he saw what an unutterably bad poker player the man was.

He sipped at his beer, watching Pickering down glass after glass of whiskey. He hadn't realized how easy this was going to be. He and Thomas needn't have spent so much time on their plan after all, he thought.

With a sigh, Will settled in for a long night of playing poker—and playing Texas Lonesome.

"Hurt your arm, Mr. Pickering? That there looks like a nasty bruise," he said at one point.

His innocent observation earned him a vicious frown from his adversary.

"Yeah. Must have bumped it on something," Pickering snarled. "Gimme two," he added with a mean glare.

Will, who was dealing, gave him two, chosen with the utmost care from the cards he had put by for the purpose. Years and years of practice had honed his card-cheating skills to perfection.

Now, as Pickering sank further and further under the hatches thanks to the combined effects of whiskey and his dislike of Will Tate, his game began to deteriorate. A sloppy card player when he was in full possession of his faculties, he became downright slovenly as the evening progressed.

Will kept the full armor of his Texas Lonesome pose in place as he played. Very carefully, without anyone's being aware of it, he eased Pickering's stake out of his grip. If Thomas Crandall had not taken a solemn oath to maintain a wooden expression no matter what happened, he would have applauded his friend's performance. Although Will never allowed himself a streak long enough to arouse suspicion, slowly but surely his winnings piled up. His winnings were evenly matched by Pickering's losses.

Pickering's personality became even more unguarded when he was under the influence of liquor and hate. "Hell," he grumbled at about one in the morning. "You bastard Texan. You're gonna have everything I own pretty damned soon."

"Shucks, Mr. Pickering," Will murmured, "I don't know what's goin' on tonight. Guess I'm just a lucky son of a gun."

One by one the other players drifted off. By three o'clock, the only two men remaining at the table were Will Tate and Clarence Pickering. Thomas Crandall, straddling a rickety wooden chair, watched, as did Abe Warner from behind the bar where he was wiping glasses with a rag.

"Well, damn it all to hell," Pickering finally muttered. "I don't have anything left to play with. You took it all, you son of a bitch."

Pickering didn't look as slick as he had when Will and Thomas first entered the saloon. His hair was mussed; his summer suit was no longer immaculate, but was wrinkled and had collected a spattering of liquor spots.

Will adopted such a woebegone expression, Thomas had to shut his eyes for a moment for fear he would burst out laughing.

"Well, gee golly, Mr. Pickering. I'm still in the mood to play. Ain't you got nothin' else we can play for? Got to give you a chance to beat me, after all. I can't just take all yer money and go away."

The glare he got was so hot with fury, it might have incinerated a person less invulnerable than Will Tate. But Will merely gazed at Pickering with eyes so wide and pure, Pickering was reduced to uttering incoherent oaths.

Then his curses abated and a crafty expression slid across his handsome face. He began to stroke his upper lip, a sure sign he was thinking evil thoughts. Since he had by now consumed an alarming quantity of hard spirits, however, his evil thought processes were not as acute as they generally were.

"Well, now, my fine Texas friend, maybe I just do have something more to play with, after all."

Will's expression brightened and he managed to look eager, despite the fact that he wanted to go to bed.

"Yes," Pickering muttered again, making slush of the word. "Maybe I just do."

With fingers that weren't quite steady, he reached into his breast pocket. "You have your eyes on our sweet li'l Emily, don't you, Tex?"

It was difficult for Will to curb his initial impulse to snap Pickering's neck. But he did and felt proud of himself.

"I'm right fond of Miss Emily, you bet," he managed to respond without even a hint of loathing.

"Well, I can tell you right here and now that you aren't gonna get her, Tex. I can tell you that right now." Pickering jabbed his forefinger on the table to emphasize his point. "Y'know why?"

"No. Why?"

"'Cause I got a lien on ev'ry damn thing those two crazy relatives of hers own, that's why."

"No!" Will succeeded in sounding positively shocked at Pickering's announcement.

"Oh, yes, I do, cowboy. Yes, I do. An' what I'm gonna do for you right now is, I'm gonna give you a chance to win some of it back." A chuckle accompanied Pickering's slurred words as he slapped a fistful of crumpled papers on the table.

Will itched to pick them up and see if they contained the paper consigning Gertrude's share of the kennel business to Pickering, but he didn't dare. He guessed he'd just have to play poker with this idiot for a while longer. Since there were so few people left in the saloon to watch, though, he decided he didn't have to be quite so clever about hiding his skill anymore. Pickering was too drunk to notice.

"Well, shucks, Mr. Pickering, I guess that would be all right, then."

Will gave his enemy what he hoped looked like a stupid smile. He noted with satisfaction that Pickering was still acting sly and superior. Good. That was just the way Will wanted him to feel.

So they played for the notes Pickering held on Gertrude's house. Although Will didn't take the time to read the documents with care, he did notice that Pickering had loaned the woman a considerable amount of money over the months. All of it was lent upon the security of Gertrude's furniture, jewels, sav-

ings, and so forth. Will felt a knot of anger form in his
chest and decided it might be fun to win more than
Gertrude Schindler's notes and the kennel from
Pickering. He wondered just what else the man might
have to stake.

Pickering lost the notes.

"Hell," he muttered.

The smile Will gave him was so contrite and sweet,
Thomas had to go visit the bar so he wouldn't hoot
with laughter and give himself away.

"Well, Mr. Pickering, I don't know what's goin'
on with me tonight. Can't seem to lose for the life
of me."

"Hell," Pickering repeated, his penchant for repar-
tee apparently having deserted him.

"Well, sir, I'm right fond o' horseflesh. Got yourself a hoss you might want to stake?"

So they played the next game for Pickering's horse.
And they continued to play as the early morning
crawled along toward dawn.

At three o'clock in the morning, when Emily, in her
innocence, was absolutely certain nobody else in San
Francisco could possibly be awake, she arose from
her bed and donned the costume she had purchased
at the charity store the prior day.

Peering at her reflection in the scratched mirror,
she decided she looked like one of those runners in
the court district.

Her assessment was not entirely correct. While
Emily was indeed wearing the requisite knickerbockers, flannel shirt, and cloth cap, not too many of the
youthful runners who scurried hither and yon for

lawyers and businessmen in San Francisco possessed her peaches-and-cream complexion. Nor did they, as a rule, appear quite as tidy as did Emily.

"Suspenders," she murmured as she stared at her reflection. "They all wear suspenders."

Since she had not thought to arm herself with suspenders, she tiptoed into her uncle's dressing room, which she could do without passing through his sleeping quarters.

It took her very little time to discover a pair of striped red suspenders. She decided they would work splendidly for her purpose. With any luck, she'd have them back in her uncle's drawer before he even realized they were missing. On her way out, she snatched a red handkerchief, deciding on the spur of the moment it would add the final, defining touch to her costume.

One last peek into her mirror assured her she looked just fine. No one, she was sure, would mistake her for a female. Perhaps a rather delicate runner, but never a female.

With that encouraging thought, and holding her shoes, which she was sure would clomp hideously, Emily descended the staircase. She slipped out the front door, blessing herself for at last having remembered to soap the hinges.

It was dark outside.

"Of course, Emily von Plotz, you silly girl, you knew it was going to be dark," she chided herself aloud. She didn't feel quite so alone when she spoke out loud. "There's no need to be timid. After all, nobody could possibly be awake at this hour."

Almost immediately the disconcerting thought hit her that *she* was awake at this hour and, what's more, she was bent upon theft. Perhaps she might more properly say that no honest, upright folks were awake at this hour. Upon that revealing thought, Emily dashed back into the house and fetched herself a stout knife from the pantry. Thus armed, she felt more secure as she began to stride briskly toward Powell Street and Clarence Pickering's lodgings.

"Now, whatever you do, Emily von Plotz, don't panic," she told herself. "Remember your plan. Jimmy the lock. Sneak into the house. If that awful man in the sling approaches you, splash him in the eye with your witch hazel and then hit him with your rock."

Emily carried a denim sack with the equipment she felt she might need. She fingered it nervously as she walked, enumerating its contents over and over again in an attempt to allay her fluttering nerves.

"Rock. Witch hazel. Door jimmy."

The houseboy, Chung Li, had let her borrow the jimmy. She hadn't asked him why he possessed such a tool, and he hadn't asked her why she needed it. Emily considered their transaction fair on both sides.

"Rope. Hand torch. Matches." She didn't know if she would need to use the rope, but she figured it might come in handy if she had to use the rock. "I guess I'm all set."

On she walked, back straight, gaze sweeping the dark street in front of her, alert to any lurking danger.

She suddenly wished she'd brought Uncle Ludwig's gun. Emily had no idea how to use a gun, but she decided—too late—that it might at least have intimidated anyone who tried to do her mischief.

Fortunately she encountered no such mischief-makers. A small band of rowdy revelers clung to one another on the corner of Pickering's street, but they did not disturb her. Perhaps the streetwise swagger she adopted as she strode by them aided her in her deception.

Taking monumental care to be quiet, Emily climbed the steps of Pickering's building, crept silently to his lodgings, and stopped to put her ear to the keyhole. She strained and strained to hear something from inside the rooms, but not a sound came to her ears.

Breathing a heartfelt sigh of relief, she set her bag of tools down on the filthy hall carpet, drew out the jimmy, and set to work. It wasn't long before she heard the distinctive click for which Chung Li had told her to listen.

Then, pausing only to remove her shoes, Emily slowly pushed the door open, praying it wouldn't squeak. It didn't. With her heart slamming against her ribcage so hard she was sure it would wake Clarence Pickering, she crept into the room.

As quietly as she could, Emily sidled across Pickering's parlor, stepping over the litter of papers, clothes, and sundry other articles strewn about. She wanted to light her little torch, but didn't dare until she'd ascertained whether or not she had company. As she went from one room to another of the five Pickering rented in the shabby building, she was relieved that no signs of him or Skates were evident.

When she did light her torch, her fastidious soul was jarred by Pickering's slovenly housekeeping. "My goodness, what a mess," she exclaimed as she eyed the formidable clutter of Pickering's desk. She began rummaging among the hodgepodge of papers until one caught her eye.

The writing on it was not completely decipherable,

but the content was explicit enough for Emily to deduce that it was indeed Pickering who had tried to burn her uncle's kennel and he who had arranged for Gustav and Helga's kidnapping. Although she had already guessed he had been behind both ill-fated attempts at her family's ruin, this concrete proof of his villainy infuriated her.

"The wicked, wicked fiend!"

Then she really dug in. Without even trying to hide the traces of her search, she scoured each sheet for anything at all having to do with her aunt. A gasp was wrenched from her when she read the beginnings of a letter Pickering had penned to a crony somewhere: "It won't be long now," the missive ran, "before I'll have little Miss Emily in my bed." Why, the *nerve* of that evil beast! To think that her aunt had actually *trusted* him!

Emily's soul blazed with fury as she ripped through the papers after discovering the letter. And the further she dug, the more evidence of Pickering's criminal activities she unearthed.

"Well, will you just look at this!"

Shocked, Emily reread the clever forgery of a birth certificate as she held it up to her torch. She knew it was a forgery because she had already seen the sheets and sheets of paper Pickering had practiced on, as well as the obituary notice, clipped from the *Call*, that had undoubtedly prompted the piece of subterfuge. She surmised he was going to try to pass himself off as that poor man's heir.

Never had Emily been exposed to such out-and-out knavery. Until right this minute, she'd never guessed it existed.

She decided then and there that she'd rather be

poor and honest than have all the money in the world, if this was how one had to go about it. She was sure, however, that Will Tate hadn't had to sink to such depths to make his fortune. But that was only one of many differences between him and Clarence Pickering.

That thought acted as a spur to Emily's industry, and soon papers were flying. There was no organization to Pickering's criminal activities, but Emily eventually found envelopes filled with her aunt's bills underneath betting tickets and on top of pawnshop receipts. It wasn't long before she had amassed a tidy bundle of her aunt's debts to Clarence Pickering.

The size of the bundle alarmed her. She had had no idea how deeply Aunt Gertrude was into this creature's clutches. "I'm glad I came here tonight." She said it defiantly, as though she'd been arguing with her conscience about the dubious merits of breaking and entering.

Emily was still riffling through papers when she heard a key scrape in the lock of Pickering's front door.

In a panic, her brain considered and discarded options with the speed of greased lightning. It was no good hiding behind the tatty drapes, as they weren't long enough to conceal her feet. She was too big to hide under or behind the sofa. There was no way to get to Pickering's bedroom and slide under his bed or tuck herself away in his closet. Besides, in the split second she had to consider her choices, the idea of hiding out in Clarence Pickering's bedroom sent cold shivers up her spine.

When she heard the front door open and then the rumble of male voices through the closed door of

Pickering's office, Emily's heart nearly leapt into her throat. In one desperate movement she swept up her aunt's papers, shoved them into her denim sack, blew out her torch, and dove into the kneehole of Pickering's desk, praying frantically that the men—whoever they were—weren't headed into this room.

It took all of her control not to burst into hysterical sobs when the office door indeed opened. She heard the clump of booted feet—one stride firm, the other hesitant—walk close to the desk under which she cowered.

Then she heard Will Tate's voice, and she nearly squealed in astonishment. A million thoughts spun in her brain when he spoke, none of them coherent.

Why was he there? Did he know of her attempt at thievery? Had he discovered Gertrude's idiocy in giving Pickering the kennel papers? Was he—God forbid—in league with the dastardly man? The last possibility was so distressing, Emily stamped it out as she might a cinder on the rug. Stuffing a fist as far into her mouth as it would fit in order to keep from screaming, she scrunched herself into the corner of the kneehole and listened.

"Well, shucks, Mr. Pickering, I hate to discommode you this way, but my pappy always told me to finish a job before I go to bed at night. Otherwise it might not get done. Now, I trust you like I trust my own self, you bein' Miss Emily's friend and all. But I figgered I'd best get them papers I won off you right now. Don't want no misunderstandings to rear up in the morning."

Emily was astonished. Will Tate hadn't sounded this bumpkinish since she first met him in the park. Come to think of it, it was only after he'd admitted to being Texas Lonesome that he'd begun to sound countrified. As she hid and listened, Emily's eyes narrowed in concentration.

"Yeah, yeah, yeah," Pickering mumbled, obviously cranky as all get-out as well as very drunk. He took no pains with his delivery now, and he didn't sound at all sincere, only incredibly mean. "Well, c'mere and I'll give you the goddamned papers."

"Thank you kindly, Mr. Pickering. I appreciate it." There was no honey on earth sweeter than Will's voice. "And don't forget your saddle neither, please, sir."

Emily couldn't see the two men, but she heard Pickering's explicit curse, and her cheeks went hot as she huddled in the shadows. What a terrible man Clarence Pickering was.

Then she thought about the words she had just heard her darling Will utter.

The papers. Now what papers could Pickering possibly have that Will might want? Surely Will Tate was too good a businessman to have fallen victim to Clarence Pickering. And Pickering's saddle? Emily's confusion was almost as great as her trepidation.

"Hell, I know they're here somewhere."

Emily could hear Pickering shove papers aside as he searched the desk for whatever it was he wanted.

"Want me to look for you, Mr. Pickering?" Will asked sweetly.

Another curse greeted Will's suggestion. "You won every goddamned thing I own, damn your soul to hell. I'll be goddamned if I'll let you mess with my desk. Goddamned poker-playin' Texan."

His words were indistinct, but Emily heard him plainly. He had won everything he owned? *Will* had won everything *Mr. Pickering* owned? Good gracious.

Her own sweet Will Tate, a gambling man? The idea
appalled her, and Emily's heart stopped thundering
and sank like lead.

All at once, Will's patience snapped like a dry twig.
He was tired, damn it, and he wanted to go to bed.
He had half carried Pickering from Abe Warner's,
with himself and Thomas each propping up a shoulder. Thomas now stood guard outside, just in case
Bill Skates or another one of Pickering's cronies
showed up.

"Get the hell out of the way, Pickering," he commanded. "I'm sick of your drunken fumbling. I'll find
the damned papers myself."

"No. You get back, you Texas scum."

Pickering assumed a fighter's stance, the effect of
which was considerably diminished by his unsteady
footing. He squealed when Will picked him up by his
collar as if he were nothing but a slight impediment
and flung him roughly aside.

"I said get out of my way, Pickering. I'm through
playing with you. You hurt my Emily, damn your eyes,
and you should be grateful all I'm taking is your pos-
sessions. I'll be happy to rid the world of your scummy
presence forever if you get in my way again. Now
where are the papers Mrs. Schindler gave you when
you cheated her out of her share of the kennel?"

"Don't hurt me. Don't hurt me!"

Pickering's words sounded muffled, and Emily
wondered why. She had no way of knowing that
Will's powerful thrust had landed him upside down
on the sofa and he was now sniveling through a
cushion.

"I'm going to do more than hurt you, you son of a
bitch, if you don't give me those papers right now."

Emily was startled by Will's sudden change in temperament. She certainly hoped she never angered him once they were married. He sounded positively furious.

Then she remembered they couldn't be married, and a tear slid down her cheek.

As Pickering continued to sniffle and not answer him, Will took two powerful strides toward the sofa. Tired of dallying, he planned to shake Pickering until he either convinced the man to hand over the papers or broke his neck.

"No! Don't hurt me!" Pickering shrieked. "I'll give 'em to you. I just can't find 'em. Honest."

"Honest? Don't make me laugh, you pitiful puddle of tobacco spit. Get up on your two hind legs and give me those papers now."

"I will. I will."

Emily could hear assorted scufflings and shufflings as Clarence Pickering stood up. His unsteady, dragging footsteps made their way back to the desk, and she heard him begin to shuffle papers again.

"I can't find 'em," he whimpered.

"I want those kennel papers, Pickering, and I'm not going to wait much longer. Either hand them over right now or die."

The warning sounded ominous even to Emily as she huddled under the desk. Of course, she knew that Pickering couldn't find the papers Will wanted because she had them packed away in her sack, but she wasn't quite sure how to go about announcing her presence. She was sure she looked a sight, and she wasn't at all certain she wanted her beloved Will to see her in such a state.

And he *was* her beloved Will, too. Whatever he

was doing with this evil man, it was for her benefit. She knew that from the conversation she'd just overheard.

"I tell you, they're not here." A distinctly whiny note had crept into Pickering's voice. It made Emily wince even as her muscles began to cramp from being squashed under the desk.

"Listen to me, Pickering, and listen well. You damned near ruined the life of the only woman I've ever loved. If you don't give me those papers right now, you're not going to get the chance to ruin anybody else's. That's a promise. You cheated Emily's aunt and uncle out of nearly everything they owned, and you tried to kill her uncle Ludwig's dogs.

"You have no honor, Pickering, no soul, no heart, and no guts. You're not a man; you're barely human, and I'm sure the world won't mourn you. If you aggravate me any more, you're going straight out that window over there, and I don't plan to open it first. Either you give me those papers right now, or you're on your way to hell."

Will sounded as though he meant it, and Emily's heart leapt. All this for her! Try as she might to hold them at bay, tears of wonder and happiness began to trickle out of her eyes.

"B-B-But they're not here," Pickering wailed. "Here. Here's the rest of 'em. Everything I own. Everything. Over there's my saddle. The horse is in the livery down the street. There's the receipt. Here's my money. Every cent I have in the world."

Although Emily could not see him, Pickering's fumbling fingers were turning his pockets inside out as he frantically tried to keep Will Tate from murdering him.

"Where are the papers, goddamn it?"

Will's bellow flung Pickering backward into a dead faint on the sofa and sent Emily springing out of hiding as though she'd been shot from a gun. Sobbing with joy, she catapulted herself into Will's astonished arms.

"Will. Oh, Will darling, how I love you!"

Although Will had been primed for homicide, the now-familiar feeling of Emily's body against his smothered the unworthy impulse in an instant. His arms closed around her and he squeezed with gratitude, even though his brain was rattled at her sudden appearance in the very lair of her worst enemy.

"Emily? What on earth are you doing here?" Even as he spoke he nuzzled her soft cheek, trying to avoid contact with the scratchy wool cap she wore. "What on earth are you wearing?"

Will allowed himself another moment close to her and then gently pried Emily's arms from his shoulders. He held her a little bit away from him. "What's the matter, Emily, love? Why are you crying?"

"Oh, Will!" was as far as Emily got before she was interrupted by another flood of tears. After she wiped them away with the red kerchief knotted around her neck, she tried again.

"I found out Aunt Gertrude had given this beastly man her share in the kennel and I came here to steal the papers back again because he wouldn't give them to me when I asked politely and he wanted me to do despicable things with him."

"He *what?*"

Will shoved Emily away and stomped toward the sofa. Death sounded like the only logical answer now. It sounded too good, in fact.

But Emily thwarted him by the simple expedient of wrapping her arms around him once more. As soon as he felt her firm, perky breasts pressing into his back, Will stopped in midstride, even though he was not entirely satisfied at having his plan foiled.

"Please, Emily?"

"You'll get into trouble, Will. He's not worth it."

"But he's vermin, Emily. People pay a lot of money to have vermin exterminated."

"I know it, darling, but not everybody feels the same way about vermin people as they do about vermin rodents."

"But he's a rodent, too."

"You're right, Will, but please don't kill him. For me?"

"Well . . . "

"Please, Will?"

The effect of Emily's stretching up on her tiptoes, thereby rubbing her bosom against him, was such that Will decided he didn't need to kill Pickering after all. At least, not right this minute.

"Oh, God, Emily, I love you."

And with that, he wrapped her up and kissed her so soundly, neither one of them noticed when Thomas Crandall entered the room.

"Did you find the papers?" he asked before he spotted Will and Emily entwined with each other. When he did, he stopped dead in his tracks and stared, aghast.

"Will Tate, why in God's name are you kissing that boy?"

17

Their attention diverted by Thomas's loud intrusion, the lovers broke their impassioned embrace.

"Miss von Plotz? Good God, it's you!"

Thomas's astonishment reminded Emily of her state of dress, and she felt her cheeks heat up. She withdrew from Will's arms, abashed as much at her overt display of affection in front of another person as at her attire. As she had cautioned Will often enough, such displays were frowned upon in polite society.

"Good evening, Mr. Crandall. I hope all is well with you."

Emily realized her attempt at manners had fallen somewhat short of its intended goal when Thomas cried, "Good God, what are you dressed like that for?"

It was a crying shame more young ladies and gentlemen had not been taught the rudiments of polite behavior by sticklers like her aunt Gertrude,

Emily decided. Thomas's question, while understandable, was very rude. It was also not easily
answered, unless she were to confess to having
committed a crime.

"She came here to steal the papers from Pickering,
Thomas."

Will still had his arm wrapped securely around her
shoulder. Emily stared up at him in surprise, not so
much at his words as at the way he said them. He
sounded as though he were proud of her.

"Did you, by damn?"

Good heavens. Thomas Crandall seemed proud of
her, too. Even though the idea confused her, it
pleased her as well. She offered a tiny smile. Her
smile grew enormously when he strode up to shake
her hand.

"Well, by God, I'd say that was mighty enterprising of you, Miss von Plotz. I swear, I didn't think
there was a woman on earth who was good enough
for Will Tate, but you've proved me wrong. By God,
you have."

Thomas pumped Emily's arm so hard her smile
began to wrinkle up into a grimace of pain, but she
didn't mind. She'd been so worried Will would think
her a terrible person if he found out about this
escapade. But he actually seemed to approve. Life
certainly was full of surprises.

As Thomas, Will, and Emily chatted, exchanging
versions of the evening's events, Clarence Pickering
regained consciousness. With a stifled groan, he
cracked his eyes open and peered at the trio in his
room with loathing.

Then, feeling more than a little sick and no longer
one whit sincere, he slunk out of the room. He didn't

even look around to find his hat, which had fallen behind the sofa.

Once out of the office, he ran down the stairs and out into the crisp San Francisco morning. He was so afraid of Will Tate that he actually made it to the corner of Powell and Market before he regurgitated the evening's excesses and began to wonder where he could escape to now in order to earn his foul living.

Without another moment's hesitation, he slunk to the dock and crawled onto a steamer heading toward Sacramento. He knew he'd recover eventually. Clarence Pickering might not be as smart as some people, but his instincts were as base as the worst of them. Eventually he'd find some other poor lamb to fleece, he just knew it. Come to think of it, he might even try politics. Those guys really made out like bandits. As the foggy night swallowed up the steamer, Pickering's spirits began to revive.

Back in Pickering's office, Emily's cheeks warmed at the honest approbation being showered upon her by Will and Thomas.

"I—I didn't think you'd approve of my trying to steal the papers, Will," she admitted shyly.

"Not approve? My God, Emily, the only thing I'm annoyed about is that you didn't trust me enough to tell me about the problem in the first place." Will had to kiss her to show her how sincere he was. "Don't ever keep secrets from me again, love. Promise?"

"I promise." Emily rendered her promise in a quivery whisper. She so loved this man! How could she ever part with him again? Yet honor demanded it. She knew it did.

"I swear, the two of you are a matched set. A matched set." Thomas shook his head and smiled at Will and Emily.

"Oh, no, Mr. Crandall," Emily breathed. "Mr. Tate would never have stooped to underhanded methods the way I did. He's such an honorable man."

She felt slightly disgruntled when both men succumbed to gales of laughter.

"Will, don't tell me you haven't told her about your colorful past yet."

"Colorful past?" Emily repeated, blinking up at Will.

"I guess there's still a few things you don't know about me, love, but we have all night to talk about it." The way Emily was pressing her enticing bosom against his arm and peering at him with those angelic blue eyes was causing Will to lose track of their conversation.

"All night!" All at once, Emily dropped Will's arm like a hot rock, and her eyes widened enormously. "My land, what time is it?"

Thomas pulled out his pocket watch and squinted at it. "Around five, it looks like."

"Oh, good gracious! I have to get home. If Aunt Gertrude wakes and finds me gone, she'll be worried to death."

"I'll take you home, darling. Don't worry about a thing," said Will.

"I'll take care of Pickering for you, Will," Thomas offered.

But when he glanced at the sofa, expecting to find Pickering still sprawled on its cushions, he uttered a sharp expletive. "Damn! Where'd he go?"

"Who?" Will had been so involved in staring into Emily's adoring eyes, he had completely forgotten about the enemy. He glanced at the sofa. "Oh, yeah. Pickering. Well, hell."

"Mercy, he's gone!" Emily added, as if to clarify the matter.

Thomas frowned. "Well, what do we do now? Go after him?"

Although Will had spent most of the past several hours wishing he could strangle Clarence Pickering, the thought of pursuing the bastard now was not appealing. He pursed his lips in concentration for several seconds.

Finally he said, "The man's a filthy skunk and a low-down pile of horse poop, Thomas, but I don't really feel like wasting any more of my energy on him." He glanced quickly at Emily. "Unless you want me to, love. If you want me to break his neck for you, I'll still be happy to do it."

Emily could tell he was in earnest. "Oh, Will, no. Please. As long as you don't think he'll come back to plague us, why not just let him go?"

"Don't worry about him coming back, Miss von Plotz," Thomas assured her. "Pickering won't dare set foot in San Francisco again. I'm sure of it."

"Yes. That's the truth." Will chuckled with glee. "I think I really scared him."

"You scared him to death," Emily confirmed in an awe-filled voice. "You were wonderful. I heard it all."

"Where were you, Miss von Plotz? I gather you were hiding when Will and Pickering came back here to get the papers."

Will chuckled. "It's a long story, Thomas. I'll tell you when I get back to your place. Right now I have to get Emily home. Will you be able to take care of all this by yourself?" His gesture was meant to encompass every room of Pickering's rented lodgings, as well as any other assets the man might have left behind.

"I know what to do, Will. Don't worry. I'll send a runner to fetch help, and we'll have all traces of Clarence Pickering and his dealings with Miss Emily's family wiped off the face of the earth in no time at all."

"Bless your heart, Thomas. I owe you a big one for this."

Emily concurred. She shook Thomas's hand fervently and said, "Yes, Mr. Crandall. God bless you for your help. I can't tell you how much it means to me."

Thomas, who, in spite of his lectures to Will, was unused to dealing with truly nice ladies, blushed to the roots of his hair. "Shucks, ma'am, it's nothing. Really."

But to Emily, who was used to fighting against almost unfathomable odds all by herself, it wasn't nothing. Someone who was willing to help her and her darling Will was a hero, and that was all there was to it.

It was almost six o'clock when Will and Emily reached the Schindler home. She quietly unlatched the front door and peeked in before allowing Will entry. She wasn't about to let him just leave her there. If she never saw him again in her life, they still had this morning. She aimed to make the most of it.

"Let me write Aunt Gertrude a little note, Will, so she won't disturb us like she did before. Wait a minute."

Just like that, Will thought, grinning. His little Emily was such a delightfully decisive creature. Well, good. He planned to show her exac.ly how much she meant to him, and he didn't particularly want any interruptions during his demonstration. She'd change her mind and marry him now. He knew it.

It took Emily no time at all to pen an appropriate note. Then she took Will by the hand and led him up the wide staircase, hurrying up the last several steps when she heard Mrs. Blodgett beginning to stir in the kitchen below.

As an added precaution, she locked her door as soon as they were inside. Then she whirled around and flung herself into Will's arms.

"Oh, Will, how wonderful you were to play poker with that man for my aunt's papers. You must be a splendid poker player."

Will answered in between the scrumptious kisses he bestowed upon her. "My uncle Mel was the slyest poker cheat this side of the Hudson River, love. He taught me every trick he ever knew before we parted company. I'm afraid I cheated Clarence Pickering out of those papers. I hope you won't hold it against me."

"You cheated him?" Emily pulled back.

For a heart-stopping second, Will was afraid she was going to take exception to the way he'd regained possession of her aunt's debts. As it turned out, of course, it didn't matter, because Emily herself had already unlawfully regained possession of them, but Will hadn't known that at the time.

But Emily didn't scold. Instead, her expression glittered on the brink of something indefinable for a second or two; then she threw back her head and laughed and laughed. When she finally found her voice, she hugged Will tightly and said, "How I love you, Will. How I do love you."

Then she realized what she had just said and knew her time had come. She couldn't deceive this wonderful man a single second longer. She stepped back and took a deep breath. Her heart ached when she said softly, "But Will, I—I have a confession."

"A confession?"

Emily nodded and dropped her gaze. "Yes." She felt as though somebody had stuffed a boulder into her throat. "Oh, Will, I know you'll hate me when you find out!"

She sounded so pathetically unhappy, Will didn't dare laugh. Hate her? It was all he could do to keep from ravishing her on the spot. Not, he reminded himself with a flush of guilt, that that meant much. Any man would want to ravish his Emily. But nobody except him ever would. He'd see to it.

"I could never hate you, Emily, love. You haven't done anything wrong. You could never do anything wrong." He gently drew her toward him.

Her hand feathered a caress down his cheek, and he wished he'd taken the time to shave. His beard was scratchy, and he didn't want to hurt Emily's tender skin.

"Oh, but Will, I have wronged you terribly. I pretended to be something I'm not."

Swamped by shame, Emily hung her head. Will had to nudge her under the chin to make her look at him. His heart clenched when he saw the misery in her eyes.

"You're not Emily von Plotz?" he asked with a little smile.

Emily blinked at him, confused. "Well, of course I am."

"I see. But you aren't Aunt Emily from the newspaper?"

Even more confused, Emily could only nod and respond, "Yes, I am."

"Well, then, that's about all you ever said you were. I don't see how you can say you pretended to be something you're not."

When her exquisite face began to crumple, Will was afraid for a moment she would start to cry on his leather vest again. It still had a splotch from the last time. He quickly repositioned her so her tears would fall on his shirt.

With a monumental effort, Emily swallowed her urge to burst into tears. "It's worse than you think, Will darling. I—" She choked to a momentary stop, took a deep, sustaining breath, and continued, "I deliberately set out to entrap you into marriage in order to use your money to rescue my family from financial ruin."

The words came out of her mouth with the solemnity of a funeral march. She couldn't look at him, but clasped her hands together in front of her and directed her gaze at the floor. She felt Will's soft lips on her neck and shivered with the millions of tiny wildfires his touch ignited within her.

Will recognized gooseflesh when he saw it. He smiled. "And you did a spectacular job of entrapping me, too, love. I've never seen anything fall as hard as I fell for you."

Emily gasped when she felt his huge, warm palm cup her breast. His words didn't register immediately. When they did, she wasn't sure she understood exactly what he meant by them.

"You're the prettiest thing I've ever seen, love. Just the prettiest thing."

When his lips nipped lightly at her earlobe, Emily almost shrieked.

"But Will," she managed to say, "don't you hate me for it?"

His soft chuckle against the skin of her shoulder where he had pushed her shirt back made her feel weak with desire. She wondered just what kind of fallen hussy she must be to take such incredible pleasure in a man's touch. Especially one who could never be hers.

"Hate you for it? Now why on earth do you think I could possibly hate you for doing such a sensible thing?"

"S-Sensible?"

"Absolutely. The most sensible thing in the world."

His tongue slid to her neck, and Emily arched against him. "But I deceived you wickedly, Will." The sentence took a long time to get out past many fluttering sighs and gasps.

"You couldn't possibly ever do anything wicked. Besides, you didn't deceive me. I already knew."

Emily stiffened up like a poker, bumping Will's chin with her scratchy hat. "You already knew?"

He rubbed his chin. What *was* that thing, anyway? "I'm sorry, my love. I didn't want to say anything because I knew it might hurt your feelings, but I could tell you were, ah, struggling with money problems."

"Oh, Will, you don't need lessons in proper behavior. You should be *giving* them."

Emily cast him such a forlorn look that he had to kiss her. The pleasant activity did much to soothe her troubled expression, but it almost left Will too breathless to explain himself.

"Believe me, Emily, it's nothing you did. It's that I grew up the same way, trying to use everything five or six times, reweaving the straw in my hats, blacking my shoes with coal dust and water, turning collars, stuffing newspapers into my shoes." He didn't add to his list illicit things such as cheating at cards, selling cigars hand-rolled from cow dung and mud, riding rail cars, and eluding the law.

There was something in his tone of voice that cut Emily to the heart. The very sketchy picture he had painted of his childhood—parentless, poor, and always on the move—tugged at her feelings. Suddenly Emily didn't feel so sorry for herself anymore; she only hurt for the poor little boy Will Tate must have been.

"Oh, Will. Oh, Will, my darling, I'm so sorry." She flung her arms around him and drew his face to hers. Then she kissed him with such determined thoroughness, they were both breathless when she finally let him up for air.

"So, will you marry me now, Emily? Knowing you didn't fool me?"

"Oh, Will! I just can't believe it. Even though you know what a wicked person I am, you still want to marry me," Emily gasped.

"I know it's hard to understand, sweetheart. At least Thomas thinks so, but . . . Well, my uncle Mel taught me to appreciate a finely crafted fraud. Not," he hastened to amend, "that I think you're a fraud. You're you. And I love you."

His words were a soothing balm to Emily's bruised spirits. She drew him to her again for another passionate kiss.

Emily's dreamy "Oh, Will" drifted into his ears and settled like honey on his soul. He found it amazing how such honey could soften his heart while it hardened his desire to an almost painful state.

He needed no further encouragement to enfold her in his strong arms and ravish her lips. As he did so, his hand found her ridiculous cloth cap and tugged it from her head. He was delighted with the fall of hair cascading over his hand.

"Lord above, Emily, you're beautiful." In a deft move, he picked her up, carried her over to the bed, and plopped her down on it. "You don't weigh more than a mite, either," he added when he noticed her bounce up and down, causing a suspender to slide off one of her delicate shoulders. "Where on earth did you get those clothes?"

He stood beside the bed, hands on his hips, and relished the sight of his prim little Emily in her knickerbockers and woolen stockings. The devilish look in her pretty blue eyes and the wicked smile on her enchanting mouth only added spice to the picture she made.

"Do you like them?" she asked with a twinkle.

"I think I'll like them better when you take them off."

She blushed, then shed her suspenders in one graceful move and began to unbutton her plaid flannel shirt slowly. He felt his mouth get dry even as his palms started to sweat. His trousers soon felt too small to hold his growing excitement.

"Emily, are you sure your aunt won't interrupt us?"

"She won't interrupt us, Will. I made sure of it."

Emily swept off her flannel shirt, revealing two perfect ivory breasts. Then she reached for Will's trouser buttons. That was all he could take standing up, so as soon as she had undone them, he joined her on the bed.

Their mating was exquisite. Will mapped Emily's body with his large hands as though he wanted to memorize every tantalizing inch of her. Her knickerbockers and woolen stockings vanished in a trice. She purred like a kitten when his finger finally dipped into her damp treasure.

"It's not fair, Will."

"What's not fair?" Will could barely speak.

"You're torturing me."

"*You're* torturing *me.*"

"No, I'm not. Here."

To his initial dismay, Emily wriggled away from his grasp. When she pressed his shoulders back onto her pillows and he found himself lying on his back, however, his dismay vaporized in an instant. When she began her own tactile survey of his body, he was pretty sure he wouldn't survive, but he resolved to try. Then she climbed on top of him and lowered herself onto him, and he decided that he was already dead and must be in heaven.

"My God, Emily, this is too good. It's too good."

"Nothing's too good for you, Will."

Then she began to nibble on his lower lip as she rocked up and down, up and down, until her own control was overtaken by her spiraling need. She made no protest when Will rolled them over and he was again on top. He made no protest when her teeth found his shoulder at the very moment he felt her rippling contractions beckoning to him like a siren's song to join her. So he did, with a cry he barely managed to muffle.

Several minutes later, Will had just enough strength left to take her with him when he rolled to his side. Thus they went to sleep, Will still buried inside her, Emily's head tucked neatly under his chin.

It was after noon when they finally woke up. Emily's eyes were the first to open.

She awoke with a song in her heart and a tuft of Will's springy chest hair tickling her chin. Very gently she unwrapped herself from his embrace so she could stretch and greet the marvelous day. She glanced toward the window and realized it was raining outside. How wonderful nature was, she thought, to spare her the trouble of watering her beautiful new rosebush today.

The hysterical yapping of Gustav and Helga wafted its way to her ears from the backyard. She thanked God for making such sturdy, alert little creatures to keep her aunt and uncle safe from housebreakers. The muted sound of the telephone's shrill ring came to her from the new office, and she thanked Him for sending Will Tate to rescue her family from the evil clutches of Clarence Pickering.

The very, very faint sound of an elocution lesson being carried out in the second-best parlor reached Emily's ears as well. She thanked her lucky stars for giving her a loving aunt and uncle. What did it matter if they were eccentric? They loved her. Her heart clutched momentarily when she considered the poor little boy Will Tate must have been, with no home and no one to care for him.

"I'll make it up to you, Will darling," she whispered as she nuzzled his muscular arm. She felt so good, she stretched again like a cat, languidly, happily.

"Keep that up and you'll never get me out of this bed," a deep voice growled near her ear.

Emily turned to find her beloved's gaze raking her naked body, and she laughed. It was a happy, delighted laugh as she considered how wonderful it would be to wake up next to Will for the rest of her life. Oh, how she loved him.

Will couldn't just lie there with Emily stretching and flaunting her perfect little body and laughing at him. He grabbed her and wrapped her in his embrace once more.

"I love you, Emily von Plotz, soon to be Emily Tate, and I'll never let you go again."

"I'm so glad, Will Tate. I'm so glad."

They demonstrated exactly how much they loved each other for another forty-five minutes or so. When Will had finally recovered his composure and his breath, he said, "Well, love, I suppose I'd better get back to Thomas's and make sure everything's all right. I'm sure he's taken care of all traces of Clarence Pickering, but I want to make certain."

"I wish you didn't ever have to leave, Will," Emily sighed. "But I guess you must. And I just can't thank you and Mr. Crandall enough. You saved my family from disaster."

Will gave her a smacking kiss. "You were doing pretty well on your own," he laughed. "But you're right. Thomas is my best friend, and I have to go thank him properly. He'll be best man at our wedding."

A quick survey of the room yielded a dressing gown for Emily. "Here. You probably don't want to go down and meet your aunt and uncle dressed like a ragamuffin today, sweetness, especially since we're going to tell them we're getting married."

Speaking of their marriage brought something else to Will's mind. He paused in the act of putting on his trousers, thereby giving Emily a splendid picture of his many masculine attributes. She smiled her appreciation as she tied the belt to her robe.

"Where do you want to live, Emily?"

His question surprised her. "Why, I thought we were going to live in Texas."

"Only if you want to, Emily. I don't want to take you away from everything you love just because I like it there. If you want to live here, we can work something out." The thought of giving up his new mansion near San Antonio didn't appeal to him much. But Will liked San Francisco well enough, he guessed, to be happy there, as long as Emily was with him.

"Will, wherever you are is where I want to be. If you like Texas, I'll live in Texas. I suppose I can come visit Aunt Gertrude and Uncle Ludwig every so often."

Her slightly wistful note did not escape Will's attention. All at once he had a brilliant idea.

"Well, hell," he said. "I don't know what I'm worried about. Barring Thomas Crandall, I'm the richest man I know. We can have a home here and a home there. Besides, now that I'm partnered up with your uncle, I'll have to spend some time here keeping up with the business. At least, I'd better. Not that I don't like your uncle Ludwig, my love, but I think he needs a keeper almost as much as those dogs of his do."

He was unprepared for Emily's enthusiastic approval of his idea. She flung herself at him so hard they both ended up on the bed again. This time, though, Will didn't succumb to temptation, much to her disappointment.

"If I don't go to Thomas's now, I'll never get out of here. You get yourself all gussied up, and I'll be back around five o'clock. We'll talk to your aunt and uncle then."

So Emily floated her way through the afternoon, counting the hours until she would see her Will again.

Since she had neglected her column the day before, she made up for it now by concentrating very hard on her answers. When she came to one particular letter, she smiled.

"Dear Aunt Emily: You have been mortal kind to me as I have fumbled around San Francisco. Since I ain't had no other luck, maybe would you marry me? I think I love you. Love, Texas Lonesome."

Her heart sang as she penned her response.

"My beloved Texas Lonesome: And, as you know, I love you, too. I shall be the happiest of women when we marry. Love, Aunt Emily."

"How funny that he still sends me these silly, wistful letters," she mused aloud. With a deep sigh, she decided it was just Will's way. Just his wonderful, romantic way.

When she felt she had done her duty as Aunt Emily

sufficiently, she gathered her correspondence into a tidy stack, ready for the following day, when she would take it to Mr. Kaplan. Then she skipped down the stairs.

Gertrude was heavily into communication with the Raja Kinjiput when Emily entered the parlor.

"Good day, Aunt," she said brightly.

Startled, Gertrude uttered a little shriek and covered her crystal ball. "Emily! What are you— I mean— Oh, dear, don't scold me again today, Emily. I don't think I could bear another scolding."

A tear quivered on one of Gertrude's eyelashes and made Emily feel like the most ungrateful wretch in the world. She flung herself on her knees in front of her aunt, causing Gertrude to flinch.

"Oh, Aunt Gertrude, please forgive me. I was horrid to you yesterday. I had no business scolding you. I'm so sorry."

Gertrude looked doubtful for a moment. "Well, Emily, I suppose you might have had *some* cause to be upset with me. I had no idea those dogs of your uncle's meant so much to you, or I never would have traded them to Mr. Pickering. And Emily," said her aunt, more sure of her ground and warming up now, "I really do think you owe him an apology. Poor Mr. Pickering. He tries so hard for us."

Suddenly Emily remembered why it was she had been so aggravated with her aunt the day before. Stifling her urge to scream, she said, "No, I don't, Aunt. I don't owe Clarence Pickering one teeny-weeny syllable of apology. The man was a horrid criminal, Aunt Gertrude. He was a thief and a forger and a drunk."

"Why Emily, dear! What terrible things to say. How on earth can you possibly assert such things about him?"

Emily realized that her aunt was honestly shocked at her ill-chosen words. She also knew she couldn't confess how she had come by her firsthand knowledge of Pickering's villainy. "I know it because Mr. Tate has found out *everything* about Mr. Pickering, Aunt. And believe me, Mr. Pickering was a fiend."

Gertrude gasped. "A *fiend?*"

"A fiend." Emily's legs had begun to cramp, so she stood once more. "He was an awful fiend who tried to ruin Uncle Ludwig's dachshund business—and you too, Aunt Gertrude. But Mr. Tate got rid of him for us. And he got all the papers back for Uncle Ludwig's business and everything else you've ever owed him. You're debt-free now, Aunt, thanks to Mr. Tate."

"Really?"

From the way her aunt stared at her, Emily was sure Gertrude had no idea how close to disaster she had been. She had been teetering on the very brink of ruin, of losing her home and everything she held dear. But Gertrude, Emily realized, who never liked to think about unpleasant things, had never allowed herself to think about the consequences of her improvidence, in spite of all Emily's efforts and lectures. Emily sighed heavily, knowing it would be useless to try to make her understand now.

"Yes, Aunt. Really. But don't worry about it. Everything is all right again."

Gertrude smiled, content once more. "Oh, good.

See? I just knew that everything would be all right."

With a sad shake of her head, Emily said only, "Yes, Aunt Gertrude."

Now that Emily didn't seem inclined to scold her any longer, Gertrude was much more serene. She patted the sofa next to her.

"Sit down, Emily darling. Let me tell you what the raja has been saying to me."

Emily complied. "All right, Aunt Gertrude," she said with resignation. "Tell me all about the raja."

So Gertrude eagerly regaled Emily with tales of Raja Kinjiput until five o'clock, when a knock came at the front door. Emily jumped up from the sofa at once, secure in the knowledge the knock came from the knuckles of her beloved Will.

She was not disappointed when old Blodgett opened the parlor door and ushered Uncle Ludwig, Gustav, Helga, and Will Tate into the room.

Emily ran up to Will and kissed his cheek. He gave her hands a meaningful squeeze, and the two of them turned to smile at Gertrude and Ludwig. Gertrude looked as though she was trying not to appear disapproving at their overt display of affection. Gustav and Helga jumped up on Will's trouser legs ecstatically. He finally had to release Emily long enough to kneel down and greet them.

"Well, what's what here, Emily? Your Mr. Tate says the two of you have something to tell us." Ludwig's voice held its usual friendly chuckle.

"Oh, yes, Uncle Ludwig. We do have something to tell you," Emily replied.

Will stood once more. "We sure do, Mr. von Plotz, Mrs. Schindler."

"My goodness, Mr. Blake, whatever is it?"

"Well, ma'am, sir, your niece has done me the honor of agreeing to marry me."

Gertrude raised two plump palms to her face. "Oh, Emily! How wonderful!"

She forgot she was holding her crystal ball and stood, sending the ball crashing to the floor and rolling away. Gustav yipped in terror, jumped onto the sofa, and buried himself so deeply among the cushions that only his quivering brown tail was left exposed. Helga snarled viciously and dove after the ball.

"Well, well, well, this is wonderful news!" Ludwig stepped up to the two lovebirds and pumped Will's hand with his usual enthusiasm.

Then he kissed Emily's cheek. She was surprised and touched to see her uncle's eyes bright with tears.

"You take good care of our Emily, Mr. Tate. We wouldn't give her to just anybody, you know."

"I know, Mr. von Plotz. Thank you. I will. I'll take the best care of her anybody ever could."

"I'm sure of it, Mr. Tate." Ludwig hauled out a huge white handkerchief and dabbed his eyes with it, then blew his nose loudly. "I know you'll be happy together." He thought of something else and added, "I shall give you one of Gustav and Helga's puppies. You can have the pick of the litter. My gift to you. The best dogs in the world. You take the puppy to Texas and show those Texans how wonderful these dachshunds are."

"Thank you, Mr. von Plotz," Will said, genuinely touched.

"Thank you, Uncle Ludwig. If they ever have any puppies." Emily looked from dog to dog and sighed.

"Oh, they will have puppies. Yah. They will have puppies. Gustav, he has been at her all day long ever since last Tuesday. They will have puppies this time, you may be sure."

Ludwig's frank announcement cost Emily a deep blush, but Will only laughed.

18

My dear readers:
  It is with mixed emotions that I take pen in hand to write to you today.

"That's a blatant lie," Emily told herself, chewing on the end of her pen. "I don't have mixed emotions at all. I'm absolutely the happiest woman in the whole wide world."

Pausing only to sigh and decide that under the circumstances a little fib would not be too sinful, Emily continued.

I shall be leaving San Francisco soon, as the bride of a wonderful man.

Well, that's the truth, at any rate.

And I hope you wish me well, as I do you. You might be pleased to learn that I met him

*through the agency of this column, as he wrote
to me for advice. I must tell you that although I
did offer him one or two suggestions regarding
his dilemma, he has given me, and continues to
give me, so much more than I could ever give
him.*

*So let this be a lesson to you, dear readers.
No matter how humble one believes oneself to
be, one can always be of service to one's fellow
man. Let my own dear Texas Lonesome shine
as your example, as he is mine. My best
thoughts and wishes go with you all.*

Love,
Aunt Emily

Emily scanned her missive thoughtfully, contem-
plating word order and phrasing, for a long time.

Uncle Ludwig was right. By the time of the wedding,
planned for a sunny mid-August day in Thomas
Crandall's beautiful garden on Nob Hill, Helga
looked as though she had swallowed a balloon, and
Ludwig was walking on air. They had been invited
to the ceremony, as had Fred, since they were the
means by which Emily and Will had met.

Ludwig decided he liked Fred all right, considering he wasn't a dachshund. But to make his joy complete, he had just received word from Germany that
four more dogs, two males and two females, were on
the boat and headed for San Francisco.

Business was so good, Ludwig already had more
than two hundred orders for his dogs. People were
flocking from all over California and Nevada to see

the little creatures and place orders. They didn't even seem to mind when told they might have to wait as long as a year or two to get their pets.

Before the ceremony, Ludwig cornered Will and emoted with such determination about dachshunds that he almost made Will late to his own wedding.

It was Thomas Crandall who finally pried Ludwig's hand off Will's shoulder and made Ludwig go back to the gazebo, where Emily awaited him. Ludwig was going to escort her down the aisle and give her away.

The aisle had been fashioned from a bolt of white satin. It had taken a good deal of coaxing on Will's part to make the thrifty Emily believe that treading on such an expensive piece of goods wasn't outright desecration.

"But Will, it's so beautiful. And so *expensive*. I could make a million things with it. I can't bear the thought of *walking* on it."

"Emily, my darling, I can buy you a dozen bolts of white satin if you want them. This one is for you to walk on. Please? For me? I'll never ask you to waste anything again, I promise. I just want to see you walking toward me on that shiny satin. Please?"

"Well . . ."

Emily, of course, could no more resist Will's cajoling than she could stop the sun from rising. Besides, the white satin would be the same as that used to make her gown. Emily knew how pretty a picture she and the aisle would make together.

Thus it was, when the melodious string trio Thomas had hired for the occasion began to play, that she stepped down the satin aisle, a shimmering angel on a cloud of gleaming white. Her gown was created in the very latest fashion, with a flared skirt, a draped bodice coming to a short point in front, a demure, pearl-encrusted high collar, and huge corkscrew sleeves.

In a daring departure from the established mode, Emily wore a large white hat atop her shimmering locks. The hat was liberally bedecked with clusters of tiny blooms from Will and Emily's favorite rose, Cecile Brunner. The long tulle veil coming down from the hat's brim was detachable, a feature Emily had insisted upon. She wasn't about to lug an armful of crushed white tulle around with her during the reception.

To Will she looked like a delicate fairy princess as she came toward him, her tiny feet treading daintily on the satin aisle spread between the lustily blooming roses Will had forced Thomas to plant for the occasion. Apparently the guests agreed. They all sighed in unison at the vision Emily created.

She looked radiant, a fact that shouldn't have surprised Will but did. He still had not become accustomed to the way she made his heart perform calisthenics in his chest, or the way his pride swelled every time he looked at her and knew she was his. As she stepped slowly toward him, she smiled shyly at him through her veil.

Will didn't think he could be happier. When Emily joined him at the altar Thomas had had built for the purpose, his heart was full to overflowing. As they recited their vows his voice shook with emotion, and so did hers.

So involved were they with each other, in fact, that neither of them dreamed anything could possibly be amiss. Then the Reverend Mr. Phelps intoned the obligatory words, "If any man can show just cause why these two cannot be joined together in holy matrimony, speak now or forever hold his peace," and a loud voice slurred, "Me! I do."

The ceremony came to a halt, and Mr. Phelps muttered, "Well, I'll be damned. This has never happened before."

Will's face lost its expression of unalloyed bliss, and he held Emily's arm securely tucked into his when he turned to face his guests. He wasn't about to let her get away from him now, no matter what this interruption turned out to be.

As for Emily, it took her a while to assimilate the surprising information that somebody was actually objecting to her marriage to Will. As she turned with him to peer over the crowd of well-wishers, she couldn't help but recall the dreadful scene in her favorite novel, *Jane Eyre,* during which Mr. Rochester's brother-in-law shows up to reveal the existence of Mr. Rochester's mad wife. The perfectly awful thought that Will Tate might have another spouse tucked away in an attic somewhere flitted through her brain. She clutched his arm tightly.

What they saw made them both stare. There before them, staggering down the aisle—his broad Stetson hat atilt, his boots muddy, and his face florid with drink—was a man neither one of them had ever seen before.

Will eyed the big six-shooter sheathed in a holster at the man's hip with nervous foreboding. From long experience, he didn't like having drunks and guns in the same vicinity.

The intruder had now taken to slurring, over and over again, "I objec'. I objec'."

Thomas Crandall finally gathered his scattered wits and accosted the stranger. "Who the devil are you, and what the devil are you doing here? This is a private ceremony!"

"Private cer'mony, my hind leg!" the stranger bellowed. "That there's s'posed t'be *my* wife!"

"*What?*" Will stared at the interloper in astonishment. Then he shot a quick glance at Emily.

The obvious befuddlement in her expression reassured him she didn't know this person, and he turned once more to the intruder.

"What on earth are you talking about, cowboy?"

"Don' call me no cowboy, you—you—you rustler! This here paper says Aun' Em'ly is gonna marry *me* today. *Me!* I'm the one. I'm Texas Lonesome, dammit. *I'm* the one she's marryin'."

The stranger waved a crumpled copy of the *San Francisco Call* above his head and pointed to Aunt Emily's column. Will realized it was the column imparting the news of her impending marriage to Texas Lonesome.

"Oh, hell," he murmured.

"Damn," said Thomas. He shot Will a disgruntled scowl. "You were supposed to tell her before now."

Will shrugged. "I forgot" was all he could think of to say—because it was the truth.

"Tell me what, Will darling?" came Emily's startled whisper. "What is this man talking about? You're Texas Lonesome. Aren't you?"

"Oh, Lord, Emily, I meant to tell you. Honest, I did. But it slipped my mind, what with all the preparations and everything."

"Tell me what, Will?" Emily asked again, a little perturbed now.

"It's all right, Miss Emily. I'll take care of everything."

Thomas cast one more glare at Will and stepped forward to intercept the belligerent stranger reeling down the once-pristine white satin aisle. The glossy fabric was now stained with muddy boot prints.

"All right, pal, let's just you and me go outside and talk about this for a minute." Thomas tried to sound friendly, but the cowboy wasn't buying it. Nor did he seem to notice the incongruity in Thomas's words. After all, they already were technically outside.

"But Will," Emily said, gazing into his eyes, her brain a whirl of confusion, "why is that man saying *he* is Texas Lonesome?"

Will was about to explain when he noticed that the confrontation between Thomas and the authentic Texas Lonesome had by now degenerated into a shoving match. The drunken cowboy was trying to find his gun. Thomas kept knocking his hands out of the way of his hip holster and eventually took the gun himself. Will, unwilling to let what was supposed to be the happiest day of his life turn into a shoot-out, ran over to retrieve it from him. Then Thomas tried to guide Texas Lonesome away from the celebration, but the recalcitrant cowboy dug in his heels.

Emily was horrified to see the pretty white satin aisle pleat up under his boot heels like a gypsy's concertina. Her hands flew to her veiled cheeks. "Oh, please, stop it! You're ruining all that expensive satin!"

All at once a booming voice rang out from in back of the rows of guests.

"I'll take care of this little matter," the voice said.

Will's face paled, and his mouth dropped open. "Oh, my God," he whispered. Until this minute he'd believed Texas Lonesome's intrusion was to be the worst horror he would have to face on his wedding day.

Emily still clutched his arm, her fingers digging into his flesh like a vise. "Who's that, Will?"

Will's mouth was so dry, he could barely form words as he stared at the one person on earth he'd hoped never to see again.

But, oddly enough, as he watched the old faker stride forward, the swaggering form Will remembered so well a little softened by age and suet, the barricades that he'd erected around his heart years and years before began to melt. All the gruff, uneasy, but genuine tenderness he remembered from his childhood suddenly overwhelmed the miseries and embarrassments.

Will didn't understand it, but the closer Melchior Tate strode toward Texas Lonesome, the more Will felt like crying—and not from hurt or leftover anger, but from love.

Finally he found a tattered shred of his voice. "That's my uncle Mel, Emily," he managed to force past the lump in his throat.

"Your uncle Mel?" Emily stared at the portly man who had by now taken custody of Texas Lonesome and begun to sweet-talk him out of the garden.

Will could only nod mutely. His heart was too full for words.

"Your uncle Mel and another Texas Lonesome?"

Emily shook her head slowly. "I don't think I quite understand it all, Will."

Her own voice was very small but, Will noted with relief, not at all angry. At least she didn't seem to be mad at him, even though she had every right to be. He stared after the retreating form of his uncle, who had one arm draped over Texas Lonesome's shoulder, and was unable to speak.

It was the minister who called them all back to attention with a loud "Ahem."

Will felt numb as he and Emily finished reciting their vows. He meant it, though, with every fiber of his being, when he told Emily he was hers, to have and to hold, in sickness and in health, till death did them part.

So did Emily when she repeated the vows.

When Mr. Phelps finally pronounced them man and wife, a cheer went up from the assembled guests, composed in equal measure of delight and relief. When Will thrust Emily's veil aside and kissed his brand-new wife, several elegant beaver hats were tossed into the air in celebration, and another hearty cheer accompanied the kiss.

The cheering kept on as the musical trio struck up a happy tune and Will and Emily walked arm in arm back down the aisle. They smiled, both still feeling confused, but blatantly delighted about becoming Mr. and Mrs. William Melchior Tate.

The reception was to be an alfresco affair, held on Thomas Crandall's elaborately tented grounds and catered by Chef Levant from the Palace, who still remembered Will Tate fondly. When Will and Emily, arm in arm, preceded the wedding party into the area reserved for the reception, the only two people there besides the caterers were Texas Lonesome and Melchior Tate.

It appeared to Emily as though Uncle Mel was trying to console the sobbing cowboy. When he looked up from his task, Mel's expression held a blend of good humor and trepidation. Emily noticed he and Will held each other's gaze for several long seconds.

Finally Uncle Mel cried, "Will, my lad!" His voice broke a little at the end.

"How—" Will broke off and cleared his throat. "How on earth did you know I was getting married today?"

Uncle Mel licked his lips nervously. "Read about it in the paper, my boy." With a shrug toward Texas Lonesome, he added, "Reckon this poor fellow did, too. Abe Warner told me the name of Aunt Emily's intended."

"I'll be damned," Will whispered. He stood as if rooted to the spot for a few more moments. Then, spurred on by a gentle nudge from his beautiful bride, he covered the distance between himself and his only living relative with two or three long strides. Mel met Will halfway, and the two men embraced in a hug that made every person in the wedding party discreetly dab at moist eyes, if they weren't bawling outright.

When they finally broke apart, Will took his uncle by the arm and fairly dragged him over to meet Emily. She waited for them with the sweetest expression he had ever seen. Lord above, he thought as he looked at her, he loved her.

And polite? Will laughed out loud when he beheld his darling wife hold out a delicate, white-gloved hand, smile her charming smile, and say in all sincerity, "It's such a pleasure to meet you, Mr. Tate. Will has told me so much about you."

That, at least, was the truth. Emily politely neglected to mention exactly what Will had said. After all, whatever his sins, Melchior Tate was her beloved Will's only family. That was all Emily needed to know in order for her to accept him gladly.

Great God in heaven, his wife was a saint. Not for the first time, Will thanked whatever benevolent spirit had been hovering overhead that day in Golden Gate Park when they met. Because there was no doubt in his mind that he didn't deserve her.

"Uncle Mel, this is Emily, my wife."

The last two words came out wobbly. It sounded as though he was trying to reassure himself of their validity. Emily glowed at him.

With a grand gesture only slightly hampered by his bulk, Melchior Tate swept a courtly bow, then took Emily's gloved hand in his and kissed it. The brightness in his eyes when he looked at her afterward might have been a twinkle, but Emily suspected tears.

"My dear, I can't tell you what a pleasure this is."

"I'm so happy you could join us, Mr. Tate."

"You are?"

Uncle Mel was obviously astounded, and Emily's tender heart went out to him. And to Will.

"Why, of course I am. After all, you're the only family my darling Will has, and I think it would be a shame if he had no family here today of all days."

She gave Mel a smile so glorious it would have

leveled a lesser man. He only gazed at her in blank astonishment for several seconds, overcome by her sweetness. Ultimately Will had to jerk him out of his stupor.

"Well, come along, Uncle Mel. Come along and meet Emily's family. And Thomas! Hell, you haven't seen Thomas these last six years or more."

Before Will could lead his uncle away, Emily tugged gently at his coat sleeve. When she had his attention, she gestured with her little chin toward Texas Lonesome, who was now propped under a spreading oak, sound asleep. Gustav had curled up at his side and was snoring peacefully. A rotund Helga had not yet finished with her inspection of the stranger. Her quivering snout now sniffed with grave suspicion at the poor man's left boot.

"What do you suppose we should do with him?"

Will took a look at the sleeping man under the tree, and his conscience smote him mightily.

"Oh, Lord, Emily, I'm sorry. I meant to tell you weeks ago I wasn't really Texas Lonesome, but I forgot. It's just that I wanted to be with you so much that when you asked me if I was, I lied." He gazed down into her sparkling blue eyes, as bright and beautiful as the summer sky, and asked meekly, "Can you ever forgive me?"

The only thing preventing Emily from melting into a puddle of love on the spot was her corset, which was laced up as tightly as her aunt Gertrude had been able to manage. "Oh, Will darling, of course I forgive you. What a sweet, wonderful little fib."

A tear glistened on one perfect lash, and Will caught it with his finger.

"You mean it, Emily?" His heart was near to bursting with adoration.

"Of course I mean it, Will."

He hugged her close, defying proper etiquette entirely, and said, "Well, then, I opt for letting Texas Lonesome sleep it off and then giving him a big dinner and a bottle of champagne and our eternal thanks. If it weren't for him, we wouldn't be here now."

Emily's giggle was muffled in the layers of his white stock as he crushed her body to his.

"I'll go with you to introduce your uncle to Gertrude and Ludwig, Will. Sometimes my relatives require a little explaining."

The laugh with which Will greeted her words was music to her ears. "*Your* relatives need explaining? Emily, my sweet, haven't I told you enough about Uncle Mel to cure you of any embarrassment about your kin?"

Emily took his arm in her two hands, wondering if she'd ever tire of the feel of him. She gave one last look to the slumbering Texas Lonesome before she and Will left to introduce their relatives.

"You know, Will, when Texas Lonesome first wrote to me, he said he didn't drink overmuch. I wonder if he could possibly have been prevaricating."

Thomas Crandall, watching Will and Emily skip hand in hand toward a table laden with enough food for three wedding parties, decided he had never seen a more perfectly matched pair in his entire life.

Let HarperMonogram Sweep You Away!

Dancing On Air by Susan Wiggs
Over one million copies of her books in print. After losing her family and her aristocratic name, Philipa de Lacey is reduced to becoming a London street performer. Entranced with Philipa, the dashing Irish Lord of Castleross vows to help her—but his tarnished past threatens their love.

Straight from the Heart by Pamela Wallace
Academy Award-Winning Author. Answering a personal ad on a dare, city girl Zoey Donovan meets a handsome Wyoming rancher. Widower Tyler Ross is the answer to any woman's fantasy, but he will have to let go of the past before he can savor love's sweet bounty.

Treasured Vows by Cathy Maxwell
When English banker Grant Morgan becomes the guardian of impoverished heiress Phadra Abbott, he quickly falls under the reckless beauty's spell. Phadra is determined to upset Grant's well-ordered life to find her spendthrift father—despite the passion Grant unleashes in her.

Texas Lonesome by Alice Duncan
In 1890s San Francisco, Emily von Plotz gives advice to the lovelorn in her weekly newspaper column. A reader who calls himself "Texas Lonesome" seems to be the man for her, but wealthy rancher Will Tate is more than willing to show her who the real expert is in matters of the heart.

And in case you missed last month's selections . . .

Simply Heaven by Patricia Hagan
New York Times *bestselling author with over ten million copies in print.* Steve Maddox is determined to bring his friend's estranged daughter Raven home to Alabama. But after setting eyes on the tempestuous half-Tonkawa Indian, Steve yearns to tame the wild beauty and make Raven his.

Home Fires by Susan Kay Law

Golden Heart Award-Winning Author. Escaping with her young son from an unhappy marriage, lovely Amanda Sellington finds peace in a small Minnesota town—and the handsome Jakob Hall. Amanda longs to give in to happiness, but the past threatens to destroy the love she has so recently found.

The Bandit's Lady by Maureen Child

Schoolmarm Winifred Matthews is delighted when bank robber Quinn Hawkins takes her on a flight of fancy across Texas. They're running from the law, but already captured in love's sweet embrace.

When Midnight Comes by Robin Burcell

Time Travel Romance. A boating accident sends detective Kendra Browning sailing back to the year 1830, and into the arms of Captain Brice Montgomery. The ecstasy she feels at his touch beckons to Kendra like a siren's song, but murder threatens to steer their love off course.

*M*arper
*M*onogram